Mistaken Intention

BIG MISTAKES SERIES - BOOK THREE

by

SUZIE PETERS

Copyright © Suzie Peters, 2024.

The right of Suzie Peters as the Author of the Work has been asserted by her in accordance with the Copyright, Designs and Patents Act, 1988.

First Published in 2024
by GWL Publishing
an imprint of Great War Literature Publishing LLP

Produced in United Kingdom

Cover designs and artwork by GWL Creative.

Apart from any use permitted under UK copyright law, this publication may only be reproduced, stored or transmitted, in any form, or by any means, with prior permission in writing of the publishers or, in the case of reprographic production, in accordance with the terms of licences issued by the Copyright Licensing Agency.

All characters in this publication, with the exception of any obvious historical characters, are fictitious and any resemblance to real persons, either living or dead, is purely coincidental.

ISBN 978-1-915109-35-4 Paperback Edition

GWL Publishing
Chichester, United Kingdom

www.gwlpublishing.co.uk

Dedication

For S.

Chapter One

Josie

"I know it's a huge ask, but it would only be for one night."

I sit back on the couch, trying to get comfortable, although that's impossible. Not because my couch isn't cozy, but because this phone call is about as uncomfortable as they get.

That said, it's not a huge ask. Not really. Lexi is my sister and all she's asking is if she and her baby daughter can visit for the first time since Maisie's birth. It's no big deal at all.

Except that in those four months, we haven't seen each other. We've barely spoken, either… and we both know that's of my doing, not hers. Admittedly, Lexi and I have never been close. We're not even proper sisters. We're step-sisters, not related in the slightest, and during our late teens and into our very early twenties, we went for years without seeing or hearing from each other. That was because of her father, and the way he treated my mom. It had nothing to do with this most recent self-enforced exile.

That's much more personal.

"Are you still there, Josie?" she says.

"Yes." I hate that she sounds like she's begging, like she expects me to say 'no'. "Of course you can come."

"Oh, thank you. That's gonna make things so much easier."

"It is?" She hasn't given me a reason for this visit, but I think she's about to.

"Drew's flying back from Rome the day after tomorrow, and we've arranged that I'll meet him at the airport and then drive him down to Newport for a few days, so he can spend some time with Maisie."

I can hear every word she's saying, but they're all muddling around in my head. That's because her sentence started with 'Drew'... Maisie's father, Drew Bennett. Just hearing his name is enough to send my mind and body into a maelstrom, because he's the man I've been in love with ever since Lexi brought him to Ingrid's birthday party last summer.

It's a night I'll never forget, because it changed my life... forever.

I didn't see them arrive to start with. In fact, I didn't even hear the doorbell ring. I was busy enjoying myself. Someone let them in, though, and when I looked up, I saw him. It was like a scene out of a romance novel. Our eyes met across a crowded room and despite the cliché, I couldn't help falling for him. He was tall... around six foot two, with dark brown hair and a chiseled, clean-shaven jaw. Someone who was standing between us stepped aside, and I was able to see the rest of him then... his broad shoulders, narrow waist, toned chest and long legs, encased in stonewashed denim. I felt a shiver run through me, even though there was a warmth building right at my core. As I raised my eyes to his, I found he was staring too, and the heat in his eyes was breathtaking.

At that moment, Ingrid walked up to Lexi and dragged her off to the kitchen. Not that I cared. My focus remained on this most perfect stranger, and although I was rooted to the spot, he moved closer, his eyes never leaving mine, until he was standing right in front of me.

"Hi." His voice sent shivers down my spine, and I swallowed hard.

"Hello."

"I'm Drew."

"I'm Josie."

He took my elbow, steering me to a quiet corner of the living room, where I leaned against the wall, looking up as he stood so close I could feel him.

We talked.

That was all we did, all evening. We just talked.

He told me he was a photographer. I told him I was a nurse, and as the evening wore on, we discovered a shared passion for what we did… and for each other. He couldn't take his eyes from mine, and I was breathless in his presence. We didn't kiss, or touch, but I could feel the anticipation coursing between us, and I know he could, too. It was written in his sparkling, coffee-colored eyes.

I think I could have stayed like that forever, pinned against the wall, just gazing at him and listening to the sound of his soothing voice washing over me… right until Lexi interrupted us. It had been years since I'd seen her, although I'd have known her anywhere. As she came up to us, the thing I noticed first was the dress she was almost wearing. As a model she could get away with more daring clothes than the rest of us, but on that evening, she'd gone all out, in the shortest dress I'd ever seen, that was so low cut it left very little to the imagination.

"I see you've met my big sister." She put her arm through Drew's and that was when the startling realization dawned, and I knew 'Drew' wasn't just 'Drew'.

When I'd arrived at the party, Ingrid had pulled me aside and told me she'd also invited Lexi. I'd have liked a bit more warning… preferably enough that I could have avoided attending, but it was too late to back out and I'd just nodded my head.

"She's bringing her boyfriend," she said. "Or a guy she called her 'kind-of boyfriend', anyway."

"What does that mean?"

She shrugged her shoulders. "Don't ask me. You know what Lexi's like."

She disappeared then and left me wondering, although I didn't worry too much. Just like Ingrid, I knew Lexi's capacity for trying to be enigmatic. But, standing there, looking at the two of them, it suddenly made sense. The man before me, the man whose expression had suddenly gone from adoring to sheepish, was my sister's boyfriend – or kind-of boyfriend, whatever that was – and the dress she was wearing was obviously for his benefit.

She leaned up, looking at Drew, even though his eyes were locked on mine. "I'm gonna go to the bathroom, and then we should probably head off. I've got an early start."

He nodded his head a little aimlessly, and Lexi disappeared again.

"Y—You're Lexi's boyfriend?"

"Sort of."

There it was again... that doubt about his status. I wanted to ask him what that meant, but I couldn't. I was struggling to breathe, let alone talk, and I just gazed into his eyes one last time, and ducked away from him. The bathroom was occupied by my sister, so I went into one of the bedrooms, grateful it was empty, and sat down on the edge of the mattress, fighting my tears. How could life be so cruel? Why did I have to meet the perfect man, only to find he was already taken... by my sister? And why had he flirted with me? How could he do something like that? I wanted to be angry. I tried really hard, but it hurt too much.

When I came out, they'd gone, and I didn't know whether to be happy or sad. Sad won over, because even though I knew it was wrong, even though there was still a hint of anger underneath all that hurt, I couldn't help loving Drew.

And it was love.

I may never have experienced it before, but I knew what it was, and it hit me like a freight train.

"We'll probably get to you around six, if that's okay?" I realize Lexi's still talking, and I try to pay attention, even though the memory of those painful days is still so fresh.

"That's fine," I say. "I finish work around five, so I'll be back by then."

"Great. You can help me give Maisie her bath."

I can't reply through the lump rising in my throat as I imagine Drew doing exactly that… bathing his young daughter.

Of course, none of us knew Lexi was pregnant when Drew and I first met. That came later. What happened first was I heard from Ingrid that Lexi and Drew had split up.

"It was always on the cards," she said.

"Why?" Was there something wrong with him? I found it hard to believe, but my acquaintance with him was too brief for me to judge, even if I had fallen for him.

"Because they met in the Caribbean, on a shoot that went horribly wrong."

"And? What difference does that make?"

"All the difference in the world. It was like a holiday romance, really. And like almost all holiday romances, it didn't work when they got back home."

"Is that what she meant when she said he was her 'kind-of' boyfriend?"

"I guess. Although it was him that ended it, not her."

"Really?"

"Yeah… and on the night of my party, too, straight after they got home."

So soon? I tried very hard not to overthink that. What did the timing matter? It didn't... did it?

Of course it did. It had to mean something.

I had to mean something.

I wondered. Did he feel the same way I did? Had he broken up with Lexi so he could be with me?

I drove myself crazy trying to work it out, in between missing him, wanting him... needing him.

Then, out of the blue, I got a phone call. I didn't recognize the number, but answered anyway, and I knew it was Drew as soon as I heard his voice.

"I'm sorry about what happened... the... the misunderstanding."

"That's okay." I couldn't blame him anymore. My anger was a thing of the past, if it had ever truly existed. I loved him. Nothing else mattered.

"Lexi and I have split up now."

"I know. I heard."

"Oh, I see. So, um... would you like to meet up for coffee?"

I wasn't sure what he meant. Was he asking me on a date? Was that even relevant? I said 'yes'. I wanted to see him again, and when I did, the following day, the spark was still there. It fanned into flames the moment he sat opposite me and our eyes met. Nothing had changed, and although all we did was talk – yet again – I knew a minute of talking with him would be more fulfilling than a lifetime of romance with anyone else.

Of course, I hoped for more. Especially when he asked if we could meet up again... and again.

After that third meeting, which I was still refusing to think of as a date, I allowed myself a glimmer of hope... just the tiniest of flickers, which I carried in my heart.

We didn't arrange our next meeting, because Drew was going away to do some work in Hawaii and his schedule was a little unpredictable.

"If the weather's bad, I might have to stay over an extra day or two. I don't wanna make plans for Friday night and then let you down."

I liked that, even though I was still trying not to overthink everything he said.

"I'm working all weekend, anyway," I told him, and I struggled not to smile when I saw the disappointment in his eyes.

"Okay. Why don't I call you when I get back? We can set something up then?"

I nodded my head. He sounded keen, so I wasn't surprised when my phone rang late at night a few days later.

What did surprise me was that the call was from Lexi. I hadn't seen her since Ingrid's party, and she hadn't called me in years. I'd even forgotten I still had her number on my phone and for a moment or two I wondered about ignoring her, mostly because I felt guilty about my feelings for her ex-boyfriend. In the end, though, I picked up… and immediately wished I hadn't.

"I'm pregnant."

Her words astonished me, blurted out like that. "I'm sorry?"

"I said I'm pregnant."

"I didn't realize you'd met someone, let alone…"

"I haven't met anyone. At least, not anyone new. It's Drew's."

I was standing in my kitchen at the time, fetching some water, but I sank to my knees, my heart fracturing in my chest, the pieces scattering, like the glass that shattered on the floor as I dropped it.

"D—Drew's?"

"Yeah… remember? The guy I brought to Ingrid's party."

Of course I remembered him. I was in love with him. "Oh, yeah. But you broke up, didn't you?" Surely Ingrid hadn't been wrong, had she? Drew hadn't been lying? He hadn't been meeting up with me and sleeping with my sister? He couldn't have been.

"We did, but… it's complicated." I wanted to tell her it was a darn sight more complicated than she knew, but I held my tongue, listening as she let out a long sigh, before she said, "I don't think I told you about the assignment in the Caribbean earlier in the year."

"No, you didn't."

"Well, it was a disaster. I got sick the day we arrived… and I mean sick. It was horrible. Drew turned up a couple of days later, by which time I was better, but the other models were dropping like flies. There was a storm forecast, and he and I had nothing else to do, so we… we got together."

"I see." I wished I didn't, but she'd painted a vivid enough picture for me.

"The problem was, because I'd been sick, my birth control pills didn't work, so…" Her voice faded, my brain switching into neutral as I realized that, even if Drew hadn't cheated – on either of us – any hopes I'd had of being with him had floundered in the aftermath of an affair neither party even cared about.

"It was an accident?" I said once she'd stopped talking.

"Yeah. Only now I don't know what to do. I told Dad, and he's fuming, and… oh, God, Josie… what am I gonna do?"

I didn't need to ask her why she'd called me anymore. If her father wasn't being supportive of her, it made sense she might turn to me instead.

"What do you want to do?"

"I don't know. I can't tell Drew. What if he thinks I did it on purpose?"

"Why on earth would he think that?"

"Because he's a multi-millionaire."

I sat up, confusion tangling my brain. "He is?"

"Yeah."

"But I thought he was a photographer."

"He is. But only because he loves doing it so much. He doesn't need the money. Everyone in the industry knows that."

I wasn't in the 'industry'. It excused my ignorance, although it made slightly less sense of her father's attitude. I'd have understood it better if Drew had been a no-hoper, but a multi-millionaire? Surely, as the father to his grandchild, that ought to have been acceptable?

"What difference does it make, though?" I asked. "Why would Drew think you'd got pregnant on purpose?"

"He might assume I'd done it to trap him into marriage, or at the very least, to get money from him."

The thought of the two of them getting married sent chills down my spine and made my eyes sting with unshed tears, but I couldn't see why they would. Not in this day and age. They didn't love each other, and just because Lexi was pregnant, didn't mean marriage was the automatic conclusion to their situation.

"But you've just explained it was an accident. And if he was that worried, he could've used a condom, couldn't he?"

There was a slight pause. "To be honest, we were both a little drunk. Contraception wasn't top of our list of priorities."

I wasn't sure I needed that much information. "You need to tell him, Lexi."

"That I'm pregnant?"

"Yes." *What else?*

"How?"

"Just call him up and tell him. He has a right to know."

I knew I was driving a nail into the coffin of any hope I had of being with Drew myself. I was going to be his child's aunt. What future was there for us?

None…

"I'm sorry we haven't been able to see each other since Maisie was born." Lexi's words bring me back to reality with a bump and I sit up, still struggling with the whole comfort thing. I pull out the pillow from behind me and throw it to the other end of the couch before settling back again, staring through the window on the far wall, at the apartment block opposite. It's a rare thing for me to have a day off work, and I'd intended catching up with my laundry, not sitting around talking to my sister, recalling things best forgotten.

"It's not your fault. I've been busy at work."

"I don't know how you do it. I could never be a nurse."

It's my vocation, so I don't have an answer. It's not something I even think about. Besides, it's not as though I have anything else in my life, so I don't mind it filling all my time.

"I could never be a model," I say, rather than justifying my career choices.

"Yes, you could. You're far prettier than I am… and you've got a better figure."

"Not a model's figure."

"Hmm… maybe not." We both know my curves would be no match on the catwalk for Lexi's svelte lines. "It's strange, isn't it… the last time I saw you face-to-face, I was the size of a house, puffing and panting, giving birth to Maisie."

Lexi has never been the size of a house, even when she was pregnant, but I nod my head anyway, regardless of the fact that she can't see me, and whisper, "Yes."

I've done my best to forget that fateful day, even though I welcomed the safe arrival of my niece.

Lexi and I may have grown up together, my mom having met her dad when I was three and she was two, neither of us remembering a life without the other in it, but we always knew we weren't really sisters. We always knew there was a void between us, which only became wider as we grew up. Still, her pregnancy, her fears about raising a child by herself, her father's blank refusal to accept the situation, and her need to share the experience with someone else brought us closer together. It was hard, but I supported her, and she came to stay with me every so often, partly so she could see Drew, and partly for a change of scene, I think. The last such visit occurred just a week before the baby was due, and although I thought she was mad for coming, I couldn't talk her out of it. Neither of us expected her to go into labor while she was here, though, and I was just relieved I had enough nursing experience to know what to do, and to stay calm while doing it, taking her to the hospital in my car.

"Stay with me." She clutched at my hand as she was taken to a delivery room, her eyes pleading with mine. "Don't leave."

"Of course I'm not gonna leave."

"And call Drew." She handed me her phone, putting me in the unbearable position of having to tell the man I loved that his child was about to be born.

I found his number in her contacts and, as she breathed her way through another contraction, I waited for him to pick up.

"Lexi? What's wrong?"

"It's not Lexi. It's Josie."

"Oh, my God." His voice was a whisper, and hearing it broke my heart. "H—Has something happened?"

"Lexi's gone into labor. I've brought her to Mass General. We're…"

"Don't worry. I'll find you."

He hung up then, and I braced myself for what I knew was to come.

Drew arrived about twenty minutes later, looking concerned, and he took my place by Lexi's side. She made it clear she wanted me to stay, despite his presence, and I watched, playing the dutiful sister and would-be aunt, while she gave birth to the daughter of the only man I was ever going to love.

Watching him cry when he looked at his newborn daughter was too painful for words. But I painted on a smile and made all the right noises, offering to let Lexi come back to my place, but giving in more than gracefully when she accepted Drew's invitation to stay at his city apartment for a few days instead.

"I know it's small, but…"

She smiled at him. "Yeah, I remember."

That was an unwanted reminder of their time together… that she'd stayed there before.

He didn't smile back, but just nodded his head. "You're welcome to use the guest bedroom for as long as you like."

"Okay." She stared up at him, and I knew I was intruding.

I made myself scarce, but heard from Lexi a week later that she'd gone back to New York. They were falling over each other in Drew's apartment, and it was causing tension between them. I tried not to feel triumphant, although it was hard.

"He's come back with me," she said, bursting my bubble.

"He's staying at your apartment?"

"No, at a hotel around the corner. The one he always stays at when he visits."

"Oh."

"We kinda planned it this way. Except I was supposed to give birth here, and Drew was gonna stay on for a while afterwards, to spend time with Maisie."

They had plans. They had a life together, even if they weren't a couple anymore, and I knew then that it was too late for me and Drew. We'd had our chance and lost it.

I cried myself to sleep every night for a week or more. My tears weren't just for Drew, though. I missed him and I wanted him, but that wasn't the only reason my heart ached. I might have been an aunt, but I'd never be a mother, and for the first time in a very long time, that hurt…

"Are you still there?" I jump, realizing I've fallen silent for far too long.

"Yes. Sorry. I was just thinking."

"Well, don't. It's bad for you."

She's not wrong.

"What time does Drew's flight get in?" I ask, just to show an interest.

"Around three, I think. He's sent me the details, so I'll check the flights are on time before I leave your place. The last thing I need is to be waiting at the airport for hours when I've got Maisie with me."

I don't doubt that. "Assuming he's coming in on time, I won't get home from work before you leave."

"No, but if it's okay with you, I'll be coming back."

"Oh? When?"

"I can't be sure yet. I've left it up to Drew how long he wants us to stay with him, but once we're through there, I need to spend some time in Boston."

"You do?"

"Yes. It's kinda complicated and I haven't talked it all through with Drew yet. He knows I'm coming back to Boston, but not why, so…"

"Y—You're not getting back together with him, are you?" My stomach lurches at the thought. I might not be able to be with him myself, but the idea of him and Lexi getting together again is more than I can contemplate.

"Of course not." I try to disguise my sigh, hoping she won't hear it. "It's nothing like that. We like things just as they are. He always makes us welcome when we visit him in Newport, and we've got our own rooms in his house."

"And does he still stay at that hotel when he comes to you in New York?"

"Yes. It works better that way."

Better than what, I'm not sure, but she seems happy enough.

"Why do you need to come back to Boston?" I ask.

"I'll explain when I see you. Like I say, it's kinda complicated, and Maisie's due to wake up any minute now."

"Okay."

"We'll see you tomorrow evening."

We end our call, and I put my phone on the couch, letting my head rock back. My stomach's churning with nerves… not about seeing my step-sister or her daughter, but about whatever it is she's planning, how it might involve Drew, and if it might involve me, too.

Drew

"Is everything okay?" Hunter asks.

"Sure it is."

Why wouldn't it be? I'm sitting in the Presidential Suite of the Hotel d'Estate in Rome, surrounded by wood-paneled walls, an ornately carved ceiling, plush carpets and the softest of furnishings. Through the open windows I can see across the domed rooftops of Italy's capital city, and the doors to my left reveal a king-sized bedroom and marble bathroom. What's not to like? Why would my brother think I'm anything but okay?

Maybe because Josie's not here with me, and because I miss her more than I can say.

I miss my daughter Maisie, too, but it's Josie who's filling my thoughts. It's Josie who haunts my dreams… who I want and can't have.

"Did you have a reason for calling me from Rome? Not that I'm not thrilled to hear from you…"

"I just wanted to let you know I'm coming home the day after tomorrow."

"Do you need me to collect you from the airport?"

"No, it's fine. Lexi's picking me up. She's gonna bring Maisie with her and drive us all down to Newport for a few days."

"How's that gonna work?" he asks. "Surely your car's in Boston, isn't it?"

"Yeah. It's at my apartment. But Lexi needs to be in Boston for some reason, so when we're finished in Newport, she'll drive me back again."

"I see. And what about your equipment?" he asks.

"It'll fit in the trunk of Lexi's car. I've been over here doing a travel shoot, so I didn't need to bring that much."

"Okay. So you don't need me to do anything?"

"Other than ask Pat to stock up the refrigerator at the cottage for me, no. I don't wanna waste my time going to the grocery store when I get back there."

"Because you'd rather spend it with Maisie?"

"Of course."

"Have you been missing her?"

"I have. Ten days is a lifetime when she's so little. She'll have changed so much."

"Do you wish you could spend more time with her?" he asks.

"Of course. But it's not practical. I might not have to work, but I have responsibilities to clients, and Lexi and I aren't together, so…"

"There's no chance of a change in that situation?" he says, his question surprising me. "I mean, there's no way the two of you would get back together?"

What made him ask that? "No. I told you, we both knew we weren't suited to each other. Our time in the Caribbean was fun, but…"

"It was too much fun, if Maisie's presence in the world is anything to go by."

"Maybe, but that was an accident. I didn't know Lexi had been sick, and she didn't realize her birth control wouldn't work. It couldn't be helped. Both of us know that. Neither of us blames the other for what happened, and we've got absolutely no intention of getting back together."

"Okay. Message received. You're not getting back together with Lexi. She's just picking you up from the airport and taking you to Newport."

"Yeah. So I can spend some time with Maisie, which we can't do in Boston, because as we discovered when Maisie was born, the three of us in a confined space didn't work well."

"Was that when they came to stay with you?"

"Yeah. I'm not gonna say it was a disaster, but it would have been if we hadn't realized where we were heading. That's why I stay in a hotel when I visit them in New York."

"You haven't considered buying yourself a place close to Lexi's?"

"I have, but first I'd need to find the time. Whenever I'm there, I just wanna be with Maisie."

He chuckles, and I can't help smiling. I don't think either of us would have thought I'd be this dedicated to being a father, but I am, and I love it. I love Maisie. She's adorable, and I can't wait to see her again.

"Would you change things if you could?" he asks, surprising me yet again.

"How do you mean?"

"I mean, would you go back?"

"To not get Lexi pregnant, you mean? To not have Maisie?"

"Yeah."

I take a moment, thinking that one through. "That's a tough question to answer. I love Maisie and I wouldn't change her for the world, but…"

"Lexi's sister?" he says, and I wrestle against the familiar pain… the one that eats at me every moment of the day, gnawing at my soul.

"Yeah." *Josie*… "How's Ella?" I ask, to change the subject, to relieve the ache in my chest. "How's Henry?"

My sister's baby was born on the day I flew out here, and that's another reason I can't wait to get home to Newport and not Boston. Ella's pregnancy was a little rocky to begin with. She'd broken up with her boyfriend before she discovered she was pregnant, and there were echoes of my situation with Lexi, except of course that Ella was in love with Mac, and missing him like mad. I could see how sad she was, and given the similarities in our circumstances, I did what I could to help her. I might have only been someone to talk to, and a pair of fairly broad shoulders to cry on, but I could see how much she needed them… and me.

Even though she and Mac are back together now, and he's moved his life from London to Newport just to be with her, I still feel responsible for my little sister. I want to make sure she's okay.

"They're both doing great," Hunter says. "Ella's a little sleep deprived and is likely to bite your head off if you suggest there's not an 'R' in the month… or there is one, for that matter."

I chuckle, remembering what it was like to step on those same eggshells when Maisie had just been born, and Lexi held me responsible for everything that was wrong with the world.

"But she's happy?"

"Yeah, she is." He pauses. "Are you?"

I'd hoped we'd successfully changed the subject. It seems I was wrong, and there's no point in trying to deceive my brother. He knows me too well.

"Happiness would be sharing my life with the woman I love, so no, I'm not happy."

"I guess there's no hope for that."

"Probably not."

"Why only 'probably'?" he says. "Surely, after everything that's happened…"

"I know, I know… and I really mustn't get my hopes up, but…"

"But what?"

"It was just something Lexi said the last time I spoke to her."

"About what?"

"I was trying to make some arrangements with her for when I get back to the States, you know? We might have fixed up what we're doing immediately after my return, but I wanted to work out when I could next go to see them in New York."

"And?"

"And she was being kinda cagey about it. No matter how hard I tried to set a date, she kept saying it could wait. There was something about it… about the way she was talking. I got the feeling something's going on."

"What kind of something?"

"I don't know. But I wondered if maybe she'd met someone and she needed to check things out with him first, before she could commit to dates and times with me."

"You don't think you could be reading too much into it?" he says, adding a heavy hint of reality to the conversation.

"Probably." I sigh, feeling like my hopes are being dashed before me. "I just thought if she'd met another guy, it might make things easier."

"It sounds to me like it'll make them a lot more complicated, trying to tie in three schedules instead of two."

"That's not what I meant. I was talking about the fact that, if Lexi is dating someone, then maybe I could, too."

"Even if that 'someone' is her sister?" He sounds skeptical, and I can't say I blame him. I'm clutching at straws here, and I know it.

"I know it wouldn't be as straightforward as me dating a stranger, but I also got the impression Lexi and her sister aren't as close as I thought they were."

"Really?"

"Yeah. I mentioned it to Ella the last time I spoke with her, but what I didn't realize then was that Lexi and her sister haven't seen each other since Maisie was born."

"They haven't?" I can hear the surprise in his voice.

"No. Lexi told me that just the other day, when I was talking to her about coming to pick me up from the airport. She said she's gonna arrange to stay at her sister's place in Boston the night before I get back, to save driving up from New York, and then having to go to Newport all in one day. She seemed a little nervous about asking, and I wondered why, which was when she told me she hadn't seen her sister since she stayed there just before Maisie was born."

"But that was four months ago," he says.

"I know. I can't imagine going that long without seeing you and Ella. We might have done it before, but only because of work commitments, or when Ella was studying in Europe."

"Exactly. They don't even live very far apart, and yet…"

"And yet, they're obviously not that close."

There's a brief pause and I can almost hear him thinking, working out the significance of what I've just said. "What are you gonna do about it?" he asks.

"I'm gonna talk to Lexi when I get home."

"About her sister?"

"Not exactly. I can hardly come straight out and say I've been in love with her all this time, but I'll probably see what's going on with Lexi… try to find out if she's got another guy in her life, and take it from there."

"You're not worried about Lexi getting involved with someone else, then?"

"Of course not. She's a free agent. As long as she doesn't stop me from seeing Maisie, she can do whatever she wants." He chuckles. "What's wrong?"

"Nothing. It's just you're so different."

"Yeah. That's what fatherhood does for you." I stop talking, realizing what I've just said, and how insensitive it sounded. He and Livia have been trying to get pregnant for a while. Hunter told me shortly after Maisie was born, when I noticed how subdued Livia was and asked if she was okay. I was worried she might be sick, but he told me they'd been trying for a baby since before their wedding, and getting nowhere. The look in his eyes gave away how much he wanted it, too, so I doubt he needs reminding of the joys of being a dad… not when he so desperately wants to become one himself. "I'm sorry, Hunter. That wasn't very subtle of me, was it?"

"It's okay," he says, although I can tell it isn't.

"I take it there's still nothing happening?"

"Not for want of trying." I can't help smiling, relieved he can't see me.

"Would it be better if I kept Maisie out of the way while we're at the house?" I ask, wondering how I'm gonna manage that, considering I've already promised Lexi I'll take Maisie swimming in the pool.

"No, it's fine," Hunter says. "Henry's at Newport, and Livia's handling it just fine. Having Maisie there won't be an issue. And besides, Ella's excited for Henry to meet his cousin."

"I'm excited to meet Henry myself."

"He's enormous compared to Maisie when she was that age," he says, and then he pauses for a second or two. "There's just one thing…"

"What's that?"

"Don't tell Ella about Livia and me."

"That you're trying for a baby, you mean?"

"Yeah."

"I assumed she already knew."

"No. I only told you because you noticed something wasn't quite right with Livia, and I didn't want you to think she was sick. The thing is…" He's struggling to talk and takes a moment. "The thing is, I think we both thought it would just happen, you know? She told me she'd had problems with her periods, and that was why she was taking birth control pills. But in that dumb, naïve way people have of believing in something, just because they want it to be true, we thought she'd stop taking them, and instantly get pregnant. We didn't see the need to broadcast our efforts, because we thought we'd be telling people she was pregnant within weeks. And now, the longer it goes on, the harder it is to talk about."

"Are you seeing anyone? Professionally?"

"A doctor?"

"Yeah."

"It's too soon, evidently," he says. "Although it doesn't feel too soon to us."

I'm sure it doesn't, but I don't know what to say to him… not when he's thousands of miles away. He coughs and I can feel the emotion in the sigh that follows, even from here.

"It'll be okay, Hunter," I say, my words sounding hollow, even to me.

"I hope so." He hesitates and then says, "Oh, and it's probably only fair to warn you, Livia and I are spending more time at the house these days."

"You are?"

"Yeah. For the last few weeks, we've been leaving Boston just after lunch on Fridays and not coming back to the city again until late on Monday. We feel relaxed in Newport, and although I

21

know it shouldn't make any difference where we are, we value the time we can spend away from it all."

"I can understand that." I know if I could be with Josie, I'd want us to live in Newport. It's the perfect place to unwind, and to raise a family… or try to start one.

I strike the thought. It hurts too much to think like that.

"I guess I'd better let you do some work," Hunter says, and he's not wrong.

"I've still got a few shots to take before I come home, and I need the evening light, which will be perfect in about an hour." I look out the window at the pale orange glow settling on the terracotta rooftops, and nod my head. It's pretty good even now. Give it an hour and it'll be exactly what I need.

"Okay. We'll see you when you get back."

"Sure…" I hesitate, just for a second. "Hunter?"

"Yeah?"

"I've said this before, but if you need to talk, you know where I am."

He chuckles. "It's usually the other way around between us, isn't it?"

"Yeah, it is. I know I'm normally the one who comes to you, but I also know you're having to be strong for Livia right now… and I just want you to remember, if you need someone to be strong for you, I'm here."

"Th—Thanks, Drew."

We end our call, and I sit back, resting my head against the sumptuous pillow behind me. I know I should get my equipment ready and go out to take this final set of shots… but I need a few moments to myself first.

My earbuds are lying on the table, and I lean forward, picking them up and playing them between my fingers before I connect them to my phone. I know what I'm doing will hurt like hell, but

I do it anyway, going to my streaming service, and selecting the piece of music I've been listening to, over and over for the last year. I have it set up at home in my apartment, too, so I can hear it whenever I want… so I can punish myself by remembering how it felt to see Josie for the first time, this piece of music playing in the background as I lost my heart.

Putting it onto repeat, the melody washes over me as I close my eyes and recall that night…

It was someone's birthday party. I don't know her name, but she was a friend of Lexi's, I think, and I didn't want to be there. I didn't want to be with Lexi at all, although we were still together, in the loosest of terms. We'd met when we were working in the Caribbean, on a disastrous assignment, where everything that could go wrong went wrong. The weather was shocking and all the models I was there to photograph got sick… except for Lexi. Thrown together like that, just the two of us, on a paradise island where clothes seemed to be optional, we did what came naturally, and we both enjoyed it. Okay, so I made the mistake of forgetting to use a condom… but it was only that first time, and to be fair, I was drunk. Lexi assured me she was on birth control, so neither of us worried about it, and we carried on having fun… and being more careful about it. I'm not saying we had wild, passionate sex all the time. In fact, it was quite tame. Not that I was complaining. It was better than staring at four walls. When the assignment was canceled and we went our separate ways, Lexi surprised me by calling and inviting me to stay with her in New York. I had nothing else to do, and didn't see the harm, but I think we both realized pretty quickly that it wasn't going to work. Even the sex felt different, and we had nothing in common… nothing to talk about. Neither of us was under any illusions, and it was just a matter of time before one of us jumped ship.

The one to jump was me. Only rather than breaking it off with her, I made the excuse of needing to return to Boston, little realizing she was going there herself. My plan having backfired, I could hardly get out of letting her come back with me, or her request to stay at my apartment. I tried to get out of the party, though. It was the last thing I felt like doing with a woman I was on the verge of leaving. The problem was, Lexi had sprung the invitation on me at the last minute, and I couldn't think of a single logical reason not to go.

"We won't have to stay for long," Lexi said as she practically dragged me from my apartment.

"I'm not dressed for a party."

She looked me up and down, and although her eyes still lit up, there was no longer that hunger she'd so often displayed when we were in the Caribbean. I was grateful for that. The sex had become boring by then and I was all out of excuses for not jumping into bed with her.

"It's not the kind of party where you need to get dressed up."

I wondered, in that case, why she was wearing such a revealing dress, but I didn't comment. I just assumed she was looking for someone to replace me, and I was grateful for that, too.

When Lexi knocked on the door of her friend's apartment, I was still trying to think of excuses to leave. The noise coming from inside was enough to make me hope no-one would hear us, but someone must have done and they opened the door, letting us in to a spacious living area, which was rammed full of people. I turned to close the door and then spun around, my eyes catching those of the most beautiful woman I'd ever seen in my life. She was standing, watching me, her dark blonde hair tied loosely behind her head, with just a few stands framing her perfect face. There were dozens of people between us, but one in particular was blocking my view of her, and when they moved aside, it was like time stood still. The room seemed to fall silent and my heart stopped beating. She was perfect. Just perfect. Her bright red dress had a fitted bodice and flowing skirt which showed off her curves, and while I admired her, I felt her eyes rake up and down my body in a slow, sexy appraisal. When she looked up again, I did the same and our eyes met once more. She blushed slightly. I didn't. There was nothing to blush about. I wanted her… like I'd never wanted anyone or anything in my life.

A woman came up to us and dragged Lexi away, neither of them looking back, or requiring my presence. The woman in the red dress was still staring at me, though, and there was no way I was passing up the chance to find out more… to get to know her. I walked over, until I was standing so close, we were almost touching… close enough for me to see that her eyes were a gray-blue color, and that they sparkled when she smiled. We introduced ourselves. Her name was Josie, but there were too many people around for us to talk properly, so I took her elbow and moved us to the corner of the room, where it was quiet enough to have a conversation.

And we talked.

Man, did we talk. I wanted to touch her, to caress her soft cheeks and kiss her tender lips, and tell her I'd found the one woman in the world who was meant for me. It was too soon for declarations like that, so I limited myself to talking about my work, and listening to her rave about hers. She clearly enjoyed being a nurse, and I loved her passion… almost as much as I loved her.

And I did love her. I knew it, even though I'd never experienced it before.

Josie was it for me, and no-one else was ever going to come close.

I was so enthralled, I didn't notice Lexi coming over... not until she linked her arm through mine, my body stiffening at the unwelcome intrusion.

"I see you've met my big sister."

My heart stopped for a second time.

Josie was her sister?

I looked down and saw a moment of realization as it flickered across her eyes. Lexi said something else, although I don't know what it was, and I nodded my head before she left again. I stared at Josie, unsure what to say or do to make it better.

"Y—You're Lexi's boyfriend?"

I could hear doubt and confusion in Josie's voice, but I still couldn't think what to say, so I just murmured, "Sort of."

I wasn't. Not really... and even if I was, I didn't want to be.

Josie frowned and nodded her head, and I noticed her eyes glistening. This wasn't the same sparkle she got when she smiled. This was different... like she was going to cry. I wanted to reach out to her, but before I could, she moved away, rushing across the room and ducking inside a door, closing it behind her. I stared. Should I go after her? What would I say if I did? She was bound to be angry with me. Even if she hadn't known of my connection with her sister, I had... and although I hadn't known who she was, I knew I wasn't exactly available.

I pushed my fingers back through my hair.

God, what a mess.

"Where's Josie?" I turned at the sound of Lexi's voice.

"I—I don't know."

She looked around and shrugged. "Oh, well. We'd better get going."

I wondered why she didn't seem very interested in talking to her sister, or even saying goodbye to her, but I wasn't about to comment, and I let her lead me from the apartment.

We made a silent journey back to my place, and once we were there, I closed the door and turned to her.

"Can we talk?" I said, and she raised her eyes to mine.

"Now? I told you, I've got an early start tomorrow."

Had she told me that? I couldn't remember, but I'd barely listened to a word she'd said all evening. "I know," I lied. "But this won't take long."

"Okay."

I walked away, into the living room, knowing she'd follow, and she did, sitting down on the couch, while I paced back and forth a couple of times and then stopped in front of her.

"I can't keep seeing you." I couldn't think how else to phrase it, and the words just poured out of me.

"Oh."

Although nothing had been the same since we'd returned from the Caribbean, she seemed surprised. But maybe it wasn't what I'd said so much as the way I'd said it.

"I'm sorry, Lexi. It's just not working."

"No, it's not."

At least she wasn't trying to pretend there was anything between us. She looked around, and it only took me a moment to realize what was wrong. "If you're stuck for somewhere to stay while you're in Boston, you can use the guest room."

She stared up at me. "You're sure?"

"Of course. There's no reason for us to be uncivilized."

She nodded her head and got to her feet. "Thanks, Drew."

I wasn't sure what she was thanking me for, but it didn't matter, and once I'd made up a bed for her, I went to my room and sat on the mattress, trying to work out what to do.

I'd fallen for Josie. My heart was hers. My body was hers too, and I wanted her so much I ached… but I couldn't see a way forward. I was so desperate, I even spoke to Hunter and Ella about it. They advised me to wait, to let the dust settle. Hunter suggested I try befriending Josie rather than dating her… at least to start with. It was going to be a novel approach for me, but when I thought it through, it made sense.

Waiting was fine in theory, but in principle, it was impossible. I couldn't handle it. So, I made up a truly lame excuse to get Josie's number from her sister. I said something about her having mentioned someone I thought I knew and wanting to check if it was the same person. Fortunately, Lexi was back at work by then, too busy to wonder about my reasons, and after plucking up my courage, I made the call.

"Hi."

"Oh… Hi, Drew."

She knew it was me? I didn't know how, but I couldn't help smiling.

"I'm sorry about what happened… the… the misunderstanding." I'd never stammered so much in my life. But then I'd never been more nervous, either.

"That's okay," she said, although I wondered if it was, or if she was just saying that.

"Lexi and I have split up now." I thought I needed to get that out there, right from the get-go.

"I know. I heard."

"Oh… I see." I was surprised by that. Had she been checking up on me? It was a nice idea. "So, um… would you like to meet up for coffee?"

The whole 'friendship' thing was getting to me. If I'd been asking her to dinner, as a date, I don't think I'd have struggled half as much, but I felt I was being dishonest, treating her like a friend, when I wanted so much more.

She agreed, regardless of my stammering, and we arranged to meet the following day.

I was nervous… more nervous than I'd ever been for any other date, even though I kept telling myself it was no such thing. When I got to the coffee shop, Josie was already there, and I sat opposite her, our eyes meeting, a smile tugging at her lips, and I knew that if friendship was all we were ever going to have, it would be enough.

We talked for hours, until she had to leave, but we arranged to meet again… and then again a few days later. I was due to fly to Hawaii after that, so I said I'd call her when I got back. She seemed enthusiastic and while I was away, I wondered what she might do if I kissed her. I played out the scene in my head… meeting her somewhere when I got home, telling her I'd missed her, and taking her in my arms. Would she welcome me? Or was it too soon?

My flight home was delayed by a few hours and when I eventually got back, I went straight down to Newport. I needed some rest, and I knew Josie was working over the weekend. Newport seemed like the best place to be. Hunter would be there too, and I figured some brotherly advice might not go amiss. He might be able to tell me if I was being too ambitious, thinking about kisses after just three dates that weren't even dates, or if I needed to hold off a little longer.

I was sitting on the couch, pretending to read, and waiting for Hunter and Livia to drive down from Boston, when my phone rang. I was surprised to see Lexi's name on the screen, but I answered, because I had no reason not to.

"Are you sitting down?" she asked, which felt like an odd greeting, even by Lexi's standards.

"Why?"

"Because I've got something to tell you."

"And I need to sit down for this because…?"

She sucked in a breath loud enough for me to hear. "Because it's gonna come as a shock."

"Just tell me, Lexi."

I heard her sigh, or maybe she was letting out that breath. It was hard to tell. "I'm pregnant."

The ground shifted beneath me, my life, my future and all my hopes altering beyond recognition with those two words. "Y— You're pregnant?"

"Yeah."

I thought for a moment. It had been a while since we'd broken up… and a while longer since the sole time we'd had unprotected sex. But I remembered… she'd assured me she was on birth control, so how could this be happening?

"It's yours," she said, like she'd read my mind. "I know you're probably wondering, but I haven't slept with anyone since we were together."

"But you were on birth control. You told me."

"Yeah." I heard her swallow. "Do you remember everyone getting sick when we were in the Caribbean?"

"Of course."

"Well… I was sick myself, a couple of days before you arrived." I felt my stomach churn, knowing what was coming next. "My birth control pills didn't work."

"No, they wouldn't." I couldn't blame her. I should have used a condom. And in any case, it was too late to play the blame game. Except… "Why have you waited until now to tell me?"

"Because I've only just found out. I've never been very… um… regular, but I've just returned from an assignment in California and I while I was out there, I started feeling really nauseous. It was mostly in the mornings, but sometimes later in the day, too. I thought nothing of it. I've been busy, not eating regularly, and I assumed I was just over-tired, because I've been so sleepy, too. When I got back home, my agent had sent me an email notifying me of another assignment in Miami, and I needed to check the dates on my calendar, which was when I noticed how long it had been since my last period. Like I say, that's not unusual for me, but then I put two and two together with the nausea and the tiredness, and I thought I should probably do a test…"

"And it was positive?" I didn't know why I asked that question, when I already knew the answer. I guess it was nerves… or fear.

"Yeah. I'm sorry, Drew."

I wasn't sure why she was apologizing and, despite everything, I felt guilty. "Don't apologize. It's not your fault."

"It's not yours either. You didn't know I'd been sick, and I promise, there's been no-one else."

"It's okay. I believe you." I did… even if the knowledge was killing me, and any hope of being with Josie.

"I'm not asking you for anything," she said. "But I thought you should know."

"What do you mean, you're not asking me for anything?"

"I know how this must seem to you, Drew. You're a multi-millionaire. Everyone in the business knows that. But I need you to believe me, I didn't do this on purpose."

"I believe you. But I still don't understand why you said you're not asking for anything."

"Because I don't want you to feel like you owe me."

"It's not about owing you. It's about being responsible. I'm responsible for what happened, and I'm responsible for making sure you're okay. Both of you."

"Y—You don't have to." Her voice cracked, and I felt sorry for her. She hadn't asked for this, any more than I had, and it was going to change her life a lot more than it was going to change mine. Any fool could see that.

"Yes, I do," I said. "I'll come down to New York tomorrow. We can talk."

She thanked me, which felt as wrong as her apology, and we ended our call.

I was in shock… about to become a father, and nursing a broken heart at the same time. I couldn't think straight and, to be honest, I didn't even try. There was no point in contacting Josie. Any hopes I might have been harboring for a future with her had just been blown out of the water, and my destiny lay down a completely different path.

Since then, I've done my duty by Lexi… and not just financially. I've attended doctor's appointments, gone to scans, fitted out a nursery in her apartment, and at the house in Newport, and been there when she needed me. And, of course, I was with her at Maisie's birth, which came as a surprise to both of us. Or maybe I should say to all of us… because Josie was there, too. She was the one who called and told me Lexi had gone into labor, and at the time, I didn't know whether to be more shocked at hearing her voice or knowing that my daughter was about to be born slightly ahead of schedule… and in Boston, not New York.

Standing in the delivery room, holding Lexi's hand, trying my best to support her through the agonies of childbirth, I wanted so much to be able to look over at Josie. I couldn't, of course. It would have broken me completely.

We haven't seen each other since. We haven't even spoken, and I guess that's not surprising. The situation is awkward, to say the least. What is surprising, though, is that she hasn't seen Lexi, either. That came as news to me, and it's news I intend getting to the bottom of. If the two of them aren't that close, and if Lexi really does have someone else in her life, then maybe there's a chance.

I keep telling myself not to hope, but after all this time, what else can I do?

Chapter Two

Josie

"You look amazing." She does. It's not a lie, or a platitude. Lexi's lost all the weight she gained when she was pregnant and has returned to her former slim build. That said, her bump was tiny. I can remember thinking, when she came for that last visit – the one when she went into labor – that she didn't look more than six months pregnant, and if I hadn't been counting every painful moment since she broke the news of her pregnancy, I'd have doubted she was due to give birth.

Of course, she did… that very weekend, and the evidence is now cradled in her arms, the two of them standing just inside my apartment.

"Thanks." We both look down at Maisie, who's gazing up at me, like the stranger I am. She looks nothing like her mom, whose hair is a shade or two blonder than mine, and who has pale blue eyes. Instead, she has Drew's coloring, although Maisie's dark hair isn't as thick as his, and she has the beginnings of a very cute curl at the ends. At the moment, her eyes are a startling blue, but they could still change to be more like her father's… more like that rich milk chocolate color I remember so well. "She's been asleep for the last couple of hours."

"Is that a good thing, or a bad thing?"

Lexi smiles. "It's a good thing. It means she won't be too grumpy when I give her a bath, and you'll be able to spend some time with her before she goes to bed."

I nod my head, trying to look enthusiastic. I know I should want to be with my niece, especially as this is the first time I've seen her since she was born, but it's hard not to feel jealous.

We move further into the apartment and Lexi puts down the diaper bag that's slung over her shoulder, letting it rest on the end of the couch, before she turns to me.

"I need to grab Maisie's things from the car. Do you wanna take her for me?"

I'd rather run down to the car and fetch whatever Lexi needs. Frankly, I'd rather do almost anything than hold Drew's baby, but I can't say that, and I can't decline, either. She'll think I don't care… and I do. I'm just finding this hard.

"Sure."

She places Maisie in my arms, kissing her forehead.

"Mommy won't be a minute. You be a good girl for Aunty Josie."

She gives me a wink and a smile, then rushes to the door, letting herself out.

I stare after her, hoping she won't be long, but then Maisie wriggles in my arms, and I look down at her.

"Hi," I whisper, and she frowns, her forehead creasing. "Please don't cry." She stops pulling faces, listening to the sound of my voice, I think, and then she raises her hands, bringing them together, as she smiles, melting my heart, but somehow breaking it at the same time.

Tears well in my eyes and although I try to stop them from falling, I can't. This is so much harder than I'd expected, but maybe that's because it's not just about Drew. I swallow down the lump in my throat. *Dammit.*

I thought I'd put this behind me… gotten used to the idea that this kind of thing isn't for me.

Except it seems not.

I bend awkwardly, grabbing a Kleenex from the box on the coffee table, and dab at my eyes, which seems to confuse Maisie, and her smile fades while she watches me.

"It's okay," I whisper. "I'm just being silly… wanting what I can't have." That frown wrinkles her brow again, only this time, she yawns, and I have to say, it's the cutest thing I've ever seen. "Are you still tired?" She stares up at me and I brush my finger down her soft cheek. "You're very beautiful, you know?" Her smile returns and I chuckle. Did she know I was talking about her? I guess she must have done. Despite all my good intentions, it's impossible not to fall in love with her, and even though it hurts my heart to do it, I let her in.

The knocking at the door makes Maisie startle and I hold her a little closer. "It's okay. It's just Mommy." I wander over, opening the door and stare in shock at the amount of bags and equipment Lexi's carrying.

"Are you okay?" she asks as she comes in and dumps everything at the end of the couch.

"Sure. Why do you ask?"

"It's just you look like you've been crying." I don't answer and after just a second or two, she comes over. "Sorry, Josie. I should have been more sensitive. It wasn't fair of me to thrust Maisie at you, when you can't…"

"It's okay," I say, before she goes any further. I don't need reminding of my inadequacies, and I make a point of looking down at all the things she just brought in with her, in the hope she'll let me change the subject. "Don't take this the wrong way, but how long are you staying?"

She turns, smiling. "Just the one night," she says, shrugging her shoulders as she takes Maisie from me, and looks down at her, kissing her forehead again. "Who'd have thought someone this small could need so many things and take up so much space?"

"What's that?" I point to a dark gray case. It's a little under two feet square and roughly six inches deep.

"That's the travel crib."

Travel crib? I hadn't even realized Maisie would need one. I guess that just goes to show what I know.

"Shall I set it up in the guest room?" I ask.

"No, don't worry. It only takes about thirty seconds."

Maisie makes a grizzling sound, and Lexi looks down at her. "What's wrong?" I ask, none the wiser.

"She's hungry." I'm not sure how Lexi knows that, but I guess experience counts for a lot.

"Do you need me to do anything?"

"No, it's fine. I brought some pre-made formula, just for tonight and tomorrow. It's easier than mixing it up."

"I see."

She looks over at me as she wrestles with one of the bags, and I step closer, helping her open it.

"I gave up trying to breastfeed. It wasn't for me." I nod my head as she finds the carton of formula and hands it over, along with a bottle. "Can you measure out five ounces for me?"

"Sure." I go over to the kitchen area and stand at the end of the breakfast bar, doing as instructed, holding up the bottle to check the measurement. "Where do I put the rest of the formula?"

"In the refrigerator."

"Okay."

Once it's safely tucked away, I return with the bottle and hand it to Lexi, who's now relaxing in the corner of my pale gray couch. I sit down, watching as she feeds her daughter, who's certainly hungry, and takes to her bottle like she's been starved for a week, gazing up into her mommy's eyes.

I'm fascinated by the bond, but I'm also still intrigued by Lexi's plans, and rather than sitting in silence, I decide to ask her outright why she's coming back to Boston after she's been to Newport. Maybe it's because we're sitting so close together, or because I'm studying her while she feeds Maisie, but I can't fail to notice the blush creeping over her face when she looks up at me.

"I—I've met someone," she says.

I don't know what I expected, but this wasn't it, and I struggle to hide my surprise.

"You have?"

"Yeah." She smiles, her eyes lighting up. "He's perfect, Josie. He's everything I ever wanted, and never thought I'd have… not now." She glances down at Maisie and her blush deepens. "Don't get me wrong, I love every hair on her head, but I'll admit, there was a time when I thought I'd never be with a man again."

That's a feeling I know only too well, and I nod my head. "Does he live in Boston?" To start with, that question makes sense, but as I finish saying it, I realize how silly I'm being. If he lived here, she'd probably be staying with him tonight, and not me.

She shakes her head, proving me right. "He's not even American. He's Spanish."

"But he lives here, right?"

"Yeah."

"What's his name?" I ask.

"Manuel."

She's being a little cagey, and I want to know why.

"What does he do?"

"He's a model. I first met him a couple of years ago when we worked together on a photo shoot in Tahiti, and our paths have crossed a few times since."

"Professionally?"

"Oh, yeah. There was nothing between us… until now."

"So what changed?"

She shrugs her shoulders. "I don't know, really. He'd been working in Europe for a while and we bumped into each other at a party and got talking and…"

"One thing led to another?"

She smiles. "You could say that."

"Does he know about Maisie?"

"Of course. I'd left her with a babysitter on the night of the party, but I told him all about her."

"That night?"

"Yeah. I had to be honest with him."

"How did he react?"

"He was fine about it. He wanted to know about Maisie's father, so I explained what had happened with Drew and how things are set up between us now."

"Does Drew know about Manuel?"

She looks a little embarrassed. "I'm going to tell him tomorrow when I collect him from the airport."

"And how does Manuel feel about you going down to Newport and staying with your ex?"

She stares at me for a moment, blinking. "He's not entirely happy about it, to be honest… and that's one of the reasons we're thinking of moving to Boston."

She's moving here? I don't know how I feel about the idea of my sister and my niece living nearby, although that's not the biggest bombshell. "We?"

"Yeah."

"So Manuel would move here with you?"

"Of course. If we do this, we'd be buying somewhere together."

I can't help the slight cough that escapes my lips. "Together? How long have you been with this guy?"

She frowns. "Four weeks."

"Four weeks? And you're talking about buying an apartment together?"

"Why not? He's practically living at my place, anyway." I shake my head, and her frown turns into a glare. "Can I take it you disapprove?"

"It's not my place to approve or disapprove, but I think you should have run it by Drew first."

"Why? We're not together. I can do what I like with my life. I don't ask him what he does, so what right does he…?"

I hold my hand up and she stops talking… the thought of Drew with another woman filtering through my head, unbidden, crushing my already broken heart.

"I—I'm not saying you're not both free agents, and that you can't do whatever you want."

"Then what are you saying?"

"That if another man is living with his daughter, Drew has a right to know."

She blushes again. "Manuel doesn't actually live with me. H—He just stays over a lot. And, in any case, like I said, I'm gonna tell Drew all about it tomorrow. I'll sweeten it by telling him Manuel and I will be moving to Boston soon, and he'll be able to see more of Maisie that way." She glances down at her daughter. "He can have her stay over at his place, if he wants."

I notice that even she thinks the deal needs 'sweetening'. "So this move is definite, then?"

"It is if we can find somewhere to live."

"Is Manuel gonna come look at apartments with you?"

She shakes her head. "No. He's working in Arizona at the moment, so I'm gonna look around and see what's available, and if I find something I like, we'll come back and take another look together."

"What about your father? How does he feel about this?"

He lives in New York and as far as I know, he has done all his life. I'm intrigued by how he's going to respond to his precious daughter moving away. I imagine he'll do everything he can to stop her. That's the kind of man he is. He's all about power, and he's good at wielding it.

"I've got no idea. We're not talking."

"Seriously?"

"Yeah. You remember me saying how badly he reacted when I told him I was pregnant?"

"Of course, although you never said why."

She shakes her head. "Because he didn't give me a logical explanation. He just flew into a rage. I wondered if it was something to do with my mother. She died giving birth, and I thought maybe he was worried the same thing was gonna happen to me."

"You don't think that would have made him concerned, rather than angry?"

"Probably."

"Did you try talking to him?"

"He wouldn't listen to anything I had to say. Even when I told him Drew could provide for us, and that it wasn't gonna cost him a dime…" Her voice falters and she swallows hard.

"Surely when Maisie was born, though…"

She sighs. "I know," she says. "I hoped he'd come around then. Although why I thought he'd change his mind, I don't know. You remember how stubborn he is? Still, I sent him a picture of her, and text messages asking him to call."

"And did he?"

"No. I—I'm still waiting to hear from him."

"I'm sorry."

She shakes her head. "It's his loss. He's the one who's missing out." Her words sound good, but I can tell he's hurt her.

That's something else he excels at… hurting people.

Maisie finishes her milk and Lexi puts the bottle on the table in front of us, sitting up slightly. As she does, her daughter lets out an enormous belch, and we both laugh, which helps lighten the oppressive atmosphere a little.

Thank God…

Maisie had her bath a while ago, and then Lexi took her into the guest bedroom so she could have some quiet time, before she put her down to sleep in the travel crib. It's a little tight on space in there, but she reassured me it would be fine, and I left her to it.

"She's gone to sleep at last," she says, coming out and closing the door quietly behind her.

I'm putting the finishing touches to our dinner, which is just a simple salad, made from roasted butternut squash, apples, pecans and cranberries, served with mixed leaves and feta cheese, and an orange vinaigrette. After Lexi's call last night, I spent ages trying to decide what to serve, knowing from experience that she adheres to a strict diet, limits her proteins and carbs, and although she's not a vegetarian, might as well be. I look up as I put the salad bowl on the breakfast bar, alongside the dishes, wine glasses and silverware.

"The travel crib was really simple to put together. Did you buy that just to come here? Or do you use it at Drew's place?"

She sits down and I copy her, pushing the salad bowl in her direction and watching as she helps herself to a small portion. "No, Maisie has a fully equipped nursery in Newport."

"So you bought the crib just to come here?"

She blushes as I dish up my salad, taking considerably more than she did. "No. I have friends I sometimes stay over with, and once or twice we've slept at Manuel's place."

"Oh."

She picks up her fork, but then puts it straight back down again and turns to me. "I know this isn't ideal, but nothing in this situation is ideal, is it?" she says.

"No." It certainly isn't… not when I'm in love with Maisie's father. I turn away to hide my blushes. "I'm not judging you, Lexi."

"Good… because I didn't ask for this any more than Drew did. And if I'm being honest, I think we're doing okay. As dysfunctional families go, I think we're better than most… and before you say anything, I know most of that is down to Drew. He's an amazing father."

I turn back again. "I'm sure he is, and I wasn't going to say anything."

She sighs, shaking her head. "D—Do you think we could try to be friends?" she says, surprising me.

"Friends? We're step-sisters."

"I know, but we've never acted like it, have we?"

I can't deny that. "No. I guess not."

She leans a little closer, nudging in to me. "I'll always be grateful you were there for me when I found out I was pregnant. After Dad reacted the way he did, I had no-one else to turn to, and even though Drew stepped up, I relied on you, Josie. I don't think you know how much. Please don't think I'm ungrateful for what you did. I—I'm sorry I didn't stay in touch after Maisie was born, but… well, life's complicated."

It's a lot more complicated than she thinks. "I know."

She smiles. "It's just, if I'm gonna move here, it'd be nice to think we could see more of each other, maybe build a relationship? We never really tried before, did we?"

"When we were growing up, you mean?"

"Yeah," she says.

"I guess we never spent that much time together."

She smiles. "No. You were always too busy with horse riding and martial arts."

I chuckle, recalling the long-forgotten interests of my youth. "Yeah… and you were only interested in ballet and dance classes."

"God… yeah. I was obsessed."

"You looked great in a tutu, though."

She laughs, although it quickly fades, and she stares at me for a moment. "Of course, everything changed, didn't it, when…"

"When I got sick?"

"Yeah." She moves her hand closer to mine, although I don't think she expects me to take it. "I didn't approve of what my dad did," she says in a quiet whisper. "I thought he treated your mom really badly."

"He'd never treated her well, Lexi."

"No. He's not the easiest of people. I—I guess he was jealous of the time she spent with you."

"I was in the hospital. What did he want her to do? Abandon me?"

She pulls her hand away, holding it up. "I'm not trying to excuse him, or what he did."

"He broke her heart." I can hear the crack in my voice and I cough to cover it. "When she found out about his affair, on top of everything else she had to cope with, it was… it was too much for her."

Lexi nods her head and I look down at my plate of untouched food, my appetite gone as I recall those dark days of my illness and the aftermath. My mom had thought life had thrown its worst at her when her boyfriend abandoned her after she told him she was pregnant with me. My illness knocked her sideways, hitting her harder still. Lexi's father had never been the kindest of men. He had a temper and could say the cruelest of things when riled, but I don't think Mom ever believed he was capable of such deception.

Except, it seems, he was.

And it broke her.

In my opinion, it killed her… and although none of that was Lexi's fault, it's hard to forgive her father for what he did.

Neither of us ate very much last night, and after we'd cleared away, Lexi said she was tired and went to bed. I didn't blame her. The atmosphere between us was too frosty for words.

I came to bed myself, unwilling to do anything that might make a noise and wake Maisie, although I struggled to sleep, unable to forget our conversations, and rid my mind of all those memories of my mom and her dad, and my illness… and Drew.

I heard Maisie wake in the early hours, and I listened as Lexi fumbled around in the kitchen. For a while, I contemplated getting up and offering to help, but the noises quietened down after a few minutes and I settled back into bed, and eventually, I guess I must have drifted off to sleep…

My shift is due to start at eight, and I check my watch. I've only got a few minutes until I need to leave, and I pull on my jacket as I swallow down the last of my coffee, looking over at the couch, where Lexi is sitting, feeding Maisie, who's wearing light blue leggings and a white t-shirt, that has a dolphin on the front. She looks adorable, and I know I need to take my chance. They'll be gone by the time I get back this evening. I need to say something… to make up for the awful tone there's been between Lexi and me.

"About last night," Lexi says, looking up at me, and I put down my cup. She beat me to it.

"Yeah?"

"I'm sorry if I said anything that upset you."

"You didn't. It's just the memories of Mom."

She nods her head. "I know. But do you think we could put all that behind us? I'd really like for us to be friends."

I wander over and sit beside her. "I'd like that, too."

She isn't her father. She might look like him in a certain light, but she isn't him. Memories of the fights between him and my mom are just that… memories. It's too late to change any of it now.

"We'll agree not to talk about my dad, shall we?" she says.

"I think that might be wise." I smile. It wasn't just his affair, it was the way he used to shout at mom, the way he'd sometimes belittle her to make him feel better about himself. I used to hear him doing it, putting her down and calling her names, and I'd run and hide, vowing silently that I'd never let a man do that to me.

Lexi and I have never talked about it, and we probably never will, but I wouldn't be surprised if she felt the same. She must have heard them fighting, too… and even though he was her father, I can't believe she felt good about what he was doing.

That's all in the past, though. It's another country, and we need to leave it behind us… not just the ancient past with her father, but the more recent past with Drew. She knows nothing about that, but it's time I came to terms with the fact that nothing can ever happen between us. I'll always love him, but I can't see any way for us to be together… not now.

"I'll call and let you know when I'm coming back from Newport."

"Okay."

"And I'll leave the travel crib here, if that's okay with you?"

"Sure." I check my watch. "God… I'm gonna be late." I jump to my feet and rush to the kitchen to grab my phone, unplugging it from the charger. I don't have time to check it, and I shove it into my jacket pocket.

"We'll see you soon," Lexi calls from the couch.

"Yeah. Take care, won't you?"

"We will."

She looks down at Maisie, who's gazing up at her, and even though that pang of jealousy is still there, I have to smile. She's so damn happy.

"Motherhood suits you, you know?"

She grins. "Yeah. It shocks me sometimes, how much I love her."

I wander back over, bending down to kiss Maisie's forehead. She glances up, her eyes locking with mine for a second, and I fight the pain in my chest… the knowledge that the only way forward is to put her father behind me, no matter how hard it is.

Drew

There's a baby crying in the corner of the departure lounge and even though the mom is doing her best to calm him, he's not responding to her. He's just screaming at the top of his lungs. Several people around me are rolling their eyes, or tutting, and I'm willing to admit that a few months ago, I'd have joined them.

Now, I've got a lot more tolerance. I understand that babies cry; sometimes for a good reason, and sometimes for no reason at all… or that's how it seems, anyway.

The woman behind me mutters, "Dear God," although I don't rise to her impatience, and just smile instead.

After my conversation with Hunter, I'm feeling more optimistic than I have in a long while. I think that's partly because I've got a half-baked plan for the future, and partly because I've realized I need to take my chances… no matter how small they are.

And I intend to.

I've hardly slept since then, and I don't care, because my mind is racing with thoughts that maybe – just maybe – after all this time, I might be able to do something about Josie. It won't be straightforward. In fact, I fully expect it to be the complete opposite, and a lot of what happens will depend on Lexi and whether I've mis-read things with her. But if I'm right, if she really has got someone new in her life, then there's a chance we all can move on. Lexi can be with someone who appreciates her like I never could, and I can be with Josie.

Assuming, of course, she wants to be with me…

A cloud descends, wiping out my smile and darkening my mood.

What if she doesn't?

I thought she wanted to be with me when we were at the party, at least until she found out who I was. Then, when we met at the coffee shop, our misunderstandings a thing of the past, I got the impression she wasn't averse to our friendship, and perhaps to it becoming more than that. She certainly seemed keen to meet up again. The thing is, a lot of time has passed since then. She could be with someone else…

I close my eyes, somehow blocking out all the surrounding noise, and I try to picture her. It's easy; she's filled my every thought since the moment I first laid eyes on her. I imagine her in the arms of another man, his lips on hers, his hands wandering. It hurts, but I have to contemplate the fact that this could be her reality. I might have hopes for a future with her, but she could already have a future with someone else. Unless… unless she's waiting for me. No, that's silly. Why would she? I left her with no hope of any kind of future for us. In fact, I didn't even contact her again after Lexi announced her pregnancy. It felt dishonest. And besides, I didn't know what to say. It was bad enough when she realized I was Lexi's boyfriend. To discover I was the father of her unborn child…

I couldn't face it. I couldn't face her.

So, I took the coward's way out.

If she's free, is it possible she'll still want something more than friendship, given how complicated things are? Will she even want to speak to me? Will she be able to forgive me?

I have so many questions, and not the slightest chance of any answers for at least the next eleven hours… until I touch down in the States and I can talk to Lexi. Obviously, I can't ask her outright about her sister's love life, but I can see how things lie with Lexi. It'll be a start.

In the meantime, those eleven hours are stretching before me like a death sentence, and I'm not sure I can handle it. If I'm flying back home just to find Josie's already with another man, I'm not sure what I'll do…

Josie's number is still on my phone. Rather than putting myself through hours of torture, I could just call her, couldn't I?

No, I couldn't.

Of course I couldn't.

What would I say? The last time I saw her was in the delivery room, when Maisie was born. It was one of the best, and one of the worst days of my life, watching my daughter come into this world, while the woman I loved was standing just a few feet away, so far out of reach, she might as well have been on the other side of the world.

The problem is, I honestly don't think I can survive the next eleven hours, not knowing what I'm going home to… whether I have a chance or not.

I pull out my phone, and even though I have no idea what I'm going to say, I go to her details on my contact list, my finger poised over the 'call' icon, as I take a deep breath.

"No." I say the word out loud, stopping myself just in time, and ignoring the bemused stares of my fellow passengers as I shake my head, staring at my phone. How could I be so stupid? It's three in the morning in Boston. Phoning her is out of the question.

Maybe I could text her instead…

Except text messages can often do more harm than good. They're easily misunderstood. And besides, I want her to hear my voice, so she'll understand how I feel.

Of course…

A voice message.

I glance around the room, spying a quiet corner, as far away as possible from the crying baby, and I pick up my bag, making my way over there. Turning my back on the room, I find Josie's details again, and this time, click on the message app, and then I take a breath, preparing myself, putting an image of Josie in my mind as I press and hold the voice recording icon.

"Hi, Josie. It's me, Drew. It's been a long time, and I know I should've been in touch before now, but… the… the thing is, I —I wanted to ask if we could meet up? I'm at the airport. I'm flying back from Rome today, and going down to Newport with Maisie and… and her mom, but I wondered… can I call you? We need to talk, or I think we do. Obviously, if I mis-read everything, you'll be wondering what on earth I'm talking about, in which case I apologize for disturbing you, and it's probably best if you stop listening now…" I pause for a second and then continue, "If you're still listening, I guess I didn't mis-read things, so the next question is, do you want to see me again? If you've moved on, or you're with someone else now, or you just don't want to have anything more to do with me, after everything that's happened, that's fine… well, it isn't, but I'll understand. This is complicated, and it's a lot harder for you than it is for me. I get that, and I'm sorry. Truly, I am. I should have said that a long time ago, but I'm really sorry, Josie." I cough, fighting my emotions. "The timing was dreadful, and if it's all too much for you, then just ignore me. I'll get the message and I won't hassle you." I pause for a second. "But if you think you'd like to meet up, call me. I'll fit in with whatever you need… whatever you want. I just wanna see you again, Josie." I've rambled on for long enough, and probably said more than I intended. Should I add anything else, though? I can't say, 'I love you,' over a voice message, so instead I just say, "Call me… please," and release my thumb from the recording icon. The message is longer than I'd expected, but I press 'send' anyway, my heart flipping over in my chest.

I know she's as likely to say 'no', as she is to say 'yes', for all kinds of reasons, but at least I've set the wheels in motion and I guess I'll know soon enough what my future holds.

"How can she have grown so much in just ten days?"

I keep looking around at Maisie, in the back of Lexi's car, marveling at the changes in her.

"Because she's a greedy little miss. She does nothing but eat."

"Her hair seems more curly, too."

"Does it? I can't say I've noticed."

It seems curlier to me, and I smile at my beautiful daughter before I turn around and face the front again.

"Thanks for coming to get me."

I think that's about the fifth time I've said that since I came out into the arrivals hall, and Maisie greeted me with the most perfect little smile that lit up my heart. Lexi handed her straight to me, and I held her against my chest, only fully appreciating then how much I'd missed her.

"It's okay. I just wish I'd remembered how much luggage you were gonna have with you."

"That's my fault. I should've thought about all the things you usually have to bring with you for Maisie, and realized how hard it was gonna be fitting my equipment into the trunk."

We had to empty everything out and re-arrange it all again, and while we got there in the end, it took forever.

The traffic's heavy and we're sitting nose-to-tail, waiting for the cars in front to move. I pull out my phone, checking to see if there are any messages or missed calls. I know I'd have heard it if there had been, but I'm desperate to hear from Josie, although I console myself that, at this time of day, she'll be at work. That'll be it. She's not really ignoring me.

"Do you have any plans for the next few days?" Lexi's voice interrupts my thoughts and I put my phone on my lap, turning to look at her, surprised by her question.

"Just to spend some time with Maisie, and to meet my new nephew. Why?"

She's biting on her bottom lip, looking worried, and I twist around a little further, giving her my undivided attention. "W— We need to talk, Drew."

"You're right, we do."

She glances over at me, frowning. "You want to talk as well? What about?"

"You can go first, if you like."

"No… it's fine."

I was going to wait until we got to the house, but I guess there's no time like the present.

"I—I was wondering… that's to say, I got the feeling you might be seeing someone… as in a man. Is that true?"

I notice the blush creep up her cheeks and smile to myself. I was right.

"It is, but how did you know?"

"I didn't. I guessed."

"You're not gonna tell me you have a problem with it, are you?"

"No. Of course not. I... um... I just wanted to say that I've been thinking about seeing someone, too."

She looks at me a little harder, then as the traffic moves, she turns back and focuses on the road again. "You have?"

"Yeah."

"But..."

"But what?"

"Well... I'd assumed you'd been seeing people all along. I mean, why wouldn't you?"

"Because I met someone a while ago. We couldn't get together then because the timing was off. But I really want to now."

"Then why don't you? There's nothing between us, Drew. I know other people find it hard to understand our set-up, but Maisie's the only link between us, and if you wanna see someone else, that's fine by me."

I nod my head. "Would you feel the same way if I told you the 'someone' in question was your sister?"

I hold my breath, waiting, watching as she works it out in her head. "Josie?"

"Yeah."

She laughs, throwing her head back. "Well... who'd have thought? Does she know?"

"I've got no idea. I met her at that party you dragged me to, and to be honest, I fell for her the moment I saw her."

"Just like that?"

"Yeah. Just like that. I felt bad, though, because you and I were still together, and..."

"Oh, come on. We were just playing at being together. We both knew that whatever we'd had in the Caribbean hadn't survived the flight home."

"No, it hadn't, but I still felt bad. That's why I broke up with you that night."

"So you could be with Josie?"

"Yeah. Not straight away, obviously. I thought I'd give it some time, only…"

"Only then I told you I was pregnant?"

I nod my head. There's no point in telling her about my 'dates' with Josie. Aside from the fact that they weren't really dates, they happened before Lexi discovered she was pregnant. Everything was different back then.

"Exactly," I say. "And what was already awkward became impossible."

"Hmm… I can see how it would be difficult for both of you."

I turn slightly, facing her. "Does Josie ever mention me?"

"No, but we've never been great at sharing secrets… about men, or anything else, for that matter."

I frown at her, wondering if she's lying, trying to make me feel better. "Seriously? Isn't that the kind of thing sisters normally share?"

"I don't know. Josie and I aren't sisters."

I sit up, my phone falling into the footwell. I ignore it, leaving it where it is, my attention fixed on Lexi. "What are you saying?"

"We're step-sisters. My mom died giving birth to me, and when I was two, my dad met Josie's mom. Josie was three at the time, and although we probably should have been close, we never were. We never had very much in common and lived quite separate lives… which were divided even further when our parents divorced."

"When did that happen?"

"When I was fourteen. She and her mom moved to Boston and Dad and I stayed in New York."

"S—So you're not even related?"

"No." She looks over at me again, just briefly. The traffic's moving a lot faster now and she needs to concentrate on the road. "Don't read too much into Josie not talking about you. I don't know her that well, but I know her well enough to understand she's a very private person, and I think you'd be good for her."

"You do?"

"Yeah. Her life's been kinda lonely. She needs someone like you… someone who'll be there for her."

I like the sound of being there for Josie, although I'm not so keen on the idea of her being lonely. "I—I've left her a message, asking her to call, but I didn't want to do anything definite without talking to you first. The situation is… well… it's delicate."

"I know. And thank you for asking."

I heave out a sigh of relief. "What was it you wanted to talk to me about?"

She takes a breath, letting it out slowly. "I—I'm thinking of moving to Boston."

That's the very last thing I expected her to say. "Even though you've met someone?"

"Yes. It's all connected."

"Oh? Does he live here then?"

"No. He lives in New York… with me most of the time. But we're thinking…"

"Whoa. Back up a second. Did you just say he lives with you?"

"Most of the time." She bites on her lip again, and I can sense her anxiety. It's well founded.

"How long has this been going on?"

"I've been seeing him for about four weeks."

"And he's living with you already?"

"Practically."

We both know that means 'yes', and I wish she'd just be honest. "Why didn't you tell me about him before?"

"I don't know," she says.

"Is it serious? I guess it must be, if he's living with you."

"Yeah, it's serious." I suck in a breath, and she glances over at me. "Are you mad at me, Drew?"

"No. Although I'd have liked to have known what was going on. I don't have the right to dictate how you live your life, Lexi, but Maisie's my daughter, and I don't understand why you didn't tell me something as important as this. I've done everything you've asked of me since the moment you told me you were pregnant."

"I know you have. You've gone above and beyond. I never asked you to pay off my mortgage, or to give me such a generous allowance."

"You didn't need to ask. Whatever you and Maisie need, it's yours. It just would've been nice if you'd trusted me with this… if you'd kept me informed. I asked you about Josie before I even…"

"Okay, okay. I'm sorry. I should've told you," she says. "It was wrong of me to keep it from you." I shake my head, turning away. "You don't need to feel threatened, Drew."

I look back at her again. "You think? Some guy moves into your apartment. He's living there with my daughter, who no doubt sees a damn sight more of him than she does of me. You decide not to tell me about it… and you tell me I shouldn't feel threatened by him?"

"No. If anything, it's the other way around."

"What are you talking about?"

She sighs. "He doesn't like me coming down to Newport with you… okay?"

"No, it's not okay," I say. "What does he think we're doing down there? Surely you've explained there's nothing between us anymore, other than Maisie? He gets that you've got your own rooms… that you only visit so I can see my daughter?"

"He does, but he still doesn't like it."

I shake my head. "And this is why you wanna move to Boston, is it? So I can see Maisie here, instead of in Newport?"

"Yes," she says. "Look… I know it's not the ideal way for you to find out about Manuel and me, but at least if we're all living in Boston, you can see more of Maisie. You can have her stay over at your place without me, if you want."

"More like a normal dysfunctional family, you mean?"

"I guess." She glances over, and I nod my head. "Does that mean you're okay with it?"

"It means I'm thinking."

"What about?"

"How to make it work." She smiles. "Do you love him?"

"Yes, I do."

"Does he love you?"

"He says he does, and I believe him." I can tell that from the look in her eyes.

"Okay. You're gonna have to give me some time."

"To get used to the idea?" she says, frowning.

"No. To find a house."

"A house?"

"Yeah."

"But you already have an apartment."

"I know, but that's just somewhere I live when I need to be in the city for work. You're making this move to Boston on the proviso that I'll see Maisie here, rather than at the place I consider to be my home. I can understand why, but if that's what we're gonna do, I'll need to buy a house here, so I can make it a home for her."

"I see what you mean. Well… you'll have plenty of time. Manuel and I haven't even started looking for a place of our own yet."

"Do you need any help… financially, I mean?"

"No. We're fine, thanks."

"If you change your mind…"

She shakes her head, and I know there's no point in arguing. I guess it's understandable that her boyfriend doesn't want me to buy their new home for them. In his shoes, I'd probably feel the same.

"Thank you," she says.

"What for?"

"For not being mad at me. For understanding."

"That's okay. I—I just want us to promise each other, whatever happens between you and Manuel, and me and Josie, nothing's gonna come between us and Maisie. Can we do that?"

"We can."

I nod my head, and although I still feel threatened, I guess I always knew my relationship with Lexi would come to this one day… that we'd have to make compromises if we were going to make it work.

I reach forward into the footwell for my phone, just as Maisie grizzles behind me.

"It's okay, baby," Lexi says, as I grab my phone.

I sit up. Lexi's twisted in her seat, checking on Maisie and I open my mouth to tell her to watch the road, just as a truck pulls into the lane right in front of us and brakes sharply.

"Brake! Hit the fucking brakes!"

She spins around, braking hard, but it's too late. We're going too fast, and I drop my phone, bracing for the inevitable impact. My instincts are telling me to protect Maisie, but I can't get to her. All I can do is watch, completely helpless as the back of the truck gets closer and closer, the car spinning as Lexi loses control.

She screams. I feel the jarring impact, the sound of metal on metal, my own voice calling out to Maisie that it'll be okay… and then it's silent… eerily silent, and everything fades to black.

Chapter Three

Josie

"Nurse Emerson?"

"Yes?" I turn around at the sound of my name and come face-to-face with Agatha Meadows. She's the senior RN on duty today and is in charge of the ward. At around forty, she's older than most of us, but everyone I know here gets along with her. She's the same height as me, with dark brown hair, which she wears in a short style, curled around her face, and she has a slim figure, which – like mine – is hidden by scrubs, although hers are deep blue, rather than purple.

"How's Mr. Stanford?"

I shake my head. "There's still no progress," I say as we stroll over to the nurse's station. "It doesn't make sense. His concussion wasn't that bad, but his visual processing skills are still very basic. He needs prompting to interpret even the simplest of objects."

She nods her head. "I think I'll call Doctor Sweeney. He's on the late shift today. He can come take a look." She checks her watch. "You worked through lunch today, didn't you?"

"I did. I wanted to do some more work with Kayla McQueen."

Kayla was the victim of a hit-and-run accident nearly three months ago. She's only twelve and as the result of the brain injury she suffered, she's been unable to speak ever since. Along with some of the other nurses, I've been working on her speech, and we had a breakthrough today, with her managing to say the word 'cat' several times over. The first time, I wondered if it was a fluke, but after the third, and judging by the smile on her face, I knew it was for real.

"I heard she'd done well today."

"Yeah… she did. Really well."

She smiles. "I just wanted to say, as you didn't get to take your break, you can go home early, if you want."

It's not an offer she needs to make twice.

I might love my job, but I'm exhausted, and not about to look the gift horse of an early finish to my day in the mouth.

"Are you sure?" I ask.

"Of course."

I thank her and, before she changes her mind, I head for the nurse's lounge.

This has to be the most depressing room on our floor. The patients' rooms and the hallways are brightly colored, to stimulate the senses and help recovery. In here, it's like someone lost the will to live – or at least to be cheerful – and they covered the walls with the drabbest of grays. The furniture isn't much better, being dark blue, and very uncomfortable, but I flop onto the couch and take a minute to myself before heading home.

I've been on my feet all day… although I'm not complaining. It's part of the job, and you don't go into nursing expecting to sit back and take things easy. I discovered that when I worked in the ER, and it's just the same up here, in the physical medicine and rehabilitation service. Our job is to help patients who've suffered neurotrauma to recover as many of their abilities as they can. I always think of it as physical therapy for the brain, and I'm part of the team here that works with various patients, helping them to pick up the pieces of their lives… to learn to talk, to eat, to walk again.

No two days are ever the same. No two injuries are ever the same. And that's why I love it.

I suppose it helps that I wanted to be a nurse ever since I was a teenager, when I spent so long in the hospital myself. It was like it was meant to be, and after I switched from the ER to neurotrauma, roughly a year ago, I knew I'd found my calling. Naturally, it can be tough. It's always hard work, but it's worth it. I get to make a real difference in people's lives, and that's what makes it special.

I get up again, realizing I'm wasting time sitting here daydreaming, when I could be at home, and I go over to my locker, retrieving my purse and my jacket. I came in wearing my scrubs today, so I don't need to change, and as I close my locker, I delve into my purse for my phone.

I haven't even looked at it today, but I check it now, letting out a gasp when I see I've got a message, and that it's from Drew.

"My God…" I've hardly had time to think about him all day, but it was only this morning I decided to put him behind me… to leave him in the past, no matter how much it hurt. Why is he contacting me now, of all times?

I guess there's only one way to find out, and I click on the message app and stare at the screen. It's not a normal text, but a voice message, and I sit on the couch again, putting my jacket beside me, grateful that I'm alone in here as I turn up the volume and press the 'play' button.

"Hi, Josie. It's me, Drew." His voice fills the room and my heart, warming me from within, although I can hear lots of background noise, too… people talking and a baby crying. "It's been a long time, and I know I should've been in touch before now, but… the… the thing is, I—I wanted to ask if we could meet up?" Can he really mean that? He sounds nervous, but that's understandable. I'm shaking, barely able to hold my phone, and all I'm doing is listening, not talking. "I'm at the airport… I'm flying back from Rome today, and going down to Newport with Maisie and… and her mom, but I wondered… can I call you? We need to talk, or I think we do. Obviously, if I've mis-read everything, you'll be wondering what on earth I'm talking about, in which case I apologize for disturbing you, and it's probably best if you stop listening now…" There's a slight pause, but I wait. I need to know what he's going to say next. "If you're still listening, I guess I didn't mis-read things, so the next question is, do you want to see me again? If you've moved on, or you're with someone else now, or you just don't want to have anything more to do with me, after everything that's happened, that's fine… well, it isn't, but I'll understand. This is complicated, and it's a lot harder for you than it is for me. I get that, and I'm sorry. Truly, I am. I should have said that a long time ago, but I'm really sorry, Josie." I can hear the emotion in his voice… the slight crack, and the cough he uses to cover it. "The timing was dreadful, and if it's all too much for you, then just ignore me. I'll get the message and I won't hassle you." There's a moment of silence and I use it to contemplate ignoring him. After a message like this, though, how could I? "If you think you'd like to meet up, call me. I'll fit in with whatever you need… whatever you want. I just wanna see you again, Josie." My heart is so light, I feel like it could float up to the clouds and carry me with it. "Call me… please," I hear him say, and all the background noise stops. He's finished speaking and I look down at my screen, seeing I have the option to keep the recording. I press it quickly, terrified I'll lose those precious words.

I also notice the time of the message, which is just after three this morning. He said he was at the airport in Rome, so it would have been around nine for him, although I wonder why he didn't wait until he got back. He must have been just about to board his flight, after all.

I guess he didn't feel like waiting.

But can this mean what I think it means?

He wants to see me again, that much is obvious. What's not so clear is, does he want more than coffee and conversation? I can't be sure, although he sounded really nervous, which doesn't make much sense if friendship was all he was interested in. Does someone who wants to be your friend get so anxious about it? I don't think so.

He also seemed worried that I might be with someone else, too.

As if that was ever going to happen.

So, can it be?

Can it be he wants me, like I want him?

I guess there's only one way to find out.

I check the time. It's four-forty-five.

Lexi said his flight was landing at three, so they'll be in the car by now, driving down to Newport together. It probably wouldn't be wise to call. Not when they're sitting side by side. Has he decided to throw caution to the winds and start something with me, despite his relationship with my sister… if it can be called that? I don't know. But at least he acknowledged how much harder this is for me than it is for him. Because even if he doesn't have a relationship with Lexi, I do.

So, no matter how much I want to run into his arms and say 'yes' to absolutely anything he asks of me, it's not that simple.

I have so many questions, and I know I won't be able to function properly until I get answers. Even so, I can't call him now. I can't speak to him, knowing my sister is sitting just inches away from him. Whatever I need to know, I'm going to have to wait.

I get up, pocketing my phone, and pick up my jacket, making for the door.

The elevator doors open immediately, and I step inside, my head spinning, even though I'm trying very hard not to think about Drew's message. How can I when I don't fully understand it… and given that, I think it's best to wait and speak to Drew, rather than punishing myself any more than I already have.

The quickest way to my car is through the Emergency Room and once the elevator doors open, I head straight there, going down the corridor and through the double doors.

I'm immediately hit by the noise, which is standard in this department, although it seems worse than usual today. There's a baby crying, and I'm reminded of Drew's call, and all those sounds in the background at the airport.

"Hey, Josie…" I nod at Doctor Walters, who I used to work with, and he smiles back as I make my way toward the nurse's station, the sounds of the baby's crying getting louder by the second.

Behind the desk, I spot one of my friends, Orla. She's a few years older than me, and she's holding the screaming infant against her chest, looking frazzled.

"What's going on?" I wander over, making myself heard above the din.

She shakes her auburn head, glancing down at the baby in her arms, in a signal I know only too well, and my heart sinks for the poor little thing. "There's been an RTA."

"The mom?"

"She died at the scene. The man with them hasn't regained consciousness. They're about to send him for a CT, but it's not looking good at the moment."

"And in the meantime, you've been left holding the baby?"

"Yeah… literally." She bounces the infant a little, bobbing up and down, but that just seems to make matters worse, and she rolls her eyes. "I've never been any good with babies."

"I'd offer to help, but…"

"Yeah, I know… you've got better things to do." She smiles and looks down at the baby. "Shall we try turning you around? You're probably bored with staring over my shoulder at the wall."

She maneuvers the baby, turning her, and I notice the dolphin on her t-shirt, my heart stopping in my chest, my legs weakening beneath me.

"No." I hear myself say the word, even though I'm unaware of being able to speak.

"Are you okay?" Orla looks at me, concern etched on her face.

"It can't be." I walk around the desk, almost falling over the car seat on the floor, getting closer to Orla as she turns, facing me.

"Josie?"

I look down at the baby in her arms, and I know it's true. I can see it in her bright blue eyes, and that curl at the ends of her hair. "Oh, God… Maisie."

I drop my jacket, taking Maisie in my arms, even though she's a blur, my eyes filled with tears.

"You know her?"

"Yes. Sh—She's my niece."

Maisie stops crying, staring up at me, and pulling that same face she did last night, when she furrowed her brow.

"She certainly seems to know who you are."

"Her mom is my… *was* my sister."

Orla picks up my jacket, putting it over the back of the chair and then turns it around, so I can sit.

"No, I'm fine, thanks."

She nods her head. "I'm really sorry, Josie. I had no idea."

"Why would you? Lexi and I don't have the same last name. We were step-sisters."

"I see. And the guy who was in the car with them?"

"Is his name Drew Bennett?" I hold my breath, although I already know the answer, and as she nods her head, a tear hits my cheek. "H—He's Maisie's father," I whisper.

She looks over my shoulder. "Here's Doctor Walters. He's in charge of the case."

I grab her arm. "Please don't say anything about my connection with the family."

"Are you serious?"

"Yes. I want to help… to do what I can for Maisie and Drew, but if the doctors find out who I am, they'll make me back off."

She knows I'm right, and nods her head just as Doctor Walters comes over, studying the chart in his hands. He looks across at me. "I don't know what your secret is, but if you can keep that baby from crying, you can stay as long as you like."

I smile up at him, although God knows how. "I'll do my best," I say, glancing down at the chart. "What's going on?"

He shakes his head, frowning. "It's too soon to say. We need the results of the CT before I can be sure about anything, but Mr. Bennett hasn't regained consciousness at all."

"Have the families been notified?" I ask, turning to Orla.

She nods her head. "They both had emergency contacts on their phones. Lexi… I mean, Miss Doyle's was a guy called Manuel Ortega. He's working in Arizona at the moment, but he's catching the next flight back."

"And Mr. Bennett?"

"His contact was his brother, Hunter. He works locally and said he and his wife would come straight here."

I swallow down the lump in my throat, wondering what I'm going to do. Drew's brother is bound to want to take Maisie, and

I'll have no reason to stay after that… not officially. Of course, I could reveal my true identity, but if I do, they won't let me be involved. My connection is with Lexi, not Drew, and I doubt they'll even keep me informed of what's happening with him.

I hug Maisie closer to me, her tender body tight against mine, as Doctor Walters bends his head, talking in whispers to Orla, before she nods her head and walks away.

"Excuse me?" I look up, catching my breath, when I see a tall man on the other side of the desk. He's the image of Drew, and I know this is Hunter Bennett, even before he says his name and asks for his brother. He's accompanied by a beautiful blonde woman, who I'm guessing is the wife Orla spoke of. She's wearing a tight navy blue skirt and white blouse with a jacket folded over her arm, and he's got on jeans and a white button-down shirt, their faces lined with worry as they turn to Doctor Walters.

"Would you like to come to the relatives' room? We can talk in there."

Hunter nods his head, putting his arm around his wife, and they step away. They've only gone a few paces when he stops and turns back, looking directly at me.

"I'm sorry. That's Maisie, isn't it?"

"Yes."

He nods. "I know it's an imposition, but do you think you could look after her for a little longer? I—I wanna be able to focus on my brother for a while. Is that…?"

He can't finish his sentence, his voice cracking with emotion and I smile over at him, nodding my head.

"It's fine. Maisie will be perfectly safe with me."

"Thank you."

He turns, going with Doctor Walters, and I look down at Maisie.

"It'll be okay," I whisper. "I'll make sure of it. Daddy will be okay."

He has to be. I need to tell him I got the message.

Drew

There's a humming sound in the background, like blurred, hushed voices. I don't know who's talking, but I wish they'd speak up, so I could hear them properly… and that the damned beeping would stop, too. It's persistent, regular, and really annoying.

Is this a dream? It has to be, because my eyes are closed, so I must be asleep. If that's the case, it's the strangest of dreams. There's nothing tangible about it. I'm sure my dreams are usually more coherent than this, although I can't remember any of them at the moment, which is odd, because I'm sure I must have had some amazing dreams in my time. In this instance, though, I can't work it out at all.

It's just a haze…

A loud crash startles me, and I hear someone calling out for quiet. That was clear enough, and they're quite right. A little quiet would be good.

I feel my hand being lifted… held. That's real. It's not part of a dream, and I do my best to focus on whoever's holding it. They've got a soft touch and tiny hands. It's a woman, and although I don't know who she is, I feel relaxed and let my hand rest in hers, flexing my fingers.

"Hunter?" That's a female voice coming from right beside me. The woman, perhaps?

"Yeah? What is it, baby?" Hmm… a man's voice. Not one I'm familiar with, any more than I am with his name, but he sounds friendly enough. The 'baby' tells me he's with the woman, which seems a shame. I like her hands… and her voice.

"He moved his fingers."

I try to pull my hand away, but can't. She's holding on to me, and I suddenly feel less comfortable. *Let me go!*

"I'll get a doctor." That's the man again. A doctor? Is this a hospital? I guess that would make sense of the hushed voices and beeping sounds.

"Don't get your hopes up. Sometimes it's just a reflex."

Whoa… that's a different woman. Her voice does something strange to my body, like bubbles bursting over the surface of my skin. I don't know who she is, but there's something about her…

I can hear movement, although I can't make out what it is, and I wish the woman would speak again. I liked the way she made me feel. Her voice had an aura of comfort to it.

The first woman finally lets go of me. There's a rustling sound, and then my hand is picked up again… only this time I can feel I'm being held by a man. I tense against him, unsure what's going on.

"I think you're right," he says. "There is some movement there, and some resistance." *Yeah… to you holding my hand.*

This is yet another voice. It's not the same man as earlier. Hunter, was it? This man's voice isn't so deep, so I guess maybe this is the doctor.

"Do you think he's coming round?" That's the first woman again.

"It looks like it. Mr. Bennett? Drew?" Who's he talking to? Is there another man in here? He squeezes my hand. "Can you hear me, Drew?"

He's talking to me? Why's he calling me Drew? My name's… my name's… Oh, God… what is my name?

What's going on? Panic wells inside me, bubbling beneath the surface and threatening to boil over.

"I think it might take a little longer," the doctor says, releasing my hand again.

No, it won't. It can't. I need to know what's going on here. I take a breath and attempt to open my eyes. These people obviously know who I am. They know my name and seem familiar with me. I'm sure if I can just see their faces, it'll all come back.

I crank my eyes open, blinking against the bright lights, before I slam them shut again. Maybe that wasn't such a good idea, after all.

"Did you see that?" the first woman says. She sounds excited.

"See what?" That's not the doctor. It's the other man, although I've forgotten his name already.

"He opened his eyes."

"He did?" That was the doctor, and I feel him take my hand in his once more.

I wish you'd stop doing that.

"Drew? Open your eyes."

I'm trying, dammit. And stop calling me Drew.

I ratchet my eyes open again, with a little more success this time. The lights are still bright, but not so blinding as they were before, and although my head is pounding now, I need to find out what's going on, so I ignore the pain.

I'm lying on a bed, a light above my head, and beside me is a man wearing a pale blue top with a v-neck. He's got a stethoscope around his neck, and as I focus on his face, I take in the graying hair at his temples and his steel-rimmed glasses. He must be the doctor, and he smiles down at me, nodding his head.

"You've rejoined us at last, have you?" That wasn't at all patronizing, but I can't be bothered to comment… not that he gives me the chance. "You've been unconscious for nearly six hours," he says. "You had us worried." I still don't know who 'us' is. I don't even seem to know who I am at the moment, but he's smiling, so I guess he's not as worried as he was, which is something.

I need to see the other people in the room, to find out how they know me, and if I know them. I slowly turn my head, taking my time, the pain behind my eyes distracting me, until they alight on a beautiful blonde woman. Things are definitely looking up… except she's standing in front of a very tall, dark-haired man, and he's got his arms around her, her back to his front.

Well… that's a shame. They're both smiling at me, which is unnerving, as I've never seen them before in my life. There must have been some kind of mistake here.

I open my mouth to speak, to ask what's going on, just as a movement catches my eye and I turn my head again, just a little more, my breath catching in my throat when I see the woman standing in the corner of the room. She's got dark blonde hair, tied up behind her head, and is wearing the same kind of top as the doctor – except hers is purple – and for some reason, she's holding a young baby in her arms. Her eyes are fixed on mine, and although I've never seen her before and have no idea who she is, I wish I did, because she's the most perfect creature I've ever seen in my life. Sure, the other woman is beautiful, but whoever this woman is, she's… she's something else.

Why she's here with a baby is anybody's guess. I wonder for a moment if it belongs to the couple who are standing, staring at me still, and whether she's looking after it for them, so they can concentrate on me, for some reason I haven't yet worked out. Either way, I hope she doesn't have to leave. I could happily spend the rest of my life just looking at her.

The doctor coughs and I drag my eyes back to him. He's still smiling, which ought to feel reassuring... and it would, if I knew what was going on.

"Now, Mr. Bennett... or would you rather I called you Drew?" he asks.

"I don't know. Is that my name?" My throat is dry, so my voice sounds strange... at least it does to me.

The doctor's smile becomes a frown, and he turns to the tall man, who moves away from the blonde woman, letting her go and stepping closer to the bed.

"Don't you know who you are?" he says.

"I'm evidently Mr. Bennett, but the name means nothing. Who are you?"

The man steps back, clearly shocked by my question. He opens his mouth to answer, but the doctor holds up his hand. "I think we need to talk outside." He turns to the woman in the corner... the one whose face I know I'll never forget, even if I remember nothing else. She's paled a little and is still staring at me. "I also think we need to call in someone from the Neurotrauma team, don't you?"

She nods her head. "Yes," she says. "Yes, I do." Her voice is like a comfort blanket against my skin, and I want to ask her to lay it over me in gentle caresses, like soft whispers of calm in this startling new wilderness.

Everyone moves, including her, heading for the door.

"Just get some rest," the doctor says. "And don't worry about anything."

How can I not worry? I have no idea what's going on. I don't know who I am, or why I'm here... or who these people are. My head hurts, too, and as everyone leaves, I wonder why I can't remember who I am?

What happened to make me forget myself?

Chapter Four

Josie

That had to be the longest six hours of my life.

I wish I could have spent it all by Drew's side, but Maisie needed to be fed and changed, and when she started to grizzle, Drew's brother turned to me, a worried expression on his face.

"W—What shall we do?"

"Don't worry. I'll take her up to maternity."

"You're sure?"

"Positive. You stay with your brother."

I wanted to stay myself, but Maisie needed me, and I knew Drew would have wanted me to care for his daughter, so I took her upstairs, where the staff on the maternity department were happy to help, finding me a small side room, where one of the midwives brought me some pre-made formula, a sterilized bottle, and some diapers. She left me to it, assuming I'd know what to do, and I'll admit, I was at a bit of a loss, never having attempted anything like it before. It all came naturally in the end, though, and I sat with Maisie in a chair by the window, while she took her bottle. I stared into space, thinking about what had happened, trying not to cry for Lexi, and for Maisie… and not to worry about Drew. It was all too overwhelming… too much to contemplate.

After Maisie had finished her milk, I changed her. She seemed tired, but I didn't wait for her to go to sleep and instead took her back to the ER, where Drew was still unconscious.

"Is everything okay?" Hunter said as I entered the room again.

"Everything's fine. I think she'll fall asleep soon."

He nodded his head, looking down at her as he sighed. I glanced at his wife, who he'd introduced as Livia not long after their arrival. She was looking worried and tired, even though she smiled at me.

"We're very grateful to you for helping with Maisie."

I half expected her to come and take her niece from me, but she didn't. She looked at Hunter with tears in her eyes, and he went to her, holding her in his arms, while I focused on Maisie, whose eyes were fluttering closed.

I didn't mind helping. On the contrary, I was grateful for the excuse to stick around.

Drew's eyes remained closed the entire time, his perfect face a picture of peace and calm. I wondered what I'd do when he woke up… how I'd explain my presence. He'd be bound to wonder, and I knew I'd have to come clean, to confess the connection between us to his family. And, of course, they'd be bound to ask why I'd stayed quiet about it in the meantime.

Naturally, what no-one anticipated was that when Drew finally opened his eyes, he'd have no memory of any of us… or of who he is. That came as a tremendous shock to all of us. I could see the fear in his eyes and wanted to go to him, to tell him it would be all right. I couldn't, though. Doctor Walters ushered us all out of the room before I got the chance. At least he asked my opinion first, about whether he should call in someone from the

Neurotrauma department. And I had to agree that he should, because Drew's reaction isn't normal. Not by anyone's standards.

"What's happening?" Hunter sounds worried and I look up at him, the four of us standing outside the door of Drew's room.

"Your brother seems to be suffering from amnesia." Doctor Walters's reply is a little condescending and I roll my eyes, although no-one notices.

Hunter glares down at him. "I'd worked that much out for myself. What I want to know is, is it permanent?"

"It's highly unlikely. In cases like this, it's more common for patients to suffer with short-term memory loss, not total memory loss. Even so, I'd expect it to pass, although it's impossible to say how long it will take." He turns to me. "Is Doctor Sweeney here, do you know?"

"He was earlier, but I guess he might have gone home by now."

"I'll see if I can find out."

He hurries away and Hunter turns to me. I half expect him to fire more questions at me, but he doesn't. Instead, he looks down at Maisie and holds out his hands, taking her from me.

"Thank you for everything you've done. I'm sure you've got other duties you need to get back to."

I shake my head. "No. I don't even work in the ER. I work in the Neurotrauma department."

He nestles Maisie in his arms. She's still sleeping and doesn't seem worried by the move. "Neurotrauma? Isn't that what the doctor just said?"

"Yes."

"So you deal with cases like Drew's?"

"I do. I've only been in the department for about a year, but we have patients with memory problems coming in quite often."

"And they recover?"

I wonder how to reply, knowing recovery can take many forms. "Some of them." He frowns and I know I have to reassure him… tell him more. "Give it time, Mr. Bennett. I know it's hard, and you want results, or at the very least, you want answers. But at this stage, there are none."

He stares at me for a moment and then nods his head. "So, if you don't work here, how did you come to be looking after Maisie?"

I feel myself blush, wondering whether to tell the truth, but deciding against it. He'll only wonder why I've waited until now to say something. "I—I was passing on my way home, and offered to help."

"But that must have been hours ago."

"Yes, but it's fine. Don't worry."

Maisie opens her eyes, looking straight up at him, and immediately starts crying. "Oh, hell."

"Shall I take her?" I offer.

"I'd love to say 'yes' to that, but I think it'll be more sensible if we get her home. It's not practical for you to stay here and look after her indefinitely. God knows when Drew's going to remember who he is, or that he's got a daughter, and Maisie needs to be somewhere she can be cared for properly." He looks over at Livia. "Can you take her?"

She sucks in a breath and nods her head. "Of course I can."

"I'm sorry, baby. I hate asking you to do this by yourself, but I need to stay here with Drew."

She reaches out, her hand on his bicep, looking up into his eyes. "It's okay. I understand."

She takes Maisie from him, cradling her in her arms. "I know it's a longer drive, but take her back to Newport," he says. "The apartment is impractical, and you'll have help down there. I'll call Pat and get her and Mick to move Maisie's things from the cottage into the main house."

"Mac will help, won't he?"

"I'm sure he will, and I'll ask Pat to get in some supplies… some formula and bottles, and diapers. I'm sure Drew has clothes for Maisie, but if not, we'll get some." He rests his hand on his niece's head. "Heaven knows how long we're gonna be looking after this little one."

Livia looks like she's about to burst into tears, her eyes glistening and almost brimming over, although she suddenly bites on her bottom lip, looking up at her husband.

"I don't have a car seat for her."

I step forward. "There was one at the nurse's station. I'm guessing that's hers."

Hunter nods his head, and we all wander back in that direction. I notice a man sitting in the seats opposite, his dark head bent, although I can make out his handsome, tanned features well enough. He looks dejected, his shoulders sagging, his hands resting on his knees, but I don't stop. Instead, I go behind the desk, picking up the car seat. Orla's typing on the computer and she looks up at me.

"This belongs to the Bennett baby, doesn't it?"

"Yes."

I nod my head and take it back to Hunter, handing it over to him. "Thanks," he says with a smile. He turns to his wife. "I'll come out with you and fit this, and once you've gone, I'll call Ella and let her know what's going on with Drew. She'll kill me if I don't keep her updated… and then I'll speak to Pat."

"Okay." She smiles up at him. "I'm glad we drove here in my car. I wouldn't have relished the prospect of driving back to Newport in yours." He caresses her cheek with his fingertips, and then turns to me.

"I'll be back in a minute. Will you still be here?"

"I can hang on, if you want."

"Would you mind? It's just, as Neurotrauma is your thing, it would be good to have someone around who can help me understand what's going on."

"That's fine."

He nods his head, smiling his thanks, and accompanies Livia to the main doors, his hand in the small of her back, their heads bent together. I turn to find Orla looking up at me.

"Can I assume Mr. Bennett's family don't know who you are, either?"

"You can."

"Is there a reason for that?"

Not one I'm going to explain. "It's a long story." I lean over the desk, so I can whisper, "Is the guy behind me Manuel Ortega?"

"Yes, he is. How did you know?"

Because he looks Spanish and like he'd be very at home in front of a camera. "Call it a lucky guess."

She nods. "He's only been here for about ten minutes. God knows how long he'll be waiting for Doctor Walters, though. We've just been notified of another serious RTA. We're expecting five major casualties and several minors."

"I can talk to him, if you like."

"Would you? It seems unfair to just leave the poor guy sitting there."

I couldn't agree more, and I turn away, wandering over to the seats. The man is looking up now and I wonder if he witnessed Hunter and Livia's departure, maybe recognized Maisie, or heard her name.

"Mr. Ortega?" He focuses on me and nods his head, getting to his feet. He's tall... around the same height as Drew and has an athletic build. His tanned features are worn with worry, and his dark brown eyes are filled with sadness.

"Yes. I'm waiting for the doctor." There's only a trace of a Spanish accent in his deep voice, and I can understand straight away what Lexi would have seen in him. He's lovely.

"I know. Unfortunately, there have been some complications… and another emergency." I step away, pointing to the relatives' room. "Would you like to come with me? We can talk in here. It's quieter." *And I have things to say I don't want anyone else to overhear.*

He nods his head, and I lead the way, opening the door and stepping inside. He follows and I close the door behind me, offering him a seat, which he takes. I sit beside him and he turns to face me, tilting his head. I'd already decided to come clean with him, but even if I hadn't, the look in his eyes is enough to make me want to. He needs to know the truth.

"My name is Josie, Mr. Ortega. I'm Lexi's sister."

His mouth drops open, his eyes widening. "Y—You're Josie?"

"Yes."

He glances at my uniform, and then at the door. "You were here when she was brought in?"

"No. I don't work in this department." I cough, gathering myself together. "Have you been told what happened?"

He nods his head. "Yes. The woman who called me said Lexi had been killed in a car accident." He brushes his fingers back through his dark hair, messing it up. "I—I can't believe this is happening."

"I know. It's a lot to take in."

"It is for you, too." I can't deny that. "D—Did she tell you about us?"

"Yes, she did."

"I know we hadn't been together for every long, but Lexi was… she was everything…" He stops talking, his voice catching, and he takes a moment. "Sorry."

"Don't be. It's fine, honestly."

"I—I saw her baby, just now."

"Yes."

"She's okay, isn't she?"

"Yes. Not a scratch on her."

"The man and woman who took Maisie away… are they related to her father?"

"Yes. They're going to look after her for the time being."

"Is he…? Drew Bennett, I mean… is he…?"

"He survived the crash, but as I said just now, there are complications."

"He's gonna be okay, though?" I can hear the worry in his voice and it makes me want to cry.

"He'll be fine." *He has to be.*

He sighs out his relief. "I wish I'd done things differently, you know?"

"In what way?"

"I wish I hadn't been so jealous. I knew she didn't love him. She told me so herself, but…" He shakes his head. "He did so much for her. Did you know he paid off the mortgage on her apartment?"

"No, I didn't." I'm surprised, although it sounds like the kind of thing Drew would do.

"He paid her an allowance, too. Anything she wanted, he did it for her, and I'm ashamed to say, I didn't react well to that. I saw it as interference, and I hated them seeing so much of each other. But I should've… I should've listened to her. She said…" A tear hits his cheek, and he wipes it away. "She said she loved me."

"I'm sure she did. Lexi and I weren't that close, but she wouldn't have lied about something like that."

He nods his head. "Thank you for saying that." He clears his throat. "She… she told me she wanted to build some bridges with you."

"I know. She told me so herself."

"She explained to me once about her father, and your mother, and that you barely spoke. I—I know she regretted it."

"I do too." Especially now.

He frowns, his face darkening. "Has her father been told?"

"No, I don't think so."

"I suppose I'd better find his number and call him."

"I—I can arrange for someone here to do it, if you'd prefer." It won't be me, but I'm sure Orla, or someone else, could make the call.

He looks up, his eyes connecting with mine, an even deeper sadness reflecting back at me. "Would you mind? I'm not sure I could talk to him and stay civil."

I know I couldn't and I nod my head. "I'll speak to someone."

"Thank you. I—I don't know if Lexi told you this, but her father rejected her when she found out she was pregnant."

"She mentioned it, yes, although neither of us understood why."

"I never said anything about this to Lexi, but I sometimes wondered if I wasn't the only one who suffered from jealousy."

"You think her father was jealous? What of?"

"The baby. He'd had Lexi to himself for years. Having a baby was going to take her away from him… or at least give her someone else to focus on, and if the story she told me about your mother was true, I don't think he was very good at sharing."

"No… no he wasn't."

His idea makes sense, and I wonder why I never thought of it myself.

He lets out a long sigh. "Can I see her?"

"You want to?"

"I need to say goodbye. Her father will probably arrange the funeral. I doubt he'll even let me attend… or you, for that matter."

I suddenly feel quite sick. I hadn't thought about that, but what he's saying is true. Lexi's father is bound to take charge the moment he knows, and he won't want me anywhere near her funeral. Even so, there's no way I can see Lexi myself. I've witnessed the aftermath of too many accidents to want to see the results of this one. Besides, I'd rather remember my sister how she was.

"I—I suppose not," I say. "I can arrange for someone to take you to see her, if you want."

"Thank you."

He goes back to staring at his hands, and I can't think of anything else to say. Certainly there's nothing that'll make him feel better, so I get up and leave the room.

Outside, Orla is still sitting at the desk and I go over to her. She looks up, giving me a friendly smile. "How did it go?"

"Okay. I told him who I am, and we talked. I—I think it helped."

"You, or him?"

"Both of us. He says he wants to see her."

"Your sister?"

"Yes. But I—I can't. I can't do it, Orla."

She rests her hand, just briefly, on my arm. "Hey… it's okay. I'll handle it."

"Thanks… and there's something else."

"What's that?"

"Lexi's father. He should probably be told what's happened."

"I didn't realize there was a father."

I nod my head. "Hmm… they haven't spoken for a while, but it seems only fair."

"You don't wanna tell him yourself?"

"No." My answer is quick, my voice louder than I'd expected, and she raises her eyebrows. "No… I'm sorry."

"It's okay. Her phone is still with her belongings. I'll find his details and call him."

I turn around, closing my eyes and tipping my head back, letting out a long breath. I'm exhausted. My back and legs are aching, and my feet are killing me, but I can't go home… not yet.

I open my eyes, tilting my head forward again, just as Hunter Bennett comes in through the doors. His shoulders are hunched, and he's staring down at the floor as he walks toward me.

"Are you okay?" I ask and he looks up, his eyes dark with worry.

"Ask me later, when my brother can remember who I am."

I want to tell him that may be some time away yet, but I don't get the chance. Doctor Sweeney steps out of the elevator and strides over, frowning. He's in his mid-fifties, with an attractive face and dark brown hair. As usual, he's wearing a white coat over the top of his pants and shirt, along with that cloak of superiority that shrouds him wherever he goes. He's good at what he does, which makes him popular within the hospital, but his arrogance is less of a hit, and I have to admit, I've never really enjoyed working with him.

"What are you doing here, Nurse Emerson? I should be at home myself by now, but I thought your shift finished hours ago."

"It did."

"She's been helping," Hunter says, stepping forward, and Doctor Sweeney looks up at him quizzically. "In fact, she's been invaluable."

"Who are you?"

Hunter's brow furrows. "I'm Hunter Bennett. Drew Bennett's brother."

"I see. Do you want to come in?" Hunter doesn't move, but turns to me and I look up at the doctor, suddenly realizing that he's addressing me. "There's a very good chance this patient will be transferred to our department, which means he'll probably be under your care as of tomorrow, so it might be useful if you were involved from the start. It'll save time."

I have to agree, and I nod my head. Even if I am exhausted, I don't care... not if I can spend some more time with Drew. Not if I can look after him.

We turn toward his room, Hunter following, but Doctor Sweeney looks up at him. "I'm sorry, Mr. Bennett, but my understanding is that your brother has no memory of you."

"That's correct."

"In which case, your presence is only going to confuse him at this stage. It'll possibly upset him, too."

Hunter takes a half step back, his face betraying his concern. "What should I do? Wait out here?"

Doctor Sweeney shakes his head. "To be honest, you'll be better off at home. Your brother's in safe hands."

Hunter stares at him, lost, uncertain what to do. I step a little closer, getting his attention.

"Why don't you follow your wife down to Newport?"

He shakes his head. "I can't do that. No matter how much I hate being away from her, I need to be here, with Drew." The doctor opens his mouth, but Hunter holds up his hand, silencing him. He's very commanding and we both look up at him. "You don't need to worry. I'm not suggesting I'm gonna stay here, pacing the hall. I'll make sure all of Drew's equipment has been delivered to his studio."

"What equipment would this be?" Doctor Sweeney asks.

"My brother's a photographer. He'd just come back from an assignment in Rome. I don't know exactly what he'd have taken with him, but there would have been a few bags and cases. He's very particular about his cameras. He'd want me to make sure they're all okay."

"I'm sure you're right," I say, nodding my head. "It sounds like a good idea." It'll give him something to do.

"I'll go back to my apartment afterwards." He looks me in the eye, holding my attention. "Promise you'll call me if anything happens?"

"I promise. I'll call you personally."

"Thank you... for everything."

I nod my head, and with a glance at the doctor, he leaves.

"Come on, Nurse." Doctor Sweeney sounds impatient and I turn, following him to Drew's room. He's about to open the door when he stops, turning to me, his face serious. "Don't forget, you can't prompt him. We don't know how severe his memory loss is at this stage, but we won't be helping him regain it if we tell him all about himself. He has to rediscover his past in his own time."

I want to scream at him that I know all of this already. I'm not an idiot. But I say nothing and follow him inside the room.

Drew

This room is much nicer than the other one. It has drapes across the window. They're blue with white stripes. The walls are a brighter blue, and there are abstract pictures on the wall opposite the bed... two of them. I'm not sure what they're supposed to be of, but they're certainly colorful.

It's also quieter here. There are no machines beeping, and I can't hear a single voice. I don't know where I am exactly, but I'm guessing this isn't the Emergency Room. I was there last night, and I remember a conversation about being transferred.

Most of what happened is a blur of hazy thoughts and fractured conversations. The only thing I can remember with any certainty is the woman in the purple top, who made the blur seem less scary.

She came back to see me, although she didn't bring the baby with her. She brought a different doctor... an older guy, who stood beside my bed looking down at me and frowning.

"There was a man here... with a woman," I said, sounding as vague as I felt. "Where are they?"

"Don't worry about them," the doctor said.

I remembered someone else telling me not to worry, although I couldn't remember who, or when... or what it was I wasn't supposed to worry about.

"What happened to me?"

"You're in the hospital and we're going to look after you."

"That's not an answer. Why am I in the hospital?"

"You're having a few problems with your memory."

"No shit."

The woman in the purple top was standing at the end of my bed and I noticed her put her hand over her mouth, trying not to laugh.

"Can you tell me why I'm here?" I asked, keeping my eyes fixed on her.

She lowered her hand. "You were in an accident. You hit your head, and you were unconscious for a while."

"Really?"

"Yes." The doctor glared at her, but we both ignored him. "There's nothing to be concerned about."

"Then why can't I remember anything? Why don't I know who I am?"

The doctor held up his hand. Ignoring him didn't seem to be working. "That's what I'm here to find out. Now... can you tell me how old you are?"

I shook my head, even though it hurt. "If I don't know my name, how the hell do you expect me to remember my date of birth?"

"You can't recall your age?"

"No."

"Any idea where you live?"

"What city are we in?" I asked, and he shook his head, making it clear he wouldn't give me any clues. "In that case, I don't know."

"Can you tell me who is the current President of the United States?"

"Absolutely no idea."

"Okay. What about the previous President?"

"What on earth makes you think I'd know that?"

His questions seemed pointless, and I turned to the woman at the end of the bed. "Do you understand the word President?" she said. "Do you know what it means?"

"Someone who runs the country?"

She tilted her head, which was very cute, and made me smile. "Is that a guess? Or do you know that's what it means?"

"I don't think it's a guess. It sounds right, doesn't it?" I was so unsure about everything, I felt the need to ask.

The doctor stepped back slightly, moving closer to her. "I'm going to have Mr. Bennett transferred to the neurotrauma department as soon as possible. We'll keep him under observation overnight and you can start working with him tomorrow."

She was going to be working with me? Even if I couldn't remember my own name, things were looking up.

Unfortunately, the doctor took her away then, and I haven't seen her since. I remember being moved here, and given some pain relief not long afterwards, and then I must have fallen asleep. I was woken several times, though, not that I can recall what for, and as I turn over in the bed, I wonder if this is how I'm going to live my life from now on… always in the moment, with no past and not much of a future.

The door opens, startling me, although I have to smile when the woman in the purple top comes walking in. Her hair is tied up behind her head again, and although I can now see she's wearing purple pants to match her top, I'm more distracted by her curves… by her full breasts and rounded hips, forming a perfect hourglass with her slim waist. She's carrying a small box, but she looks up and returns my smile.

"Good morning." Her voice is still soothing, just like it was yesterday, when I first heard it, and I let it wash over me in gentle waves. "How did you sleep?" She comes across to the bed as she's talking, putting down the box at the end.

"Not bad… considering."

She frowns slightly. "Considering what?"

"That people kept coming in here and waking me up."

She giggles and shivers rush down my spine. The sound is no less soothing than her voice, but the effect is different; my skin tingling, my cock twitching. "We always keep up observations on concussion patients for the first twenty-four hours, I'm afraid."

"So I'll get a better night's sleep tonight?"

"Yes, you will." She steps a little closer… close enough that I can smell her floral scent. "Now, it's time you stopped lying around in bed. We need to get you moving."

I'm not sorry about that. I'm fairly sick of lying on my back, and I smile up at her. "Okay. Let's try it." I sit up, the room swirling, nausea gripping my stomach, a sharp pain stabbing behind my eyes. I wince against it. "Oh… shit…"

She grabs my arm, steadying me. "Are you okay?"

"No… my head."

She keeps me sat up for a moment, re-arranging my pillows behind me and then helps me to lean back against them, pulling up the covers and straightening them.

"I'll get you some more painkillers, and we'll leave getting you up for a while longer."

I'm grateful for that, although I feel incredibly weak and pathetic for being unable to even sit up in my own bed.

She leaves the room, returning within moments with some tablets, which I swallow down with the water she offers.

"Am I allowed to know your name?" I ask, resting my head against the pillow.

"Yes. I'm Josie."

"That's nice."

"Thank you. Now… get some rest and I'll come back in a little while."

I want to ask her not to go, but I don't have the strength… and besides, she said she'd be back.

The door closes and I'm surprised how much I miss her already. There's something about her that makes me feel safe, and I need that at the moment. I close my eyes, which seems to ease the throbbing in my head, and try to remember…

She said there was an accident. She mentioned the word concussion, although that doesn't mean a thing to me. I know what it means, but it's like there's nothing in my head as to how I came to be concussed. It's just a void, and the harder I try to think, the worse it gets.

What if they can't help me? What if I can never remember who I am, or where I'm from, or how I came to be here? How will I live the rest of my life in this shadow world of never understanding anything?

I open my eyes again and look around the room. The light seems brighter, my head feels a little better and I realize I've been asleep, although I don't know how long for. Time doesn't seem to matter, or to mean anything, and I wonder about trying to sit up again. The problem is, I'm scared. What will I do if I feel dizzy and sick again? Will I have to spend the rest of my life lying here in bed?

The door opens and I look up, unable to stop that smile touching my lips as Josie comes back in. I remembered her name and I feel a small sense of triumph over that.

"Feeling better?" she asks.

"My headache's gone, if that's what you're asking."

"It wasn't." She comes over to the bed and looks down at me. "How are you?"

"To be honest, I'm terrified."

She nods her head. "It's okay. We don't think any of this will last."

"Y—You knew that was what I was frightened of? That I'd be like this forever?"

"Yes. I can't imagine what it must feel like, but it's got to be scary, feeling so sick and knowing nothing about yourself."

"It is. Can you remind me of my name again?"

She shakes her head. "No. I'm sorry, I can't. I'm not supposed to tell you anything. You have to try to remember for yourself. Your brain will mend itself. You just have to give it time."

"You're sure about that?"

"As sure as I can be." She smiles. "Do you want to try getting up again?"

"After last time, not particularly."

"I'm right here. I won't let anything happen."

Those are the most reassuring words I've heard so far, and I throw back the covers, deciding to try properly this time. She takes my arm, holding me while I sit up and swing my legs around until I'm perched on the edge of the bed, my feet on the floor.

"That's a weird sensation."

"It will be. But give it a minute. You'll soon get used to it."

I take a few deep breaths, and after a short while, I feel a lot better.

"Okay. I think I'm ready to stand."

"Sure?"

I nod my head, and she steps right in front of me, taking my hands. Then, looking into her eyes, I raise myself up onto my feet. I'm towering over her now, although she's a lot steadier than I am, like she's the rock and I'm the tide, swaying back and forth.

"Whoa… this really is weird."

"It's okay. I've got you."

I look down into her blue-gray eyes and kind of lose myself for a moment. I think it could become an endless moment, during which she gazes up at me, too… except I suddenly notice a strange sensation behind me. It's like a draft of cool air and I let go of her hand, reaching around to feel my bare ass.

"Um… why is there no back to this nightshirt thing?"

She purses her lips, trying very hard not to smile. "Because that's how hospital gowns are designed."

"By whom? A pervert?"

She giggles, and despite my embarrassment at having my ass exposed, my cock hardens. The sound of her giggle seems to do that to me. Or maybe it's just her presence.

"Do you wanna try taking a few steps?"

"Are you gonna peek?"

"At what?"

"My ass."

A smile tugs at her lips, her eyes sparkling. "I might."

"In that case, let's try it." I hear her slight gasp, noticing the blush on her cheeks. "Did I embarrass you?"

"Of course not. I'm a nurse. We're impossible to embarrass."

"Then why are you blushing?"

"I'm not. Now come on, right foot forward."

"Yes, boss."

She shakes her head and I move my right foot, my head spinning just slightly. I grip her hands a little tighter and take a deep breath, moving my left foot.

"Well done. Keep going."

Slowly but surely, I make it across the room, reaching the chair by the window in around five minutes… a pitiful length of time.

"You need to sit for a while."

"Is that because you're worried you might see my ass?"

She chuckles. "No. It's because you've suffered a serious concussion, and you need to rest."

I sit, looking up at her. "I hate to admit it, but I feel ludicrously tired."

"It'll get better. I promise. But before you get too comfortable, I'm gonna give you some exercises to do."

"Really? You heard the bit where I just said I'm tired, didn't you?"

"Yes, but it's not your body I'm interested in, it's your brain."

"In which case, I'm not only very disappointed, but I'm sorry to have to admit, I'm not sure I have one."

"You do. You even have a memory. We just have to find ways of triggering it."

"I'll take your word for that."

She turns, perching on the edge of the mattress, and reaches over for the box she brought in earlier. I'd forgotten all about that, and I watch as she pulls out a large book, which she holds out in front of her.

"I'm gonna show you some pictures and I want you to tell me what you think they are. If you don't know, just say so, and we'll move on."

"Okay."

She opens the book, turning it around, and flips the page. I study it for just a second and look up at her. "It's a cat."

She smiles. "And the next one."

She turns the page again. "An elephant."

"Good..." She moves on... and on, and I identify everything she shows me with no difficulty at all.

As she closes the book, I shake my head. "I don't understand. Why can I recall what all those things are, but I don't know who I am?"

"Because the brain works in mysterious ways. Don't be downhearted. The fact that you recognized everything in the book is a good sign... so cheer up."

"I'll cheer up when I can take a shower. I feel awful."

She tilts her head, which is just as cute as the last time she did it. "Who says you can't take a shower?"

"Me. I'm so dizzy."

"I know, but I can help you if you want."

She's blushing again, even as she's speaking. "Is that allowed?"

"Of course it is, if it's what you need. I'm here to look after you."

"Well... I guess you've seen it all before."

"You'd be amazed. In this line of work, we see just about everything."

"I'm not sure whether to feel relieved or scared."

She shakes her head, smiling. "Just sit there, and I'll be back in a minute."

She puts the book away and gets to her feet, going over to the door and letting herself out without another word. Once she's gone, I glance out the window, staring down at the cars in the parking lot. I wonder for a moment if I can drive, but I can't remember, and before my mind drifts off into that tortured void, I close my eyes and think of Josie instead. It's a safer place to be…

"Are you ready?" Josie's voice startles me and I open my eyes. She's back in the room and I stare across at her, unable to stop myself from smiling. Is she going to do that to me every time she comes into the room?

I hope so.

"Ready for what?"

"You said you wanted a shower."

"Did I?"

"Yes."

I don't remember that, but I can't see any reason she'd make it up, and she's carrying a towel, so I guess it must be true.

I stand, taking a moment to steady myself, and Josie comes over to offer her arm in support.

"Worried I'll fall over?"

"No. Just here to help."

I nod my head, although I wish I hadn't, but rather than making a fuss, I take her arm and let her lead me into the adjoining bathroom.

Josie pulls the light cord, and I look around. There's no bath in here, or shower cubicle, for that matter. It's more of a wet room than anything else, but there's nothing luxurious about it. The room is very functional, with what appear to be hoists hanging from the ceiling and a shower head in the corner, with a seat beneath it, and two bars on the walls, to grab hold of, I guess. *They might be useful.* There's no screen… just a big empty room, with a toilet and basin on the far wall.

"Why is the room laid out like this?" I ask as she puts down the towel and moves behind me.

"It's for people with mobility issues."

"Like me, you mean?"

I feel her reach up, undoing my gown, then pushing it forward, off of my shoulders. She walks around in front of me again, looking up into my eyes.

"Compared to most, you're lucky."

Looking down into her beguiling face, I'm feeling kinda lucky. She pulls the gown from me and I stand before her, completely naked.

My cock is bone hard, and I ought to feel vulnerable, or at the very least embarrassed.

Except I don't.

I feel alive.

And safe. Very safe.

After a moment, she steps away, moving toward the shower. She can't be unaware of my arousal, but she doesn't show any signs of awkwardness, and instead she turns on the water.

"You adjust the heat setting here," she says, pointing to the controls.

"Okay."

I go over, testing the heat and turning it down slightly, before I step underneath.

"There's some body wash on the shelf there," she says, turning away.

"You're not leaving, are you?"

"No. But I think you can handle washing yourself, don't you?"

"I'll try."

"If you get tired or dizzy, just sit down."

"Okay."

I turn around, holding onto one of the rails, and dip my head beneath the water. It feels good. I don't remember the last time I had a shower… but that's not surprising. I don't remember anything.

I take a moment before I turn back around again to find Josie's standing on the far side of the room, leaning against the wall.

She's staring at me, her thumbnail in her mouth, her eyes fixed on my chest, although they slowly wander south, widening as they go. I should wash, but I don't. I stand and watch her reactions… the flare of her nostrils, the heave of her breasts, the slight pinking of her cheeks.

She's not embarrassed; she's aroused.

I don't know how I know that, but I do.

It's an instinct, and it's one that makes me smile.

Chapter Five

Josie

Exactly as I predicted, the moment Lexi's father was made aware of what had happened, he stepped in and took over.

Fortunately, by the time he was able to get to the hospital, I'd gone home, so I didn't have to see him. Orla told me the following day that he'd made a tremendous fuss, though. He said he should have been informed immediately.

"He didn't care about her boyfriend, and he didn't even mention you." He wouldn't. In fact, I doubt he even knew of Manuel's existence, and he will have forgotten me years ago. "And then he started shouting at everyone because he wanted to take her body back to New York with him straight away."

In a way, that didn't surprise me. It was the sort of thing I'd have expected of him. "But surely he understood there has to be a post-mortem."

"He seemed to think there was no need, and even when Doctor Walters explained the protocol to him, he thought there should be some kind of exemption for him… or his daughter."

He would.

"Did he ask about Maisie?"

She shook her head. "No. Not once. I was surprised by that."

I wasn't.

"Did you arrange for Manuel Ortega to see Lexi's body?"

"Yes." I was pleased. I felt sorry for him, especially as I knew Lexi's father wouldn't allow him at the funeral… any more than he would me. At least he'd got to say goodbye. Orla was staring at me. "Are you sure you did the right thing? Not seeing her yourself, I mean?"

"Yeah. I didn't want to remember her like that."

She smiled sympathetically, although I couldn't feel sorry for myself. I still can't. I've got Maisie and Drew to think about. Lexi would have wanted me to focus on them, not grieve for her. I didn't get the chance to say any of that, because Doctor Walters came up and thanked me for taking care of Mr. Ortega the previous day.

"I'm really sorry I left you to handle that," he said.

"It's okay. I know how busy you were."

He shook his head. "Busy or not, it should have been me who spoke to him, not you."

"Am I in trouble?" I asked, slightly fearful of his answer.

"Hell, no. The poor man would have been waiting until the early hours of the morning if you hadn't dealt with everything. I imagine he was just as grateful as I am."

I couldn't be sure about that, but it was good to know I hadn't breached any kind of protocol… and that I'd hopefully given Manuel more comfort than anyone else could have done at such a horrible time.

It's been three days since the accident and although I haven't seen Maisie since Livia took her to Newport, I've seen plenty of Drew… a lot more than I anticipated, in fact.

I wondered at the wisdom of helping him shower on that first day, but it's a part of my job, and he'd have thought it strange if

I'd asked someone else to step in... especially as we'd been flirting. He started that, when he discovered the back of his hospital gown was open, and I took the chance to flirt back, which he seemed to like. Of course, I didn't expect him to say he wanted to shower, but once he had, I could hardly refuse to help... could I?

I could hardly fail to notice his arousal, either. That happens sometimes with male patients, and they usually get embarrassed, or try to hide it. Drew didn't. I wasn't sure what to make of that, but I kept it professional, helping him into the shower and showing him how to work the temperature controls.

Once he was occupied, focused on what he was doing, I took a moment, leaning back against the wall to admire him. There's no getting away from it... his body is divine. He has the broadest of shoulders, rippling abs, and a narrow waist, which lead down to the most perfectly formed penis... thick and heavy, all ridges and veins, with a bulbous head. Whenever male patients get aroused, I ignore it... but it was impossible to ignore Drew, or the effect he was having on me. I was struggling to breathe, sucking in lungfuls of air, trying to stop myself from sliding down the wall. My nipples were so hard they hurt, my pussy was slick with longing for him, and I had to bite on my thumbnail to stop myself from groaning out loud.

I've loved him for so long, but I'd never wanted him with such a visceral need.

He's been aroused several times since... and not just in the shower. But I can't act on it. Not only because I wouldn't know how to, but because it would be unprofessional, and wholly inappropriate. Besides, I can't even be sure his arousal has anything to do with me. I want it to, of course, but as I've already explained to him, the brain works in mysterious ways and his reactions may be nothing more than simple reflexes...

Although I hope they're not.

Over the last three days, his physical health has improved significantly. He can shower and dress himself now... which is a shame, although I offered to help him shave yesterday. He hadn't done so since the accident, but rather than accepting my offer, or suggesting he'd manage by himself, he simply rubbed his hand across his chin and shook his head.

"I don't know whether I used to shave before, but I kinda like this," he said.

"You do?"

"Yeah."

"Are you thinking of growing a beard?"

"I'm not sure."

I smiled at him. The stubble suited him, and I had a feeling a beard would, too.

His headache seems to have passed and although he still has occasional bouts of dizziness, they're very few and far between, and usually the result of him standing up too quickly. At the doctor's request, Hunter brought him in some clothes, so he no longer has to wear a hospital gown during the day.

"More's the pity," he said, when I gave him the holdall and explained the contents to him. I couldn't help blushing, but I don't think he noticed. I had to admit – even if only to myself – I was going to miss the sight of his delectable ass.

As for his cognitive abilities, he's still struggling. He has recall over certain things. For example, he knows what a cup of coffee is, and when I brought him one yesterday, his anticipation of how it would taste made me laugh. He knows my name and says it every time I come into his room... with the broadest of smiles on his lips. Even outside of his personal life, which is still a blank to him, there are holes, though. He can't remember the name of the President, and when I showed him a photograph of the White

House, he just said it was a big building… but he didn't recognize it for what it was. We'll keep working on it, and I'm sure he'll get there.

In the meantime, the other problem is his short-term memory, which is absolutely shocking. He can barely remember anything for more than a few minutes at a time, and yesterday I did some memory exercises with him, which he failed dismally, finding the whole thing exhausting.

We're having fun together, though. I love how his face lights up whenever I come to see him, and the way he laughs so readily… even at his own predicament. We enjoy his moments of triumph together, and on the rare occasions when it gets too much, I do my best to distract him, so he doesn't dwell on the negatives.

Of course, I realize these improvements – no matter how small – will one day lead to him being discharged from the hospital, and from my care, but I'm trying not to think about that.

"Nurse Emerson?"

I turn at the sound of Doctor Sweeney's voice, surprised to see Hunter Bennett standing beside him. I haven't seen him in person since the night of the accident. He's still wearing jeans and a button-down shirt, but he looks a lot less stressed, which isn't at all surprising. He smiles as I approach, looking down at me

"Doctor?"

"We've just been looking for you," he says with a nod of his head.

"I was on my way to Drew Bennett's room."

"Hmm… can you join us in my office for a moment?"

"Of course."

I follow them to the end of the corridor, going through the double doors that lead out of the department, and waiting while

Doctor Sweeney opens the first door on the left. It brings us into a large office. Opposite us, the windows overlook the city, while the wall to the left is lined with bookshelves. I doubt he's read very many of them. They look too new… too perfect. The wall to our right is filled with photographs and certificates and it's to that end of the room that the doctor leads us, over to his desk. There are two seats on this side of it, and Hunter waits for me to sit in one before taking the other himself, while Doctor Sweeney lowers himself into the chair opposite, gazing at me, his eyebrows raised.

"Mr. Bennett called me this morning," he says, glancing at Hunter before returning his gaze to me. "He's suggested that, rather than his brother continuing with his treatment here in the hospital, it might be better if he could go home."

I feel the panic rising inside me, my throat closing over and my palms sticky with sweat. I wrack my brain, trying to think of a reason – or an excuse – to keep Drew here, but I'm coming up blank.

"I—I see."

"I think it's an excellent idea. Drew's general health has improved. There don't seem to be any lasting physical effects from the concussion, and I can't see a reason to keep him here in the hospital. As you know, I've always believed that – where the patient can tolerate it – the introduction of familiar objects and surroundings can aid in their mental recovery."

"You think he's ready for that?" I ask.

He nods his head. "As long as it's done properly, yes," he says.

Part of me knows he's right. Doctor Sweeney has always advocated this approach, usually with outstanding success. The problem is, I know how scared Drew is. I've seen it in his eyes. And I promised I wouldn't let anything happen to him.

"In this case, though…" He holds up his hand and I stop talking.

"I haven't finished yet, Nurse. Drew is still going to need professional help, and it's obvious to everyone here, even after just a few days, that he responds better to you than he does to anyone else. So, his brother has suggested that you continue to care for him at his home."

I turn in my seat, looking at Hunter. "You want me to come and visit him every day?"

He smiles. "No. That wouldn't be practical. Drew's home is in Newport. I couldn't possibly ask you to drive down there every day to see him, as well as working here. That's why the doctor and I were wondering if you could come to stay. I'll pay you, of course, and Doctor Sweeney has agreed to release you from the staff at the hospital on a temporary basis."

"Your job will be waiting for you when you get back." I turn to the doctor, my head spinning. "I can't imagine Drew's recovery will take very long. Once he's in the comfort of his own home, I think he'll get the boost he needs for his memory to return to normal."

"What do you say?" Hunter asks and I look back at him, unable to take it all in. I'm not about to say 'no'… not if it means I get to spend more time with Drew.

"If it helps, of course I'll do it."

He smiles and Doctor Sweeney gets to his feet. "Shall we tell the patient?"

Hunter and I both stand, following him from the room. Out in the corridor, I make a point of getting ahead of them, wanting to be the first one through Drew's door. He's still nervous around other people… even other members of staff, and I don't want him to be anxious.

I open the door to his room. He's sitting in the chair by the window, wearing jeans and a t-shirt and, as usual, his eyes light up, a smile tugging at his lips.

"Hi, Josie. I wondered…" His voice fades as he sees I'm not alone, a frown settling on his face.

"It's okay." I go to him, noting the panic in his eyes as he sits back in his seat.

"Why is the doctor here?" he says. "And who's that guy?"

I consider it a minor breakthrough that he's remembered who Doctor Sweeney is, but I don't make a fuss and instead I stand beside him, my hand on his shoulder as Hunter approaches.

"Don't you remember me?" he says.

"No. Should I?"

"I was here the other night with my wife… after your accident."

"Your wife?" Drew says, frowning.

Hunter smiles. "Yes. Blonde… beautiful… surely you remember her, even if you don't remember me."

Drew shakes his head, not seeing the funny side.

"It doesn't matter now," I say, before Hunter pushes any further, and he glances at me, nodding his head, before he turns back to Drew.

"No. Of course not. What matters is, I've come to take you home."

Drew looks up at me, fear lining his face. "I—I don't want to go home."

"It's okay," I say. "I promise. I'm coming with you."

His face clears, and I hear his gentle sigh. "You're coming home with me?"

"Yes… until you get better."

He tilts his head. "Okay. But where is my home?"

Hunter steps a little closer, but Doctor Sweeney moves more quickly.

"We can't tell you that," he says. "I'm sure Josie's explained to you, it's better if you try to remember things by yourself."

Hunter shakes his head. "That's not fair, Doctor. I'm asking Drew to leave a place where he feels safe, and just take my word for it that he can trust me. He doesn't even know who I am. At the very least, let me explain where I'm taking him." The doctor hesitates for a moment, then nods his head, and Hunter crouches in front of Drew. "You have a house on our family's estate."

Drew shakes his head. "That doesn't make sense. Why would I have a house on your family's estate?"

"Because we're brothers."

Drew pushes his chair back, so it hits the wall with a thump. "No. That's not possible. I'd know if I had a brother."

Hunter stands, holding up his hands like he's surrendering, and my heart goes out to him as I take his place, kneeling rather than crouching, and looking up at Drew. "That's the whole point, though," I say. "You wouldn't know. And you're gonna have to trust us on this. Hunter is your brother."

He frowns, looking from me to Hunter, like we're mad.

"It's okay," Hunter says. "I get how confusing this must be for you, but you don't need to be scared about who I am, or about coming home. Your house is separate from the main building. You won't have to see me – or anyone else – if you don't want to." He glances at me, then looks back at Drew. "I'd have said you could go to your apartment, but that's never really been your home…"

"I have an apartment, as well as this house you're talking about?"

"Yes. It's here in the city, but it's not practical for your needs right now. It's not that big, and if Josie's going to stay with you and help you, then you'll be better off at the house. She can have her own room there, and you can walk in the grounds and use the pool…"

"There's a pool?" Drew shakes his head. "Am I rich, or something?"

Doctor Sweeney steps forward again, clearing his throat. "That'll do for now, Mr. Bennett. You've already given him more than enough information." He looks down at Drew and I get to my feet. "Are you happy to go home? We can't force you, but I think it'll help your recovery."

Drew pauses for a moment, looking from him to Hunter and then to me. "I guess. As long as Josie's with me. I mean… what choice do I have?"

That seems to be all the answer the doctor needs, and he turns toward the door, although Hunter hesitates. He glances at me, the pain in his eyes asking the silent question; is he doing the right thing? I nod my head and he moves away, following the doctor from the room.

"Don't go yet," Drew says, grabbing my hand and holding on to it.

"I won't be long. I just need to make the arrangements."

"Please wait."

"What's wrong?"

"I—I wanted to apologize."

"What for?"

"Because I think I just came across as very ungrateful. I'm sure you're all putting yourselves out for me, and I didn't mean to sound so unappreciative. It's just that, if I'm being honest, I'm even more frightened than I was before."

I kneel down again, a little closer than I was before, our locked hands between us, and I look up into his eyes. "That's understandable, but you have nothing to fear, Drew. I'll be with you every step of the way."

"I know, but… who is that guy?"

"Exactly who he said he is."

"That's ludicrous. How can I have a brother and not know him?"

"Try not to think about it."

"That's easier said than done." I go to get up, but he keeps a firm grip on my hand, pulling me back down again. "I meant what I said, Josie… about being okay with this, as long as you're with me."

"Good." I smile and he smiles back, although I can still feel his uneasiness as I get to my feet. "I need to arrange your medication and deal with all the discharge papers, which shouldn't take too long. Why don't you pack your things and get ready to leave?"

"Okay." He nods his head, releasing my hand, and I turn away, heading for the door, although when I open it and glance back, he's still sitting in the chair, staring at me.

"It'll be okay, Drew. I promise."

He smiles, and I go out into the hall, surprised to find Doctor Sweeney and Hunter are still out here, their heads bent together in conversation.

Hunter sees me and steps back slightly, shaking the doctor's hand before he turns to me, Doctor Sweeney heading for the nurse's station.

We wait until we're completely alone and he looks down at me, worry furrowed on his brow.

"Are you sure you're okay with this?" he asks.

"Of course. I'm a little intrigued by how you got Doctor Sweeney to agree to keep my job open indefinitely, but…"

He shakes his head. "Money talks, as ever. After I offered to make a very generous donation to his department, I think I could have asked for his first-born child, if I'd been so inclined." I laugh and he joins in, just briefly, although the clouds quickly return to his eyes. "I've just been talking to him about my sister."

I hadn't realized he and Drew had a sister, but I do my best to hide my surprise. "What about her?"

"Ella lives at the house in Newport, too. That's to say, she's got an apartment in the main building. She lives there with her fiancé, Mac, and their baby boy. But the doctor's just said it's probably going to be best if she keeps her distance for a while. Is that right?"

I nod my head as I recall him mentioning someone called Ella on the day of the accident. I think I heard the name 'Mac', too, although I can't be sure. "Yes," I say. "It's best to let Drew call the shots… to come to her when he's ready." He lets out a sigh. "I'm sorry. I know it's gonna be hard for her, just like it is for you, but he needs time, and to be honest, his recovery needs to be managed."

"What do you mean?"

I wonder if I should have said anything, but I've started now, so I may as well go on. "Drew's got a lot to cope with. He's got short-term and long-term memory problems."

"Is that why he couldn't remember me being here with Livia the other night?"

"Yes, and to be honest, reminding him won't help. That's why I stepped in just now. He remembered your visit at the time, because he asked about you later on that night, but the memory is gone now, and in reality, he's got bigger things to recall… like who he is, who you are, and what your relationship is to him, as opposed to why you were here."

"I see." He nods his head. "We'll be guided by you, Josie."

That's a relief. "I can't claim to be as knowledgeable as Doctor Sweeney, but I can promise to put your brother's needs first. You might not always agree with what I'm doing, but…"

"No," he says, interrupting me. "If it's in Drew's best interests, we'll do whatever it takes. I'll call ahead before we leave and let Ella and Livia know what's happening. They've been going quietly insane over the last couple of days, but hopefully, the relief that Drew's coming home will be enough to appease them for now. I'll also arrange for the kitchen at the cottage to be restocked with food."

"Re-stocked?"

"Yeah." He nods his head. "Drew asked me to get our housekeeper to stock it up for him before his flight back from Rome, but after the accident, she divided the contents of Drew's fridge between the main house and Ella's apartment, rather than just let everything go to waste."

"I see. So, can Drew cook?" I ask him.

"Yes. Why? Can't you?"

"I can. I just wondered whether he could. It might be a good trigger for him."

"Oh, I see. He likes to cook, but never had much time to do it." He pulls two phones from his back pocket, shaking his head. "I'm getting into such a muddle. They gave me Drew's phone, but it's identical to mine." He looks up. "To be honest, I'd turn his off, but I guess I shouldn't in case someone important calls, wanting to know how he is."

"It's probably wise."

He pockets one phone, looking down at the other. "I'll give you my number and if you need anything or you have any questions about him… about how he was before the accident, just call me."

"Okay." I pull out my phone, adding his number to my contacts. "Do you want to take mine, too?" He nods his head, putting it into his phone. "And I guess you'd better give me your address in Newport so I can drive down there."

He frowns. "Sorry… I kinda took it for granted you were gonna come with us. Drew would be more comfortable with you in the car, wouldn't he?"

"Yes, but I'll need to go home and collect some things."

"That's okay. I'd assumed you would. I thought we could go there first and then I'd drive us all to the house in Drew's car. It's more practical than my Ferrari, and I figured that way, he'll have a vehicle in Newport if he feels like driving anywhere himself."

I shake my head. "He won't be driving for a while, but maybe sitting in a familiar car will help. It might trigger a memory. Did he used to enjoy driving?"

"Yeah, he did. He's had quite a few cars over the years, but he bought the Range Rover because he can fit all his equipment inside."

"His photographic equipment?" I ask and he nods.

"Yeah. When Drew's ready, I'll drive us all over to your place. You can pack whatever you need, and I'll take us to Newport."

"Thank you."

He frowns, shaking his head. "Don't thank me, Josie. What you're doing for Drew… for all of us…" His voice cracks and I put my hand on his arm.

"It'll be okay."

"I know. I just hate that he has no idea who we are… or who Maisie is."

"It's hard." I hate having to keep Maisie from him, but I can't say that out loud. "What are you doing about Maisie? Will she be at the house in Newport?"

"Yes. Livia says all her things have been moved over to the main house now, so Drew isn't gonna walk into one of the bedrooms at the cottage and wonder why there's a crib in there, or anything like that. Of course, I guess there's a chance that he'll see her in the grounds, but there's nothing I can do about that. We can't keep her locked up in the main house until Drew gets better."

No, they can't. It wouldn't be fair… but then, none of this is fair. "Is your wife looking after her?"

"She is. Along with our housekeeper, Pat, and my sister, although she's got a newborn of her own, who Drew's never even met, so…" He pauses for a moment, swallowing hard. "Maisie's not short of people who care for her, but she needs her father. And I think he needs her, too."

I can't disagree with that. "Try not to worry. He'll get there."

I turn to leave, but he calls me back. "I meant to ask on the night of the accident, was Lexi's sister notified of her death?"

I suck in a breath, feeling the blush creep up my cheeks. "Yes, she was."

"Good." He smiles, a very slight twinkle in his eyes.

"What's so amusing?"

"Oh… it doesn't matter. I just hope Drew's memory comes back soon, and that when it does, he remembers her."

"Who? Lexi?"

"No, her sister." I have no idea what that means, and I can hardly ask… not without giving myself away. He looks down, his eyes fixed on mine. "Tell me… am I being selfish?"

"Selfish? No. You're doing what's best for your brother."

"Even if part of the reason I'm doing it is that my wife is in Newport, and I'm here… and I miss her."

I smile. "We all do selfish things from time to time, but that doesn't make them wrong."

I'm thinking of myself as much as him. I've chosen not to reveal my identity to Drew or his family. If anyone were to ask why, I'd give them the same reason I gave to Orla… I want to help Drew and Maisie. That's not a lie. It's exactly how I feel.

But it's not the whole truth, because I'm also doing it for myself.

Because I love him too much to leave him… or to be left behind.

Drew

I've been wandering from room to room for the last twenty minutes, and I can't take it in. How can this house be mine, and yet I can't remember it? How can I have a brother, who I don't even recognize? It doesn't make sense. Although I'll admit we look vaguely similar… I guess. He showed us around the house before he left, telling Josie where things were, probably because he knew there was no point in explaining any of it to me… not when I was unlikely to remember.

The one piece of solid information I've gained today is that my name is Drew. Drew Bennett. Hunter let that slip at the hospital, even though Josie has scrupulously avoided calling me anything for the last few days. He didn't call me 'Bennett', but that's what the doctor called him, and I assumed my last name must be the same as his, and put that together for myself.

I suppose I ought to feel grateful for small mercies. At least I've learned something… even if it doesn't seem to have got me anywhere.

Before we came here, Hunter took us to Josie's apartment so she could pack some things. She lives in a pretty little condo, and to enter it, you climb up some steps on the outside of the building. Initially, Hunter had suggested we'd wait outside for her, but I didn't want to. I felt nervous being alone with him, and I think Josie sensed that, solving the problem by inviting us in. Of course, I hadn't anticipated that I'd find the steps such a challenge, but it was the first time I'd tackled any since the accident and by the time we reached the top, I was feeling a little light-headed. Josie must have noticed, and she helped me along the balcony to her front door, opening it, and letting me inside, where she sat me down on her pale gray couch.

"Are you okay?" she asked, kneeling in front of me.

"Yeah. I'm just being pathetic… again."

She smiled. "You're not pathetic. Far from it. I should have realized the stairs would be difficult for you," she said and I shook my head, but didn't say a word, still feeling weak, and she gave me a smile and got to her feet. "I'll be as quick as I can." She went into an adjoining room, leaving me alone with the man who claimed to be my brother.

While she was gone, to avoid having to make conversation, I studied her bookcases, noting there wasn't a single photograph anywhere in her living room. I don't know why, but that felt odd to me. Hunter stared out the window, neither of us speaking… but I'm not sure what we'd have said. He's not supposed to tell me anything, and I don't know who he is.

Awkward didn't even begin to cover it.

Fortunately, Josie didn't take long at all, and within twenty minutes, we were on our way again. She held my hand as we went down the steps, Hunter carrying her bag and going ahead of us, and when we got to the car, she made sure I was sitting safely in my seat before climbing in beside me.

There's something about her that makes me feel safe, and although I want to protect her too, at the moment, I'm not sure I'm capable.

On the drive down here, I kept hoping something would trigger a memory; that I'd see my 'home', and it would all come flooding back. So far, though, nothing's happening. It all seems so grand… from the gated driveway Hunter drove us along in that enormous black Range Rover, to the extensive lawns and huge house he parked outside of, before he helped us unload the bags and walked in front of us down to this cottage I'm supposed to call home.

Everything is so strange.

Is this really what I come from?

Don't get me wrong, I like the cottage. I mean… what's not to like? The living room is large, with a cream-colored couch and two dark blue chairs, all set around an enormous fireplace, with a wooden mantel above it. There are glass doors in the far wall, leading out onto a terrace, and through an arch is a magnificent kitchen. It has off-white units and granite countertops, and has a large table in the center. A door at the end leads through to a formal dining room, with an oak table and eight chairs surrounding it, although I imagine I'd have eaten in the kitchen. I feel like I'm a 'kitchen' kind of guy.

I wander up the stairs, taking my time over climbing them, so as not to wear myself out. I know there are four bedrooms up here because Hunter showed me earlier. Mine comprises a suite at the back of the house, and it's simply furnished, and quite functional, with just a large bed, two nightstands and a couch. I also have an office, a dressing room, and a bathroom, and I go into the office, checking out the tidy desk, with a laptop sitting on its shining surface, and the couch beneath the window, on top of which, there's a black canvas bag.

I wonder what I did for a living, although there are no obvious clues here, and I go back out and into the dressing room, opening the closets to find them filled with jeans and t-shirts. I have a few shirts, a couple of suits and a tux, but for the best part, it seems I dressed informally… so I guess I didn't work in an office.

Josie's room is opposite mine, and she's in there now, unpacking her things. I looked around her room earlier. Like all the other rooms that overlook the front of the house, it has shuttered windows, which she seemed to like, and big oak furniture, with a large wet room attached. That reminded me of the wet room at the hospital and how she watched me shower in there. I didn't say anything… not in front of Hunter, but the thought crossed my mind that I'd like to watch her shower, or better still, get in there with her.

There seem to be photographs everywhere, on all the surfaces and most of the walls and, having gleaned nothing from my bedroom or office, I step outside my bedroom door, studying a black-and-white image of a cornfield, with what appears to be a stormy sky above it, when the door behind me opens and Josie comes out. She's changed out of her purple scrubs and is now wearing skin-tight, stonewashed jeans and a pale lilac t-shirt, which is molded to her breasts like a second skin. My cock is instantly hard and very uncomfortable.

"Are you okay?" she asks, looking up at me.

"I'm just confused." That's the understatement of the century. Aside from not knowing who I am, I can't work out what kind of man I am, either. I want to fuck her, so damn hard… but is that the kind of thing Drew Bennet would do? What kind of lover am I? Do I fuck, or do I make love? Do I bide my time, or am I the kind of guy who just goes for it… and if I do, am I tender, or dominant?

"That's understandable," she says. "There's a lot for you to take in."

No kidding.

She comes and stands beside me, studying the picture, and even though she's so close I could kiss her, I have to distract myself. "Is it me, or are there a lot of photographs here?"

"There are, but I like them."

"So do I. Did I take them?"

She tilts her head. "Is that a question, or a memory?"

"It's a question. I can't see why else I'd have so many."

"I agree, but I'm not allowed to tell you. You know that."

The distraction is working better than I'd expected. This is so frustrating. It's like there are memories pulling at me, nagging me to recall them, but they're too far out of reach. "Am I a photographer? Is that my job?" She stares at me, raising her eyebrows. "Okay, okay. I get it. You can't tell me. But if I was, surely I'd have equipment, wouldn't I?"

"Possibly."

"You can be really infuriating, you know?"

"It's for your own good."

"Sure it is." I turn away, but she grabs my arm. I may be a little weak still, but I'm stronger than she is, and I'm standing my ground, so instead of pulling me back, all she does is stumble into me and I reach out, holding her steady.

"Don't get mad at me, Drew."

She takes a step back, and I have to let her go. "Sorry. I don't mean to." *I'm just especially confused.* "This is so much harder than I thought."

"You imagined you'd come back here, and your memory would miraculously return?"

"Something like that." I let my head drop, staring down at the space between us.

"If only it was that easy." She moves closer again, dipping her head and crouching slightly, to get my attention in the cutest possible way, which makes me smile. "Shall we go downstairs?"

"Sure."

I let her lead the way. She knows this place about as well as I do, after all, and when we get into the living room, she turns to face me. "Can I get you anything?"

"I noticed the complicated coffee machine in the kitchen, so I guess I'm a coffee drinker."

"That's debatable."

"Why do you say that?"

"Because you seemed to enjoy the coffee I brought you in the hospital… and it's notoriously bad."

I chuckle and she joins in. "Maybe I don't have a very discerning palate."

"Or maybe you were just desperate for caffeine."

"Why don't we see if we can work out how the coffee machine functions, and maybe I'll be able to establish whether I have taste or not?"

She turns, making her way into the kitchen. "I think it's a given that you have taste," she says, over her shoulder. "This place is beautiful."

"It is kinda nice."

The coffee machine is over by the window and we head straight for it, standing for a moment and studying it.

"Are you sure you wouldn't rather have tea?" She looks up at me with a smile.

"It can't be that difficult."

I turn it on at the wall, and the control panel lights up. There are buttons all around it and I press the arrow on the right.

"What are you doing?"

"I don't know, but what's the worst that can happen?"

"It'll explode?"

I laugh, and we both look back at the control panel, which says 'flat white'. I click the arrow again and the display changes to 'single espresso'. "Ahh… so we choose the type of coffee we want." Josie nods her head and I keep scrolling through until we get back to 'flat white' again. "What do you feel like?"

"I don't know… let's try a cappuccino."

"Okay." I make the selection. "It seems you have to choose how frothy you want the milk to be."

"Seriously?"

"Yeah… look, there's a scale."

It's one to five, so we choose three, on the basis that we don't know what we're doing, but it's in the middle, and seems safest.

We need water, and I find the tank easily, filling it up… and then comes the coffee itself. The machine takes beans, which surprises Josie.

"You really do like your coffee, don't you?" she says, rooting through the kitchen cabinets, discovering where I keep my cups and bringing two back, along with a packet of coffee beans.

"I guess so."

She opens the pack, tipping them into the container. "Do you think it's ready now?"

"We just need milk."

She rolls her eyes and darts to the refrigerator, bringing back a carton, which she opens, handing it to me. There's a separate tank on the side, and I open it, filling it up to the 'max' line.

"That's gotta be everything now," she says.

"Hopefully, if it isn't, it'll tell us."

I press the start button. Nothing happens for a few seconds and I'm just wondering if we've missed a step when the machine makes a noise.

"It's doing something," Josie says, looking up at me with a smile.

"Let's hope it's making coffee."

A movement outside catches my eye and I glance through the window, noticing a blond woman walking across the grass. She's a fair distance away, so I can't make out her features very well. What I can see, though, is that she's holding a baby. Alongside her is another woman, with short dark hair, who's also cradling an infant in her arms.

"Do I know those women?" I ask Josie and she looks up. I hear her sigh and turn to face her, noting the worried expression on her face. "What's wrong?"

"Nothing."

I don't believe a word she's saying. "Am I related to them?"

She looks up at me. "Is that a question, or a memory?"

"A question."

"So you don't remember either of them?"

"No. Should I?"

She puts her hand on my arm. "Don't worry about it."

"That's not an answer, Josie."

"You know I'm not supposed to tell you anything."

"Yeah, but does that mean I can't ask questions?"

"No… no, of course not. I know it's confusing, but try not to think too much. You're not helping yourself." *I'd noticed.* "The memories are still in there, Drew."

"You've started calling me 'Drew'."

She smiles, surprised by my change of subject. "Yes. Your brother used your name earlier, at the hospital, and I couldn't see the point of keeping it from you anymore."

"Hmm… I noticed his slip-up, too."

"And you remembered your name this time?"

"Have you used it before then?"

"Quite a few people used it on the night of the accident, but you obviously forgot it, and we couldn't remind you, even when you asked."

"Did I? I don't remember asking."

"Well, you did."

"Okay… but I won't need to anymore. I'm not gonna forget it again."

Her smile widens. "Good… but don't pressure yourself. If you keep pushing, you're just gonna find it harder to get to where you want to be."

"I'll take your word for that." I nod out the window to where the two women are standing still now, talking. "Is one of those babies Hunter's? Am I an uncle?" She doesn't reply, but just continues to stare at me. "I hate this. I hate that there are so many things I don't know."

She leans a little closer. "Would it help if I told you I hate that there are so many things I can't tell you?"

Not really.

She's near enough that I could easily reach out and pull her into my arms. I want to, so badly. Not just because she's doing crazy things to my body, but because I need to feel something real… something true. My cock still hasn't recovered from that first moment I saw her come out of her room in her tight t-shirt, and having her this close is driving me insane. It's painful, too… but it's a pain I could learn to live with, and I inch closer.

The coffee machine beeps, and she looks away, breaking the moment. *Dammit.*

"Oh, look. It worked."

"Don't sound so surprised. I'm a man… it's a machine…"

"Yeah, and that's usually a recipe for disaster," she says, and I laugh. She joins in, lifting the cup to her lips and taking a sip. "Oh… oh, that's very good."

"I guess I'd better make myself one, then."

"Yeah, you had." She cradles the cup. "This one's mine… all mine."

"Okay, but remember, I'm the one who knows how to use the machine, so if you want more coffee, be nice to me."

"I'll always be nice to you."

I really hope she means that, as does my aching cock.

"Are you hungry?" I ask, looking over at Josie.

We're sitting in the living room, both of us on our second cup of coffee, but my stomach keeps rumbling.

"I am a little. Would you like me to make something?"

"Do we have food?"

She nods her head. "Hunter's had the kitchen stocked up, and before he left to go back to the main house, he said I should just let him know when we need anything."

I nod my head, and she gets up, walking into the kitchen. I follow and between us, we establish that there's enough food here to feed an army.

"I don't know what I like," I say, turning to face her.

"Why don't I just make us something simple for today, and we'll worry about likes and dislikes tomorrow?"

"Okay, but can I help at all? I mean… I don't know whether I can cook, but I seem to have a nice enough kitchen, and I can't imagine it was put in purely as a home for the coffee machine."

She smiles. "I'm sure you can cook, but it's been a tiring day for you. You need to rest."

She's not wrong. I feel exhausted, but rather than returning to the living room, I sit at the kitchen table and watch her work.

"Do you have a family?" I ask, as she gathers ingredients… an onion, some garlic, spices, tomatoes, broccoli. Her hands are full, and she looks up at me, frowning.

"No, but why do you ask?"

"Because I'm wondering how you're able to just drop everything and come live with me."

Her frown fades, a smile tugging at her lips. "Oh, I see."

"We're two of a kind, really."

"Are we?"

"Yeah. You don't have any family… and even if I do, I don't know who they are."

She sets down all the ingredients on the countertop, turning to face me again, her smile widening. "I guess…"

She stands for a moment, just staring at me… and I stare back. Within seconds, she comes to her senses, like she's scolding herself for daydreaming, and turns around to prepare our meal. I don't take my eyes from her, though. I stare at the back of her head, at the way her hair is held up in a loose arrangement, a few strands hanging down her neck, which in itself is a thing of beauty. Pale and slender, I want to brush those stray hairs aside and kiss her at that point where her neck meets her shoulder. I want to let my hands roam over her body, discovering every curve, my lips following close behind. She'll taste sweet. I know she will and I groan at the thought of unlocking her innermost secrets… with my tongue.

"Are you okay?" She turns, having clearly heard me, and I nod my head, unable to speak. She smiles. "This doesn't take long to prepare. You can set the table, if you feel up to it."

I nod again, still unsure about my voice, and she turns away. I want to ask her to turn back so I can tell her that even if I never get to kiss her, or touch her, or taste her, I need her to stay.

Because I'd be lost without her.

I don't say any of that, and instead I give myself a moment to recover from my daydreams and I set the table. I take a while to find everything, but I get there eventually, and by the time I'm done, Josie is dishing up our dinner into shallow bowls.

She brings them over to the table, sitting opposite me.

"What are we eating?"

"It's a chick-pea curry."

"It smells incredible, so I'm guessing I like curry."

She smiles, picking up her fork. I copy her, tasting the combination of spices and vegetables, which is absolutely delicious.

"Do you like it?" She looks across at me, tilting her head, like she's nervous.

"It's lovely… although I feel like there's something missing."

She laughs. "I wondered if you'd say that."

"You did?" I'm confused, and I put down my fork, staring across at her.

"Yeah." She tips her head the other way. "There's no meat."

I glance down at the bowl. "Of course. I guess this means I'm a carnivore." She nods her head. "Are you a vegetarian?"

"No. I only cooked this for us because I know how quick and easy it is, and I figured you're tired and might want to get to bed early."

She's not wrong. As much as I'd love to sit up and talk, or even just look at her, I'm worn out, and once we've finished eating, it's all I can do to keep my eyes open. Josie notices and suggests I head up to my room.

"No. I'll help clear away."

"You won't. There's a dishwasher, so I've only got to stack things into it. It won't take a moment."

"That doesn't seem fair when you've cooked."

"You can make it up to me some other time." She gets to her feet, coming around to my side of the table as I stand. "Do you need me to help you get ready for bed?"

I think about that for a moment. It's tempting to say 'yes', not just because I'm so tired I can barely function, but also because I want to be near to her. But the thing is, I want to be near to her when I'm capable of doing something about it, and when I know that's what she wants, too. Unfortunately, that means I'm better off going upstairs by myself… at least for now.

"I'll be fine, thanks."

"Okay, but call if you run into trouble."

I nod my head and make for the door, although I turn on the threshold and look back at her. She's clearing the dishes already, focused on what she's doing.

"Josie?"

She looks up. "Yeah?"

"Thank you."

"What are you thanking me for?"

"Being here." It's the truth. I'm grateful for her presence.

She blushes. "You don't have to thank me for that."

"Yeah, I do."

I turn, unable to get into an argument about the rights and wrongs of thanking her, and I make my way up the stairs to my bedroom. Closing the door, I switch on the lights and stand by the bed for a moment. When I went through the dressing room this afternoon, I didn't find any pajamas, but even if I had, I don't think I've got the energy to put them on. Instead, I pull off my clothes and tumble into bed, drawing up the covers over my body as sleep claims me.

"Do you feel like a walk?" Josie looks across the breakfast table at me. It's already gone nine-thirty, but I overslept, and then took ages in the shower… not because I'm still tired, but because the shower is so good. "You need to get some exercise."

"If you say so." She smiles and stands up. "Are you gonna object if I offer to clear away?"

She made our breakfast, but I'm still half expecting an argument. "No. I'm gonna let you clear away all by yourself while I go find my shoes."

I'm surprised but do my best to hide it and while she goes upstairs, I stack the dishwasher with our plates and cups. By the time I'm done, she's standing in the doorway, and I glance down at the flat pumps adorning her feet, my eyes wandering up over her denim-clad thighs, and resting for a moment on her full breasts, concealed behind yet another tight t-shirt… a bright pink one this time. Eventually, I make it to her face, to find she's smiling at me, seemingly unfazed by my attentions.

"Are you ready?"

"Sure."

We make our way to the front door, going outside and pulling it closed behind us. We don't need to lock it, even though Hunter left a set of keys on the cabinet by the door. This place seems secure enough without keys, and Josie looks up at me before setting off, turning to her left, away from the main house. I fall into step beside her, wishing I could hold her hand, even though I can't.

"It's beautiful here," she says.

"Yeah." She's not wrong. The grounds are extensive and well maintained. There are quite a lot of mature trees, and in the distance, I can see another building, although it's clearly still within the boundaries of the property. "What's that?" I ask her, pointing to it.

"I don't know."

"You genuinely don't know? Or you can't tell me?"

"I don't know. Your brother hasn't explained what it is, and I haven't asked."

"So, for once, we're both living in ignorance?"

"It seems that way, yes." She looks up at me, squinting slightly against the bright sunshine. "I can ask him about it, if you want… but you need to remember, if he tells me you were already aware of whatever it is, I won't be able to discuss it with you."

"In which case, there seems little point in asking." The building looks like a single-story house, although it's quite a size and if I lived here as my brother claims, I must have known about it.

She nods her head, turning away again, just as my eye catches sight of a bright red Ferrari, driving up toward the main house. I stop in my tracks.

"I—I know that car," I say.

Josie turns, facing me. "You do? You mean, you know that's your brother's car?"

"No. I just know it's a Ferrari. How do you know it's my brother's car?"

"Because he told me he drives a Ferrari," she says. "And he sent me a text message very early this morning, letting me know he was going back to the city to collect it."

"I see." I spot a second car… an SUV.

"What's that one?" she asks.

"A Mercedes." I look down at her. "But again, I don't know who it belongs to… or how I'm able to identify the car."

"As for who it belongs to, in this case, I don't know either, but I imagine it's someone who lives here, who drove your brother into the city this morning."

"And the reason I know what the car is?"

She shrugs her shoulders. "Maybe you liked cars," she says. "Maybe it's a memory, of sorts."

"You think I enjoyed driving?" She gazes up at me, raising her eyebrows. "Okay. I get it. You're not gonna tell me."

We walk on for a moment or two, while I try to fathom why I can remember the makes of cars, but have no idea who I am. Or how I seemed to know I like coffee, but couldn't remember whether I ate meat. Why are the holes in my memory so random? Why don't I know basic things, like whether I enjoyed driving… or whether I was even capable of driving, come to that?

Suddenly, a horrible thought crosses my mind, panic rising in an instant, and I stop, grabbing Josie's arm and pulling her back. "Was I driving when I had the accident?"

"I can't tell you," she says.

I pull her closer, her body almost touching mine. "I don't care about any of that. Please, Josie… I have to know, even if you can't give me details. Tell me I'm not responsible for what happened. If I hurt someone else… or… or somebody died because of what I did, you have to tell me. I need to know if I'm to blame."

She places her hand on my chest and I suck in a breath, fighting the distraction of her touch. "You're not."

The relief is almost too much for me and I keep a hold of her for a moment longer. There's nothing sexual about this. I need her support. I need her to ground me… to be my rock. Again.

"Thank you." Her brow furrows, like she doesn't understand my gratitude. "I'm not gonna ask you for details you're not allowed to give, but thank you for putting my mind at rest. That was a scary moment."

She smiles. "It's okay."

It is when I'm with you.

I let go of her and she steps away, both of us turning and continuing our walk.

"Why did my brother contact you this morning to let you know he was going into the city?" I ask. It seems like an odd thing to do.

"He wanted to know if there was anything either of us needed him to bring back. I couldn't think of anything, and didn't want to wake you, so I just said 'no'. I hope that was all right."

"I don't have a clue what I own, so I wouldn't have known what to ask for, anyway."

"That was what I figured."

The two cars have disappeared from view now, and Josie and I wander on, occasionally catching a glimpse of the harbor between the trees.

"Is this really who I am?"

"What do you mean?"

"Do I really come from a world of Ferraris and family estates with harbor views and swimming pools? Is this me?" She doesn't answer, because she can't, and I let out a sigh. "I'm sick of these one-sided conversations. Tell me about you instead."

"No," she says sharply – a little too sharply – and I stop again, turning to face her.

"Why not? I don't have anything to say. You're not allowed to answer my questions, and my brain is a void for the best part, so unless we're gonna spend our time in silence, just admiring the scenery, I suggest you talk." She giggles, which is a relief, although she soon falls quiet and stares up at me. "Don't stop laughing, Josie. The sound is…"

"It's what?"

"It's how I imagine heaven would be." She gasps and I'm so tempted to kiss her, to find my true heaven here on earth. But I don't want to scare her off, so instead, I take her hand in mine. "Please, Josie… talk to me." *You fascinate me and I want to know more.*

She keeps her eyes fixed on mine as we take baby steps together. "What do you want to know?"

Anything. Everything. "Where are you from?"

"Boston… although I lived in New York for a while."

"What made you decide to become a nurse?"

"I spent some time in the hospital as a teenager. It inspired me."

Her answers are short, factual, lacking in detail. I'm guessing she's a private person, and I can't force her to talk. But there's something I need to know… desperately. "I remember you said you don't have any family, which I'm gonna guess means you're not married?" She nods her head and I copy her, slowing us to a stop yet again and looking down at her. "Do you have a boyfriend?" I wait, but she doesn't answer and I'm in an agony of expectation. "Josie?"

"I don't have a boyfriend, no."

"Good."

"Why is that good?"

"I'm not sure it is yet, but to find out, I'm gonna have to ask you to break your rule… just once."

"My rule?"

"Yeah, the one that says you're not allowed to tell me anything. I need you to break it and give me a straight answer."

She pauses for a moment, her eyes fixed on mine, like they're searching for something. "What do you need to know?"

"Am I married? Do I have a girlfriend? I'm pretty sure she'd be here if I did... but can you tell me?"

She shakes her head, and I wonder if I'm going to have to beg her, or explain my reason for asking... that I need to be with her, but I can't if I'm with someone else. I may not know myself very well, but I don't think I'm the kind of guy who'd cheat. The thought of it feels wrong, which is why I need to know whether I'm free. I open my mouth to ask again, just as she says, "No, you're not married... and you don't have a girlfriend."

She lowers her head as she's speaking, but I place my finger beneath her chin, raising it again until her eyes lock on mine, her breath catching in her throat as she sucks it in.

"That's good too, isn't it?" I whisper, my lips no more than an inch from hers.

"Why?" She blinks hard. "Why is it good?"

I move closer. "Why do you think?"

"I—I don't know."

"Yes, you do."

Chapter Six

Josie

Do I?

Can it be that he wants me as much as I want him? It would be so easy, too…

Except it wouldn't.

I might have given him a few bare facts, but he doesn't know me. He doesn't know who I am, or my connection to his old life. And besides, he's a patient.

I take a step back, letting out a long breath.

"Sorry," he says, his voice filled with regret. "Did I say the wrong thing? Did I move too fast?"

"It's not that."

"Then what, Josie? What did I do?"

"It's just…" My phone rings, interrupting me and I curse under my breath, pulling it from my back pocket. Hunter's name is displayed on the screen, so I know I can't ignore him. "I'm sorry. I have to take this."

Drew nods his head, and I move away, connecting the call to his brother.

"I'm really sorry to interrupt you, Josie." *Not as sorry as I am.*

"What can I do for you?"

"I need you to come up to the main house."

"When?"

"Now."

He isn't giving me any options and doesn't seem to want to take 'no' for an answer.

"Okay. We're just taking a walk, so I'll have to get Drew back to the cottage, and then I'll be right over."

"Thanks."

He hangs up, and I wonder what's wrong. He seemed much more abrupt than he usually is, and I look around, trying to see if we're visible from the house… if he's been watching us, and has seen how close we came to kissing just then. That doesn't make sense, though. We're on the other side of Drew's cottage and I can't even see the main house from here, so that can't be it, although something's clearly wrong.

"Who was that?" Drew asks, breaking into my worries.

"Hunter."

"My brother?"

I hate that he needs to check, that he still doesn't know. Just like he doesn't know who I am… who his daughter is.

"Yes. He needs me to go up to the main house."

"What for?"

"He didn't say."

"And you have to go right now, do you?" His face darkens.

"I'll get you back to the cottage first."

He stares at me for a moment and then nods his head, like he's reluctant to accept the situation.

Neither of us says another word, but we retrace our steps, Drew opening the door when we get to the cottage.

"Do you need anything?" I ask him as he turns to face me.

"No. I'll be fine."

"Are you sure? I can get you a coffee, or a glass of water?"

"I'm okay."

I step closer. "Don't be mad at me."

"I'm not." He reaches out, his fingertips just skimming over my cheek. "I'm not mad at you, Josie. But this is so damn difficult."

I don't know whether he's talking about what just happened outside, or the situation as a whole, and even if I wanted to find out the answer, I don't have time to ask.

"I—I need to go."

He lets his hand fall to his side again. "Sure." He steps back and I move toward the door. "Josie?"

"Yes?" I turn back to face him.

"Don't be long," he says.

"I'll be as quick as I can."

He nods his head and, as there doesn't seem to be anything else to say, I open the door and let myself out, following the path that leads to the main house.

My mind is a whirl of indecision, my thoughts racing. I should feel happy. I know I should. This feels like a dream come true. I've wanted Drew for so long, and loved him even longer. It seems he wants me, too. But, does he even know what it means to want someone? Does he know what that entails? He obviously used to. He has a daughter to prove it. But now? Does he remember? Because if he doesn't, we're in trouble. The kind of trouble I can't resolve.

And what about love? He hasn't mentioned it, and I need him to.

Maybe that's another part of what's holding me back and stopping me from leaping into his arms... aside from the fact that he's a patient, that he has a daughter of whom he knows nothing, that her mother was my step-sister and that he doesn't know who I am, let alone who he is.

Why couldn't this be simple?

Why couldn't we just have met and fallen in love, like a 'normal' couple?

I let out a sigh, knocking on the front door of the main house. It's opened within moments by a woman who appears to be in her early sixties. She has red hair, with a few gray streaks, and she looks at me with sparkling green eyes.

"You must be Josie?" she says.

"I am."

She smiles. "I'm Pat. We haven't met yet, but I—I wanted to thank you for everything you're doing for Drew."

I don't know what to say, especially as I know how dishonest I've been about my role in his past. "You don't need to thank me."

"Oh, I think we do." She steps aside. "Come on in. Hunter's in his office."

I enter the house and she closes the door, giving me a moment or two to take in the wood flooring, the white walls, and the wide staircase that leads up to the second floor.

There's an archway to one side, but Pat opens a door opposite, waiting for me to enter Hunter's office. It's a big room, with a desk at one end and a couch by the window that overlooks the front of the house. Hunter is sitting behind the desk, but he stands the moment he sees me, walking over to greet me.

"Thanks for coming so quickly," he says, ushering me into the room. The door closes behind me, and I focus on the other person in the room. She's sitting in one of the two chairs facing Hunter's desk and she turns around to face me, revealing herself to be a very attractive woman in her mid- to late-forties, with short dark hair that frames her face. "Please, take a seat."

I sit beside the woman, who stares at me for a moment longer and then looks across the desk at Hunter. I don't know who she is. He looks a little awkward; she looks uncomfortable, and I'm just wondering if I'm going to have to ask to be introduced, when the woman turns in her seat, holding out her hand to me.

"I'm Lindsay Bennett. I'm Drew's mother."

I'm not sure how that's possible. She doesn't look old enough, but I take her slender hand in mine, using the moment to think; to remember to stay silent. Drew's never mentioned his parents to me, but even if he had, I wouldn't be able to say anything without giving myself away.

Fortunately, I don't need to. Hunter coughs and his mom withdraws her hand from mine, both of us turning to look at her son, who's frowning at her from the other side of the desk. He averts his gaze to me, his expression lightening a little.

"I'm sorry, Josie. I need your advice, but in order to ask for it, I'm gonna have to take you into my confidence… or rather into the family's confidence." He glances at his mother again. "The situation is complicated, but I hope you'll be able to help."

"I'll do whatever I can," I say, even more confused than I was before.

He nods his head and sits back. "As you know, I drove into the city this morning to fetch my car. When I got back, I found our mother here, waiting to see me."

"That's not strictly true," Mrs. Bennett says. "I asked to see Drew and the woman who let me in told me I couldn't, and I'd have to wait for you to get back first."

He stares at her for a moment and then turns back to me again. "However it happened, what you need to know is that Drew hasn't seen our mom since he was six years old, and I'm not sure if it's a good idea for him to see her now."

"Why not? He's my son." Mrs. Bennett sits forward in her seat.

"Then why the hell did you leave him? Why did you abandon him, and Ella… and me?"

I can hear the hurt in Hunter's voice, even now, over twenty years later, and I wonder what effect that abandonment had on Drew.

"I—It's hard to explain." Mrs. Bennett stumbles over her words, glancing at me and I wonder if she'd rather I wasn't here… if she'd be able to talk better if it was just her and her oldest son. The problem is, Hunter said he needed my help, so I'm staying put.

"I'm sure it is," he says, narrowing his eyes at her.

"It wasn't easy coming back to this house, after all this time." Her voice cracks, but he seems unmoved.

"Maybe you shouldn't have stayed away so long. Or better still, maybe you shouldn't have left us in the first place."

"I had no choice." She raises her voice, emotion getting the better of her, and Hunter stares at her, like he's battling his own feelings, trying to decide whether to sympathize with her, or recoil from her. Neither side seems to come out on top, and after a moment or two, he turns back to me.

"I'm sorry, Josie. This must be very difficult for you."

It's nowhere near as difficult for me as it seems to be for him, but I smile, hoping it'll help. "It's okay. I'm guessing you've asked me to be here because you want my opinion about whether it's wise for Drew to meet with his mother?"

"Yes."

I nod my head. "I don't know how Drew reacted to his mom leaving, but he was very young when it happened, so I imagine it would have been traumatic for him… for all of you."

"It was." Hunter glances at his mother again. "To be fair, I think it was harder on me than it was on Drew or Ella. I was eleven. I blamed myself."

"Hunter?" His mom's voice cracks and she reaches across the desk, although he ignores the olive branch. "It wasn't your fault."

135

"That's not the point right now, Mom. The point is, should we let you see Drew? Should we even let him know you're here?"

I sit forward and they both look at me. "Drew remembers nothing about his past yet," I say. "He's still struggling to come to terms with the idea of having a brother. He doesn't understand the setup here, or his life before the accident. We haven't even broached the concept of him having a sister, and I'm concerned this situation could cause more harm than good." I turn to Mrs. Bennett. "I'm not judging you for anything you've done in the past, and I'm not questioning your motives. All I'm saying is that, while it might make you feel better to see your son, at this point in his treatment, it won't help him."

"What should I do?" she asks.

"Wait. I'm sorry to keep saying it to everyone, but it's all you can do. Once Drew remembers things for himself, we can re-assess the situation and ascertain his state of mind a little better."

"And how long will that take?"

"I don't know. This isn't a precise process."

She turns back to Hunter, like she's about to plead with him to change my mind, but he merely shrugs his shoulders. "If that's what Josie says is best, that's how it has to be."

She seems to deflate, staring at the top of his desk for a moment, but then she raises her head again. "What about Ella? Will you let me see her?"

He shakes his head. "I don't think that's a good idea, either."

"Why on earth not? What do you think I'm going to do to her?"

"Turn her life upside down. She's grown up with no memories of you at all. You can't suddenly walk back in here and expect her to accept you. Besides, we still need to think about Drew in all of this. He hasn't met Ella yet, but when he does, the last thing we need is for her to blurt out that you're back. I know this isn't what you want to hear, but if it's gonna work, it has to be handled right."

She swallows hard, blinking rapidly, like she's trying not to cry. "Do you want this to work, Hunter? Do you want me back in your lives?"

"That depends what you want from us."

"Forgiveness."

He shakes his head. "I've always given you the benefit of the doubt, Mom. If Drew could remember anything, he'd be the first to tell you, I've always been the one to defend you. But you're asking a lot. Especially right now, with everything else we've got going on. We haven't heard a word from you in over twenty years. For you to just arrive on our doorstep, unannounced…" His voice fades and I can see, just from the look in his eyes, how hard he's finding this.

"I know." She gets to her feet, revealing that she's a little shorter than me, and is wearing a plain pale blue dress. It fits her well, but doesn't look expensive. Hunter stands up, too, and I follow suit, realizing she's about to leave. "Can I call you?" she asks, looking at him.

"What for?" He seems confused by her question.

"To stay in touch… for updates on Drew."

"I think it's best if I call you."

She tilts her head. "Will you, though?"

"I've said I will, so yes. Don't expect daily reports, or even weekly ones, but I'll call you if anything changes."

"I—I'd better give you my number."

He nods his head, picking up a pen and writing it down on a notepad, then he comes around the desk, heading for the door. When he gets there, he opens it and she crosses the room, looking up into his face.

"I'm sorry I hurt you, Hunter."

He sucks in a breath. "I'm sorry I was so abrupt. I'm just looking after Drew and Ella's interests."

"Like you've done since I left?" she says and he shrugs his shoulders.

"Maybe."

"One day, I'll be able to explain what happened, and hopefully you'll understand." He doesn't answer, and after a moment or two, she turns to me. "Thank you for taking care of Drew," she says.

"You're welcome."

She exits, Hunter following behind, and I hear the front door open and close as I deflate into my chair again. Moments later, Hunter returns, closing his office door behind him.

"I'm so sorry about that, Josie. She was here when I got back. I had no idea she was coming, and I didn't know what to do."

"It's okay. It must have been a shock for you."

He sits down opposite me again. "That's one way of putting it." He leans back, shaking his head from side to side, trying to take it in, I guess. It's easy to see he'd rather do that by himself, so I stand and he looks up at me, like he's only just remembered I'm here. "Before you go, was what you said just now completely accurate? Does Drew really not understand yet that this is his home… and that I'm his brother?"

I sit again, just perching on the edge of the seat. "He's asking questions, but so far, that's all they are. He's not drawing on memories at all."

"I thought the doctor hoped he'd pick up on things when he got back here."

"He did. But there's a lot for Drew to take in. He's trying to piece things together still."

"And not getting very far?" he says.

"He's finding it difficult."

"And nothing he's seen so far is helping?"

I shake my head. "Sometimes I think it's just confusing him further."

"In what way?" he asks.

"Well… he saw your wife in the garden, carrying Maisie. She was with Ella, and her baby, too. Drew didn't recognize any of them."

"Not even Livia?"

"Not that he said, and the babies meant nothing either. He assumed at least one of them must be yours, and that he's an uncle, not a father."

Hunter closes his eyes for a second, sucking in a breath. When he opens them again, I'm surprised by the level of pain that's staring back at me.

"This is…" He stops talking, his voice filled with too much emotion.

"He'll be okay, Hunter."

He nods his head. "I know. To be honest, that's not what's worrying me right now."

"What is then?"

"I'm concerned about Livia," he says, surprising me.

I'd half expected him to tell me something else about his mom, so I can't help the frown that forms on my face. "Livia?"

"Yes. She's really struggling with looking after Maisie."

"Is that why you're here and not at your office in Boston?" I ask. "So you can help?"

"No. I'm here because of Drew. I want to be close by while he recovers."

"In that case…"

"It's not the practicalities of looking after Maisie that are the problem for Livia, it's the fact that we're trying to start a family ourselves, and it's not working. The disappointment of that was hard enough before, but having to look after someone else's baby when it seems she can't have one of her own is breaking Livia apart. She wants to help Drew, but having to watch her go through this is… is killing me, inch by inch, every minute of the day."

I know only too well how Livia feels, and even if I'm not about to tell him that, I pull my seat a little closer to his desk. "How long have you been trying?"

"Since the New Year." He smiles, although it doesn't touch his eyes. "At least, that's when Livia came off her birth control pills. You might hear it mentioned that we only got married in February, but we talked things through and decided we wanted to start a family, and she may as well stop taking the pill straight away. Livia used to have problems with her periods being irregular, so we figured we'd give ourselves a head start, and if she was pregnant when we walked down the aisle, we didn't mind in the least."

"She has irregular periods?"

"Not anymore," he says, rolling his eyes. "They're as regular as clockwork now… worst luck."

"Hmm… that can sometimes happen. Unfortunately, a doctor would tell you it's still early days, even though I know it doesn't feel like that to you."

"No, it doesn't."

"I'm sorry – again – but there's nothing I can do to speed up the process with Drew. It's impossible for me to make him remember his life any faster. I'm gonna go back to doing some more cognitive exercises now he's settled into the cottage, but to be honest, they're more about helping with his short-term memory problems than his amnesia."

"It's okay. I wasn't expecting you to solve all my problems, and I'm grateful for everything you're doing."

I wish he wouldn't keep thanking me. It makes me feel awkward. "Can I ask a question?" I say.

"Sure."

"Does Drew have a camera here?"

He thinks for a moment. "I imagine so. He has them everywhere. Why do you wanna know?"

"Because he was asking me if he was a photographer."

Hunter's eyes spark to life. "Was that a memory?"

"No. He'd noticed all the photographs on the walls and the shelves at the cottage and asked if he'd taken them."

His face pales. "Oh… should we have removed the pictures of Maisie? There are quite a few dotted around the house."

"I noticed, but to be honest, it's best that he sees the cottage as it used to be, so he can try to make associations with his past."

"Okay." He heaves out a sigh. "He hasn't made the association of taking any of the photographs yet?"

"No… but I remembered you'd said all his equipment was taken back to his studio after the accident, and it made me think that, if he had a camera, it might just spark a memory for him."

"I see. Well… as I say, I'm pretty sure there's one here. It'll be in a canvas bag somewhere."

"Okay. I might get him to take some photographs with it, and see how it feels."

Drew

Josie's only been gone ten minutes, and I miss her already, like a part of me has gone with her. I feel incomplete and broken enough without this…

I moved too fast this morning. I know that now. She might have said I didn't, but I did.

We got along so well yesterday, making coffee and flirting… or I thought we were flirting. I didn't see the harm in trying again, and it felt right at the time. It felt like who I am, and I don't know how to be anyone else… not anymore. Pretense is beyond me. All I can do is act on instinct, and all my instincts are telling me to hold her, to kiss her… to make her mine.

The problem was, she backed off, so no matter how much I want her, I need to slow down.

I also need something to take my mind off of missing her so much. But I can't think what to do. What would I have done before? I look around the living room, my eyes settling on the photographs that line the walls. They must be relevant, surely. There's an office upstairs… maybe that will tell me something.

I head up there, ignoring my unmade bed, and wander through to the office. The laptop on the desk is the most obvious place to start, and I open it, sitting down in the chair. The screen comes to life, but it requires a password, and my mind is a blank… yet again.

I open the drawer at the front of the desk, wondering if I ever wrote down my password, but all I find are pens, a couple of notepads, a box of paperclips and a few stray elastic bands. Very useful, I'm sure, but not what I need right now.

I stand again, frustration getting the better of me as wander over to the couch, flopping down onto it. I've got a slight nagging headache, but I pull forward the canvas bag and open it. Inside, there's a camera... a very technical-looking one, and I wonder about the photographs again. Is this a hobby of mine? Or is it what I do for a living? Do I even need to earn a living when I've got enough money to live somewhere like this?

God knows...

I'm sick of questions, already — especially as there's no-one who can answer them — and I stand up again, going back out through the bedroom and down the stairs.

My eye lands on a photograph of a baby. It's on the shelf above the fireplace and I go over and pick it up, studying her closely. She's lying on what appears to be a pink blanket and looks very much like the baby the blonde woman was holding... the one I saw yesterday. She's absolutely beautiful, very cute, and I guess there's a slight resemblance to Hunter. I turn, spotting another one of the same baby on the bookcase. It's smaller, and this time she's propped up in some kind of baby seat, staring straight at the camera, with the most perfect smile on her lips. She's adorable, but what I don't understand is why I have photographs of my brother's daughter in my house. Am I that kind of uncle? Maybe Hunter and I are closer than I think. At the moment, that seems hard to imagine, but so is just about everything else when I don't know who I am.

I turn to put the first photograph back, a blinding pain searing through my head, right behind my eyes. The room spins, and I drop the picture, clutching my head as I fall to the floor...

"Drew? Wake up... please."

I open my eyes, slamming them shut again, the pain catching me unawares. "J—Josie?"

"I'm here."

I feel her hand in mine. I'm lying on my side and I'm aware she's right next to me. "My head."

"Your head hurts?"

"Yes."

"Did you hit it when you fell?"

"N—No. Don't think so. It hurt before."

"It was hurting before you fell?"

"Yes."

"Okay. Are you in pain anywhere else?"

"N—No. Just my head." I try cracking my eyes open again, but the pain is still too much.

"I can't lift you."

"Let me try…"

"No." She raises her voice slightly. "You stay exactly where you are. I'll get help."

I know when I'm beaten, and although I don't know where she's going to get help from, I can't think about that. I can't think about anything. It hurts too much.

"Hunter?" She must be on the phone, talking to my brother. The brother I don't know. "Drew's had a fall. Can you…?" She doesn't finish her sentence, but then adds, "Thanks," and says, "Hunter will be here in a minute," talking to me now.

I'd nod my head, but I'm not brave enough to try, so I just lie still. It's uncomfortable down here, but I'm not sure I care… especially as she's still holding my hand.

Within minutes, I hear the door open.

"Jesus… is he okay?" I guess that must be Hunter. He sounds concerned, and a little out of breath. Does that mean he ran here?

Josie releases my hand and stands. "He says his head hurts, but I think it's from the original concussion, not from the fall."

"He's conscious then?"

"Yes. He's in a lot of pain, though, and I need to get him upstairs to bed."

"It's a good thing I brought reinforcements, then. You two haven't met, but this is Mac."

Who the hell is Mac? Hunter doesn't explain and Josie doesn't ask, which I guess means he's significant to me and they're not about to give away his identity. I want to turn over and look at the guy, in case he rings any bells… but I can't. The pain is getting worse.

"Hi," Josie says.

"Hello." The man has a deep voice, but he doesn't sound familiar to me, although I guess that's not unusual.

"Mind the broken glass." What broken glass? What's she talking about? "Drew must have been looking at the photograph, and it broke when he fell."

"I'll get a new frame," Hunter says, and I wonder if maybe he gave it to me in the first place. The photograph inside is of his daughter, so that would make sense.

"How are we gonna do this?" Mac asks, and I notice his strange accent, which I can't place.

"The easiest thing is to put him on a chair, and lift the chair," Josie says.

"Okay." That's Hunter's voice. "I'll fetch one from the kitchen."

I hear him move away, then feel Josie kneel beside me again. "Broken glass," I mutter. "Be careful."

"It's okay. I'm fine. Hunter and Mac are going to lift you onto a chair and carry you upstairs."

"Okay."

I feel too weak to argue, or to help myself, and she stands up again.

I'm aware of someone taking her place, although whether it's Mac or Hunter, I couldn't say.

"Josie…" That's Mac, not Hunter, but his voice sounds like it's coming from behind me, not in front. "Can you pass me that throw from the couch? If we lay it down behind him, we can roll him onto his back without worrying about the glass. It should be easier to lift him from that position."

I feel someone pushing something soft against my back, and then the man in front of me leans closer. "Drew?" It's Hunter, and although his presence has made me feel uneasy every other time we've met, I suddenly feel quite safe… probably because he's my only hope of getting out of my current predicament. "We're gonna roll you onto your back, okay?"

"Fine." He eases me over, and I let out a slight groan, the pain shooting through my head.

They don't leave me lying here for long, though, and with one of them on either side, they pull me upright, into a sitting position. My head feels like it's going to explode, and I daren't open my eyes, although I'm surprised I don't feel dizzy.

"Let me just check his arm and side for cuts," Josie says. "He fell on the broken glass." She moves in, taking Hunter's place on my left side, and I feel her raise my t-shirt, her fingers brushing over my skin as she examines me. "He seems okay. You need to get him on the chair," she says, moving away again. "If I hold it, can you lift him?"

"Sure," Hunter says, sounding confident, even if I'm not so certain myself. I feel him lift my left arm, and then Mac raises my right. "We're just putting your arms around our shoulders, Drew, then we're gonna stand you up. We'll keep a hold of you, so don't worry."

That's easy for him to say.

"Okay?" Mac says, and although Hunter doesn't reply, I guess he must have given some kind of signal, because the next thing I hear is Mac giving them a 3-2-1 countdown, and then I'm being lifted onto my feet, like I weigh nothing. They pull me backwards, and then lower me again almost immediately onto a chair, and I let out a breath.

I take my courage in both hands and open my eyes. The pain is still intense, but I keep them open long enough to see my brother standing right in front of me, worry written all over his face as he pushes his fingers back through his hair. To his right is a dark-haired man, who I'm guessing is Mac. I don't recognize him at all, but he's handsome, despite the worried look in his eyes, and muscular enough that he seems like a useful guy to have around in the circumstances. Josie is standing off to one side, slightly behind the two of them. She looks scared, and I wish she'd come nearer. I need to hold her…

Mac steps forward. "Whichever one of us takes his feet is gonna be carrying the bulk of his weight once we start up the stairs."

Hunter turns to him. "In that case, I'm volunteering you for the job."

"Thanks," Mac says, smiling, and Hunter moves around behind me, while Mac steps up in front. "I suggest you close your eyes again, Drew. We're gonna tip you backwards, and it's likely to make you feel dizzy again."

I do as he suggests, tucking my arms in, because that makes sense to me. Moments later, I feel the chair falling backwards, resisting the instinct to reach out or lean forward, knowing they won't let it drop. Sure enough, it comes to a steady stop at around forty-five degrees and then Mac counts down again, and on one, I feel them lift the chair.

It's a strange sensation of being jostled, and part of me wants to open my eyes… but I decide against it and concentrate on sitting still instead.

Neither man says a word, and before long, they set me down again.

We're upstairs already?

"I'll just straighten the bed." Josie must have come up with us, and I feel guilty now for not tidying up earlier.

"I—I'm sorry."

"Don't be. I just wanna get you comfortable, give you some painkillers and make sure you're okay."

"I'm fine."

"No, you're not."

"She's right," Hunter says. "You're not. Now... let's lift you onto the bed."

He and Mac put my arms around their shoulders again and haul me off of the chair. They turn me around and sit me on the edge of the bed, and then I feel someone pulling at my shoes. I guess it must be Josie, and I crack my eyes open to find her kneeling at my feet. That feels wrong. She doesn't belong there... in fact, it should be the other way around. I should be kneeling before her.

"We'll take the chair down and clear up the glass," Hunter says.

"I can do that later," Josie replies.

"No, it's fine. Let me know if you need anything else."

"I will... and thank you."

I hear them move away, their footsteps on the stairs, their whispered voices fading into the distance.

"Let's get you into bed," Josie says, standing, as she reaches for the hem of my t-shirt, pulling it off over my head. "We'll take these things off, just in case there are any fragments of glass in them." I feel her tugging at the button on my jeans, undoing it eventually and pulling down the zipper. "If you lie down, I think I can pull them off."

She pushes me gently to my side, holding onto me until my head hits the pillow. Then she lifts my legs up onto the bed and I feel her pulling on my jeans, tugging them down and eventually, right off. I'm only wearing my trunks and, although I wouldn't object to her taking those off as well, she doesn't. Instead, she pulls up the covers.

"I'm gonna fetch you some painkillers from my room. I'll be right back."

I nestle down slightly, getting comfortable, and relaxing at last. I never thought I'd be so relieved to be horizontal.

"Here…" She's back and I feel her hand beneath my head as she raises it slightly and helps me swallow down the tablets she's brought for me. "They should start working soon, and hopefully you'll feel better."

"I don't think I could feel much worse."

The mattress sinks slightly as she sits beside me.

"I'm sorry," she whispers, the emotion in her voice cutting through me. I know it's gonna hurt, but I open my eyes. She's gazing down at me, looking so scared, it hurts me more than my head.

"What for?"

"I never should have left you alone for so long."

I pull my hand from beneath the covers and reach out, caressing her cheek with my fingertips. "It's not your fault, Josie. I'll be okay."

She sighs as I let my hand drop, although I can hear a stutter in her breath. "I'll let you rest."

"No… don't go. Please."

"Okay." She shifts back slightly, so she's sitting right up against me. It's comforting, feeling her that close and I shut my eyes again…

*

I wake in slow stages, gradually becoming aware of my body… of the fact that it feels warm and rested, and that my head doesn't hurt as much as it did. Then I notice the light, which doesn't make me want to snap my eyes closed again… and finally I realize I'm alone.

Josie isn't here.

I open my mouth to call out, but shut it again, fearful that although my head feels a little better, it's not up to raised voices yet. Instead, I sit, taking care to go slowly, and then I twist around in the bed, setting my feet on the floor.

So far, so good.

I could use a drink, and some more painkillers, but there's no clock in here. I don't know what time it is, or how long I've been sleeping. Is it too soon to take more tablets? Josie's the only one who can tell me that, and I cling to the nightstand as I get to my feet, feeling okay about being upright.

I step cautiously to the door, which is wide open, and make my way out into the hall. I can hear a shower running and I guess it must be coming from Josie's room. Her bedroom door is open, too, and I wander over, gasping when I see she hasn't closed the bathroom door, either. I guess she must have done that so she could hear me, but I've got no intention of being heard, and I stand, leaning against the doorframe…

She's facing away from me, at a slight angle, so I can see the swell of her breast and the curve of her ass. The sunlight from the open window catches in the pouring water, glistening off of her silky skin, like stardust, and snatching the breath from my lungs.

I've never seen anything so beautiful in my life and, my headache forgotten, my cock hardens, straining against my trunks.

I turn, feeling guilty for watching her, and I lean back against the wall beside the door, wondering if this is how I'd normally behave, or whether I'm the kind of man who'd walk in there and claim her. The question is still there… what kind of lover am I? Am I a man who has relationships? Or do I prefer one-night stands? I know there's a difference… just like I know there's a difference between fucking and making love. I rub my hand along the length of my cock and contemplate a one-night stand with Josie, shuddering against the thought. It would be impossible. I couldn't do it. Even if that's who I was before, I couldn't be like that with her. Just like I know I need to eat, to drink, to sleep, I know I need more than one night with her.

I need forever.

What I don't know is how Drew Bennett would go about making that happen.

"Does that matter?" I whisper to myself.

Surely, I can do whatever I want now. I can be whoever I want to be. If that happens to be the same as Drew Bennett, then so be it. But if not…

I hear the shower shut off and let my hand drop to my side. I can't let her find me here… not in my current state of arousal, so I go back to my bedroom and sit on the edge of the bed, pulling the cover over, so my erection is hidden from view.

Within a few minutes, Josie appears in the doorway, a cream-colored fluffy towel wrapped around her, just above her breasts, covering her to mid-way down her thighs.

"You're awake?"

"Yes."

I look her up and down, unable to help myself. "Sorry," she says. "I felt like a shower."

"Why are you apologizing?"

"Because I should have been here when you woke up."

"It's okay."

She takes a half step forward. "How are you feeling?"

"A little better, but I could use some more painkillers, if I'm allowed?"

"Um… I don't know what the time is." She ducks away, returning within moments, still wrapped in the towel, I'm pleased to say. "I can let you have some more. Just give me five minutes to get dressed."

I'd like to tell her not to bother, but I can't. If I was moving too fast for her this morning, I doubt anything will have changed in just a few hours.

I stare at the door, wishing she'd come back, wondering if it's always been this way for me… if I've always been this dependent, or whether I'm just feeling this lost because I'm sick…

I hear her footsteps, holding my breath, and then capturing the gasp before it leaves my mouth as she reappears in the doorway.

That's when I realize I'm not dependent at all. And this has nothing to do with being sick.

I'm not lost either.

I'm in love.

She walks over, carrying a glass of water and clutching two more tablets in her hand, which she holds out to me. Her hair is damp and loose around her shoulders, and she's wearing jeans, and another of her skin-tight t-shirts… a pale yellow one.

I swallow down the tablets and then sip at the water while Josie pulls my bed back into shape.

"You don't have to do that."

"It's fine. I don't mind." She takes the glass from me, putting it on the nightstand. "Now… get back into bed."

I do as she says, lying back on the pillows and looking up at her as she pulls the covers over me. She turns, but I grab her hand, holding on to her.

"Stay, Josie… please?"

She nods her head and sits beside me, and I keep hold of her hand, staring at her beautiful face until my eyes close…

Chapter Seven

Josie

It's hard to recognize the man sitting across from me at the breakfast table. He's so different to the man who lay in his bed yesterday, his eyes closed against the light, his face pale and drawn. Today, the color has returned to his cheeks and the sparkle to his eyes. He hasn't asked why Hunter summoned me so abruptly yesterday and I'm relieved by that, because I don't know how I'd explain it… other than to lie. Again. And I really don't want to do that.

As for what happened when I got back here…

When I found him lying on the floor, I didn't know what to do. I tried to be a nurse, to check his vital signs and stay calm. But my heart was beating so hard, I couldn't tell his pulse from mine. When I called his name and he didn't respond, it took every ounce of strength and willpower not to panic.

It was my fault. He was my responsibility, and I'd let him down. As I was calling his name over and over, squeezing his hand and rubbing his chest, I knew I'd never forgive myself, even if he came round… which he did. Eventually.

When he said his head hurt, my first thought was that he'd hit it when he'd fallen. Had he tripped, or stumbled? If only I'd been here…

Once he made it clear the headache had been there before the fall, I realized it was connected to the concussion. It wasn't an additional problem, but a legacy one.

I still should have been here, watching him, caring for him. But I knew I could beat myself up later. Getting him up off of the floor was the most important priority. Only there was no way I could do that by myself. I needed help.

So I called Hunter.

He came running... and I mean running. He was slightly out of breath when he arrived, and he brought Ella's fiancé with him, which showed he was thinking more clearly than I was.

Between them, they got Drew up the stairs and into his bedroom, and I took over from there. I could have left him in his jeans and t-shirt, but he'd broken a picture frame when he'd fallen, shattering the glass. It would have been easy for tiny fragments of it to be lodged in his clothing, and it was much safer to remove it. His t-shirt was easy enough, but I had a little more difficulty with his jeans... although I managed it in the end, lying him on the bed and tugging them off.

As I pulled the covers over him, I felt lost. I needed to draw strength from him, but he was sapped by pain. It was too much to ask him to be strong for me, too.

I apologized for leaving him and he opened his eyes, squinting against the light, focusing on my face, then he reached out and touched my cheek with his fingertips.

"It's not your fault, Josie. I'll be okay."

It was like he knew I needed to hear that... needed the reassurance.

I felt a lump form in my throat, tears pricking behind my eyes, but it was unfair to cry in front of him. "I'll let you rest."

"No... don't go. Please."

I swallowed down my emotions. I could cry later. I edged backwards, feeling the heat of his body through the covers and taking comfort from that… from the nearness of him as his eyes fluttered closed again.

I stayed with him for ages, watching the rise and fall of his chest, the occasional flinch from the pain I guessed was still rampaging through his head. He settled eventually, though, and I stood, pulling up the covers, and bent, gently kissing his forehead. He didn't even stir. I didn't mind. The kiss was for my benefit, not his.

I left him to sleep, going downstairs for a while. The living room was tidy, the broken glass all cleared away, and I poured myself a glass of orange juice and tried reading a book to relax. It didn't work. Drew might have only been upstairs, but I found it odd, being in his home without him. It made me feel restless, so I gave up with the book and went back up to my room, checking on Drew as I passed. He was still sound asleep, but I left my bedroom door open to be on the safe side, and laid down on the mattress, letting my head sink into the soft pillows.

As far as I was aware, that headache had come out of nowhere, but if it proved one thing, it was that I needed to keep a closer eye on him. I also needed to stop him from trying to remember. That was obviously what he'd been doing. The broken photograph was evidence enough of that. I could understand him wanting to know, but if this was going to be the result, I needed to find other things to keep him occupied.

I also wondered then if his headache had anything to do with what had happened between us earlier in the morning. It felt like a lifetime ago, but he'd been upset by my response – or lack of it – that much was clear.

Was I even more to blame? Should I just have let him act on his emotions… and mine?

It would have been so easy. I'd yearned to feel his lips on mine for such a long time. But there was still so much to be said… to be revealed.

I took a shower to freshen up, leaving the bathroom door open in case Drew called out for anything.

He didn't, but when I came out, having wrapped myself in a fluffy towel, I thought it best to check on him and was surprised to find he was awake and in need of painkillers.

Once I'd got dressed and fetched them for him, he swallowed them down and got back into bed, before he asked me to stay. No. He begged me to stay.

I couldn't refuse… not a plea like that. So I sat beside him, our hands locked, our eyes fixed, until he drifted off to sleep again.

"Are you okay?" Drew's words jolt me back to reality and I stare across the breakfast table at him.

"Of course. I was just… um…"

"You were thinking about yesterday, weren't you?" he says, shaking his head without a trace of pain. "I wish you'd stop beating yourself up over it."

"How did you know I was?" I ask.

"Because I know you."

"You can't say that."

He smiles. "Yes, I can. As far as I'm concerned, my life only started a few days ago, when I woke up in the hospital. You've been the one constant for me since then, and even if you haven't told me very much about yourself, I still feel like I know you better than I know anyone else."

He's obviously noticed how reticent I've been to part with any details about my private life. What he doesn't know is why. What he can't hope to understand is that our lives are already intertwined. Or how. And I can't tell him that. I wish I could, but I can't.

"I should have been here," I say instead.

"I wish you had been." He smiles. "But failing that, I should have been resting, not wandering around the house, trying to remember things."

"Oh? So you've worked that out, have you?"

"If you mean, have I finally heard what you've been saying, and realized it's better for me to let my memories come back naturally, then the answer is, yes. At least, I'm gonna try. I can't guarantee I won't still ask questions, because it's hard not to, when everything is such a mystery."

"That's understandable."

"I just don't want another repeat of yesterday."

"It was painful, wasn't it?" I ask.

"Yes, and it felt like a setback, too. But it's more than that." He takes a deep breath. "You were scared, Josie. I could see it in your eyes, and I didn't like being responsible for that."

He saw through me so easily? "I—I..."

He holds up his hand, and I stop talking. "It's okay. You don't have to explain."

That's good, because I'm not sure I can without giving myself away.

He picks up his cup, swallowing down the last of his coffee. "Shall we go for a walk? I could use some fresh air."

"We could... or you could maybe have a swim, if you like." That way we won't have to talk, and there won't be a repeat of yesterday's embarrassing situation.

"A swim? Am I up to that?"

"As long as you don't push yourself too hard."

"How do we know I can swim?" he says, tilting his head.

"We don't. But I guess there's only one way to find out."

"What? Throw me in and see if I drown?"

"No. I was thinking more about taking you over there and letting you try it out for yourself."

He looks out the window, in the vague direction of the pool. "You'll come with me?"

"Of course. I just said..."

He turns to face me, his eyes twinkling with a mischief that makes my insides melt. "No. I mean, you'll come into the pool?"

My cheeks redden under his gaze. This was supposed to be less embarrassing than yesterday, but at the moment, it feels so much worse. "I—I thought I'd stay on the side."

He shakes his head. "I think you should come into the water with me. What if I have a dizzy spell, or my headache comes back?"

"Then I'll be right there."

"Yeah. But it'll be safer if you're in the pool, won't it?"

I know I'm beaten. His smile is enough to do that to me, although I keep telling myself that just because we'll be in the pool together doesn't mean we'll have to talk. "If you insist."

"I think I do," he says, then he pauses, his smile widening. "Do you have a swimsuit?"

"Yes. When your brother said there was a pool here, I thought it wise to bring one, just in case."

"Oh… that's a shame."

"Why? I thought you wanted me to come with you."

"I do."

He stares at me until the penny drops, and I feel myself blush – yet again. I don't know why I'm bothering to plan things that will make it easier for me to be with him and not want him. How can I deny the way I feel about him? And why should I? I've wanted him for so long… and regardless of all the arguments against us being together, surely something that feels this good can't be wrong, can it?

Can it?

I get to my feet, picking up the plates, but he stands too and grabs my arm across the table. "I know I said I'd let my memories take care of themselves, but can I ask you something?"

"Sure."

I put down the plates again, studying his perfect face. "Do you think I was a flirt? Before, I mean… before the accident?"

I know perfectly well that he was. He flirted with me when we first met, and I liked it. I can remember the way he made me feel, just by looking at me… although I don't need to remember, because he's doing it again now. Except I can't tell him that.

"I don't know." It's another deception, and I feel guilty for it, even though I know it's for his own good. "Why do you ask?"

"Because I feel like I want to flirt."

I step back, forcing him to release my arm, and I struggle not to stagger, holding onto the table to right myself. "Y—You want to flirt? With women?" I'm not sure who else he'd want to flirt with, but I can't disguise my shock… and my disappointment.

"Not with women in general, no. Just with you."

I'm in even more danger of falling now, but I gaze up into his eyes, catching my breath. "I—I see."

"Shall we forget about clearing away for now and go for a swim instead?"

"Okay. Maybe we should put on our costumes underneath our clothes. It'll make things easier when we get over there."

"If you insist."

I'm not sure I'm capable of insisting on anything, but I lead the way to the stairs, and he follows.

"Oh… it looks like there's a pool house." And it appears to be large enough for changing rooms, too. We needn't have bothered putting our costumes on, after all.

"Yeah, but I suppose neither of us was to know that, were we?" Drew yanks off his t-shirt over his head.

I've brought towels from the cottage and I put them down on one of the loungers by the pool, slipping out of my shorts and top. When I turn around, Drew's already taken off his jeans and is standing in just his swim shorts, which do very little to hide his arousal.

"Sorry," he says, although the smile twitching at his lips is more playful than contrite. "I'm afraid there's nothing I can do about that."

I decide it's best not to make a fuss, but to treat it like an everyday occurrence. "I know. That's one advantage of being a nurse. I get how it works. It's a natural reaction." I need to stop talking. I might not be making a fuss, but I'm rambling.

He steps closer, making my goose-bumped skin tingle with anticipation. "Yes, but do you know what it's a natural reaction to?" I can't speak. My lips won't function and my mouth has gone dry. "I'll tell you, shall I?" he says. "It's a reaction to you. You must have noticed in the hospital that I was always hard whenever you were around?"

"Y—Yes, I did."

"Well… nothing's changed. It's what happens whenever I'm near you, or when I think about you, or hear your voice."

I stare up into his eyes, trying not to get lost in them, or his words, because I need to know… "Do you remember why you're reacting like that?"

"Yes, and no." That's not what I'd hoped to hear and I can't hide my dismay. If he can't recall what this is all about, there's no hope for us… if there's even an 'us' to hope for. "Hey… don't look so sad." He reaches out, cupping my face with his hand. "It won't be a problem."

"But if you can't remember…"

"It won't matter. You won't have to break your rules and explain it to me." That's good, because I wouldn't be able to. He smiles. "This is an instinct, Josie. It's a bone-deep instinct to be inside you." I gasp, unable to hold it in, and he steps closer, looking right down at me. "I know I made you feel uncomfortable yesterday morning, and I apologize for that, even though I don't know exactly what I did wrong. You see, not knowing who I am means I don't know how I'd normally go about this. All I is know is, it can't be wrong to want you… unless you don't feel the same…" His voice fades and I long to reach out to him, to tell him I've felt the same for longer than he's been aware of knowing me. Except that's the problem, isn't it? Even if this feels too good to be true, and even if denying him is tearing me apart, we're too bound up in secrets and deceptions. All of them mine.

He steps back, releasing me, and nods his head.

"Drew?"

"It's okay."

Without another word, he steps down into the pool and dives under the water, and although I want to call him back, I can't.

Drew

I handled it all wrong by the pool yesterday. I know I did.

Obviously, there was nothing I could do to hide my erection. Josie had just peeled off her shorts and top, and was standing in front of me, wearing nothing more than a one-piece swimsuit, in a pale blue fabric, with a butterfly print. It had high-cut legs which showed off her toned thighs, and the neckline was revealing enough to make my cock ache. What was I supposed to do?

Maybe ignore my obvious arousal? How? When she was staring at me, her eyes alight with longing. Because they were. I might not know very much, but I knew what that look meant. It was another of those instincts. In this case, one that told me she liked what she saw.

Perhaps I should have found another way of telling Josie how much I want her, though.

Because being open about it didn't seem to work.

I sit back on the couch, feeling confused... not just because Josie's insisted on clearing away the breakfast things all by herself, sending me in here 'to rest', but also because her silence at the pool yesterday was too loud to ignore. If she was just admiring, but didn't want me in the same way I want her, why didn't she say so? Why did she ask if I knew why I was aroused in that voice that was too tempting for words? And if she wanted me, why didn't she do something? All it would have taken was a step in my direction. Instead of which she neither moved nor spoke. And that's why I'm so confused... because I really thought she liked me. At least enough to be honest with me.

The signs were there... or I thought they were.

Take the day of my fall as an example. She seemed really upset by that. I heard the crack in her voice... saw the fear in her eyes. It wasn't a figment of my imagination. I even I told her I'd noticed it, and didn't like how it had made me feel. She didn't deny her reactions, either, and although she hesitated over explaining them, I didn't mind. As far as I was concerned, it was enough just to know she cared. Because she did. I could feel it.

She also seemed hurt yesterday, when I asked her if I was a flirt, and she assumed I was thinking of flirting with other women... as if that's ever going to happen. I was close enough to hear her breath catch in her throat, to see her struggling to swallow, when I told her I didn't want to flirt with anyone but her. Stupidly, I thought her response meant something. I assumed it meant she didn't like the idea of me flirting with anyone else. But evidently not.

I got it wrong… again.

If her reaction at the pool was any kind of indication, I couldn't have been more wrong.

I must have mis-read the signs, or over-reacted to them.

Maybe they weren't signs at all, and my brain is just too muddled still to know what's going on.

Let's face it, how am I supposed to understand Josie when I don't understand myself?

And, more importantly, what am I supposed to do about it?

I've agreed not to keep trying to recapture my memories… not because it hurt, as Josie suggested, but because I couldn't bear to see the fear in her eyes, knowing I'd put it there. I love her. It's my job to keep her safe, and if doing that means I have to wait a little longer to find myself, then I'll do it.

I'll do anything… once I work out what 'anything' is in Josie's world.

The problem is, we've hardly spoken since yesterday morning. We were only in the pool for about thirty minutes in the end. I found it difficult being that close to her, and Josie was so embarrassed, she couldn't look me in the eye. It seemed easier to give up on the idea of swimming, so we came back to the cottage. Once we were here, though, we went to separate rooms. Josie suggested I should rest in my bedroom for a while, and she stayed downstairs. It was probably for the best in the circumstances. In the afternoon, she did some of those picture exercises with me, but we limited our conversation to the necessary comments, and afterwards, she went to take a shower. I tried not to picture her, although it was hard, having such a fresh recollection of exactly how she'd look, and when she came down again, she insisted on cooking… by herself. Needless to say, the atmosphere between us is so tense, you could cut it with a knife, and I know that's my fault.

I can't undo the things I did yesterday, or unsay the things I said. And even if I could, I wouldn't want to. Cupping her face in my hand and gazing into her eyes felt right, and so did telling her what she does to me... how she makes me feel.

I meant every word, too... except one.

She hadn't replied to me, but she looked so pained, and right before I dived into the water, I told her it was okay, even though it wasn't. It was a white lie, but I couldn't tell her how much her silence hurt.

"Shall we go for a walk? You need some exercise."

Her voice makes me jump and I turn to see she's standing in the archway to the kitchen, looking across at me. There's something sad behind her eyes and I want to ask her about it, although I think it's best if I don't. I doubt it'll end well.

"If you like."

I stand, noting she's already wearing her flat pumps. I've got my shoes on, too, so I head for the door, stepping outside.

"Um... Drew?"

I spin around. She's standing with her hands in her pockets, near the foot of the stairs.

"Yes?"

"I think there's a camera somewhere, isn't there?" she says.

"There is. It's upstairs."

She nods her head. "Why don't you bring it?"

I don't know why she's suggesting that. Maybe so we don't have to talk, or if we do, we can talk about photography, rather than each other.

"Sure. If you want me to."

She doesn't reply, and I step back into the cottage, frowning as she moves back the moment I put my foot on the bottom step. Is she so indifferent to me she doesn't want me anywhere near her?

That thought makes my chest hurt, and as I climb, I wonder how I'm supposed to do this. How am I supposed to switch off my feelings for her?

I wander through to the office and look down at the camera bag, trying to decide whether to take the whole thing. Except it's large and cumbersome, so I grab the camera and make my way back down the stairs.

Josie has her back to me and is straightening the throw on the back of the couch, bending over slightly to give me a perfect view of her glorious ass.

Why was I thinking about switching off my feelings for her?

That's the last thing I want to do.

We've been walking for about fifteen minutes, neither of us saying a word. I'm carrying the camera, and Josie seems intent on making sure there's at least a foot of space between us, which hurts.

She didn't do this the last time we walked together. We held hands then, so clearly something has changed. I just wish I could work out what, and why… and how to put it back to where it was.

And why this has to be so fucking complicated… as if my life wasn't complicated enough already.

"How does it feel?"

I turn and look down at her, although neither of us breaks our stride. Josie's got her hands in her pockets and is staring up at me, her eyebrows raised.

"How does what feel?" *It hurts to know you can't even bear to hold my hand, but I doubt that's what you're asking.*

"The camera," she says, nodding down at it. "How does it feel to hold it?"

I stop walking, and she does, too. "Are you trying to tell me something?"

"No. I'm asking a question."

A weighted one, but a question, I'll grant her. I raise the camera, holding it in both hands. "It feels okay."

"Take a picture with it, then."

I remove the lens cover, which hangs from a short cord, and lift the camera to my face, looking through the viewfinder directly at her. The sun is shimmering off of her hair, and although there's still that sadness behind her eyes, she's too beautiful for words. Except behind her, in the distance, is the building on the far side of the grounds. There's nothing wrong with it. As buildings go, it's quite attractive, but even though it's out of focus, it spoils the composition.

I lower the camera and grab her hand.

"What are you doing?"

"If we're gonna do this, let's do it properly."

I glance around, spying a nearby tree, and pull Josie over to it, standing her in front of the wide trunk. I step away, but there's still something wrong.

"Lean back."

"Against the tree?"

"Yes."

She does as I say and I look at her through the viewfinder again. The sunlight is dappled now, gentler, but she's still the most beautiful creature I've ever seen. I take a single picture, clicking the shutter.

"Now... tilt your head."

"Which way?"

"Your left... no, not that far." She adjusts the slant of her head and I snap two more photographs before I lie down on the ground.

"What are you doing down there?"

"Getting a different angle," I say. "Don't look at me."

"Okay. What should I look at then?"

"Whatever you were looking at before."

She smiles. "I was looking at you, Drew. You're the one with the camera."

"Okay. Look at the place where I was standing."

"Even though you're not there?"

"Yes. And don't smile."

"What do you want me to do, then?" She looks confused, but just as that fades to something a little more enigmatic, I take the shot.

"Perfect."

"How do you know?"

"Because I do."

She shakes her head, and I click the shutter again. "That one's even better."

"Can I see?"

"Sure."

I get up, brushing grass from my jeans and wander over to her, adjusting the camera setting so we can view the pictures on the screen.

"You knew how to do that?" she says, looking up at me.

"It seems so."

I hold the camera between us, our heads bent together, and I scroll through the images. In the first one, she's looking right at me, and I swear to God, there's something in her eyes that isn't sadness. I don't know what it is, though, and I can't read too much into a single photograph. In the second and third images, her head is tilted, although the look is still there. Then I move on, hearing Josie's gasp when she sees the fourth shot. I don't blame her. She looks even better than I thought she would… and as for the next one…

"Oh, my God."

"What?" I turn to look at her. She's staring at me, her eyes wide, her lips slightly parted.

"How did you do that? How did you know that one would be better than the last? You didn't look at them at all while you were taking them... so how did you know?"

"Instinct, I guess."

"Instinct?" she says.

"Yes. You haven't told me if I'm a professional photographer, but I think I might be."

"Is that a memory, or a question?"

"I didn't ask a question. I stated a fact... or at least a thought," I say, holding up the camera, although I don't take my eyes from hers. "It's like I know what I'm doing with this, which is more than I can say for you."

"I'm not gonna deny it. I don't know the first thing about cameras."

I shake my head. "No, you don't understand. I meant, I don't know what I'm doing with you. You've bewitched me, body and soul, Josie, and sometimes I feel like you're the only solid foundation I've got. Then, at other times, I feel like you've cast me off... left me drifting. Except I'm not strong enough to survive. Not by myself. I don't even know if you like me..."

"I like you," she says and I suck in a breath, stepping a little closer to her.

"You do?"

"Yes."

"In what way? I mean... do you like me as a fellow human being? Or do you like me as a man who's told you he's longing to be inside you? There's a difference, Josie – even I know that – and I need to understand it. I need to understand you." She doesn't say a word, but continues to stare at me, blinking once or twice, looking lost herself. "You see... this is where it gets complicated for me. When you go silent on me like this, I don't know what to do or what to think."

I lower the camera to my side and move closer still, so there's maybe an inch of space between us. I can feel her breath mingling with mine, even though time has stood still… for both of us, I think. The lost look on her face is worrying, but she hasn't stepped back. I know I could take her silence as rejection yet again, but this doesn't feel like rejection… not this time. It feels like she doesn't know what to do.

So maybe I should do it for her… and if I'm wrong, she'll stop me.

Right?

I have to be right, because there's no way I can step back, and we can't just stand here forever.

"Oh, to hell with it."

I grab the back of her neck, holding her still, and I bend my head, covering her lips with mine. She lets out a very slight yelp, and although I half expect her to pull back, she doesn't, and I take advantage of the moment to explore her with my tongue. Her yelp becomes a moan, and then a sigh, and as I whisper her name into her mouth, I put my other arm around her waist, pulling her closer. I'm still holding the camera, but that doesn't stop me from crushing her body to mine, letting her feel my arousal. She sighs again, a little louder, and her fingers creep up my arms, her hands resting on my biceps, like she's clinging on… like she needs me.

Oh, please… let that be true.

Chapter Eight

Josie

There are so many reasons I shouldn't let this happen, but none of them seem to matter now his lips are on mine. I can't help my slight squeal of surprise, or the moan that echoes through my body as his tongue delves into my mouth, searching and inquisitive. He's more demanding than I'd expected, but I like that. I like his self-assurance. It suits my uncertainties, cancelling them out. At least, that's how it feels. He murmurs my name, without breaking the kiss, and then I feel his arm come around behind me, encircling my waist and pulling me closer to him, our bodies pressed together. He doesn't move his hips, but I can feel his erection… long and hard, and oh, so tempting. I remember how it looked and I sigh at the thought that this is what I do to him… that he wants me, maybe even needs me enough to respond like this. I let my fingers dust up his arms, bringing my hands to rest on his biceps. They flex and I hang on, my body trembling as he deepens the kiss still further. I want him so much, even though there's a small voice in the back of my head, telling me, over and over, that this is a truly bad idea. But how can that be so?

Because he doesn't know who he is yet… let alone who you are.

I know. But despite my reaction at the pool yesterday, and despite the awkward atmosphere that's shrouded us ever since, I've thought of nothing but this moment for so long. That has to make it right, doesn't it?

No.

I have to resist. It's for his benefit, even more than mine, and I swore to put his needs first. I promised…

I pull back, looking up at him.

"W—We can't do this," I say.

He frowns down at me, breathing hard. "Why not?"

I need an answer… quickly. "You're my patient, Drew."

"And? Does that mean I can't want you? Does that mean you can't want me back? Because it's no good pretending you don't anymore. Your kiss gave you away, and so did your body. I felt your need. You want this just as much as I do."

"Maybe I do." I can't deny it. There wouldn't be any point. "But it's only been a few days since your accident. You need time to recover."

He smiles, his eyes twinkling with mischief. "You'll just have to be gentle with me."

That's exactly what I might have said to him, in different circumstances, but it's the last thing I need to hear right now. It just reinforces the other reason this can't happen… why I can't let it happen.

Tears well in my eyes, and I step away, shaking my head.

"What's wrong, Josie?" he asks, his voice filled with concern.

"Nothing. It's just that it's not as simple as you think."

The first tear hits my cheek and as he reaches out to me, I break away, turning and running for the cottage.

It only takes a few minutes to get back, but as I close the door behind me, I'm out of breath… and out of ideas. He saw right through me, which I guess is no surprise. I've struggled to hide my feelings for days now. If he got close enough, he was always going to see me for who I am. And why shouldn't he? Why can't we be happy, just because of bad timing and a past he can't remember?

I suck in a breath, stepping further into the room and resting my hands on my hips.

If only it was that easy.

Even if I could ignore the past – which I'm sorely tempted to do – there's still the other problem…

The door bursts open, and I jump, turning to see Drew standing on the threshold. My lips tingle, recalling his kiss, and my stomach lurches, knowing I want more.

He comes inside, closing the door again and puts the camera on the cabinet, walking over and standing right in front of me, although he doesn't get too close, leaving a gap of nearly a foot between us.

"I'm sorry, Josie," he says.

There's an intensity in his gaze that's unnerving.

"What for?" I hope to God he's not apologizing for that kiss. That would be so humiliating.

"I'm sorry I upset you, and please don't say I didn't," he says, and he reaches out, brushing the tear away from my cheek… the evidence that makes denying his statement utterly pointless. "If I hurt you, I didn't mean to, and if I said the wrong thing again…"

"It's not your fault." I can't bear it that he keeps blaming himself.

He moves a little closer. "Maybe it is, and maybe it isn't, but I get the feeling your life would be an awful lot easier if I didn't want you so much. I mean… I have no idea how I'd go about achieving it, but would you be happier if I could somehow stop myself from needing you every minute of the day?"

I can't answer him. How can I, when I love being wanted by him? How can I, when I'm so in love with him? I just wish I knew how we could make this work. I wish I knew what to say to him.

"Answer me, Josie."

"It's not that simple."

"You said that already. What you haven't told me is why? Talk to me. Tell me why this has to be so complicated, when the simple fact is that I want you and you want me. Because you do want me, don't you?"

"Yes." There. I've said it.

He sighs and steps closer, his body pressed against mine again. Somehow, this is even more erotic, because his hands are by his sides. He's holding me in place with my own will, and the fiery look in his eyes.

"Then why did you say we can't do this?" he says. "Why did you run? What's the problem?"

"I'm the problem."

He frowns. The look is lost… and so am I. I turn and run for the stairs, bolting up them and into my room, slamming the door behind me. I've got nowhere else to go now, but how could I stay down there with him, when just the intensity of his gaze is enough for me to give myself away?

"Josie?" I clamp my hand over my mouth to stop myself from crying out. He knocks. "Josie… you've gotta stop running away from me. I'm not fit enough to keep up with you yet."

He sounds breathless and I rush over, pulling the door open. He's leaning against the doorframe, and stares down at me. "Are you okay, Drew? Your head's not hurting?"

"No. Not in the way you mean. I'm just bewildered by what's going on here, and I could use some answers. That's all." He tilts his head to the left. "Why do you think you're the problem?"

"Because I am."

"But why? I can see that me being your patient could be difficult. Not that I care. But you? You're not the problem?"

"Yes, I am. Regardless of what you say or think."

"Explain it to me, Josie."

I shake my head and push the door closed... except I can't. There's something stopping me, and I open it again to find Drew's hand pressed against the wooden surface.

"I know you think I'm weak, Josie, but I'm not that weak."

"I never said you were. I said you were recovering."

He glares down at me. "Either way, don't shut your door on me."

I swallow hard, biting on my bottom lip. His eyes fix on it, darkening, as he reaches out and frees it with his thumb.

"Y—You don't play fair, Drew."

"I don't think I ever did."

"Is that a memory?" *Please say it is. Please say it's all coming back to you and I'll be saved from having to lie anymore.*

"I don't give a fuck what it is. I need to know why you think you're the problem here, Josie. Because as far as I'm concerned, you're the solution to every goddamn problem I've ever had, and the answer to every single question I've ever asked."

Did he really just say that? "I—I am?"

"Yes. You're the only ray of light in my life right now, and you just admitted you want me, so why are you denying us something that I think we both know could be magical? You know how much I want you... so what is it? Don't you trust me?"

"Of course I do."

"Then what's stopping you? You think I'm not serious about this? You think I'm gonna make love to you and leave you, or something? Because I've gotta tell you, even if I felt inclined to leave you – which I don't – I've got nowhere to go."

"I know... and that's not it."

"Okay. So, if you trust me, and you don't think I'm gonna leave you, and you want this as much as I do, why are you holding back?" I can't answer him. I might have excellent reasons for saying 'no', but I want him just as much as he wants me, so how can I deny us this? "You've gone silent on me again," he says, pulling me so tight against his body I can hardly breathe.

"Yes, because I don't understand."

"What's not to understand? I need to be inside you, Josie." I gasp, my body tingling, trembling at the thought. He must be able to feel my reaction, his eyes widening as he sucks in a breath. "I need to hear you scream my name when I make you come. I need to make you mine."

I can't move, or think, or speak. "I...I..."

"Don't tell me it's not that simple. This is about as simple as it gets."

"I wasn't going to say that." Although I'd love to be able to explain how utterly complicated it is in reality.

"Okay. What were you going to say then?"

I don't know. How can I tell him the truth? How can I explain that this is all a lie, that I've loved him for longer than he thinks he's known me? I can't tell him anything about the past at all. But I guess I have to tell him something, even though I'd hoped it wouldn't be like this.

"You talk about all of this, like... like it's the easiest thing in the world."

"Yeah," he says, shrugging his shoulders. "Because it is."

"Not for me."

"Why not?" he asks.

"Because I don't know how."

"You don't know how to what?"

"How to do what you've just said."

The air around us stills, although it's charged with tension...

sexual tension, sparking off of his eyes, straight into mine. "You don't know how to do what I've just said?" He sounds confused. He looks it, too.

"No."

I see the moment the penny drops, his face clearing, his eyes lightening. "Are you telling me you've never had sex?" I lower my head, unable to answer him, but he places his finger beneath my chin, applying a little upward pressure, until I'm forced to look at him, our eyes locked. "Josie? Is that what you're saying?"

"Not exactly."

"Then what are you saying?" he says, frowning again.

I pause, looking up into his eyes, hoping I don't regret telling him this. "I've never done anything."

"Never done…?"

"Anything."

His frown deepens. "You've been kissed, though. Right?"

"Yes," I say and he sighs, like he's relieved. "By you… just now."

"You mean that was your first kiss?"

"It was the first one that meant anything. The first proper kiss."

"And you've never…?"

"I've never been touched, never touched a man, never been naked in front of a man."

He nods his head and puts his hands on my waist, pulling me close to him. "Why does that mean you can't now? With me?"

"For the very reason I just said. I don't know how."

Drew

I stare at her, struggling to understand how she's never had sex when she looks like she does. It doesn't make sense… but I can tell she's not lying. This isn't an excuse. It's for real, and she's embarrassed about it… and that means I need to do something. I'm done chasing around. Now I know what she tastes like, and have felt her lips on mine, I need more.

I need all of her.

"Does that matter?" I ask.

Her brow furrows. "Of course it does."

"Why? I mean… is there any reason I can't show you how it's done?"

"Do you remember how?"

I smile, moving my feet either side of hers, so she can feel my arousal pressing hard against her. "I don't need to remember. Like I said, it's a bone-deep instinct with you. And, in any case, I'm not sure memories would serve me very well right now. This feels like a fresh start… like nothing else matters except us." She blinks, gazing up into my face, and I bring my hands up from her waist, cupping her cheeks, her soft skin beneath my fingers, my lips poised above hers. "How can this be?" I ask, my voice drifting in a soft whisper between us.

"What?"

"How is it you've never had sex? I mean… you're perfect."

"I'm not, Drew," she says, shaking her head. "I'm very far from perfect."

"I beg to differ… and I still don't understand. Have I got something wrong here? Are you a lot younger than I think you are?"

"That depends how old you think I am."

"This hardly seems fair when I don't even know how old I am, but I'm gonna guess at twenty-four?"

"I'm twenty-five," she says.

"Okay… but you're not seventeen, and unless I'm mistaken, you haven't been living under a rock for the last few years, so…"

"It's a long story."

"Oh. In that case, can you tell me some other time?"

Her eyes widen slightly, her lips twitching upward at the corners. "Really? You don't want to hear it now?" she says. "You're usually so hungry for information."

"I know, but today I'm hungry for you."

I bend my head, swallowing her gasp with my kiss. The moment my tongue meets hers, it's like she forgets her inhibitions, and rather than touching my arms, she brings her hands up and lets them rest on my chest. The sensation is like tiny fireworks setting off all over my body, every nerve ending sparking beneath the surface of my skin. I lower my right arm, putting it around her and pulling her close, my hand just above her ass as I flex my hips, making sure she can feel my aching cock. I need her to know how real this is. She moans into my mouth, soft and throaty, and I deepen the kiss, moving my right hand down slightly over the swell of her ass, kneading her firm flesh. That husky moan gets louder, and she stands up on tiptoes, bringing her hands between us, up onto my shoulders, clinging to me… again.

I suck on her bottom lip, feeling the stutter of her breath, the heave of her breasts, and I pull back, looking down into her glistening eyes. Her lips are swollen, her cheeks flushed, and she's breathing hard.

"Wh—What do we do now?" she says, gazing up at me.

"We don't have to do anything."

She frowns, leaning back. "We don't? I thought you wanted me. I—I liked your need… hearing it… feeling it."

I smile down at her, flexing my hips again. "You want more?"

"Yes," she says.

"Tell me what you want."

"You."

I shake my head. "Give me more than that, baby."

Her eyes widen. "You called me baby."

"I know. Do you like it?"

"Yes," she says. "Yes, I do."

"Okay… now tell me what you want."

"I want to be yours."

I brush my lips over hers. "Would you be surprised if I told you, you already are?"

"I am?"

"Yes. There's no way I'm letting you go. You're mine, Josie. But what I meant when I said we don't have to do anything was I'll wait. I'll wait as long as you need, if…"

"No. Please, Drew," she says, clinging to me. "Don't let me think. Don't give me time to change my mind. Just…"

"Just what?"

"Just take me."

A low growl escapes my lips as I crush them against hers. She's right. Now is not the time for thinking. It's the time for doing, and I reach down, finding the hem of her t-shirt and pull it up, breaking the kiss to yank it over her head. She's wearing a white lace bra, but I pause, leaning back slightly.

"Your turn," I say.

"To do what?" She stares up at me, her face a potent mix of innocence and longing.

"Take off my t-shirt."

"Is this how it's done?" she asks, putting her hands behind me and pulling it up my back.

"I don't know. But it's how we're doing it."

She tugs further and I help her slightly, leaning forward so she can pull my t-shirt over my head. She drops it to the floor beside hers, her eyes raking over my chest, her teeth nipping at her bottom lip.

"That's sexy," I murmur.

"What is?"

"When you bite your lip like that."

"What does it make you wanna do?" she asks.

"This…" I dip my head and gently nibble on her bottom lip. She leans against me, moaning softly. There's still a barrier between us, though, so I reach behind her, unfastening her bra, and pull the straps down, letting it fall to the floor beside us. I pull her close again, feeling her soft skin against mine.

It's too much… and yet I need more.

I pull back, bending down to flick my tongue across her hardened nipple, cupping her other breast as she shudders, moaning loudly.

"Oh, Drew… that's so good."

I reach between us, unfastening her jeans, and pulling down the zipper. Her panties feel as though they're made of the same delicate lace as her bra, and I delve inside, leaning back and standing to stare down at her.

"You're shaved?"

"Yes," she says. "Is that okay? Do you prefer women to be…?"

I shake my head, and she stops talking, blinking, gazing up at me. "I don't know what I prefer, and I don't care. What matters is, you feel perfect." I kiss her, my fingers circling over her swollen clit. She squeals and bucks against me. "Easy, baby. There's no rush."

"But it feels so good."

"I know."

"How do you know?"

"I have no idea… but my body seems to know what it's doing."

"I—It certainly does…" She breathes a little harder as I circle faster, and she grasps my arm, like she needs the support. I gently pull my hand from her panties and she sighs out her disappointment, looking up at me. "You're stopping?"

"No. I'm just changing position."

I kneel before her, tucking my thumbs into the waistband of her jeans and pulling them down to her ankles. She kicks them off and I do the same with her panties, holding her steady while I help her step out of them. I look up at her, taking in her slender waist, her full, firm breasts, and her flared hips as I lean in and kiss her glistening pussy.

Her hand comes down on the back of my head and I reach up, parting her lips with my fingers as I lick her clit. She moves her legs apart and I slide closer, feasting on her, like the starving man I am. She's soaking, her juices dripping down onto my chin, but I lap them up, swallowing down her sweet nectar as she flexes her hips back and forth into me. I alternate the pressure on her clit, between soft and hard, fast and slow, until her breathing is so ragged I know instinctively she can't take much more. Her legs are trembling, her body twitching, and I grab her hips, holding her upright as she comes apart, grinding her pussy into my face, a loud scream escaping her lips. I can't make out a word she's saying. It's an incoherent jumble, but I don't care… I'm too busy drinking her down, and drowning in my love for her.

Her screams subside to mewling whispers, and once I'm sure she's steady on her feet, I release her hips and stand, looking down at her flushed face. Before she can say a word, I capture her cheeks in my hands and kiss her. Hard. She hesitates for a moment, realizing I taste of her, and then I feel her tongue dart into my mouth, her body writhing against mine. I guess she likes the way she tastes, and I reach down, lifting her into my arms. She wraps her legs around me, her arms resting on my shoulders, her hands on the back of my head as I walk across to the bed, place my knee on the mattress and, supporting her back, slowly lower her down.

She looks up at me as I stand again, reaching for my belt buckle. She's still trying to catch her breath, I think, although her eyes drop from my face to my chest, and continue downward.

"I thought I was supposed to…" she whispers, hesitating over her words, or maybe unsure what to say, or how to phrase it.

"Supposed to what?"

She blushes. "After what you just did… isn't it my turn?"

I smile, shaking my head. "It's okay. You don't have to do that."

"Even if I want to?"

I halt, gazing down at her. "Y—You want to?"

"I think so," she says. "I'd like to try, anyway."

I move my hand from my belt, holding it out to her and she takes it, letting me pull her up into a sitting position. She shimmies to the edge of the bed and, with fumbling fingers, she undoes my belt, pulling it from the belt loops and lying it on the mattress beside her. Then, with her eyes fixed firmly on mine, she unbuttons my jeans, lowering the zipper, and tugs them down. I help, pushing them to my ankles and stepping out. She bites her bottom lip and I reach forward, freeing it with my thumb.

"Unless you want me to bite that again, you need to leave it alone."

She heaves in a breath, and rubs her fingertips along the length of my cock, through the thin material of my trunks. Back and forth… back and forth, just twice, and then she tucks her fingers in the top and pulls them down, my erection almost hitting her on the chin.

She smiles, looking up at me, and I smile back, cradling her face in the palm of my hand.

"You don't have to do anything you don't want to, Josie."

She nods, pushing my trunks lower, right down my thighs to my knees. I step out of them, kicking them aside, and after just a moment's pause, she closes her hand around me, half-way down my shaft. Her eyes widen as she leans in and runs the tip of her tongue across the head of my cock, before opening her mouth wide and taking me.

I suck in a breath, gritting my teeth, watching as she swallows down the first couple of inches of my swollen dick. She dips her head back and forth, her tongue swirling over me, and then she moves her hand down to the base of my cock, letting it slide around underneath, cupping my balls.

"Oh, fuck. That's good, baby."

She takes me a little deeper, upping the pace. She looks so good with my dick in her mouth, and acting on impulse, I grab my belt, looping it around the back of her neck and holding both ends with my right hand. It's impossible for her to pull away without me letting her, and she knows it. Her eyes are on fire. She shifts closer to the edge of the bed, moaning as I flex my hips just slightly. She's letting me know she likes this, but even as I'm thinking that, and I flex my hips again, she gives my balls a gentle squeeze to remind me I don't have all the control here.

I feel a tingle at the base of my spine. There's a warmth that comes with it, spreading through my body, and I release the belt from around Josie's neck, letting it fall before I capture her face in my hands and pull out of her mouth. She looks up, blinking, and licks the corner of her lip.

"Did I do something wrong?"

"No. You were gonna make me come." She smiles, looking a little shy. "I've got no idea what my powers of recovery are like, and I've got so much more I wanna do with you."

"Like what?"

I close the gap between us, and the moment my lips hit hers, I let my hands drop from her face, lifting her from the bed and kneeling up on it before I lay her back down again, beneath me. She parts her legs, raising them up, and I support my weight on one arm, palming my cock with the other.

"This." I find her entrance, holding still, with just the tip of my dick inside her. "I'm sorry, baby. This is gonna hurt." She raises her right hand, resting her palm on my chest to get my attention. It works and I move my other hand down beside her head, then lower myself to my elbows. "What's wrong? Do you wanna stop?"

"No. I—I just need to ask a question."

"Okay."

"When you said this is gonna hurt, was that a memory?"

"No."

"Then how do you know it'll hurt?"

"In the same way I knew just now when I was about to come. It's no different to knowing when I need to eat, or drink, or sleep. It's just instinct."

"So you don't know if you've ever done this before?"

"Done what?"

"Had sex with a virgin."

I lean a little closer and dust my lips over hers. "To be honest, I can't tell you either way. I don't remember… and I don't care."

"You don't?"

"No. Because we're not having sex."

She looks utterly bewildered. "We're not?"

"No."

She frowns. "What are you doing to me, then?"

"I'm making love with you. There's a difference."

"And how do you know that?" she says. "Have you made love before… as opposed to having sex, I mean?"

"I don't know, and even if I did, it wouldn't matter. Whatever secrets my past holds, they mean nothing… and you mean everything. Absolutely everything." I cradle her head in my hands as she blinks up at me, and I can't hold back any longer. "I love you, Josie." She opens her mouth, but nothing comes out and her eyes fill with tears, which even I know isn't the best reaction to what I've just said. "It's okay, baby. I know it's early days to be saying things like that, and I don't expect you to feel the same way."

She puts her arms around my neck, pulling me down, our tongues meeting before our lips mold together. She's not ready to say the words, and that's okay. It's enough that she knows how I feel… that this isn't just about want and need. It's more than that.

She rolls her hips, her natural instincts getting the better of her natural reserve and, holding her tight, I push all the way inside her, swallowing her cry. I wait, absolutely still, other than my lips sweeping over hers, my tongue occasionally dipping, tasting.

Eventually, curiosity gets the better of me, and I break the kiss, leaning up, and looking down at her. She's smiling, her cheeks flushed, her eyes a little glazed.

"Okay?"

She nods. "It stretches."

"Has the pain stopped?"

I feel her muscles clench along the length of my cock, like she's checking. "Yes."

"And the stretch? How does that feel? It's not too much?"

"No. I like it." I smile and pull back out of her, almost all the way, then slide back in again. She sighs, bringing her legs up higher, gasping as I go a little deeper on the next stroke, and the next. "That's so good, Drew…"

She raises her hands, clinging to my shoulders, her body writhing, twisting, craving more. She's like the tide, ebbing and flowing, alternating between breathless need and soft inquisitive desire. I can feel her washing over me, the depth of my emotions catching me unaware, a lump forming in my throat as I watch her uncoil, sense the building surge within her.

I don't know if this is the kind of lover I used to be. I don't know if I've ever been this connected before. But this is who I want to be with Josie.

I take her slow, but hard… tender, but deep. She's gripping my cock tighter and tighter, and I feel a gentle quivering right at her core. She tenses, and I know she's about to come. I also know I won't be able to hold back, and as she thrashes against me, arching her back, breathing fast, climbing to the precipice, I swivel my hips into her.

"Now, baby… please."

She clamps around me, her nails digging into my arms as she throws back her head, letting out a low moan that builds and builds to the crescendo of a scream, and I thrust into her one last time, howling out her name and losing what's left of my mind as I fill her with everything I've got.

She's rolling beneath me, her body rising and then falling again, as her orgasm slowly subsides. "Please…" she whimpers. "Please don't stop, Drew." There's no way I'm ever going to stop. I'm still hard and I need to move again. I need more, too.

I lower myself down, resting my forehead against hers as I plunge deep inside her, letting her know this isn't over. This will never be over. "I can't stop," I murmur, dusting my lips across hers. I lower my hand behind her, resting it on her ass, and I lift her off of the bed, just slightly. That changes the angle, and within moments, she tips over the edge once more.

I'm nowhere near coming again, and I gaze down at her perfect face, a picture of ecstasy as her body writhes into mine, stretching and contracting, her eyes closed tight, her lips moving, even though this time, there's no sound coming from them. She's saying something, and I need to know what it is. I bend my head a little closer to hers, so my ear is right beside her lips, and I know I've truly lost my mind when I hear her whisper, "I love you, Drew. I've always loved you…"

Chapter Nine

Josie

Drew stops moving.

He can't have heard me, can he?

I whispered my love for him, so very quietly… how can he have heard?

I hope to God he didn't, because I've just stupidly said I've always loved him, and even if that's true, it's bound to raise questions I can't answer.

It's bound to complicate things.

I meant to wait until he got his memory back. That's why I didn't respond when he said he loved me… even though I wanted to. Those were the words I've waited to hear for so long, and I was desperate to tell him I feel exactly the same way. Except it felt wrong to say it when he doesn't know who he is… or who I am, or that we have a history of sorts.

Why am I worrying about that, though?

I didn't intend making love with him either… and yet, we just have.

And it felt so good.

Too good not to want to do it again… and again… and again.

Except he's stopped.

I flex my hips up into his, but he pulls back... not all the way out of me, but enough to let me know he's in control of what happens next, and I open my eyes, gazing up into his puzzled face.

"You just said you love me."

Damn. He heard.

"Yes." I can't lie to him now... not about this. I'm lying about everything else, but in this I have to be honest.

He lowers himself down so his body is resting against mine. Not his entire weight, just his body. I can feel his skin against mine, thigh to thigh, hip to hip, breast to chest. He brushes a hair from my cheek, tucking it behind my ear.

"Tell me you meant it," he says. "Tell me it wasn't just a heat of the moment thing."

I still can't lie. "I meant it."

He blinks, his eyes sparkling, as he sucks in a stuttered breath. "Y—You love me?"

"Yes."

"You just said you've always loved me... but we've only known each other for a few days, so how can that be?"

What am I supposed to say now? I can't tell him we've known each other for a lot longer...

"It just feels like I've always loved you," I say, hoping that sounds real. It's certainly true.

He smiles. "I know what you mean... but then my memories begin and end with you."

I wish he hadn't said that. It's a lovely, romantic thing to have said, but it's a reminder of everything I'm keeping from him... all the secrets, and all the lies.

Except, when it comes down to it, I love him and he loves me, and that's the only truth that matters.

He dips his head, his tongue sweeping into my mouth, his lips crushed to mine as he starts to move again. I match his rhythm, raising my hips to his, loving not only him, but the way he feels, the way he loves me. He's gentle, but assertive, taking me just as I hoped he would… showing me how good this can be.

He breaks the kiss, breathless, his eyes on fire, as he kneels up, lifting my right leg onto his shoulder and twisting me at my waist, so my hips are at an angle, but my shoulders are still flat on the mattress. Changing position, he straddles my left leg, going even deeper inside me, my breath catching in my throat as he pumps into me, harder and harder, until a sheen of sweat forms on his chest. With one arm clamped around my thigh, he moves the other hand down, his thumb circling over my clitoris.

"More, Drew. Give me more."

He rubs harder, taking me deeper, controlling my body… my destiny.

"You want more?"

"I want everything." I'm not altogether sure I know what 'everything' is, but I know I want it all with him.

"I'll give you everything," he whispers. "Everything I have."

He increases the pace, both of us breathing hard, oblivious to everything except our bodies pitching, plunging, hurtling to their journey's end.

I reach the precipice with no warning this time… no quivering, no tingling… just falling unbounded, tumbling down through mists and stars, wrapped in a bliss of whispered love as Drew's body stiffens. I open my eyes long enough to see the rapture on his face, to watch his lips move as he echoes back his love for me, to see his muscles tense as he pushes deep inside me. Then I feel it… the moment of his release. It's like absolution, washing over me… like all my lies are forgiven.

If only that could be true.

I cling to him, unwilling to let go, and he lowers my leg and turns us onto our sides, facing each other, still connected.

"You okay?" he asks, his voice hoarse, filled with emotion.

"Yes. You?"

"Better than I ever thought I'd be." He smiles, brushing his fingertips down my cheek, his eyes wandering over my face, like the stranger he thinks I am. "God, I love you."

"I love you."

He wraps his leg around me, pulling me closer. He's still hard inside me, but neither of us is in a hurry to do anything about that. For myself, I'm bone tired, happy to lie here enfolded in his arms. Drew seems contented too, just looking at me. I don't feel embarrassed by his gaze. It feels as though I'm the center of his world… and I love that.

He hasn't said anything about contraception. He didn't ask if he needed to use it, and he hasn't acknowledged the fact that he didn't. Obviously, it doesn't matter, but he doesn't know that… and I wonder if I should bring it up myself, to put his mind at rest.

Except he's clearly not worried.

And I'm not sure how I'd go about explaining. I'm hiding so much from him already, but this deceit feels like the worst of all. Unlike my other lies, this isn't about him; it's about me. And it isn't about the past, either. It's about the future. A future he might want to have one day… but which I can never give him.

"What's wrong?" He breaks into my thoughts.

"Nothing. How could anything be wrong when I'm lying here like this?" He smiles. "What made you ask?"

"The sadness in your eyes."

I hadn't realized I looked sad, and I smile up at him, kissing him back when his lips touch mine and doing my best to reconcile the lies and the regrets.

I can't regret this, though. I could never regret this.

I just wish it didn't have to be so shrouded in pretense.

He pulls back and I gaze into his eyes, willing him to remember… not just me, but all of it. Drew regaining his memory will almost certainly complicate things even more, and take us down an unpredictable path. He's bound to be upset about the secrets I've kept. But, if we're going to be together, then his past coming back to our present, and forming a future for us both, is the only hope we've got.

I wake with a start, and although I'm still in a haze of sleep, I'm aware of being alone… no longer swathed in Drew. A shiver of fear runs through me and I lean up on my elbows, his name on my lips, as I see him, sitting on the mattress, leaning against the end of the bed. He's unashamedly naked, utterly perfect, his legs bent up, his arms resting on his knees as he gazes at me.

"What are you doing there?"

"Watching you."

I crawl over and he parts his legs, making space for me to nestle between them as he brings his arms around me. "You didn't want to lie here and hold me, then?"

"Yes. And I did, for a while." I look up at him and he smiles, leaning down to kiss me. "You're very cute when you're asleep. Did you know that?"

"No."

"Well, you are," he says.

"Then why did you get up?"

"Because there was something I wanted to do."

"Oh?"

He lowers one arm, reaching down beside him, and then brings it back up again, holding his camera.

"I went downstairs to get this."

"Your camera?" He nods and I sit up slightly. "Have you been taking photographs of me?"

"Yes." He keeps a firm hold of me as I try to pull away. "Before you get upset, or insulted… please don't. They're not explicit."

"Really? I've got no clothes on, Drew."

"I noticed." He pulls me back into his arms, turning the camera around and showing me the screen. "I'd never do anything that made you uncomfortable… but please, will you look? And will you trust me?"

I can't say 'no' to that, and I settle against him as he flicks through the images. The first is of my eyes, shut and fast asleep, so close I could count the lashes. The second of my lips, pink and swollen from his kisses. He moves on, showing me my fingers, flat against the surface of the pillow, and the nape of my neck. In all the photographs, the sunlight shimmers off of my skin, even in the one he's taken of my foot, hanging over the edge of the bed.

"What's this?" I ask, gazing at the screen. The top corner of the frame is filled with white sheet, and the rest is taken up with skin. I can see a dip and a curve, but I can't make out what I'm looking at.

He pushes me forward gently, putting down the camera, and rubs his hands down my back in a slow, sensual movement.

"It's this bit… right here." He lets them come to rest, just above my ass.

"Oh."

"Are you okay with that?"

"I guess."

He pulls me back against his chest again, his left arm coming tight around me as he picks up the camera again, showing me the next photograph.

"And this?" I ask, seeing yet another shot that's just filled with me… or with my flesh, even though I'm once again, unsure which part of me this is.

"That's right… here." He puts the camera down, and lowers his right hand, skimming down my side until he reaches the very top of my thigh, running his fingertips from the outside in. "This part that leads from your hip inward."

"That's quite intimate."

"I know. It's as close as I was willing to go without you being aware of what I was doing."

I twist my head, looking up at him. "You won't show them to anyone else, will you?"

"Of course not. I took them for me, Josie."

"Why?"

"Because you're so beautiful."

"But why do you need a photograph? I'm not going anywhere."

He smiles. "That's good to know," he says. "But I took them because I didn't want to lose this moment among all my other forgotten memories. It's too precious. You're too precious. I wanted to be able to lock this time away forever."

"That's so lovely."

"I probably should have asked your permission first, but I didn't want to wake you… and I didn't want you to feel self-conscious about having your photograph taken. It wouldn't have been the same."

"You must have had to wait for me to turn over… to get in the right positions."

"I did. But watching you sleep could never be dull, baby." I smile and he smiles back. "Besides, seeing you through a viewfinder has kinda sparked something."

I sit up, turning to face him. "A memory?"

He shrugs his shoulders. "I don't know. I'm fairly sure I've taken photographs before, though."

"Like this? Photographs of naked women?"

I'm pretty sure he hasn't, but I'm interested to see what he says. "Not naked, no… but women, yes. There was something about the sun on your skin that was familiar. It wasn't anything specific, it was just a flash of something. And I have to say, I'm feeling more and more at home with a camera in my hand, so although I still can't be sure whether I was a professional, or not, I think photography played a big part in my life." I open my mouth to tell him he's right, but he clamps his fingers over my lips. "It's okay. I know you're not allowed to tell me… and I don't mind. I can wait for the memory to come back in a more lucid form."

I pull his hand away. "You don't want me to answer any questions?"

"Just one." He twists me around again, so I'm sitting with my back to his front, and brings his arms around me, lowering his hands.

"What's that?"

"How would you like me to make you come?"

He parts my legs as far as his will allow and as his fingers touch against my clitoris, I wriggle back into him. "Any way you like."

"You're not sore?"

I shake my head. "No… please, Drew." I sound desperate, but that's because I am.

He lets out a low growl, dropping his legs to the bed and moving them under me so they're inside mine. Then he pulls me up onto his lap, so I can feel his arousal pressing into me from behind, before he parts his legs again, taking mine with them. I'm spread wide open, but it seems he likes me that way and without a second's hesitation, he finds my swollen nub, rubbing it hard with the tips of his fingers.

He brings his left hand up, cupping my breast, then gently squeezes and pinches my hardened nipple, making me squeal and squirm against him. His fingers circle and delve, curling me into a mass of stretched nerve endings, desperate for release.

"Please, Drew…"

"Please what?"

"Make me come. I need to come."

He pushes two fingers inside me, leaving his thumb to do the work on my clitoris and suddenly it's like the sun has exploded behind my eyes. My body contorts, bucking against something new… something different. It's too strong for me. I'm not falling this time, I'm fighting.

"Go with it, baby," Drew whispers in my ear, holding on to me and I give up the struggle, letting it take me. This is more intense than anything that's gone before, the pleasure bordering on pain as it drives through me, leaving me spent.

Drew cradles me for ages while I calm, catching my breath, my body still twitching as the shocks continue to rock through me.

"Oh, God…" I whisper, settling back onto him. "That was so good."

"It was."

I twist, looking up at him. "Can I have more?"

He smiles. "You want to come again?"

"I want you inside me."

"Then take me," he says.

"How?"

His smile widens. "Just sit up a little." I do as he says, and he pulls me back slightly, and lowers me right onto his erection.

I let out a gasp as he impales me, stretching me again, and then I settle on to him, so he's as deep as he can go, before he pulls me back into his arms.

"Better?" he says and I nod my head.

"Much better."

Holding me close, he raises his legs a little, steadies his feet, and starts to move beneath me. He can't pull out very far, but he goes so deep, I don't care… the movement is enough, and when he lets his fingers play gently over my clitoris again, it sends me over the edge. This time, there's less tension in my body, and I let it fall through realm after realm while he hammers into me, only slowing when I start to calm.

"Y—You didn't come," I stutter, getting my breath back.

"No. I don't need to… not every time. Just watching you is enough." He grasps my chin, turning my head and tipping it back so he can kiss me. "Just loving you is enough."

I sink into him, losing myself in his kisses, ignoring the nagging doubt at the back of my mind… the one that says he might not feel that way when he finds out the truth.

Drew

I meant it when I said loving Josie is enough.

It is.

It's all I'm ever going to want… although that doesn't mean I've had my fill of her yet.

I need more.

I think I'll always need more. I break the kiss, holding her steady as I look down into her upturned face.

"Would you like to shower with me?"

"Shower? Together?"

"Sure. Why not?"

Her eyes sparkle, giving me her answer before she's even said, "Yes," which she does with a husky nuance to her voice.

With great reluctance, I lift her off of me, sliding out from under her, and shifting to the edge of the bed. I stand, looking back, as she lies where I left her, and for a moment, I wonder about suggesting we leave it for a while, so she can rest, but then she glances up at me, seeming to come back to life, and I offer my hand. She accepts it, letting me pull her from the bed and into the bathroom.

I've only been in this room once, when I briefly looked around on the day Josie and I arrived back from the hospital, but I remember it better from the other day, when I stood and watched her shower, the sun dappling off of her perfect skin. I may have wondered then about striding in here and claiming her, but in reality, I never thought that dream would come true. It seemed too much to hope for that I'd be in here with her, or that I'd have been able to tell her I love her, and that she'd love me back.

But here we are…

I lead her underneath the enormous waterfall shower head, turning it on, as Josie raises her head, her gaze raking over my chest, pausing for a while on my lips, and then settling on my eyes.

"I love you so much," she whispers, leaning against me, her breasts crushed against my chest. I bring one arm around her, holding her close, while cupping her cheek with my other hand.

"I love you, too."

I cover her lips with mine in a frantic kiss, our tongues clashing, our hands everywhere. I was only inside her a few minutes ago, but it doesn't feel like it. This kiss feels more like we've been starved of one another, like our lives depend on the connection I'm about to make between us.

Without breaking the kiss, I walk her backwards until she hits the white-tiled wall, raising her left leg and hooking it over my right arm. Then I bend slightly, and I slide inside her. She gasps into my mouth, bringing her arms up around my neck as I start to move.

I lean back, parting my lips from hers, and gaze down into her wondrous face. Her eyes are sparkling, her lips swollen, her cheeks flushed… and still, I want more.

"Hold my shoulders," I say, surprised by the rasp in my voice.

She does as I ask, and I lean down, hooking my arm under her right leg and lifting her up. She yelps in surprise, but settles onto me and, once I've given her a moment or two to get used to the feeling, I use the wall for support and hammer into her, harder and faster, giving her my entire length with every stroke.

Her eyes are locked on mine, our lips almost touching, the room filled with my guttural groans and her breathless sighs… and still, it's not enough.

Resting my hands under her ass, I turn us around, so my back is to the wall now, and I brace my feet on the floor, water pooling in the valley between our two bodies.

"Don't let go, baby. Whatever I do, don't let go of me. Okay?"

She nods her head, her eyes alight, and I pull her down onto me, then lift her, and slam her down again.

"Oh… God…" She grinds out the words through gritted teeth. "That's so good."

"Tell me you're mine."

She looks into my eyes. "I'm yours."

"Tell me you'll always be mine."

"I'll always be yours."

I watch her expression as I move my right hand slightly, brushing the tip of my middle finger across her tight anus. She sucks in a breath, her eyes widening as her body shudders against mine.

"You wanted everything… remember?"

She nods her head, and as I raise her up again, she kisses me. I circle my finger over her puckered hole and she breathes hard, moaning into my mouth and then breaks the kiss, throwing her head back as she screams out a shattering orgasm. She bucks and writhes against me, so close, I can feel the strain in every sinew of her body as she clings on to me.

As she slowly calms, I kiss her neck and trace a slow, delicate line of kisses up to her ear.

"That was so hot," I whisper and she nods her head, incapable of speech, I think. "We can stop if you want…" The shake of her head renders me silent, and I lift her off of me, smiling at the worried frown on her face. "This isn't over, babe."

Her frown fades, although she still looks a little confused… which I guess is because she doesn't know what's happening… and I like that.

I step out, so she's facing the tiled wall, and I move around behind her. Then, with gentle pressure on her back, I tip her forward.

"Put your hands out flat on the wall." She does as I say, supporting herself, and looking over her shoulder at me, with a slight smile on her lips as she arches her back. This has the natural effect of tipping her ass upwards, and I run my hands over her rounded cheeks, letting my fingers slide lazily between them. I hover over her anus and she wiggles her ass, letting out a soft moan, before I move my fingers down between her legs, her swollen lips parting to my touch. She sucks in a sharp breath, raising her ass as I circle around her clit.

I move in close behind her, nudging her feet a little further apart with my own, and place the tip of my cock at her entrance. I pause, teasing her, tempting her as she squirms back, trying to get more.

"Please, Drew… please."

I slam into her, giving her what she wants, what I need. I don't give her time to adjust. My need is too great, and so is hers. I can feel it, not just in my cock, but right down in my core. I lunge into her, each thrust more powerful than the last.

"Take me, Josie. Take all of me."

She looks over her shoulder, her eyes connecting with mine. "Give me everything… please, Drew. Everything."

I know what she means… what she wants, and without slowing my pace, I flatten my right hand at the top of her ass, letting my thumb rest against her anus.

"You want everything?"

"Yes!"

I slip my thumb inside her tightest hole and she explodes. Her body rages against mine, bucking and contorting as she rocks back onto me, wanting more… always more. My name is a long scream on her lips as she clamps around my cock, and it's all too much for me. I let go, as deep as I can inside her, the rhythmic clenching of her inner muscles milking me dry.

As I carefully pull my thumb from her, I realize her shoulders are shaking, convulsing… her body going with them, and I grab her, spinning her around as she lets out a sob that shatters my heart.

Oh, god… what have I done?

"Josie… baby," I say, holding her close to my chest, caressing her hair as she weeps against me, her body so small and soft and delicate. "I'm sorry. I'm so sorry."

She shakes her head, pulling away, and looks up into my eyes. "No."

"No, what?" *I'm dying here. Give me more than 'no', for the love of God.*

She rests her hands on my chest. "D—D—Don't be sorry." She's struggling against her tears.

"But I hurt you."

"No."

I capture her face with my hands, my body pressed hard against hers. "Tell me. Tell me why you're crying."

She sucks in a deep breath, and then another, trying to calm herself. It doesn't work. Tears are still rolling down her cheeks, but the look in her eyes isn't one of pain or hurt. It's one of love… the kind of love that makes the sun rise and the moon shine. The kind of love that draws two hearts together, knowing that to part would break them both.

"I—I can't help it," she says, still struggling.

I nod my head. "Are these good tears?"

"Yes. At least, they're overwhelming tears." She takes another breath. "I—I thought what you did to me earlier, on the bed, was as intense as it could get… but what you did just now…"

"It was good?"

She smiles, choking back her tears in a half laugh. "Good isn't a strong enough word. I feel like my body isn't mine anymore. Like it's in pieces on the floor…"

I kiss her, my lips playing across hers. "Then let me help you."

"Do you think you can?"

I stare into her eyes. "Yes."

"How?"

"I don't know, but I'd tear myself apart to put you back together."

Tears trickle from her eyes, and she throws her arms around my neck. "I love you so much, Drew."

"I'll always love you more."

I turn off the water, wrapping her in a towel and I hold her for a very long time, until it feels like she's whole again, her breathing quite normal, her body relaxed in my arms.

I grab a towel for myself, fastening it just above my hips, and then I lift her into my arms. She rests her head against my chest and I carry her back into the bedroom, laying her down on the mattress.

"You okay?" I lie beside her, pushing damp hairs from her face.

"I am now," she says. "Sorry about that."

"Don't be."

She smiles. "You looked really scared."

"I was. I thought I'd hurt you."

She shakes her head, her smile fading. "Can I ask you a question?"

"Sure." I pull her into my arms, lying on my back, and she nestles against me.

"That… that thing you did to me… is that something you've done before?" I know what she's talking about, even if she's not being altogether clear.

"I don't know. Like everything else, it's a mystery."

"Then why did you…?"

"Because you said you wanted everything, and so do I. I want all of you to be mine… every inch of you." I reach down, placing my finger beneath her chin and raise her face to mine. "Was that okay?" Her smile returns, her eyes twinkling as she bites on her bottom lip, looking a little shy. "Can I take that as a 'yes'?"

"You can," she says and I chuckle, closing the gap between us and covering her lips with mine. She pulls back after just a few seconds, though, staring up into my eyes. "Would you think badly of me if I suggested we get dressed?"

"I could never think badly of you."

"And you wouldn't mind getting dressed?"

"Not if that's what you want."

I'm struggling to hide my disappointment, especially as I'm hard again already, and her lips twitch up into a smile. "It's not necessarily what I want. It's just that I'm hungry."

"You're hungry? Why didn't you say?"

"Because we've had better things to do than think about food… but I'm pretty sure we've missed lunch."

I turn, checking the time on the clock beside the bed, and let out a laugh. "We've missed it by a mile."

"Why? What time is it?"

"Nearly five."

"You mean we've been up here for seven hours?"

"Yeah. But you were asleep for some of it." She nods her head, biting on her bottom lip again. "If you wanna eat anytime today, you need to stop doing that."

"Why?" She's teasing and we both know it.

"Because it makes me wanna roll you over on your back, part your legs and bury myself deep inside you." She blinks a few times, still biting on her lip, and I tilt my head, raising my eyebrows. "What's it to be, babe?"

"I'm very tempted to stay up here, but…"

"You're hungry?"

"Yes. I'm sorry."

"Hey. Don't apologize." I kiss her forehead, then her nose and then her lips before I slide off of the bed, getting to my feet. "Do we really need to get dressed, though?"

She blushes, sitting up on the edge of the mattress. "Would you mind if we did? It's just that I think I'd feel more comfortable wearing clothes if we're going downstairs. If your brother came knocking on the door, I'd…"

I take her hands, pulling her to her feet, the towel loosening and falling around her ankles, so I can put my hands on her ass and pull her closer.

"If that's what you want, then I'm fine with it. Besides, I kinda like the idea that I'm the only man who's seen you like this." I kiss her, nibbling at her bottom lip, which makes her moan. "I wanna keep it that way, too."

"Hmm… so do I."

I step back, looking down at our clothes in a pile on the floor. "I'm gonna go find some shorts."

"Okay." She bends down, picking up our clothes, giving me a view of perfection, and I pat her ass, making her squeal.

"Biting your lip isn't the only thing that could delay you getting fed, you know?"

"I had to pick up our clothes."

"Yeah… and flaunt your delectable ass at me."

She turns, hugging my jeans and hers to her chest. "Delectable?"

"Yeah… or delicious… delightful… desirable."

"Are you limited to adjectives that start with a 'd'?"

"Not at all… I could just as easily call your ass adorable or beautiful, captivating or divine, enticing or f—"

"Stop it," she says, giggling. "You're just working your way through the alphabet now."

"I know… but you're supposed to be impressed."

"What was 'f' going to be, then?"

"I'll show you later," I say as her eyes widen and she licks her bottom lip. "Still wanna go eat?"

"You're such a tease, Drew Bennett."

"I know. And yet, you love me."

She dumps the clothes on the bed and turns to me, resting her hands on my chest. "I do."

"Good. Now, I guess we'd better feed you, or you won't have any energy for later."

"Later?"

I step away, walking backwards to the door, my eyes not leaving hers. "Yeah… when I show you what 'f' means."

I can hear her gasp, even as I get to the door, and turn around, crossing the threshold and going over to my room.

I can't stop smiling, but that's hardly surprising. I've dreamed about this for days. Ever since the moment I first woke up in the hospital and set eyes on Josie, I've wanted her… and now she's mine. And I'm hers. Entirely.

I don't want to spend too much time in here. Just a few seconds is enough to make me miss her, and I wander into my dressing room, going through the drawers until I find a pair of cargo shorts. They're dark gray, and I pull them on, doing up the zipper and button. I could put on a t-shirt, but I enjoy feeling Josie against my skin… and even if my brother comes over for some reason, I don't care if he sees me half-naked. It's Josie I'd be worried about.

I close the drawer again, and head back out into the bedroom, noticing I didn't make the bed… again. My eyes drift over to the door, my mind roaming beyond that to Josie's room… and I wonder if she'll want to sleep with me tonight. God, I hope so. The thought of holding her all night, of waking up beside her, of her face being the first thing I see tomorrow morning… it makes my skin tingle.

I hurry over and pull up the covers, straightening them, and puff up the pillows, so it looks like I made an effort… just in case.

I've been gone too long, so I make my way back to Josie's room, where I find her dressed in denim shorts and a sleeveless blouse, which is cinched in at the waist. She turns as I approach and I swallow down my groan. She's not wearing a bra, her nipples straining against the pretty floral material, and I reach out, pulling her into my arms.

"Are you trying to tease me to death?"

"I could ask you the same question." She lets her hands roam over my bare chest. "You didn't think a t-shirt was necessary?"

"No."

She chuckles, shaking her head. "Okay," she says. "Let's go get something to eat."

I'm tempted to say that everything I need is standing right in front of me, but I know she's hungry, so I let her lead me from the room and down the stairs.

In the kitchen, she opens the refrigerator door, peering inside and I stand, open-mouthed, staring at her rounded ass, encased in tight denim. It's too much for me, and I wander over, rubbing my hands over her in soft circular movements. She squirms into me and then shimmies back, closing the refrigerator again, before bringing her arm up around the back of my head as I bend to kiss her neck. My hands roam around in front of her shorts, and I unfasten them, delving inside to find there's no barrier between me and her swollen pussy lips.

"You're not wearing any underwear?"

"No." She rotates her hips, rubbing her ass against my hard-on. "I couldn't see the point."

"Neither could I."

I take her hand from behind my head, bringing it between us, and holding it against my erection. She strokes along my length as I dip a finger inside her soaking entrance.

We're both breathing hard, desperate for each other again, but Josie sees sense, and after a few minutes of urgent fondling, she steps away, turning to face me. Her cheeks are glowing, her eyes on fire, and with her shorts undone, she looks like sex on legs. I reach for her again, but she holds up her hand.

"We need to eat."

I raise my hand, licking her juices from my fingers. "Should I consider this the appetizer?"

She watches me, her breasts heaving, her eyes fixed on my lips as she says, "The main course will follow later… I hope?"

I move closer, lowering my hand and clasping the back of her neck, holding her still. "You can count on it, baby."

I know I could easily tempt her to more, but I need to take care of her in other ways, too… ways that include food. So, I re-fasten her shorts, shutting away temptation… for now.

"What have we got to eat that takes no time at all to prepare?" I ask, reaching around her and opening the refrigerator again.

"I don't know. I was just wondering that."

We stand side by side, arm in arm, and check out our supplies. "We've got cold chicken." I pull it out, handing it to Josie to put on the countertop.

"There's some salad, too." She opens the drawer at the bottom, finding lettuce, tomatoes, radishes, cucumber, some olives, and a red onion. "We can make something out of this."

"Something quick?"

She smiles up at me. "Yes. Something quick."

We gather the ingredients, and between us, we chop them up into a large bowl. Josie prepares a dressing while I set the table, and before I know it, we're sitting opposite each other, ready to eat.

"This looks good."

She nods her head. "It does."

"Not as good as you, though."

She smiles, dishing up the salad into two bowls, and handing one to me. I pour us a glass of chilled water each, and smile as Josie tucks in with gusto.

I join her, and after a couple of mouthfuls, she looks up at me.

"What are you going to do with those photographs?"

"The ones I took of you, you mean?"

"Yes."

I shrug my shoulders, spearing a slice of cucumber. "I'm not sure."

"You're not?" she says, frowning at me.

"No. I'm guessing I must have had software of some kind for editing photographs, but it would have been on my laptop, and I can't remember the password yet."

"You want to edit them?" She looks disappointed now and I have to smile.

"Yes, but not because I don't love the way you look. I just think the images would look great in black and white. I think the contrast of your skin and the sunlight will look amazing."

"You're not thinking of displaying them, are you?" She puts down her fork, her frown deepening to the point where she looks worried.

"Not if you don't want me to… but even if I did, it would have to be somewhere private, where only I could see them."

"Oh… okay." She starts eating again, happy with my answer, I guess… not that I've decided what to do with the photographs yet. I need to know the password for my laptop first, and I've got no idea how to go about working that out.

"Have you ever done any photography?" I ask her, taking a sip of water.

"Not really. I don't have time. Obviously, I've taken pictures on my phone, like everyone else, but…"

"Your phone?"

She nods her head. "Yes."

I sit back, a memory flashing through my mind… a screen, long and narrow, different to the one on my camera. It's fleeting and I can't quite grasp it or see the image on the screen, but for the first time in ages, I feel the need to ask a question. "Do I have a phone?"

Josie drops her fork this time, a blush creeping up her cheeks. "Yes, you do."

"Do you know where it is?"

"Why do you ask?"

"Because I think I might have taken photographs on it, and if I did, there might be clues… things, or people, or places I'll recognize. I checked the disk that's in the camera while you were asleep earlier, and there's nothing on it, other than the pictures I've taken today."

"I see." She frowns. "I wish you hadn't done that."

"Done what?"

"Checked the camera, without me being present… and awake."

"Why?"

"What if you'd found something? What if it had triggered an adverse reaction?"

"It didn't, though, did it?"

"No," she says. "But that's not the point, Drew. I know things have changed between us today, but you're still my patient. I'm still supposed to be managing your recovery."

"Okay. I'm sorry."

She smiles, although it's a little half-hearted. "It's fine. There's no harm done."

"Maybe not, but I'd still like to know where my phone is."

"Your brother has it. He was given it at the hospital after the accident, and he's had it ever since."

"And I'm guessing you're not gonna let him give it back to me?"

She sighs, leaning forward. "I thought you said you were gonna let things happen naturally."

"I know. But isn't this a natural progression?"

"No. This is you, trying to force a progression." I shake my head, looking at the salad bowl. "Don't be mad at me, Drew… please," she says.

I look up again, then reach across the table, taking her hand in mine.

"I'm not mad. I'm frustrated."

"I know. But can't you see? You're asking me to do something that has the potential to send you into a spiral of confusion. There could be names and numbers in your contacts list, and pictures on your phone that mean absolutely nothing to you… and they'll just add to the list of things you've already got rattling around your brain. You need to process what you've got before you add anything new."

She's right, and I know it. Overloading my brain won't help, and based on what happened the last time I tried too hard, it could even hinder my recovery.

"I'm sorry."

"You don't have to be sorry," she says.

"Yes, I do. I know you're only acting in my best interests."

"Yeah… and I know you want to get your memories back." I can hear something in her voice… something wretched. It matches the sorrow in her eyes and I get up, going around the table to crouch beside her.

"Hey…" She turns, looking at me. "Please don't think I'm unhappy with where I am… with where we are. I know it might seem like I'm obsessed with the past sometimes, but that's only because I don't have one. And just because I'm trying to find out who I am, doesn't mean I don't already know you're everything I need, Josie. You're everything I want. You're the only thing that's right in my life."

She leans in to me. "I hope so."

"You are. Trust me. And I meant it… I'm sorry. I shouldn't have taken my frustrations out on you."

I kiss her, just gently, and she returns my smile as I get to my feet, walking back to my seat. I wish I'd never mentioned the damn phone now. Even if she had given it to me – or gotten Hunter to give it to me – I doubt its contents would have meant anything. Nothing else has. All I've done is make Josie unhappy, by doubting her loyalty… and that's the last thing I wanted to do.

My appetite has waned, and it seems Josie's has, too. Neither of us finishes our meal, but we do a passable job, and once we've both had enough, we clear away, stacking the dishes into the dishwasher, before I pull her into my arms, looking down into her eyes.

"Spend the night with me?"

"You want me to?" she says, sounding doubtful.

"Of course. I'm sorry if I've ruined our evening, but please don't let my stupidity ruin our night as well."

"You haven't ruined anything. And it's not stupidity."

"Yeah, it is. But I'd like to make it up to you… if you'll let me?"

She smiles. "You don't need to make anything up to me, and I'd love to spend the night with you."

I take her hand, leading her to the stairs, and we climb them together. At the top, I pull her toward my room, but she tugs me back.

"We're going to your room?"

"Yeah. Is that a problem?"

She glances over my shoulder at the closed door. "N—No."

I'm not sure I believe her, but she smiles, leaning up and kissing me. "If you'd rather we slept in your room…?"

She shakes her head. "No… it's fine."

She reaches around me, opening the door, and I turn and lead her inside.

Chapter Ten

Josie

What an evening. What a day.

Drew's fast asleep now. I'm lying beside him, my back to his front, his arms wrapped around me, and even though I can't see his face, I know his eyes are closed and he's lost to the land of dreams. I can feel his rhythmic breathing, and there's something oddly comforting about matching it with my own. We may never have done this before, but it feels familiar… and I like it.

I'm not surprised by his tiredness. I'm exhausted myself, even though I slept for a few hours this afternoon. He didn't, and he's recovering from concussion, too. Not that you'd know there was anything wrong with Drew, based on today's performance.

I've lost count of the number of times we've made love… and each time seems different from the last. He's very energetic, and although I'm an innocent when it comes to men, I'm also a nurse, and I know it's not necessarily normal for a man to be able to keep going like he can. I wonder if he's like this all the time, but there's no-one who can tell me that… not even Drew. He doesn't remember anything, even though he seems to know exactly what he's doing. He says it's an instinct, and I have to believe him, because he certainly has a talent for this… one that makes my body sing to his tune.

It makes my body ache, too. I've discovered muscles I hadn't even realized I had… and I've used them to their limits. I can feel it now, in my legs and hips, in my shoulders and back. Snuggling into him makes it feel better, though, as do the memories…

I didn't feel too good when he brought me up here after dinner. He'd asked me to spend the night with him, and while I wanted to, more than anything, I was plagued with guilt.

We'd come close to having an argument about his phone, and I wished I'd never mentioned taking photographs on mine, even though it was innocently done. I knew as soon as he asked about having a phone himself that it was going to be an issue. He had that look on his face… the same one he'd worn when we first got back here and he was trying to figure everything out, all at once. Alarm bells were ringing in my head. I knew I'd have to deny him access to his phone… for the exact reasons I gave him. What I didn't know was how he'd react.

He got angry. He said he wasn't, but there was no escaping it. His eyes gave him away, and I'll admit, that worried me. Not in terms of what Drew might do, but because of what it meant for us.

I was being completely truthful with him, for once. I firmly believed – and I still do – that giving him back his phone wasn't a good idea. Not yet. If I'd thought he might benefit from having it, I'd have called Hunter and asked him to bring it over. But, like I said to Drew, it's early days, and while I want him to regain his memories, I don't think he's ready for the wealth of information his phone is bound to contain. Introducing something like that needs to be managed carefully… like everything else in his recovery.

The problem was, not only did my answer frustrate him, it also turned me back into his nurse. Our roles became clouded, just like I knew they would. It was one of the reasons I'd given him for not getting involved… not that it matters now, because we're more than involved.

We're in love.

That was why it was so hard, watching him struggle with the past he can't remember. He might not be aware of exactly how much I know… but he realizes that my knowledge of him and his past is greater than his own. It feels like a void between us, even if he tried to patch over the cracks. His apology was heartfelt, and I know he meant every word he said, but until his memory returns, there's always going to be a blank space neither of us can fill.

That's what worries me the most in terms of our relationship. The longer this takes, the harder I think it will be for us to dance around that space; him in the dark, and me in the shadow of my lies. I'm scared that when we come out into the light, he won't like what he finds…

I don't doubt his love for me, but it's new to him. There's no history to it, like there is in my love for him. Will that new love be strong enough to survive when he knows what I've done? Will he be able to forgive me for keeping so much from him? Not just about us and our past together, but also about the future we can't have, his family, his mother's reappearance… and, most important of all, his daughter.

I shudder at the thought of how he might react and, even though he's fast asleep, he tightens his grip on me, like he can sense my fear.

I caress his arm, brushing along it with my fingertips, wishing I could talk to him… wishing I could tell him the truth, and ask at least some of the questions that are rattling around my head; questions he can't answer.

There are so many… which makes it even more bizarre that, for a brief moment this evening, I added another one. Because

I couldn't help wondering what's gone before… or rather who has gone before.

I hadn't thought about that all day, not during all the times we'd made love, but after I'd said 'yes' to spending the night with him, he assumed I'd be okay with sleeping in his bed. We got to the top of the stairs and I hesitated when I realized where he was taking me.

He noticed, and to prove I was okay with it, I opened the door and let him lead me inside.

I may have been in his room before, but that was in my role as his nurse. This was different, and as I stepped through the door, waiting for him to close it behind us, the only thing I saw was the bed. It seemed to dominate the room, and my mind. Just as I expected, I was awash with questions. Had he brought other women here? Had he loved them like he loved me? Was Lexi among them? I struck the thought. Lexi had always told me they weren't in love, that it had been a fling, and while I knew she'd been here after Maisie was born, she'd never mentioned visiting Drew here before then.

I stared at the bed, thinking about his past, realizing that, while I knew more than he did, I still knew very little. He'd had other lovers, but how many and over how long was anybody's guess.

He came up behind me, snaking his arms around my waist, and dropped a kiss onto my neck.

"Are you sure you're okay with this?"

I turned in his arms, looking up at him, seeing the worry in his eyes. He cared. He really cared, and I smiled, resting against him.

"I'm fine, Drew."

I was. He'd told me I was everything he needed… everything he wanted. I felt exactly the same, and we were living proof that the past doesn't matter.

I brought my hands up, clasping his stubbled jaw and pulled his head down, my lips meeting his in a fiery kiss, ignited by our almost-argument, and fueled by that mutual need. He pulled me close, flexing his hips and letting me feel his erection. I don't know why I was surprised by his arousal. It had been over an hour since we'd last made love, after all… and it seemed like an hour was more than enough for Drew.

"There's something I need to show you," he whispered, leaning up and looking down into my eyes.

"There is?"

He smiled, pulling me over to the bed. "Yeah…" He spun me around, so I was facing the mattress, then he stood right behind me, his body tight against mine, and reached around, unfastening my shorts, pushing them down over my hips. His lips brushed over my neck, while his hands came between us, cupping my ass, squeezing gently. "Alluring," he murmured between kisses. "Beautiful… captivating… delightful." He may not have been using the same words, but I knew where he was going, and a slight shiver coursed through me. He was leading me to 'f'… or to the meaning of it, and although I'd loved everything he'd done to me, I wasn't sure if I was ready to be taken *there*. I wasn't ruling it out – not forever – but it felt too soon.

He must have felt my uncertainty, or at least sensed it.

"It's okay," he whispered. "You can trust me."

"I do."

"Then you know I won't do anything you're not ready for."

I twisted my head around, looking up at him. "I know."

He smiled, a wicked, sexy kind of smile and then bent me over the mattress, his middle finger tracing a line from the base of my spine, across my tight anus and further down, resting at my entrance.

"F stands for fingers," he murmured as he pushed two of them inside me and I chuckled. I was pretty sure that wasn't what he'd meant earlier. It didn't make sense in the context he'd been using, and 'fingers' weren't an adjective. But it didn't matter. He was doing such incredible things to me, I didn't care anymore.

He made love to me for hours, never once pushing me outside of my boundaries, but testing them all the time, taking me beyond my wildest dreams and into the realms of fantasy…

I wake to darkness, my body tingling even before I'm aware I'm being touched… intimately. I concentrate on the sensations, piecing them together.

Something is inside me.

Drew's fingers.

They're sliding gently in and out, from tip to knuckle.

There's no urgency; just a soft, rhythmic sway. It's soothing and arousing. I could easily fall asleep again, but my body craves more.

My back is to his front still, and I wriggle my ass into him, feeling his arousal.

He moans.

I sigh.

And then everything changes.

Without a sound, he withdraws his fingers, rolling me onto my front. My arms are caught beneath me, but it's not uncomfortable.

He straddles me, my legs quite close together for once, and then he raises my ass off of the mattress, just a little. I feel the head of his erection rub against me, finding my entrance, and then he's inside me… so deep it makes me gasp.

I arch my back, wanting more and he leans over me, his hands on my waist, holding me down as he thrusts into me, harder and faster. There's something different about this. There's something desperate and powerful behind each stroke, behind each guttural groan.

"Take my cock..." he says, with an urgency in his voice.

"Give me more."

We're both feeling this, both needing it.

He plunges into me, setting my body on fire. "Tell me you're close, Josie."

"I'm close... please, Drew. Please make me come."

He leans over me even more, so I can feel his weight, and swivels his hips, grinding into me. That's all I need to plummet, pleasure chasing me, catching me, consuming me...

I surface, aware that he's still now, that the moment has passed for him, too. He's spent, as am I, and he lies on top of me for a moment, dragging air into his lungs before he pulls out of me and rolls onto his side, turning me, so I'm facing him.

I feel a fingertip on my cheek, a kiss against my lips.

"I'm sorry."

How can he be apologizing after that? "Why?"

"Because yesterday was tiring," he says. "I should have let you sleep."

"I can't think of a nicer way to be woken up."

He chuckles. "Neither can I. I found you in my arms and I had to touch you... had to have you."

"I'm not complaining, Drew," I say, nestling against him. "I liked the feeling of being wanted so much."

"You are. I think you always were."

I lean back, even though he keeps a hold of me. "Is that a memory?" Can it be? Is it possible he's recalled something about us, or about our past?

"No. But it's like when you said you've always loved me. I feel the same way. I might have only known you for a few days, but it's like you've always been here." He takes my hand, resting it against his chest, over his heart. "I don't want that to change, Josie. I don't want this to end."

"Who says it has to end?"

"No-one. But after what happened earlier – about my phone and my frustrations – I want you to know, if the price I have to pay for keeping you here is never getting my memory back, then I'll pay it."

I move closer to him, raising my leg and wrapping it around his. "No, Drew. I don't want that for you. I want you to remember."

"So do I. But what I'm trying to say is, if I had to choose between you and my past… or you and my life as it used to be, then I'd choose you. Every. Single. Time."

Tears well in my eyes, and even though he can't see me, it's like he knows they're there and he holds me tighter. "You can't say that. You don't know what you're sacrificing."

"I know I love you. I know I want to spend forever loving you."

"Forever?" I can't help smiling.

"Yes. Forever. Although how our kids are gonna feel about having the most forgetful father in history is anyone's guess."

My smile fades, my dreams shatter, crumbling to dust in that one brief sentence.

"K—Kids?"

"Yeah. I love you so much, I can't imagine not being a family with you… not having children with you. I don't know if that's something I ever considered before, and I don't care. It's something I want with you, Josie. It feels right."

Oh, God… this isn't a dream. It's my worst nightmare.

I can't answer him. I don't have the words. Luckily, because I'm lying on my side, my tears fall onto the pillow, so he doesn't notice them when he leans in and kisses me, his lips skimming over mine.

"I'm not pressuring you." He leans back, clearly noticing my silence. "There's no rush. I'm just putting it out there."

I nod my head, knowing he expects a response, and it's the best I can do. If I speak, he'll hear the emotion in my voice. He'll ask questions. And I don't have any answers.

He settles down, getting comfortable, holding me against him, and although I'm so tense my muscles are aching even more than they were before, I lie still and wait… and wait…

Within a few minutes, his breathing changes and I know he's asleep.

There's no chance of sleep for me, though, and I can't just lie here, living yet another lie. Not this time. It's too much.

I slip out of his grip, sliding from the bed and I stand for a moment, getting my bearings, deciding where the door is, and then, treading on my tiptoes, I sneak out of the room.

The hall isn't so dark. There are no drapes covering the windows and the moonlight floods in, so I can see the open door to my bedroom and I cross over to it, closing it softly behind me and switching on the lights.

My bed is a mess. We didn't re-make it earlier, and the pillows are scattered, the covers screwed up and pushed off of the edge. I pull them back, straightening them, and return the pillows to their rightful place, destroying the physical evidence of what happened in here today. That won't help me forget it. I can't. But I don't want to face it at the moment. I don't want to think about how unfair this is.

Drew wants children. He just said so. And why wouldn't he? It makes perfect sense that it would feel 'right' to him. He's already a father, even if he doesn't know it. But as for us being a family? That's the one thing we can't have. It's the one thing I can't give him. And it's the one secret I wish I hadn't had to keep, above all the others.

I hadn't realized it would mean so much to him. Let's face it, Maisie's conception was hardly intentional. But it seems I got that wrong. He wants this, and I can't deny him his future… especially not when he's still wrestling with his past.

I wander to the closet and pull out a pair of jeans and a t-shirt, finding some underwear in the dresser. It only takes a few minutes to get dressed, and once I'm done, I grab my bag from the bottom of the closet, dumping it on the bed and filling it with my things. I don't fold them, or take any care in packing them. I just load up my bag, and once it's done, I slip on my shoes and check I haven't left anything behind. Obviously, I have, because my shorts and top are in Drew's room, but that's where they'll have to stay. I daren't risk going in there, in case I wake him… and I can live without them.

Even if I'm not sure I can live without him.

Still… what choice do I have?

I grab my bag, switching off the lights, and haul it down the stairs, taking care to make as little noise as possible. At the bottom, I pick up my purse from the living room, check my phone is inside, and quietly open the front door.

There's a slight chill in the air, the wind catching my hair, stinging at my eyes as I let the tears fall, but I close the door anyway, and lug my bag down the path toward the main house. I won't be going in there, but I need to follow the path in the moonlight, and then join the main driveway that leads to the gates.

Hunter explained how the gates work on the day we arrived, so I know a cab won't be able to get in without someone granting them access. That means my only choice is to walk the length of the driveway and exit through the small side gate. Like the main gate, it needs someone to let you in from the main house, but there's a button on the wall that you can press to get out… thank God.

The plan comes to me with a cool logic, born of the need to get away, and I trudge along, putting one foot in front of the other, not looking up or back, until I reach my destiny. The gate opens with a creak, but I'm far enough away from the buildings and the people sleeping in them not to worry, and once I'm outside, I look up the number for a local 24-hour cab company.

I realize, as I'm placing the call, that I don't know exactly where I am. Hunter didn't give me the address. But I'm able to describe the house and its location to the man on the phone.

"Oh... you mean Theodore Bennett's place."

"*Theodore* Bennett?"

"Yeah. He's dead now, of course. His kids live there, but that's the place right enough."

He tells me he can get a cab to me within fifteen minutes, and I lean back against the wall by the gate and wait.

I can't see Drew's house from here. It's too far away, and still too dark, although I can see the beginnings of the dawn on the horizon. Even if I could see the house, it wouldn't change anything. I have to leave, and deep down, I think I always knew it would come to this. I've always known, if my lies didn't ruin everything, my secrets would.

I've only been away for a few days, but my apartment feels different. Or maybe that's me.

Maybe it's that I know I'll never be the same again.

How can I be, after everything I've done... everything I've been... everything I've lost?

The cab driver realized after five minutes of attempted conversation that I wasn't in the mood to talk, and let me sit in silence for the journey back to Boston. I cried for some of the time, but he didn't seem to notice, or if he did, he didn't say anything, and once I'd paid him, he drove away, presumably keen to get home again.

I can't say I blame him.

I'm not great company.

I dump my bag in the living room and flop onto the couch, pulling my phone from my purse. It's gone six, the sun is up, and although I'd rather put this off a little longer, I know I have to make the call.

"Josie?" Hunter sounds sleepy, but that's not surprising, really. "Has something happened?"

"Yes, in a way."

He yawns. "Do you need me to come over?"

"No. I'm not at the cottage."

"Where are you?" he says, suddenly sounding more awake.

"I'm in Boston."

"What the fu…" He stops talking. "Sorry. I mean, what's going on? How did you get to Boston, for Christ's sake?"

"I called a cab."

"In the middle of the night?"

"Yeah."

"But how did they get in through the gates?"

"They didn't. I waited outside."

"You did what?"

"I waited outside. Sorry, Hunter. I couldn't stay anymore."

"Why not? Did Drew do something?"

"No. At least, nothing I didn't want him to do."

There's a moment's silence and then he says, "Oh. I see."

"I don't think you do." I don't see how he can. "Either way, I couldn't stay. I'm sorry. I know this is gonna be difficult for you, and it's not very professional of me, but I'm sure if you contact Doctor Sweeney, he'll be able to suggest another nurse who can look after Drew."

"You think he'll be happy with another nurse?"

"In the long run, once he knows the truth, I think he might be."

"You're not making any sense, Josie."

"I know, but I can't explain it. I'm sorry. Just look after him for me…" A tear hits my cheek and I let out a sob, hanging up the call so he won't hear my heart breaking.

Drew

The smile is on my lips before my eyes are even open, the memory of last night, and of yesterday, too fresh for anything other than smiles and lasting happiness.

It's not just about memories, though. Not anymore. It's about a future I've sometimes doubted I could have… and it's lying right beside me.

I turn over. "Good morn—"

The bed is empty, and I sit up, looking around the room. The sun, peeping between the edges of the drapes, gives me enough light to see the top Josie was wearing yesterday evening is still lying over the end of the bed, where it landed after I eventually pulled it off of her. I lean over the edge and see her shorts on the floor beside my own.

She must be here somewhere.

"Josie?" I climb out of bed and wander to the door, pulling it open. The house feels eerily hushed. I can't hear her downstairs, and I step across the hall.

Josie's door is ajar and I push it open and go inside.

"Are you in here?" There's no reply. The room is empty.

With a rising sense of panic, I go back out into the hall and run down the stairs, checking the living room and kitchen, and even looking out onto the terrace.

She's nowhere to be seen.

"Josie?" My shout is met with silence and I stand for a moment, pushing my fingers back through my hair. Where can she be?

Surely, if Hunter had asked to see her, like he did the other day, she'd have woken me and told me… wouldn't she? And why on earth would he have asked to see her so early in the morning? What could have been so important he'd have had to drag her out of bed? It's not even seven yet

Unless he didn't ask to see her at all…

I run back up the stairs, stopping at the top, and slowly turn to my left, going into her room again. My feet lead me over to her closet and, with a shaking hand, I pull it open.

"No!" My voice echoes around the empty room.

There's nothing here.

She's gone.

My legs feel weak and the room spins, but I grab the closet door, holding on, as I take a few deep breaths.

This can't be happening.

Why would she leave?

After everything we said and did yesterday, why would she leave?

I don't know. I can't think, and standing here won't help. The answers aren't in the back of her closet, or anywhere else in this house. They're wherever Josie is.

I need to find her. Now.

I steady myself, turning slowly and, once I'm sure I'm in control, I walk back to my room, taking care to make sure I don't fall, even though my legs still don't feel very stable. Inside, I go straight to my dressing room, grabbing some jeans and a t-shirt, which I pull on, along with some shoes.

I might not understand what's going on here. I may not have any answers, but if I'm going to find them – or to find Josie – I need help. This isn't something I can do alone, and I only know one person who I can turn to, even if I don't feel like I 'know' him at all.

As I leave the house and make my way along the path, I wonder if I should go to the front door or make my way around the back. An image flits across my brain and I stop in my tracks, trying to grab hold of it, to stop it from passing through unnoticed. I have a vague memory of making this walk before. The circumstances elude me, but I know this isn't the first time I've trodden this path. I'm not thinking about when I came over to the pool with Josie, either. In my mind's eye, I'm alone.

I wish I had time to focus… to see what else I can recall. But I don't. And besides, forcing memories hasn't worked very well for me in the past.

I continue on my way, following the path to the rear of the house and going around by the pool to the glass doors that lead to the kitchen.

"Kitchen?" I mutter the word out loud, a slight shiver running through me as I tap on the glass, looking through and seeing that – just as I'd expected – the room on the other side is an enormous kitchen. How did I know this would be here? I've never been to the house before. Not knowingly.

Maybe it's an instinct, rather than a memory.

And yet, it feels like more than that.

The door opens, startling me, and I look up into the face of the man everyone says is my older brother. He's dressed in jeans and a button-down shirt, his hair damp at the ends, and he frowns down at me.

"What are you doing here? I was just coming to see you."

"What about?" Hunter hasn't been near the cottage, or me, since my fall the other day. Why would he choose today of all days for a visit? And at this time of the morning?

"Josie."

"That's why I'm here. She's gone." I step closer, my foot on the threshold, my anger rising. "Do you know something about that? Have you fired her?" I can't see why he would have done, but I can't think of another reason she would have left.

"Of course not." He steps back. "Come inside. We can talk more easily."

I hesitate for a moment. That's not because I have no memory of this man who claims to be my brother, but because I'd rather be looking for Josie. Even so, I'm aware of the fact that I can't hope to find her without him, so I step into the house.

The room is not only enormous, but it's stylishly furnished, with white cabinets and pale gray countertops, none of which are familiar to me. There's an island unit, with four wicker chairs tucked underneath it, and Hunter pulls one out.

"Have a seat. I'll fix us some coffee."

I do as he says, my legs still a little unstable, and I watch as he makes us both a cup of coffee, bringing them over. He stands on the other side of the island unit, looking at me, a puzzled expression on his face.

"What's wrong?"

"Nothing. It's just odd to see you sitting there again."

"I don't remember sitting here before."

"No." He takes a sip of coffee.

"You said you were coming to see me about Josie?"

"Yeah. She's gone."

"I know that. Where is she?"

"She's in Boston."

I grab the edge of the countertop, steadying myself. "Boston? How do you know this?"

"Because she called me early this morning to tell me she'd gone home."

"She was already there?"

"Yes."

"She didn't call to tell you she was leaving?"

"No. If she had, I'd have tried to stop her." He purses his lips and then says, "Has something happened between the two of you?"

I stare up at him. "You mean like a fight?"

He shakes his head. "No... I mean, like sex."

How does he know? "Why do you ask?"

"Because of what Josie said when I asked if she was leaving so suddenly because of something you'd done."

"What the hell did you think I would have done?" I say, raising my voice a little. "You know me, even if I don't. What kind of guy do you think I am?"

He shakes his head. "I didn't mean it like that. I wasn't accusing you of anything. It just felt strange, when she's been so concerned for you, that she'd walk away like this."

"No shit..." I shake my head. "So? What did she say?"

"She said you hadn't done anything she didn't want you to. It implied..."

"I know what it implied."

"And? Did you sleep with her?"

"Yes. But, like she said, she wanted me to."

He tilts his head to one side, narrowing his eyes. "This matters, doesn't it?"

"She matters, yes."

His eyes widen, although I'm not sure what that means, any more than the slight shake of his head. "She suggested I should contact Doctor Sweeney at the hospital to get a replacement nurse, but when I said I didn't think you'd want that, she said she thought you would, once you knew the truth. What was that about?"

"I don't know. Did she say anything else?"

"Not really. She was crying when she hung up, though. I could hear her. I don't think she wanted to leave, and she asked me… no, she practically begged me to look after you."

"I don't need looking after. I just need her," I say, struggling to control the emotion in my voice. Hunter leans over, resting his elbows on the countertop.

"Do you want me to take you to her apartment?"

"Yes. I need to talk to her. I have to know why she's done this, and what I have to do to get her to come back to me."

"Okay."

I get up, making for the front of the house, but he calls me back. "Not so fast. You need to go shower first. You look like a wreck."

"You think I care?"

"You will when you see her again. We know where she lives. She won't have disappeared by the time we get there. Just go back to the cottage and smarten yourself up." He smiles. "You could consider taming that beard a little, too."

I rub my hand over my chin. "I would, if I had anything to tame it with. So far, I've only found a razor and some shaving cream, so I'm guessing I was clean-shaven before the accident?"

He doesn't confirm or deny, but just chuckles, rubbing his hand over his own stubbled jaw. "I'll get you a beard trimmer. Then you can decide how far you wanna go with your facial hair, but in the meantime, go shower. I'll let Livia know what's going on, and I'll bring your car around front."

"I have a car?"

"Yeah. It's the Range Rover I drove you here in the other day." I nod my head. "Do you remember it?" he asks.

"From the other day? Yes. From before? No."

He shrugs. "Don't worry about it."

"I'm not going to. I've got more important things on my mind."

Like getting to Josie and asking her what I did to make her leave.

I've showered and put on a shirt, rather than the t-shirt I had on before. Hunter seemed to think appearances mattered, although personally, I think standing in front of Josie, asking her the pressing question of 'why', is more important.

It hasn't taken me long, and less than fifteen minutes after leaving him in the kitchen of the main house, I open the cottage door to find Hunter standing there, waiting.

"I thought I'd walk with you to the car," he says, falling into step beside me.

"In case I couldn't remember the way?"

He smiles, but doesn't reply, and we walk together to the front of the house, where he's parked a black Range Rover. This may be my car, but there's nothing familiar about it, even when I open the passenger door and climb in.

"Are you getting anything?" Hunter asks as I look around the interior.

"No."

"Well, I'm not sure you ever sat in that seat, so I guess that's not surprising."

He has a point, but I don't want to waste time trying out the driver's position, just to see if it brings back any memories.

It seems to take forever to get down the long driveway, but when we finally reach the end, the gates open automatically, and I remember him saying something about sensors, and a button on the wall, which I guess is how Josie got out of here this morning. Having checked for traffic, he turns right onto a fairly quiet highway.

"How long will it take to get to Boston?" I ask him.

"At this time of day, with this little traffic, probably around an hour and fifteen minutes."

I nod my head, wishing it could be faster. My life feels disjointed enough as it is without losing Josie.

Losing Josie?

That can't happen. I can't even think about letting it happen. I need to think about something else.

Anything…

I turn in my seat, so I'm facing Hunter. "You know, earlier in your kitchen, when I asked what kind of guy you think I am? Can you tell me?"

"Tell you what?"

"What am I like, or what was I like before… with women?"

"You know I'm not allowed to answer questions like that."

"Okay, but I'm in love with Josie. Was that something I did all the time?"

He sucks in a breath, and I notice him gripping the steering wheel a little tighter. "No, you didn't."

I don't understand his reaction, but I'm relieved by his answer. Josie feels special. She feels different. It's good to know I got that right, at least.

"Would I have told you if I did? Were we the kind of brothers who talked about things like that?"

"Yes," he says, smiling now. "Didn't you notice just then, how easy it was to tell me you're in love with her?"

"Yeah… I guess." I hadn't noticed, but now he's mentioned it, I didn't even hesitate before telling him how I feel.

"Does that mean I've discussed my relationships with you before?"

"No."

I'm confused now. "But I thought you just said…"

"You didn't have any relationships to discuss," he says, his smile widening.

"I didn't?"

"No."

"But… but I've had sex, right? Before yesterday, I mean…"

"Yeah," he says, making it sound like that's a foregone conclusion.

"That's a relief."

"Why?" His brow furrows.

"Because I knew what to do… with Josie."

"It wasn't a memory?"

"No, it was an instinct, but it's good to know it comes from somewhere."

He grips the steering wheel again. "Do you have any idea why she might have left?"

"No. I mean, we had a kind of fight yesterday evening."

"A kind of fight?" he says.

"Yeah."

"What about? Or was it personal… something you can't tell me?"

"It wasn't personal, no. Not in the way you mean. We were talking about photography."

"Oh?" He flips his head around.

"Yeah. I think I might have been a photographer. Josie wouldn't confirm it, but I feel at home with a camera in my hand, and it's another instinct… like I know what I'm doing, and how to do it."

"I see." He doesn't say anything else and I get the feeling he's not about to give me any more clues, either. "Why were you fighting about that?"

"We weren't. Josie mentioned that the only photographs she'd ever taken were on her phone, and I asked if I had one."

"A phone?" he says.

"Yeah."

He nods his head. "I've got it."

"I know. At least, I know now. Josie told me. She said I couldn't have it back yet… not until I've recovered a bit more."

"I agree with her," he says. "After the way you reacted to looking at photographs the other day, I think she made the right call."

"I know. I can understand that now, but at the time, I got a little frustrated."

He looks over at me, just briefly. "What did you do?"

"Nothing. It was difficult, though. I thought having my phone back might prompt some fresh memories, but Josie argued it could be too much for me. She said I was trying to force my progress instead of letting it happen naturally. And she was right."

"She cares about you."

"I know. I knew it before, but it hit home when I realized how upset she was. That was when I stopped arguing with her. It wasn't worth hurting her."

"So, you made up?" he asks.

"Yes. Like I say, we didn't even argue. Not really. And I know she was okay about it afterwards."

"How? Did she tell you?"

"She didn't need to. She came to bed with me."

He nods his head, unfazed by my confession. "Okay. It must be something else, then."

"I know. But the question is, what?"

"Well… we know she cares, but does caring translate into love? Just because you're in love with her doesn't mean she feels the same way. Maybe it was all too much for her."

"I can't believe that. She told me she loves me too. She said the weirdest thing to me... she said she's always loved me, and although I know I only met her a few days ago, and that shouldn't make sense, it does to me. I feel exactly the same. I told her that last night... that she's always been in my heart. It's like she belongs there." I cough, swallowing down the lump in my throat, trying not to think about last night... about how it felt to wake in the darkness with such a burning desire for her, it could only be quenched by taking her, there and then. Was that too much? "Oh, God..."

"What?"

What if I went too far? But no, that can't be. She enjoyed it. She told me afterwards.

"It's nothing," I say. "It's okay."

"What is?"

"It was just something I did last night. I wasn't sure for a moment if I'd gone too far with her... but I just remembered how happy she was afterwards. We talked about having kids..."

"Jesus... what did you do? Propose to her?"

"No." *I woke her up and fucked her senseless, if you must know.* But she liked it. She liked how wanted it made her feel. I remember her saying that.

"But you had the children talk?" he says, sounding a little shocked.

"Is that a problem?" I ask.

"I don't know, but Livia and I didn't discuss having kids – at least not properly – until just a couple of months before we got married."

"You didn't?"

"No."

"What did you say? Maybe I got it wrong?"

He shrugs. "I didn't really say anything. It was just something that came up."

"Do you think Josie felt rushed? I told her that wasn't my intention, but I only met her a few days ago. I made love to her for the first time yesterday morning and started talking about having kids together in the middle of last night." When I put it like that, it sounds like the definition of 'rushed'.

He shakes his head. "She might have thought things were going a little too fast. But I guess there's only one way to find out… and that's to ask her."

It doesn't take much longer to drive through the city and park in the quiet street outside Josie's apartment. I'm a little nervous now, but I'm still desperate to see her, to talk to her, and I get out of the car, following Hunter up the steps and onto the balcony.

I feel dizzy again, but this time it's got nothing to do with my concussion, or the stairs. This time it's because I'm scared.

Hunter takes charge, leading the way to her front door, where he pauses, looking at me.

"Ready?"

I nod my head, and he knocks. We both wait and after a few seconds, the door opens. Josie's eyes dart from him to me, and although I have a moment to take in her red-rimmed eyes and tear-streaked cheeks, it's only a moment, before she raises her hand to her mouth and pushes the door closed.

Fortunately, my reactions are fairly quick, and I hold up my hand, resting it against the door, just before it shuts tight, pushing back against it and stepping over the threshold.

"I told you not to shut your door on me," I whisper and she looks up, blinking back more tears.

"Why are you here?"

"Because I need to know why, Josie. I need to understand why you left me."

"Don't say it like that."

"Like what?"

"Don't say I left you."

"Why not? It's what you did. You packed your bags and ran out in the middle of the night without a word. I need to know what I did wrong."

"You didn't do anything wrong," she says.

"Then explain to me why I woke up to an empty bed this morning."

She stares at me for what feels like a lifetime and then her shoulders drop, like she's admitting defeat. "You'd better come in." She steps back, opening the door wide.

"Would you prefer if I waited in the car?" Hunter says, and she looks up at him.

"No. I think I'd like you to stay."

Personally, I'd rather he left. I have a feeling this conversation could get intimate, and while I seem quite comfortable around my brother, I'm not sure I'm all that comfortable. Still, if Josie wants him here, I'm not going to argue.

We step inside and wait while she closes the door.

Initially, I wonder if she's going to invite us to sit on her pale gray couch, but she doesn't. She just stands in front of me and puts her hands in her pockets. Hunter steps back, leaning against the door, leaving the two of us facing each other.

"I'm sorry," I say before Josie can even open her mouth.

She frowns, shaking her head. "Why are you sorry?"

"I don't know. But I must have done something to make you leave, and whatever it was, I'm sorry."

"I—I told you, you didn't do anything wrong."

"Then why did you run? I told you yesterday, you've gotta stop doing that."

"This is different."

"How? Explain it to me."

She sucks in a breath, pulling one hand from her pocket and pushing her fingers back through her hair. She musses it up and

I reach out, pushing a stray strand from her face. Her eyes fix on mine, brimming with unshed tears.

"What is it, Josie? Tell me."

"Y—You said you wanted us to have children," she whispers.

"Yes. One day. Not right away. I said, there's no rush. You didn't have to…" My brain suddenly switches a gear and I grab her shoulders, holding on to her, grounding myself. "I—I've just realized something."

"What's that?"

"I don't know how many times we've made love, but I haven't used a condom, have I? Not once." I let my head rock back, staring at the ceiling for a moment, before I look back at her. She's wide-eyed, but I can't believe this is news to her. "How could I have done that to you? I mean, what the hell is wrong with me? I'm so sorry, Josie." I turn to Hunter. "Don't give me any bullshit. I need to know I haven't put Josie in danger."

"How the hell am I supposed to tell you that?"

"By answering a straight question for once."

"What question would that be?"

"Did I used to sleep around?"

Hunter stares at me for a moment and then looks at Josie, just briefly, before returning his gaze to me. "You hadn't slept with anyone for over a year before the accident."

"You're sure?"

"Positive."

"And do I have regular medicals?"

"You do."

"When was the last one?"

He thinks for a moment. "It would have been late June or early July, I think, but I'm sure we can find out."

"We don't need to… as long as it was recent and everything was okay." He nods his head, and I turn back to Josie. "That's one weight off of my mind. But I still can't believe I allowed this to happen. Or that I had a conversation with you about having children, and didn't realize the consequences of what I'd already done."

"Will you stop panicking?" she says. "There are no consequences."

"You… you mean you're on birth control?"

"No."

"Then I don't understand."

"I can't have children, Drew."

Her words seem to echo around my head. "You can't?"

"No."

"How do you know?" I ask, and she steps away, turning and looking toward the window.

"It's not something I talk about very often," she says, her voice little more than a whisper. "But when I was thirteen, I got sick."

A shiver runs down my spine. "How sick?"

"Very. It started with headaches. They were pretty fierce, but for a while everyone assumed it was because my periods had just started and my hormones were all over the place. After a few months, though, they got worse and my mom took me to see a doctor. I had some tests and a scan, and they found I had a brain tumor."

"Oh, my God." I reach out and pull her into my arms, holding her close. She doesn't object, although she doesn't hug me back either. I don't care. The urge to protect her is overwhelming… even if it is ten years too late. After a few minutes, I lean back, although I still keep a hold of her. "What happened?"

"They operated to remove the tumor."

"So, when you said you spent some time in hospital as a child…"

"Yeah. It was being in the neuro rehab unit for so long that made me decide to become a nurse. I didn't anticipate going into neurotrauma, but now I have, I love it."

"I know you do. But what I don't understand is why something that happened over ten years ago means you can't have children."

She tilts her head just slightly, gazing into my eyes. "Because of the chemo." Her answer seems obvious to her, but it's only just adding up to me. "It left me infertile."

That's such a big word, and it stretches between us, hovering, threatening, like the doubt in her eyes.

"Aside from that, you're okay now, though… right? The tumor's gone. It's not gonna come back?"

"No. I'm fine now."

"Then why did you leave?"

She frowns. "I've just explained."

"No. You've just told me you were really sick when you were a teenager. You haven't told me why that's a reason to run away from me in the middle of the night."

She breaks free of me, and I let her, watching as she steps back, my hands falling to my sides. "Because you want something I can't give you, and I won't ruin your life."

"Ruin my life?"

"Yes. I can't take this from you."

"You think having children is more important to me than being with you?" She looks up at me, blinking, and I pull her back into my arms again, cupping her face with one hand while the other rests in the small of her back, holding her against me. "The only way you could ruin my life would be to let this stand in the way of our happiness."

"But…"

"But nothing. If we can't have children, then we can't have children."

"Y—You said 'we'," she whispers.

"Yeah. Because we're in this together."

She shakes her head. "No. That's not right."

"Why not?"

"Because you can have children."

"You don't know that. Not for sure." She glances at Hunter and then looks back at me. "And even if I could have children, I wouldn't want them with anyone but you."

She bursts into tears, loud sobs building somewhere deep inside her, rising to escape her lips.

"I'll wait in the car," Hunter says, opening the door and slipping out through it.

I hold Josie's head against my chest, stroking her hair as she weeps and weeps.

"Hey… baby…" She looks up, tears still flowing, and I smile down at her. "Don't cry. Please. It'll be okay. I love you. I can't lose you."

"But what if you change your mind?"

"About loving you? It's more likely that hell will freeze over."

"I meant, what if you change your mind about having children?"

"It still won't change how I feel about you."

"You really mean that?"

"Yes. If we decide we want to have children in the future, we'll find a way."

"There is no medical way for me to make that dream come true."

"I know. I get that. But there are other options. I just wish you'd told me, rather than running away."

"You know I'm not allowed to tell you anything."

I lean back, looking down at her. "But this is about you, not about me. Surely the rules don't apply."

A pop of red flushes on her cheeks. "N—No, they don't."

"Okay… so next time, talk to me."

"Next time? Y—You want me to come back with you?"

"Of course I do. You're my family." I pull her closer, moving my hand behind her head and I dust my lips across hers, swallowing her whimper as I deepen the kiss.

Chapter Eleven

Josie

I think Drew was tempted to take me to bed after that kiss. If he'd suggested it, I wouldn't have said 'no'. If he'd asked the way to my bedroom, I'd have told him.

I felt guilty for all the misery I'd caused, and I wanted to make it up to him. But it was more than that. I wanted to prove to myself that what we have means more than all the secrets and lies that seem to be the foundation of our relationship. Except all I've done is add to the lies.

He asked me why I hadn't told him my secret, and all I could say was that I wasn't allowed to. I couldn't think of another excuse, although we both knew that wasn't true. Even as he was asking me to come clean with him 'next time', I was thinking that I might not be able to… not if telling him meant revealing parts of his life he's not supposed to know about. But what could I say? How could I explain without revealing our past connection? It had been hard enough telling him my story while keeping Lexi and Maisie out of it.

I'd wondered, just briefly, if things would come to a natural head when Drew said he might not be able to have children himself. Naturally, I knew that wasn't true, and I glanced over at Hunter to see how he reacted, hoping he might say something… perhaps decide to enlighten Drew about his daughter. He looked a little pained, but didn't say a word. I guess because he's taking his lead from me, and not the other way around. Before I could decide what to do for the best, though, Drew carried on talking, saying he only wanted to have children with me. How was I supposed to answer that? How could I tell him that, even though I might be infertile, he already has a daughter? And that her mother was my sister?

The problem is, not telling him feels like I'm just making things worse, because I'm denying him something I now know he wants… and already has.

Telling him would be selfish, though. I'd be doing it for myself, because I'm uncomfortable with the lies, not because it's in Drew's best interests.

I worked that out before Drew even broke the kiss, which he did eventually, staring down into my eyes.

"Where are your things?"

"In my bag. I haven't unpacked yet."

"Good. We can go now, then."

"You're sure this is what you want?"

"Yes."

He went to pull away, but I grabbed his hand, pulling him back. "I mean it, Drew. You need to be absolutely certain. I couldn't bear it if I came back with you and it all went wrong."

He cupped my face in his hands. "Were you listening to me at all last night?"

"Yes."

"Then you'll have heard me say you're everything I want… everything I need."

"I did. But that was before you knew that having children with me won't be possible."

"It makes no difference. I love you because you're you. Not because you can carry a child."

"That's good. Because I can't."

"I know... and I'm sorry."

I blinked back my tears. "So am I. It's never really bothered me before, but for the first time, I'm truly sorry I can't have children."

He kissed my lips. "This doesn't define you, Josie. It doesn't alter who you are."

He put his arms around me and I rested against him, letting his strength seep into me. He didn't suggest we go to bed, or ask the way to my bedroom, but after a while, he leaned back, a smile etched on his lips.

"Shall we go?"

"Okay."

He carried my bag out to the car where we found Hunter waiting for us, as promised. We climbed into the back and sat, side by side on the journey to Newport. Hunter didn't say a word, and Drew spent most of the time just staring at me, like he was scared if he took his eyes from me, I'd disappear.

My thoughts were all over the place. That mixture of fear and worry about the lies was ever-present, but there was something else.

It was hope.

That wasn't just because of the things he'd said about us and our future.

It was more than that.

I remembered about five minutes into our journey that Drew had forced an admission out of Hunter that he hadn't slept with anyone for over a year before the accident. He wanted to know because he was worried he might have put me in danger by not using a condom. That thought had never occurred to me, although I don't know why. It ought to have done. But I guess I had other things on my mind. I'd waited for Hunter's answer with bated breath, knowing that, while it wouldn't change how I feel about Drew, it might make things difficult for both of us when he finally remembers his past. He'd sent me a message before the accident, saying he wanted to see me again, but I didn't know why, or what about. I had no idea what he'd been doing while Lexi was pregnant and during those early months of Maisie's life, but it seemed unreasonable to hope that our meeting had meant as much to him as it had to me. It seemed unfair to hope he'd have missed me, like I'd missed him... until Hunter said there had been no-one else.

Could it be?

Could it be that he'd been waiting?

Waiting and hoping that maybe our time would come?

I didn't want to get my hopes up, but it was impossible not to dream.

When we got back, we left Hunter by the car, Drew thanking him for his help. I felt embarrassed and didn't say a word. I just let Drew lead me back to the cottage.

Once inside, he dumped my bag and captured my lips with his.

"Don't ever do that to me again. Okay?" he growled, and I nodded.

And that was when he took me to bed.

I don't feel like Drew's nurse anymore. I might have enjoyed that role, but I much prefer being Drew's lover.

We've spent the last five days, since he brought me back here, just being together. We haven't left the house... in fact, we've barely left his bedroom, except when someone knocked on the door the day before yesterday. Drew went to answer it, and came back up to the bedroom, smiling, a package in his hand.

"What's that?" I asked as he opened it.

"Hunter left it on the doorstep. It's his way of telling me to smarten up my facial hair."

He pulled out a box, containing a beard trimmer, and we both laughed. I watched him shave, getting his stubble to the length he wanted, pointing out the bits he'd missed, and when he was finished, he kissed me.

"It's not too rough against your skin, is it?" he asked, gazing down at me.

"No."

He smiled then and kissed his way down my body…

When we're not making love, or snatching moments of sleep, wrapped up together, we simply stare at each other, like neither of us can believe this is really happening. I know I can't. I spent too many months living without him, knowing he had to put his daughter first, believing we'd never get the chance to be together. Now we are, it feels like a spell has been cast over us, and even though we're bound by it, I'm aware it's a spell that could break so easily.

I want to make the most of it, just in case this is all we ever have.

Just in case he can't forgive me once he knows everything.

I'm lying across the bed, my head on Drew's stomach, his fingers playing gently over the side of my breast. We showered and ate breakfast a while ago, before coming back to bed, but I've lost track of time.

"We really should go out, you know?" I say.

"Why?"

I turn over onto my front, resting my chin against him, and I smile up into his perfect face. "Because you need some exercise."

He smiles. "Sex counts as exercise, doesn't it?"

I feel like it should, after the last five days. My muscles certainly feel as though they've been pushed to their limits. "Probably. But we need some fresh air, too."

"Okay… if you insist."

I kneel up. "Come on, then."

He reaches out, tweaking my nipple between his forefinger and thumb. "I can't tempt you to a little indoor exercise before we go?"

"We can do that when we get back."

"Okay. I'll hold you to that."

"Good."

He grins and gets out of bed, offering me his hand. I crawl over and take it, getting to my feet and he pulls me into his arms, our bodies fused, his erection pressing into me.

"I love you, Josie. You know that, don't you?"

"Yes." I couldn't doubt it. He tells me all the time. "And I love you."

He smiles, his eyes roaming over my face in that way they sometimes do, like they did after the first time we made love… like I'm new to him, even though I'm not.

It's a strange sensation, being studied in this way and sometimes, when he does it, I wonder if he's trying to remember.

Except he has no idea I'm a memory.

Not like he is to me.

When we came back the other day, after we'd made love, Drew went downstairs and fetched my bag, bringing it back up. He took it into his dressing room and made space for my things… a sign, perhaps, that he wanted me to stay. I haven't used the guest bedroom since, and we both like it that way; sharing our space, along with everything else.

I fetch us both some clothes, bringing them back, and sit on the bed, watching him dress, while I pull on jeans and a t-shirt, neither of us bothering with underwear, although after I've dragged my t-shirt over my head, I look up at him and smile.

"Do you think I need to wear a bra?"

He studies me, taking far longer than necessary. "That depends."

"On what?"

"On whether you want this to be a long walk, or a really short one. If you don't put a bra on, I swear to God, I'm gonna drag you back here within five minutes, and rip your clothes off."

"And if I do?"

"I might last thirty minutes…" He tilts his head one way and then the other. "Maybe twenty…"

"You're incorrigible, you know that?"

"Yeah… but you love me."

"I do." I stand, pulling off my t-shirt again as I walk back into the dressing room. "And I'm gonna find a bra."

I open the drawer where I put my underwear, pulling out a white lace bra, which I put on, along with my t-shirt, and go back out to find Drew sitting on the bed, fully clothed, his shoes already on his feet.

"You're keen," I say.

"I know, but the sooner we go, the sooner we can get back." He stands, coming over, and pulls me into his arms. "You're so sexy… you know that?"

I rest my hands on his chest, feeling his muscles flex. "You're the sexy one."

He groans, grinding his hips into mine. "If we don't go now, we're never gonna make it."

I chuckle and take his hand, leading him down the stairs.

Outside, it's warm enough, despite the slight breeze that keeps catching my hair, and I wish now I'd taken the time to put it up. Drew walks beside me across the grass, taking my hand and looking down at me, a smile twitching at his lips.

"Are you okay?" I ask.

"Yes. Sorry for staring… it's just my short-term memory still has a habit of developing holes, and I know I won't remember every look, or word, or sound. I want to do my best to imprint as many of them as I can onto my brain."

I rest my head on his shoulder. "That's a lovely thing to say."

He kisses the top of my head and we both breathe in a deep breath at the same time, letting it out slowly.

We're walking toward the main house, but from where we are, we can see the pool, my eyes caught by the opening of the glass doors, and the arrival outside of Livia and Maisie, and Ella and her baby boy. They're talking, unaware of our presence, and they sit on loungers, holding the babies, deep in conversation.

"That dark-haired woman seems to spend a lot of time here," Drew says and I realize he's noticed them, too.

"Yes." I can't tell him that's because she lives here… because she's his sister.

"I guess that makes sense if she's a friend of Livia's."

"You remember Livia?" I say, turning to face him.

"No. But I remember Hunter telling me his wife's called Livia, and that she's blonde. I'm just putting two and two together." He shakes his head. "You'd think I'd remember things like that… things like my brother having a baby, wouldn't you? But there's nothing there… not even the baby's name."

"It's Maisie." I blink back my tears, realizing I probably shouldn't have told him that. I let my emotions get the better of common sense and professionalism, and now they're about to overwhelm me.

"Oh, God, Josie. I'm sorry." He stops walking, pulling me into a hug.

"What for?"

"That was really insensitive of me. It must be hard enough for you, being here and seeing other people's babies, without me talking about it as well."

"It's okay." It isn't, but how can I explain?

"No, it's not." He turns us both around so my back is to the house. I guess he wants to protect me from having to see the baby he thinks is his brother's... the one he thinks is upsetting me, when the reality is, I'm upset because she's his, and he doesn't know it. "Why don't we go away?"

"On vacation, you mean?"

"No. For good. I can hardly expect my brother to leave, but I can see how hard this is for you."

I pull away from him, shaking my head. "No, Drew... no."

"But..."

"No!"

I turn and run, but I've only gone a few paces when I feel him tug at my arm, pulling me back and turning me around to face him.

"Stop it. Stop running, for Christ's sake."

"I hate conflict. I always have. Can't you see that? Don't you get it?"

"This isn't a conflict, Josie. I just want what's best for you."

"And you think that's leaving here?"

"Yes," he says.

"But this is your home."

"Yeah. A home of which I have almost no memory."

Did I hear that right? "What do you mean 'almost'?"

He shakes his head, like he's confused. "Don't change the subject."

"I'm not."

"Yes, you are."

"I'm really not. I just need you to tell me why you said 'almost' just now. Have you remembered something? Tell me, Drew. It's important."

Especially now. If his memory is coming back, it could change everything.

He sighs. "Okay. But I don't know if it meant anything."

"What happened?"

"It was just, the other day, when you left, I went over to the main house to find Hunter. I needed his help, and as I was walking there, I got the feeling I'd made that journey before."

"You had. With me, when we went swimming."

He shakes his head. "No. This was different. And it was more than that. When I got there, I knew straight away that the glass doors led to the kitchen."

"Like you'd gone into the house that way before?"

"I don't know. It didn't feel like a memory, if that's what you're asking, and I'm not reading too much into it. I just knew that's where the kitchen was, although when I got inside, there was nothing familiar about the room."

"This is exactly why you have to stay, Drew. It might not feel like a memory to you, but it's a fragment of one. It's a start, and being here will help you remember the rest."

"I don't care about that."

"Then you should." *More than you know.*

He moves closer, holding me. "I told you the other day, before you left, if I have to give up my past to keep you, then I'll do it."

"No. You can't do that."

"I'll do anything for you."

We're both breathing hard, staring at each other, and I know now, beyond any doubt, that it's vital he remembers… and remembers soon. He needs to know Maisie is his daughter and that abandoning her, even for me, is out of the question.

I might want to keep him in this perfect little bubble of ours, hiding away in the cottage and pretending the rest of the world doesn't exist, but how can I? How can I deny him his one chance at fatherhood?

I have to do whatever it takes to help him…

He cups my face with his hands. "Love is about making sacrifices, isn't it?"

"I don't know. I've never been in love before. But even if it is, I don't think it's about sacrificing your life."

"I've never been in love before either, but I wouldn't consider myself as having sacrificed my life, as long as I can be with you."

My brain feels like thick molasses, and is working just as slowly. "Wait a second. Did you just say you've never been in love before?"

"Yes, I did."

"But how do you know that? Is this another memory you haven't told me about? Because I'm still your nurse, you know, even if it doesn't feel like it most of the time."

"I know. And it's not a memory. It's something Hunter told me."

Is he serious? "When was this?"

"The other day, when we were driving into the city to find you. I asked him to tell me what I was like before."

"In what way?"

He sighs, pursing his lips. "With women. You'd left me. I couldn't work out why. I guess I was looking for clues."

"In your past?"

"Yes. I don't have anything to go on."

"What did he tell you?" I ask.

"Not very much. He refused to answer me. So I told him I'm in love with you and asked if that was something I did all the time."

"I—I see. And he told you it wasn't?"

"Yeah, he did."

A thought suddenly occurs to me, and I lean back slightly in his arms. "How do you know he's right? I mean... I know he said the other day that you hadn't slept with anyone for over a year before the accident, but how would he have known? Did you used to talk to him about things like that?"

I might have had a sister until a short while ago, but we rarely talked about relationships. That evening when she told me about Manuel was a first for us.

Drew chuckles, and I frown at him. "I asked him the same question," he says.

"And how did he reply?"

"He said we used to talk… a lot."

"About relationships? Because talking a lot could have meant you discussed cars, or sport, or food… or anything."

"No. I specifically asked him if I'd discussed my relationships with him."

"And he said you had?"

"No. He said I hadn't."

"Then why…"

"Let me finish. He said I hadn't, because there hadn't been any relationships to discuss. Evidently, I hadn't had any."

"None at all?"

"Well… I'm guessing he meant serious ones, worthy of discussion, but that was what he said."

I lick my bottom lip, only aware of the action when the breeze chills against its surface. "So you've never had a serious relationship?"

He drags his eyes up from my mouth to my eyes. "Not until now, no. He said I'd had sex, though." He winces slightly. "Sorry."

"Why? I think it's pretty obvious I wasn't your first."

"Was it obvious?" He frowns, and I realize how close I've come to making a mistake… to letting it slip that the evidence of his sexual history is sitting with his sister-in-law, beside the pool, behind me.

"Yes."

"How?"

"Because you knew what to do. You said it was an instinct, but it felt like more than that… like there was a wealth of experience behind everything you did."

That's not a lie, even if I am still hiding the truth.

"Wealth of experience?" He tilts his head to one side. "I'm not sure I like how that makes me sound."

"Does it matter? It's in the past now. It can't be changed."

"I know. Hell… I can't even remember it, so what chance do I have of changing it? But I think finding out I hadn't been in a relationship before made me wonder if I'd screwed up in some way… if I'd done something to make you run."

"Like what?"

"Like talking about having kids when we'd only been together for a few hours. When I told Hunter that, he asked if maybe I'd made you feel pressured."

"You told him what you'd said?"

"Yeah. Sorry. I know it was personal, but I needed his help."

"It's okay. You weren't to know the real reason I'd gone."

"No. At the time, he made me think I'd gone too far, too fast. He told me he and Livia hadn't discussed having children until just before they got married." He looks over my shoulder, presumably studying her and Maisie. "When was that, by the way? He didn't say."

"It was in February."

"This year?"

"Yes. He told me the other day, when he asked me over to the house…" I stop talking, realizing I'd been about to say 'when your mother was here'. What's wrong with me? I know I said my brain was moving as slow as molasses, but how could I have almost let that slip? He nods his head, his brow furrowing, and

I wonder how I'm going to explain myself. "I don't remember how we ended up talking about it…" That's another lie. I remember it perfectly. It was when Hunter asked how long it would take for Drew to get his memory back, because Livia was struggling with looking after Maisie. I can hardly say that either, though, can I?

"That doesn't make sense," he says.

"What doesn't? I just said, I can't even remember how…"

"No. You're missing the point. Hunter told me he and Livia only talked about having kids a few weeks before their wedding. You've just told me that was only six months ago. So how can they have a baby already? That's not possible. Even I know that."

My blood has frozen in my veins, my skin prickling with fear.

I've come so close to giving the game away in the last few minutes, but it seems Hunter is the one who's been careless, not me. The question is, what should I do? I can't lie. Not now. The lie would be too calculated. That means I have to tell him. But how will he react? Is he ready to hear it all? And am I ready for the bubble to burst?

"I—I…"

His eyes switch over my other shoulder, and his frown deepens. "Who's that?" he says and I turn, relieved I've been saved from having to answer… for now.

There's an enormous car driving toward the house, the sun gleaming off of the bright metal grille at the front. From here, neither of us can see who's inside, or even how many people there are, but I'm relieved to have the distraction… the momentary delay in having to explain who Maisie is. Ideally, I'd rather do that with Hunter present, so he can help me and maybe mitigate some of the fallout. Except, with this new arrival, it seems that might not be possible.

We watch as the car pulls to a stop at the front of the house, the door slowly opening, and I gasp as a man climbs out. Even from here, I know who he is, although it's been years since I last saw him.

"What's wrong?" Drew turns to me, his eyes betraying his concern as he moves closer to me. "Josie? You've gone as white as a sheet." I nod my head, although my voice won't work and Drew looks back at the man, who's now standing by the front door. "Do you know him?"

I nod my head again, knowing I don't need to worry about explaining who Maisie is anymore.

The bubble has already burst, and my entire world is about to come tumbling down.

Drew

What the hell is going on here?

I was confused enough before. I didn't think my brain could get any more disoriented. But it seems it could, because I honestly don't know which way is up right now.

I hadn't even begun to get my head around how Hunter could have a baby who was conceived before he and Livia even talked about having kids together. Josie didn't look too keen on explaining that to me, either. But I wasn't going to take 'no' for an answer. I was going to make her tell me… at least, I was, until that enormous car pulled onto the property. It had the look about it of someone who means business… if a car can have 'a look'.

There was something menacing about its shiny black angles and the way the sun glinted off of it, like it was trying to blind you to whoever was inside.

I decided I could wait a minute or so for Josie's explanation... until the guy inside the car climbed out and I heard her gasp, then saw the look on her face. Her skin paled to a grayish-white and her eyes were filled with fear, like nothing I've ever seen before.

She knows the guy and now nothing else matters to me, except the need to understand who he is, and why his presence here seems to scare her so much.

My brother opens the front door, and the two of them talk for a moment before Hunter steps outside, pulling the door closed. He didn't invite the guy in? I don't know my brother, but he doesn't strike me as inhospitable.

I look down at Josie. She's shaking, her body trembling beside me, and I pull her into my arms.

"What's going on, baby? Talk to me."

"I—I can't."

I lean back, looking into her tear-filled eyes. "Are you serious?"

"Please, Drew. Let's just go back to the cottage."

I'm about to say 'no', when I hear raised voices and turn back to the house. Hunter's waving his arm toward the gate, presumably telling the guy to leave, and the stranger is standing up to him, wagging a finger in his face. Any hope Josie had of persuading me back to the cottage just vaporized. I step away from her.

"I'm gonna see if Hunter needs any help with this."

"No!" She grabs me by the arm, pulling me back. "Hunter will be fine."

"How do you know that?" I shake my head at her. "Something's wrong here. It doesn't add up. You're scared of this guy, but you won't tell me who he is, and Hunter clearly wants him gone. Is he connected to me in some way?"

"Please, Drew… for my sake. Don't go."

I notice she didn't answer me and I stare down at her. "Tell me who he is, Josie."

"I—I can't."

"Then I'm gonna find out for myself."

I move away, but she runs around, standing in my path. "Don't… please, I'm begging you."

I shake my head. "I'm done with all this bullshit, Josie. The stories you and Hunter are telling me don't even add up anymore, and I wanna know the truth. I know you think you're protecting me, but you're not, and if you won't tell me what's happening here, maybe this guy will."

"No, he won't." I can hear the desperation in her voice, but I mean every word I say. Holding things back from me might have felt like a good idea to her and the doctor. I might even have agreed with it for a while, but it's not working anymore. There are too many nagging doubts; too many questions. I need answers, and I don't care where I get them from.

"Well… let's go ask, shall we?"

I dodge around her and stride toward the house, the sound of raised voices greeting me.

"You lied to my housekeeper to get onto my property," Hunter says. "And if you don't leave now, I'm gonna call the cops." He sounds mad. He looks it, too… but I focus on the other guy.

He's around six feet tall, with light brown hair peppered with gray. I'd say he's in his mid-fifties, wearing an expensive-looking suit and what appear to be handmade shoes. A man of business, by the looks of things, and for a moment, I wonder if this has nothing to do with me at all… whether it's related to Hunter and his job.

Except Josie knows him.

"I'm not going anywhere until I've seen her."

He wants to see Josie? What the hell for? And why is Hunter so riled up about it? If anyone should be defending my girlfriend, it's me.

"Can I help you?" I wade in, Hunter flipping around, the shocked expression on his face taking me by surprise. He glances over my shoulder, and I turn to see Josie just a few feet behind me. Despite her reluctance, she must have followed me, although the fear in her eyes has been amplified about a hundred times over.

The man turns, facing me, and then looks at Josie, tilting his head. There's no obvious sign of recognition, and I wonder for a second if Josie's made a mistake.

"This doesn't concern you, Drew," Hunter says. "This man is just leaving."

"Like hell I am." The guy turns back to Hunter. "I told you. I wanna see my granddaughter."

"Who's your granddaughter?" I ask, quickly working out the math in my head. It can't be Josie. That wouldn't add up. But who else can it be? And whoever his granddaughter is, why is she here? And what's the connection between this guy and my girlfriend? "Is she here?"

"Of course she's here." He gives me a withering look. "She's been here ever since she was kidnapped from the hospital after my daughter was killed in that accident."

This gets more confusing by the minute. His daughter was killed? And someone here kidnapped his granddaughter? That doesn't make sense. The people here might be unknown to me, but they've been kind. They're not kidnappers. I open my mouth to say so, just as Josie steps up, passing me and walking straight up to the stranger. The color is back in her cheeks and I barely have time to see the spark in her eyes before she turns and points a finger at him.

"What makes you think you have a right to see her?"

The man looks down at her, a smirk touching at his lips, like she's no more significant than a fly he'd swat away. "What's it got to do with you?"

"Answer the goddamn question? Why do you think you have a right to see her?"

"Because she's my flesh and blood," he says, raising his voice.

"You weren't too worried about that when you found out your daughter was pregnant, were you? You disowned her."

I glance at Hunter, to see he's looking as confused as I feel, and the stranger is just the same, frowning down at Josie.

"How do you know about that?"

She takes a deep, stuttering breath and looks over at me, tears filling her eyes. "I'm sorry, Drew," she says, puzzling me still further. "I'm so sorry." And then she turns back to the man. "You don't even recognize me, do you?"

He shrugs. "Why? Should I?"

"Yes. I lived with you…"

I step forward, and Josie stops talking, my movement grabbing her attention. "Wait a second. You lived with this guy?"

She nods her head. "Yes. But not in the way you think." What does that mean? I don't know what to think anymore. She blinks a few times, biting on her lip and then says, "This is my step-father."

The ground shifts and I feel myself stumble. Hunter moves closer and Josie reaches out, but I hold up my hands, halting them both. "Your step-father?"

"Yes. He married my mom when I was three years old."

For a split second, I feel the tug of a memory… a story, told to me by someone else, but I can't hold on to it, and I've got more important things to think about.

The man studies her again, frowning, his eyes narrowed. "You mean, you're Josie?"

"Yes," she says.

"What are you doing here?" He looks up at the house behind her.

"Good question," I say and they both turn to me. I'm captured by the sadness in Josie's eyes. It fractures my heart, splintering it into fragments that stab at me… painfully. She doesn't say a word to me, though, but turns back to her step-father.

"It's none of your business what I'm doing here."

"Oh? You don't think you owe me an explanation?"

"No. I owe other people explanations – and apologies – but I owe you nothing."

He opens his mouth, then closes it again, brushing his hand down his face.

"Fine. But these people don't have the right to keep my granddaughter here against my will."

"Yes, they do," Josie says, even as Hunter steps forward again. "They have every right to keep her here and to look after her. They're related to her."

"So am I," he thunders. Josie takes a half step back and on instinct, I move closer to her. I might not know who she is right now, but the need to protect her is still flowing through me as strongly as the blood through my veins.

"Then why didn't you ask after her at the hospital? Why did you disown her mom when she got pregnant? Why did you ignore her, instead of giving her the support she asked you for?" she says, her voice stronger and louder than I'd expected. "I'll tell you why… it's because you've always had to be the center of attention. Everything has to be about you. It was the same with my mom. When you married her, you expected her to make you the focus of her world. And she did it, because she thought you loved her as much as she loved you. She ignored the way you put her down, and the tantrums, and the bullying. She ignored all of it."

"Huh... so that's why she divorced me, is it?" he says, raising his chin.

"No. She divorced you because you had an affair when I was sick in the hospital. You resented me for taking her away from you, and you punished her by sleeping with her best friend... the only person she had left to turn to." Josie steps up close to him, glaring into his face. "She thought I was gonna die, but were you there, helping her, holding her hand, comforting her? No. You were thinking of yourself and taking from her the only other person she cared about in the world."

"That's ancient history." He waves his hand, dismissing her.

"Yes, it is. But I won't let you try to control Maisie's life and then drop her when it doesn't go your way."

Hunter steps forward, looking down at Josie. "Neither will I."

I'm beyond confused now. What has any of this got to do with Maisie? She's Hunter's daughter, and surely can't have anything to do with this guy... or with Josie.

"Whatever you think your rights are," Josie says, "Maisie's place is here."

"Yes, it is." Hunter turns to me and Josie does too, both of them looking right into my eyes. "With her father."

Everything stops. The wind, the heat from the sun, the birds singing in the trees... the pain in my chest. It all ceases at once.

Her father?

I focus on Josie. It's obvious from the guilty look in her eyes and the way she's biting on her bottom lip that she's known about this all along. The baby I've assumed to be my brother's, who I've talked about and discussed with her as belonging to him and Livia, is mine. I can tell just from the look on Hunter's face. Josie's kept that from me, and built a web of lies so great, I can't see beyond it.

How could she?

Part of me wants to take a leaf from her book… to run away, to hide, to pretend this isn't happening. But I can't.

I'm suddenly overwhelmed by a much stronger force than self-perseveration… a need to protect my daughter, even though I don't remember her.

I step forward, ignoring Josie and put myself in front of her step-father.

"Maisie is my daughter." The words sound alien on my lips, but I give them enough conviction to fool him, and he raises his eyebrows. "She belongs here, with me."

"What about me?" he says, sounding pitiful. "I'm her family, too."

"You should have thought about that when you had the chance. You're not gonna take my daughter from me, especially if all you want is to make her dance to your tune. No-one will ever do that to her. If my daughter wants to dance, she'll make up her own goddamn tune, and sing it at the top of her voice."

"But…"

"But nothing. I have nothing more to say to you… now get off of my property."

I glare at him and he stands his ground for a moment or two longer before he lets out a huff and strides back to his car, getting in and driving away with a screech of his tires.

I wait until he's disappeared from view, so I know he won't be able to see us in his rear-view mirror, and then I turn around.

Hunter is right behind me, and Josie's to my left, just a foot or so away. My brother is the one to step forward, but I push him away.

"Fuck off, Hunter."

He stumbles back, righting himself quickly enough, his eyes wide, and Josie steps away, like she thinks I might lay a hand on her. *As if that would ever happen.*

"Please, Drew," she whispers.

"Please, Drew, what?" I growl, and she stills, her bottom lip trembling.

"Don't be mad."

"Are you fucking serious? You lied to me."

"I had no choice."

Hunter stands beside her. "We had no choice," he says.

"You lied to me," I yell. "You kept my own daughter from me."

Hunter moves forward again, but I push him back, although he keeps his footing this time. "What else were we supposed to do? The doctors told us…"

"Bullshit. I don't care what the doctors told you. You've been pretending my daughter is yours all this time. You're supposed to be my brother, but you're playing happy goddamn families with my daughter."

"That's not fair, Drew," Josie says, shaking her head. "Hunter and Livia volunteered to take care of Maisie when there was no-one else to do it. They're not playing at anything."

There was no-one else. The words play over and over in my head. "Maisie's mom, that guy's daughter… she was in the car with me?" Hunter nods his head, looking miserable, but I ignore him, my eyes fixed on Josie. "How could you? You told me I wasn't responsible… that I didn't kill anyone. But Maisie's mom is dead."

"Yes. But I didn't lie. You didn't kill her. She was driving. It was her car that crashed."

"She died at the scene," Hunter says. "There was nothing they could do for her."

This is too much to take in... and yet I need to know more. I need to know all of it, even if I'm struggling to fit the pieces together.

"What was her name?"

"Lexi Doyle," Josie says. "We never shared the same name. Her father didn't adopt me or anything like that."

Hunter turns to her. "But she was your step-sister?"

"Yes." She blushes. "I'm sorry I didn't tell you before."

He shakes his head, frowning. "I remember asking you whether Lexi's sister had been informed about her death. You could have told me then, couldn't you?"

"Not really. I'd already lied to the doctors about the connection between us."

"Why?" he asks. "Why did you do that?"

"I was scared they wouldn't let me stay with Drew if I told them the truth. I'd have had no way of knowing how he was, either. By the time you asked me, we were on the verge of leaving the hospital, and I thought you might not let me come here and help him."

I feel like we're getting side-tracked. "Can I just confirm something?" They both turn to me. "Are you saying I had a relationship with your sister? Because according to my brother, I didn't used to do relationships. Or was that a lie, too?"

Hunter shakes his head. "No, it wasn't a lie. You didn't have a relationship with Lexi."

Josie sighs. "But you did sleep with her. And she was my step-sister, not my sister. We weren't that close."

"Was there a reason for that?" I ask, my head spinning.

"We liked different things, and we were very different people. When we were growing up, we had nothing in common, and then I got sick and, like I just said, her dad resented my mom having to spend so much time with me at the hospital."

"And he had an affair with her best friend?"

"Yes. Her name was Hannah. I'd known her all my life. She and Mom had been friends since high school, and Hannah had helped mom through her pregnancy, when her boyfriend walked out on her. She'd been there throughout those first three years until Mom met Lexi's dad and moved to New York. They stayed in touch, though, and when I got sick Hannah came to stay, to help out. Mom spent a lot of time with me at the hospital, but she went home one afternoon to take a shower and get a change of clothes and found Hannah and my step-father in bed together. She didn't breathe a word about it to me… not then. She knew how sick I was, and she kept it to herself, but when I came out of the hospital, we didn't go home. We went to a hotel, and then after a few weeks, when I was a little better, we moved back to Boston… and we never saw Hannah again."

"And your step-father?" Hunter asks.

"I never saw him again, either. Mom divorced him."

"How did you find out about his affair?"

"Mom told me before she died."

"She died?" Hunter says.

"Yeah. She was diagnosed with cancer just after my seventeenth birthday, and died six months later. Not long before that, she told me what he'd done and made me promise never to let a man do that to me." She blinks away her tears. "H—He'd broken her, and I don't think she ever recovered from it."

"And Lexi?" he asks.

"She'd stayed with her dad in New York. I didn't hear from her again until just a few years ago."

"I have no memory of her," I say, and they both turn to face me. "What happened between us? I get that we didn't have a relationship, but how long did I date her for?"

Josie shrugs, looking uncomfortable. "I honestly don't know."

"It wasn't for very long," Hunter says. "And I'm not sure you could even say you dated her."

"What did I do then?"

"You met her last year, in the summer, when you were working together in the Caribbean."

"Working at what?"

He glances at Josie, and she nods her head.

"You're a photographer," he says. "Just like you thought you were. The assignment you were on then was a fashion shoot, and Lexi was one of the models. From what you said at the time, the shoot went horribly wrong. The weather was terrible and all the models except for Lexi got sick. There wasn't very much the two of you could do, so…"

"We found other ways of amusing ourselves?" I say and he nods. I glance at Josie and note the blush on her cheeks, and the way she curls in on herself, but what can I do? What can I say? I get that hearing me say things like that can't be easy, and I wish I didn't have to. But the thing is, she's kept so much from me. She owes me the truth, even if it is uncomfortable.

"Yes. Eventually the agency who were employing you abandoned the project, and you came home."

"With Lexi?"

He nods his head. "Except things didn't translate well when you got back to the States. The way you told it to me, it wasn't serious for either of you, and you were both thinking of breaking up when…" He stops talking and glances at Josie, frowning, although his face quickly clears, and for some reason, he smiles.

"When what? She found out she was pregnant?" I say.

"No, that came later."

Josie clears her throat. "I think what your brother is trying to tell you is, you and Lexi were both thinking of breaking up with each other when she took you to a friend's birthday party, and you met me."

I stare at her for a moment, my brain clouding, fogging with yet more confusion. "Y—You mean I knew you before? Before the accident?"

She sucks in a breath. "Yes. But not until that party."

Chapter Twelve

Josie

This is all going so wrong.

Why did I suggest coming out? Things were fine at the cottage. They were perfect, in fact. If we'd just stayed there, naked and happy in bed, none of this would have happened. Drew wouldn't have seen Livia and Maisie, and put two and two together about the timing of her birth. We'd never have noticed my step-father's arrival, either. I didn't see that coming… not even in my worst nightmares. But if we'd just stayed at the cottage, it would all have gone on without us. Hunter would have dealt with him and we'd have been none the wiser.

Everyone could have carried on living in ignorant bliss.

Hunter would never have needed to know I'm Lexi's step-sister, and Drew wouldn't have had to find out about his daughter, and our past… such as it is. Judging by the look on his face, I'm not sure he was ready to hear all of that, and I doubt he'll be able to forgive me for lying to him.

That magic spell that bound us so closely isn't just breaking; it's fracturing into so many pieces, I know I'll never be able to put them back together again.

"So, you're not just my nurse?" He frowns, shaking his head slowly from side to side.

I can't begin to tell him how much that hurts. Since when was I just his nurse? Since now, I guess. If I needed a hint that we're over, I just got it, and for a second or two, I can't answer. I refuse to cry in front of him, but it's a struggle to swallow down my tears and croak out the word, "No."

"And we met at a party?"

"Yes. It was at an apartment in Boston."

"I don't remember it."

I nod my head. "You walked in the door and I took one look at you and fell in love." *Because, whatever you might think, I've never been just your nurse.* "I didn't realize straight away that you were with Lexi – not romantically – and we spent the evening together, just talking. Then she came over and made it clear the two of you were together, and I—I thought that was the end of it… that nothing could ever happen between us."

He holds up his right hand. "Hold on…" A frown settles on his face. "Is that what you meant when you said you'd always loved me, the first time we had sex?" I flinch at his words. It's interesting that he's saying we had sex now. We didn't make love. And although he spots my reaction, his frown deepening, he doesn't say anything else and just stares at me, waiting for an answer.

"Y—Yes."

"So, rather than proving that love by telling me the truth, you perpetuated the lie?"

"It's not a lie."

"This whole thing is a fucking lie, Josie," he yells, and I swallow down my tears.

"No, it's not. I—I love you."

"You love her, too," Hunter says, stepping forward. "And in case you're having any doubts about it, you always did."

Drew turns to him. "How would you know?"

"Because you told me." Hunter takes a deep breath, stepping closer to Drew, trying to calm both him and the situation, I think. "When you asked me about your past the other day, I told you that love wasn't something you did very often. I wasn't exaggerating. As far as I'm aware, it was something you'd only done once before, with the woman I knew as Lexi's sister." He turns his head, looking at me, and smiles, just slightly. "I didn't know her name. You never told me," he says, clearly still talking to Drew. "But I remember when I was asking Josie if Lexi's sister had been notified about the accident. She told me she had, and I said I hoped you'd remember her when you got your memory back." He looks back at Drew again. "I had a reason for saying that."

"Yeah?"

"Yes. I knew how much you loved her… Lexi's sister, that is. You'd told us…"

"Us?" Drew interrupts. "Who's us?"

Hunter sighs and glances at me, shrugging his shoulders. "We've come this far. We might as well tell him everything." Drew frowns and tilts his head.

"What now?" he says.

"Us is me and Ella."

"And who is Ella?" Drew asks.

"She's our sister… yours and mine. She lives here, in an apartment in the main property."

Drew turns away, looking up at the house, like he's hoping it'll spark a memory. I'm not sure if it does, but after a few seconds, he looks back at us. "Is she the woman with the short, dark hair and the baby?"

"Yes." Hunter nods his head. "That's Henry."

"Jesus Christ… how many more secrets?" Drew pushes his fingers back through his hair, glaring at me.

"They're not secrets." Hunter says. "We were told not to tell you anything for your own good."

Drew turns to his brother. "Really? It doesn't feel like this is doing me much good right now. I've got a daughter, and a sister, and a nephew I didn't know about. I can't even remember my daughter's mom, and it seems like this isn't love at first sight for me and Josie, but love at second sight... if there is such a thing."

Hunter moves a little closer to Drew. "I get that you're confused and angry, but don't blame Josie."

Drew narrows his eyes and my skin prickles against the distant icy memories of a life without him.

Please don't let it come to that.

"What did I tell you? You and Ella?" Drew asks.

"That Lexi had dragged you to a party, against your will. That you'd gone to be polite, met Lexi's sister and fallen for her. Ella made fun of you, because that's what she does... and because you'd never been in love before. It was a golden opportunity for her, and she wasn't about to pass it up."

"I don't get why I told you. Was that the kind of thing I did? Was I renowned for discussing my love life?"

Hunter smiles. "You didn't really have a love life. You had a sex life." He glances at me, looking a little sheepish, but then turns back to Drew. "And you told us because you needed advice."

"What about?"

"How to ask Josie out. You'd already broken things off with Lexi by then, and you'd worked out that Josie was the one for you. Only you didn't know what to do about it."

"What did you suggest?"

"We both told you that you needed to wait. And I said you could try making friends with Josie, rather than dating her... at least to start with."

"And is that what I did?" Drew says, turning to me.

"You didn't wait very long, but you called, and we met up for coffee. It was lovely."

"Romantic?" he says, tilting his head, like he's trying to work out if that's what we had before… whether it was different to how we've been since the accident.

"No, not especially. I think you must have heeded your brother's advice and decided to go down the friendship route. Not that I minded. As far as I was concerned, I was just so relieved to hear from you, and so happy to see you… to talk to you. I hoped it might lead to something more… eventually. All I wanted was to spend time with you, and if I had to wait for Lexi to be a little further in the past, I didn't mind in the least."

Drew sighs, his brow furrowing, like he's thinking through what I've just said. "Did we meet again?"

"Yes. Twice more."

"And?"

"Each time was better than the last."

"Did we do more than meet up and talk? Did we kiss, or…?"

"No, but I wanted to. We seemed to be getting closer, but after that third meeting, you had to go to Hawaii. You weren't sure when you'd be back, and I was working over the weekend, so you said you'd call. You seemed keen to see me again, and I wanted to see you. I was looking forward to hearing from you… at least until I got that call from Lexi."

"She called you?"

"Yes."

"Had someone told her about us? Did she have a problem with it?"

"No. There wasn't an 'us' to speak about. Not really. She called me because she'd found out she was pregnant."

"Oh." He lets his head fall, and I can feel the anger and confusion pouring off of him.

"I didn't understand why she was confiding in me. Like I said, we weren't close, and it didn't make sense that she'd come to me... until she explained that her father was livid. He wasn't talking to her. She needed someone, and I guess she turned to me."

"Not me?" He looks up, bewildered.

I shake my head. "You were still in Hawaii at the time... not that she knew that. She didn't call you straight away because she didn't want you to think she was trying to trap you."

"Trap me?"

"Yes. You're a multi-millionaire, Drew. She thought you might assume she'd done it on purpose."

"How? Presumably I'd had some involvement? Or did I routinely go around having sex and not taking precautions?"

"No," Hunter says, shaking his head. "As far as I know, that was a first for you. The way you told us the story was that you were drunk and forgot to use a condom. You said Lexi was on birth control, but she'd been sick, so it hadn't worked."

Drew looks up at his brother. "I told you that? You and Ella?"

"No. You told me, and Ella... and Livia."

Drew's eyes widen. "And Livia?"

"Yeah. You were in shock. Lexi had only just broken the news to you. I don't think you knew what you were saying."

"Lexi told me the same thing, Drew." He looks back at me. "She was fearful that you'd think she'd either been lying about the birth control, or that she'd gotten sick on purpose, or something. I pointed out that you could've used a condom, and she said you were both a little drunk... that it hadn't been top of your list of priorities." I can feel myself blush, but I owe him details... and a lot more besides.

Drew sighs. "What made her change her mind... about telling me, I mean?"

"I did."

He frowns. "You did?"

"Yes. I knew it would mean the end of any hope for us, but I couldn't deny you the right to be a father to your child, knowing that, even if we got together, that was the one thing I could n— never give you." My voice cracks, although there's nothing I can do about that.

His eyes darken, and he steps closer, facing me. I might have hoped for kindness, given what I've just said, but there's none in his face. Instead, I'm looking at nothing but unbridled rage. "How can you say that?" I cower against his thunderous voice and Hunter grabs his arm. Drew shakes him off, his anger getting the better of him. "How can you say you couldn't deny me the right to be a father to my child when you've been doing precisely that ever since the accident?"

"It wasn't just Josie who did that," Hunter says, putting himself between us, protecting me from his brother's fury. "That was my decision, too. So, if you wanna get mad at someone, get mad at me."

"I am mad at you."

"Fine. Carry on. Don't let me stop you if it makes you feel better. But are you honestly suggesting we should have let you look after Maisie? You think you've been in a fit state to do that? Caring for a baby is a full-time job, and it's damn hard work. You've been recovering from the accident while trying to figure out who you are. Do you really think you could have factored Maisie into that?"

"No, but that's not the point."

"Then what is?" Hunter raises his voice, exasperated.

"That you kept her *existence* from me. Can't you see?"

"Of course we can," I say, stepping out from behind Hunter, so I'm standing beside him, looking up at Drew. "We're not inhuman, you know? This hasn't been easy for either of us."

He shakes his head at me. "Oh, I'm sorry. I didn't realize this was all about you."

"Oh, grow up, will you?" Hunter says, standing up to his full height.

"Drew, please." I reach out and touch his arm, but he pulls back and tears fill my eyes. "How do you think I felt when I told you I can't have children? Do you think I enjoyed telling you that, knowing you already have a child of your own, but that being parents is something we can never share? It's been difficult for Hunter, too. And for Livia. These weren't decisions we took lightly… believe me. Keeping things from you hurt us, too. But we were just doing what we were told, and what we believed was best for you. The doctor said we couldn't tell you about your past. He said it might harm your recovery if we revealed things you weren't ready for."

"Do I look like I'm ready now?"

"No. If you want me to be honest, the way you're reacting is evidence that the doctor was probably right. Finding out hasn't done you any favors… especially not in this way, with all the information coming at you in an avalanche. I was supposed to manage your recovery, and I've failed dismally."

I step back, but Hunter reaches out and grabs my arm just above the wrist. "You haven't failed, Josie. This is no-one's fault. You couldn't foresee that scene with your step-father. No-one could have seen that coming."

"No, but it was going to unravel anyway, even before he arrived."

Hunter frowns. "It was?"

"Yes. Drew had worked out that Maisie isn't yours." I turn to him. "Hadn't you?"

"Yes," Drew says.

Hunter looks at his brother. "How?"

"Because you told me you and Livia discussed having a baby for the first time just a few weeks before your wedding. Then Josie told me you and Livia have only been married since February. It was a simple matter of doing the math. Maisie can't be yours. Obviously, I didn't realize she was mine, but…"

"He'd put two and two together," I say.

"Yeah. I just hadn't quite made four yet."

"So, I'm as much to blame as anyone," Hunter says, still focused on his brother. "I slipped up. But do you know what? I'm human. So is Josie. In an ideal world, we'd never have let this happen. We'd have found a way of releasing the information to you in a more controlled way, when you were ready for it."

Drew stares at him for a moment or two and then turns to me. "Now we've come this far, can you tell me what happened?"

"When?"

"You were saying you persuaded Lexi to tell me about the pregnancy."

"Yes."

"And after she did? What did I do then?"

"I don't really know. I didn't hear from Lexi for a while."

"You drove down to New York to see her," Hunter says, filling in the gaps for him. "You offered to support her."

"Financially?" Drew raises his eyebrows.

"In any way she wanted."

He turns to me. "Did I contact you?"

I shake my head. "I didn't hear from you again."

He frowns. "Y—You mean I didn't even call you? Not at all?"

"No. What were you going to say? It was a horrible situation… for all of us, I think. And like I said, when I persuaded Lexi to tell you she was pregnant, I knew it would mean the end for us, so I wasn't surprised."

"So, we didn't see each other between then and the accident?"

"We saw each other once… on the day Maisie was born."

Hunter closes his eyes for a second, shaking his head just slightly and I guess he must already know this story; that Drew must have told him before.

"Really?" Drew says, frowning. "How did that happen?"

"Lexi came to stay with me just before Maisie's due date. My step-father was still refusing to have anything to do with her and she found that kinda tough. She used to come to Boston every so often to see you…"

Drew holds up a hand and I stop talking. "We… we weren't involved, were we? Lexi and I, I mean?"

"No. But you saw as much of her as you could. Sometimes you'd go to New York, and sometimes she'd stay with me in Boston, and you'd meet up there."

"And that's where she was when Maisie was born?"

"Yes. She was at my apartment. I had to call you, and we both wound up being present for Maisie's birth." I swallow down the lump in my throat, reliving the memory, and regretting that he can't. "It wasn't easy and I'm not gonna say it was. I was happy for Lexi, but seeing you hold your newborn daughter for the first time… it broke my heart." My voice cracks and he frowns, like he's struggling.

"Did Lexi ever find out about us?"

"Not from me."

He turns to Hunter. "Do you know if I told her?" he asks.

"I don't know. I think you intended to."

"What does that mean?"

"A couple of days before the accident, we spoke on the phone. You said you'd had a conversation with Lexi and you thought she might be seeing someone else."

"Did that worry me? Was I jealous?" I hate that he's so unsure of himself… so lost.

"No. Not in the slightest. You were pleased about it. You thought it might open the way for you to get together with Josie."

"Even though she and Lexi were sisters?" Drew says, his brow furrowing.

"Yes. You said you didn't think Lexi and her sister were very close, because they hadn't met up since Maisie was born."

Drew turns to me. "Is that true?"

"Yes. I found it hard, seeing her and Maisie and knowing I couldn't have that life with you."

"You told me you were gonna talk to Lexi," Hunter says. "You said you were gonna find out if she really had another guy in her life, and if she did, you were gonna take it from there. Whether you got the chance to do any of that before the accident, I don't know."

Drew keeps his eyes trained on me. "Was she seeing someone?"

"Yes, she was. His name is Manuel Ortega, and he's a model, like she was. The way Lexi explained it to me, they hadn't been together for very long, but they'd known each other for a while… and it was serious. That's probably how you picked up on it."

"It was serious?" he says.

"Yes. They were thinking of moving to Boston."

"Together?"

"Yes. Lexi thought it would make things easier for you."

"Why?"

"Because you used to drive to New York and stay in a hotel so you could see Maisie. It was difficult for everyone, I think, and…"

"And what?"

"And Manuel didn't like her coming to Newport to stay with you."

Drew raises his eyebrows. "She used to come here?"

"Yes."

"With Maisie?"

"Yes," Hunter says, taking over. "It wasn't something you did all the time, but they had their own rooms in the cottage, and you brought them here whenever it suited your schedule."

Drew tips his head to one side, looking over Hunter's shoulder toward the cottage. "I don't get it. If Maisie has a room at the cottage, where are all her things?"

"We moved everything over here," Hunter says, nodding toward the main house. "After the accident, it was obvious someone other than you was gonna have to take care of her for a while, so we moved the contents of Maisie's nursery from the cottage over to one of the guest rooms."

Drew pushes his fingers back through his hair, one hand on either side of his head. "And Lexi had her own room, too?"

"Yes."

"Did I look after her? Lexi, I mean?"

Hunter nods his head, moving a little closer to Drew. "You did everything for her. Anything she asked of you, you did it."

"Was I happy?"

"No."

Drew shakes his head, like he doesn't understand. "So, I didn't want to have a child?"

"That's not what I said. You asked if you were happy, and I said 'no'. But the reason you were unhappy had nothing to do with Maisie… not really. It was because you wanted to be with Josie, and you couldn't. It broke you when you had to stop seeing her, but you put Lexi and Maisie first, last and everywhere in between."

"I see. And Maisie? What was I like with her?"

Hunter smiles and, despite everything, I can't help my lips from twisting up a little, too. "When she was born, you became a man," Hunter says. "You switched your entire career around… your entire life around, to accommodate her. I honestly don't think you could have done any more."

Drew averts his gaze to me. "It's true," I tell him. "Lexi may have met someone else, but she was grateful for how you were with her and Maisie, and for everything you did. That's one of the reasons she wanted to move to Boston. She was trying to keep Manuel happy, but she wanted to make things easier for you, too. I think she knew you didn't enjoy staying in a hotel when you went to New York, and she said that at least if she moved to Boston, then Maisie could stay at your apartment there… just the two of you."

"She was gonna let me have Maisie by myself?"

"Yes. That's what she said. You'd done so much for her…" I let my voice fade, wondering if I should have started that sentence.

"What's wrong?" he says, moving closer. "You were gonna say something."

I guess there's no point in trying to hide it. "It's just that Lexi hadn't explained to you about Manuel. From what she said, he was practically living with her, and I told her she should have kept you informed. We nearly had an argument about it."

"Why? Didn't she want to tell me? What did she think I'd do?"

"I don't think she was worried about that. Her reasoning was that she didn't pry into your sex life, so you had no right to know about hers. I told that if she was bringing another man into Maisie's life, as Maisie's father, you had a right to know."

"And she agreed?"

"Eventually, yes. She took some persuading, but she said she was gonna tell you. Obviously, I don't know if she was able to before…"

He nods his head, understanding my meaning without me needing to say the words.

"This Manuel guy... does he know about the accident?"

"Yes, he does. He was Lexi's emergency contact on her phone, so they called him when it happened. I spoke to him at the hospital."

"You did?" Hunter's surprised.

"Yes. I—I told him my true identity."

"Why did you tell him and not us?" he asks, and I wonder if he's offended.

"Because it made him more comfortable. It meant he had someone who he could talk to about Lexi... someone who understood. And I wanted him to know I was looking out for Maisie."

Hunter nods his head, while Drew tilts his. "You liked him?"

"Yes. He was a nice guy. He was devastated about Lexi, but he wanted to know Maisie was okay... and you, too."

"Why? Had I met him?"

"No, but I think he felt bad for doubting Lexi's motives in seeing so much of you. He was jealous of the time you spent together, even though I think he knew, deep down, he had no cause. She loved him, and he knew it. He told me you'd paid off the mortgage on Lexi's apartment, and that you gave her an allowance, too. He said that was part of what made him so resentful... even though there was no need."

Hunter stares at Drew, shaking his head slightly. "I didn't know you'd paid off her mortgage."

"Neither did I," Drew says. "Obviously."

"There's probably a lot more that you don't know, and that even we can't tell you," I say and Drew looks at me, frowning. "Hunter knows a lot about your past, but I'm sure he doesn't know everything... and I only know some of Lexi's side of the story. I'm only aware of the things she told me in that last meeting we had before the accident. You're gonna have to fill in the blanks for yourself, when it all comes back to you."

He shakes his head. "I'm not sure I can handle anything else."

"Then don't think about it."

He looks at me, incredulously. "How can I not think about it, after everything you've just said?"

"No. You don't understand. What I mean is, don't think about the blanks. Just come to terms with what you know for now... if you can."

He takes a deep breath. "That's gonna take some doing."

"There's no rush."

"Really? You think I enjoy having all these holes in my memory still? I'm not sure it wasn't easier to live in total ignorance than to have a half-baked idea of my past."

"Which is why I should have managed this better. I'm sorry, Drew. I wish it hadn't all come out like this."

He sighs and rubs his hand down his face. "I need some time by myself." Hunter steps forward, but Drew holds up a hand, halting him. "I know what you're gonna say. I get that I'm a father and I have responsibilities, but I can't deal with them yet. Okay? I'm not ready. First, I need to take in at least some of what you've told me." He turns, looking down at me, although I can't read his face. "I'm going for a walk."

"Do you want me to come with you?" I ask, but he shakes his head. Why would he? I'm just his nurse.

He takes a step away, but I reach out, grabbing his arm. This time he doesn't shake me off, but he looks at my hand, pale against his darker skin, and then raises his eyes to mine. "Do you hate me?" I ask.

"Of course not. I can't hate you."

"Do you still love me?"

He stares at me for a long moment and then pulls his arm away. Tears prick my eyes, and he cups my face in his hand, sighing deeply, like he wants to do more, but can't. "I need some time... okay?"

He moves away again. "Drew… wait."

He turns back. "What is it?" He sounds a little impatient, like he's desperate to be somewhere else… anywhere else.

"I—I need to play you something, before you go."

"Play me something?"

"Yes." I pull out my phone. "It's a recording of a message you sent me." I find it quickly and turn up the volume, holding my phone between us, so he can hear…

"Hi, Josie. It's me, Drew. It's been a long time, and I know I should've been in touch before now, but… the… the thing is, I —I wanted to ask if we could meet up? I'm at the airport. I'm flying back from Rome today, and going down to Newport with Maisie and… and her mom, but I wondered… can I call you? We need to talk, or I think we do. Obviously, if I've mis-read everything, you'll be wondering what on earth I'm talking about, in which case I apologize for disturbing you, and it's probably best if you stop listening now…" While the recording pauses, I look up at Drew's face. He seems bewildered, his mouth slightly open, like he's trying to remember a time when he might have said these words. "If you're still listening, I guess I didn't mis-read things, so the next question is, do you want to see me again? If you've moved on, or you're with someone else now, or you just don't want to have anything more to do with me, after everything that's happened, that's fine… well, it isn't, but I'll understand. This is complicated, and it's a lot harder for you than it is for me. I get that, and I'm sorry. Truly, I am. I should have said that a long time ago, but I'm really sorry, Josie." I hold my phone a little tighter at the sound of Drew's cough, and the emotion I know is behind it. "The timing was dreadful, and if it's all too much for you, then just ignore me. I'll get the message and I won't hassle you. If you think you'd like to meet up, call me. I'll fit in with whatever you need… whatever you want. I just wanna see you again, Josie." There's a pause, but I wait, knowing there's more to come. "Call me… please." The message ends and I lower my phone, looking up into his face.

"I picked that up right before I found out about the accident. I'd just finished my shift and your message was on my phone. It had been there all day, but I hadn't had time to look. I listened to it and I let myself hope that maybe you wanted more than friendship… that somehow, we could be together."

He nods his head. "That makes sense. Obviously I can't be sure of my meaning, but I'd said I wanted to see you again, and from the tone of my voice, it sounded like I was looking for something more than we'd had before."

I nod my head.

"That was what I thought. I wondered if I should call you. I wanted to, so badly… but I realized you'd be in the car with Lexi, driving to Newport, so I waited. Then I went down in the elevator, thinking I'd call you when I got home, and on my way through the ER, I saw Maisie, and they told me about the accident." I look up into his bewildered eyes. "I know I could have come clean. It wouldn't have been easy, but I could have admitted who I was to the doctors, and to your family. Except my sister had just died, and even if she and I weren't that close, I wanted to be with Maisie, to hold on to her, and take care of her for Lexi, and for you… and I wanted to be with you, too. It all happened so fast, I didn't have time to think clearly about the trouble I was storing up for both of us. I just wanted to cling to the love I'd come so close to tasting. And then, when I realized what was wrong with you, I wanted to help you. Because I knew I could." I move a little closer. "I made a mistake, Drew. A big one. I took advantage of the situation… and of you. It wasn't done to hurt you, though. It was done with the best of intentions. You have to believe me. You were there, and you needed me, and I—I couldn't risk losing you again."

He doesn't say a word. Instead, he just stares at me, breathing steadily in and out, and I know it's too late.

There's no way back for us.

I turn, running for the cottage, tears streaming down my cheeks, because this time, I know he won't follow.

I'm on my own.

Right where I deserve to be.

Drew

I watch Josie go, and while my heart is telling me to follow, my head is holding me back.

I want to talk to her, to tell her we'll be okay, to reassure her that, even though I couldn't say the words just now, I still love her, more than anything. But first, I need to be alone. I need to be sure that when I say the words, they come out right, with no anger, or frustration, or blame attached to them.

And that's going to take some time.

"I'm gonna go for that walk."

Hunter steps up in front of me, blocking my path. "You don't think you should talk to Josie first?"

"No. I will talk to her… but not yet. Please, Hunter. I need to be by myself for a while."

He nods his head, stepping aside, and I stride off, heading across the grass, away from the cottage.

Right now, there are so many thoughts and emotions rolling around inside of me. I'm mad. I'm boiling mad. But I'm also confused and scared and disappointed. Josie was right. I need to come to terms with the information I've been given before I can do anything else.

I don't know where I'm going, but I put one foot in front of the other, and I keep on doing that, the steady, monotonous rhythm giving order to my thoughts.

First and foremost, I'm a father.

The little girl whose picture is in my house, is my daughter. She's not my niece, and I guess, when I think about it, that makes sense. I would have pictures of my own child, wouldn't I? And while I might not have any memory of her, I know she's beautiful, with a shock of dark hair and the clearest of blue eyes. I try to picture myself holding her, but I can't. It's an alien feeling, but I guess it's one I'll have to get used to.

Because she's mine.

I also have a sister. Ella. And I'm an uncle, too. That's not quite such a shock. I believed myself to be an uncle already, to the baby who, it seems, is my own.

My baby…

I shake my head, struggling to get my head around the idea that I have a child… that there's a small person on this planet for whom I'm responsible.

It's strange. I told Josie I wanted us to have children together, and I meant every word. I was excited at the prospect of the two of us becoming parents, even though I thought we'd only known each other for a few days. Pictures formed in my head of a pregnant Josie lying in my arms, of me cradling her bump… our child. I imagined us holding our newborn baby between us, kissing and marveling at the life we'd created… until it all came tumbling down, when she told me she can't have children.

Now, it seems that dream is already a reality… at least for me.

Only I don't know what to do with it.

I don't know what to do with Josie, either.

No… that's not true. I know I'll always love her, just like I loved her in the past, it seems, before all this.

But as for her deception…

There's so much of it, it's hard to know where fantasy ends and reality begins.

I know she was doing what the doctor told her… as was Hunter. But whether it was in my best interests, I have yet to be convinced. It doesn't feel like it at the moment.

I still have too many unanswered questions. I've been given so much information, and yet there's still more I don't know, and while it's okay for Josie to tell me not to think about the blanks, that's easier said than done. Especially as the blanks feel so huge… and so vital to my understanding of who I am.

I suppose that's the thing that worries me the most.

Who am I?

Despite everything I've been told, I still don't feel any closer to knowing the answer to that. It's been plaguing me for ages. Even before today's revelations, I've wondered what kind of man I was before the accident.

The fact that I got Lexi pregnant doesn't augur too well. Hunter may have said it wasn't something I routinely did, but when you bear in mind, I made love with Josie countless times before I remembered I hadn't used a condom, it doesn't fill me with confidence. Obviously, in Lexi's case, she was sick, and it sounds like I was unaware of that. And in Josie's case, I wasn't to know she couldn't have children. I was just reckless with her safety…

Was I always like that?

Does my brother know me as well as he thinks he does?

Is he right when he says it was a first for me, or was I really an inconsiderate asshole?

Questions, questions, questions. There are so many of them. How is that I belong here on this lovely property?

I have money, but where did it come from? And what did I used to spend it on?

Hunter confirmed I'm a photographer, but why? Why would I work, when I have all this?

I sigh, stopping, and look over at the building in the distance. I still don't know what that's about, either. It's another blank.

I'm struggling to focus on anything, my thoughts drifting from one unknown detail to another. Regardless of what Josie said, I feel like I won't be able to think straight until I've bridged at least some of the gaps in my past, and that being the case, I need answers.

I turn, surprised by how far I've walked, and start to re-trace my steps, taking them more slowly this time.

Obviously, I could go back to the cottage and speak to Josie, but it seems unlikely she'll be able to give me the information I need. I think there's only one person who will, and I head for the main house, hoping my brother is still feeling communicative.

He's lying on a lounger by the pool and sits up when he hears me approach, swinging his legs around so he's perched on the edge.

"I wasn't expecting to see you again so soon," he says.

"I know. But there are things I can't work out… things I need to know."

He nods his head and waves his arm toward the lounger beside him. "Sit down. I'll tell you what I can."

I do as he says, facing him, my hands resting on my knees. "I'm gonna start with a question I've already asked you once before."

"Which is…?"

"What was I like? The last time I asked that, you said you couldn't answer, but you can now. You've told me I didn't have relationships. So, what was I? Some kind of player?"

He tilts his head, like he's thinking about that description, which makes me a little uneasy. "I don't know I'd go that far. I'd say you avoided taking things too seriously, and there's nothing wrong with that. You were a guy, like any other guy… trying to find your way. You had your fair share of women, as did I."

"Did I hurt anyone?"

"There were a few casualties."

I shake my head. "I'm not sure I like the sound of who I was back then."

"Why?"

"I hurt people."

"In situations that couldn't be avoided, and that weren't necessarily of your own making."

"Such as?"

"The one I know most about was a woman called Keira."

"What did I do to her?"

"You dated her for a while, but then you got the chance to go to Australia on a long-term assignment and she didn't want you to go."

"I'm guessing I took the job?"

"Yeah. I think you were just having fun with Keira, like you did with all the other women you dated. Only she thought it was more than that. She didn't take it well."

"How do you know that?"

"Because she used to call me from time to time, just to talk."

I'm liking myself even less. "Was I that serious about my career?"

"Yes."

"But why? That's another thing I don't understand. You say we're rich, and this property kinda proves that. But if that's the case, why do I need to work?"

"You don't need to. Like me, you choose to."

"So you work too?"

"Yes."

"And Ella?"

"She did, before she had Henry."

I nod my head. "So, what did she do before she became a mom?"

"She trained as a chef and worked on a TV show as a culinary consultant. She's also written a cookery book."

"And you?" I ask.

"I'm the CEO of an advertising agency. It was started by our father…" He stares at me, waiting for my reaction, I guess.

"Our father? You haven't mentioned him before."

"No." His eyes darken, his face clouding. "He was a hard man, and he's one of the reasons we all choose to work."

"What does that mean?"

He sucks in a deep breath. "It's complicated."

"I'm not going anywhere, and I need to know, Hunter. I need to understand where I come from… who I am. I'm struggling to get my head around being a father and a lover, because I don't know the first thing about myself as a man."

"Okay, okay. I'll tell you. It's just…"

"Just what?"

"Some of this won't be easy to hear."

"None of this has been a walk in the park."

He pauses for a moment and shakes his head. "I guess not." He leans back slightly, looking at the house, and then turns to me again. "He died nearly two and a half years ago."

"He's dead?"

"Yes. But don't get upset about it. You weren't at the time. Neither was I."

"And Ella?"

He shakes his head. "Our father barely acknowledged any of us when he was alive. It was kinda hard to acknowledge him when he died."

"This place was his?" I say, looking around.

"Yes. Along with the money he left us."

"He left us some money, too?"

"Don't you remember Josie telling you that you're a multi-millionaire?"

"Oh, yeah." I'd forgotten that.

"Hmm… our father left us around fifteen million dollars each."

I cough, unable to help myself and then struggle to regain control… to breathe. "F—Fifteen million?"

"Yeah. Sorry. I probably should have prepared you for that."

"When Josie said 'multi-millionaire', I thought she was exaggerating."

"No. I don't think she knows exactly how much you're worth, not unless you told her when you knew her before, or you told Lexi and Lexi told her. I've certainly never mentioned it to her, and it's not public knowledge as far as I'm aware."

I shake my head, struggling to take it all in. "In that case, I'm even more confused."

"About what?"

"Why we'd choose to work."

"To begin with, for you and me, it was because we wanted to prove a point."

"To whom?"

"Ourselves mostly. Our father had never given us any support, and we wanted to prove we didn't need it… that we could make it on our own. Later, once we'd inherited, I think we carried on because we wanted to prove we were worthy of the lives we were suddenly able to live."

I nod my head. "I see. And are we? Worthy, I mean?"

"We try to be."

"Did we make it?" I ask, wishing I already knew the answer to that.

"Yes. Dad never saw Ella make a success of her career, but she did."

"And me?"

He smiles. "You're a damn talented photographer, with a great reputation, and a bank balance to match."

"You said I worked in fashion? Or that was what I was doing when I met Lexi?"

"Yeah. It's what you used to do. You traveled all over the world, photographing some of the most beautiful women on the planet."

"Please tell me I didn't sleep with them… at least, not all of them?"

He smiles. "No, you didn't. In fact, you usually steered well clear. I think the thing with Lexi was born out of boredom."

I'm not sure that makes me feel any better, but I don't want to lose track of our conversation.

"Is that what I was doing in Rome? Photographing beautiful women, I mean… not sleeping with them."

"No. That was a travel shoot, and one you didn't want to do. After Maisie was born, you started doing more studio work, because you didn't like being away from her. But a client asked you to go to Rome for them, and you didn't feel like you could say 'no'. You hated it, though, and you couldn't wait to come home."

"I see. And do I have a studio of my own?"

"Yes. It's in Boston. Close to your apartment."

"Okay. And what about you?"

"What about me?"

"You said you're the CEO of our father's advertising agency. Was that something you chose to do, or did he choose it for you?"

"No. As I said, he didn't care enough about us to worry what we did. It was my decision to go into advertising, although I haven't always worked for TBA."

"TBA?"

"Theodore Bennett Associates. Dad named the company after himself."

"His name was Theodore?"

"Yes."

I delve into the recesses of my mind, but I'm not coming up with anything. "I don't remember him."

"I shouldn't worry. Like I said, he wasn't an easy man to live with."

"He was presumably a successful one, though, if he made so much money."

Hunter tilts his head. "The bulk of his cash didn't come from hard work. It came from taking the company public. He did that not long after his cancer was diagnosed, and netted a small fortune."

"So you don't own the family firm?"

"No. That was intentional on Dad's part. He put me in charge, but made sure I had no control. When he died, he left us his shares, so between us, we have a controlling interest, but the company is owned by all of its shareholders, not just the Bennett family."

"Why did he do that? I mean, why did he put you in charge, but tie your hands at the same time?"

"Because that's the kind of man he was. Not that I care anymore. Livia's taught me that trying to work out his motives isn't worth it. I can't change what he did, so I don't think about it anymore."

I sit in silence for a moment, trying to work things out in my head. "If our father was such a terrible man, why did he leave us so much money, as well as the shares in the company and this house?"

"I don't know. I imagine he left us the house because he didn't know what else to do with it. It's not as though he spent very much time here, so I doubt it had any sentimental value for him. As for the shares, I expect that was because he didn't like the idea of TBA falling outside of Bennett hands, even if it's no longer owned by us entirely."

"And the money?"

"I've always believed that was because he expected us to give up our careers and blow it all."

"Just like that? Did he never allow for the fact that we might enjoy what we do?"

"He never allowed for anything. I'm speculating here. In all honesty, I've got no idea why he did the things he did… and like I say, since I've met Livia, the past isn't something I spend too much of my time dwelling on."

I guess that makes sense… except I don't have a past, and there are things I still need to know.

"What about our mother? Where does she feature in all of this?"

"That's a little more difficult to explain," he says, frowning.

"Like I said, I'm not going anywhere."

"I know, but in this instance, even I don't have all the answers." He looks down at his hands and I wait, knowing he'll tell me what he can. "Mom left us when you were six years old."

"Six?"

"Yeah."

"Sorry," I say. "I'm struggling with context here. Nobody's told me how old I am yet."

He smiles. "You're twenty-eight."

"And you're…?"

"I'm thirty-three."

"So you were eleven when Mom left?"

"Yeah."

"Do you remember what happened?"

"Not very much, and to be honest, even when you had all your faculties, you didn't remember her very well at all. Ella doesn't either. She was only three at the time."

"So she's twenty-five now? The same age as Josie?"

"Yes."

I nod my head, taking it all in as best I can. "Didn't our father spend more time with us after Mom left?"

He snorts out a half-laugh. "No. He did the opposite. He hired Pat and Mick to take care of us."

"Pat and Mick?"

"Yeah. Pat's the housekeeper, and Mick takes care of all the maintenance around the property. Pat effectively raised us. She was more like a mom to you and Ella than our real mom was."

I close my eyes, trying to picture her, but I can't. "She's not there," I whisper, opening my eyes again.

"Don't worry. She's still here now. She's helping Livia to look after Maisie."

"So I'll meet her?"

"Of course. She can't wait. She's been itching to see you. So has Ella."

"But you've held them back?"

"We had to. The doctor told us to let you remember things for yourself before we introduced you to anyone else from your past."

"I see." I'm not sure I do. It feels unfair to everyone… not just me. But it's not his fault. I have to keep telling myself that. It's not anyone's fault. "Why did Mom leave?" I ask, getting us back onto our original topic of conversation.

"I don't know. She didn't say."

I shrug my shoulders. "I guess that's not surprising. It probably wasn't something she wanted to discuss with a child."

Hunter shakes his head. "No. But she was here the other day. She could have told me then."

"Sh—She was here? She came back, after all this time?"

"Yes. She read about your accident and wanted to see you."

"Then why am I only hearing about this now?"

"Because Josie thought it would be too upsetting for you, and I agreed."

"You asked Josie?"

"Yeah. I had to. I didn't know what to do. Mom arrived out of the blue, asking to see you… and Ella. And I wasn't sure what was in your best interests. I called Josie and asked her to come over."

"Oh… that was the morning she dropped everything and came dashing over here?"

"Yes. She listened to what Mom had to say and then said she didn't think it was a good idea for Mom to see you."

"Was that her call to make?"

"Yes. I trusted her judgement. I still do. She told me she'd always put your interests first, and I believed her. I know why she said that now, but that doesn't make it any less true. She only wants what's best for you, Drew. You knew nothing about yourself or your past. The last thing you needed was our mother adding to the confusion. Josie told her she'd have to wait until you were well enough."

"So she visited with Ella instead?"

"No. I decided that, if she couldn't see you, then she couldn't see Ella, either. Ella doesn't even know Mom was here. I assumed you'd recover and meet Ella before meeting Mom, and I didn't think it would be very helpful if Ella blurted out that Mom had been visiting."

"You mean you sent her away again?"

"I told her I'd call her if the situation changed," he says and I nod my head, although he just stares at me. "I won't be calling her just yet, Drew. You've got too many other things to work out in your head before we bring our mom into the equation."

"You don't think that's a little unfair? She obviously wanted to see us all."

"Maybe she did, but she's the one who left." He sits up, his back straight, his shoulders square. "We didn't hear a word from her for over twenty years, and while she may have a good reason for that, I've yet to hear it. I've always tried to see things from her side, Drew, even if I don't know why she left us, but if she wants back in, she'll do it on my terms."

"Your terms?"

"Yes. It's not just about you, Drew. It's about Ella as well. I have to think about how she's gonna react."

Something sparks in my memory... something distant, shadowy. I can't work out what it is, but I feel safe and comfortable with the thought, and I smile across at him.

"You've always been protective, haven't you? Of me and Ella, I mean."

His face lights up. "Yes. Why? Have you remembered something?"

"Nothing specific. It's just a feeling, that's all."

He smiles. "Then hang onto it. You never know where it might lead."

He's not wrong. I feel the need to clutch a hold of every little taint of memory, just in case it takes me on to something else... something more tangible.

"Is Ella married?" I ask.

"No. She's engaged... to an English guy called Mac. Remember him? You met him the other day. He helped me to lift you up the stairs."

"I wouldn't say I met him. I glimpsed him when I was brave enough to open my eyes."

"Hmm... well, he was useful to have around."

I'm not about to disagree. I can still remember how easy he made it look, carrying me up to my room, when my legs wouldn't work. Obviously, I didn't realize he was engaged to my sister… but I guess I didn't know I had a sister at the time, so…"

"That building on the far side of the grounds… is that where Pat and Mick live?"

"No. They've got an apartment above the garage."

"Is it for Ella and Mac, then? Do they need somewhere bigger now they've got a baby?"

He shrugs his shoulders. "To be honest, I don't know. They seem happy where they are right now. Henry's still tiny, and two bedrooms are enough for the time being. If they needed more space, or wanted to have more kids, they could build something larger here, or they might move to another house sometime. I don't know what their plans are. We haven't talked about it."

"Because of me?"

He smiles. "We have been kinda preoccupied with you, yeah."

"Sorry about that."

"It wasn't your fault," he says.

"Are we sure about that?"

"Absolutely."

"I definitely wasn't driving the car? You're not just saying that to make me feel better."

"You weren't driving, Drew. You'd arranged for Lexi to pick you up in her car and bring you here."

"Okay." I can't tell him how relieved I am, although judging by the look on his face, I think he might already know. "So… that building…?"

"Livia's parents live there."

"Oh?"

"Yeah. Her father had a stroke a few years ago, and her mom was finding things hard, having to work and care for him. They lived in Maine and Livia hated being so far away from them, so I had a home built for them here."

"That was generous of you."

"Not at all. I love my wife. I've loved her since the moment I met her. You felt the same way about Josie, and when you get your memory back, you'll remember how it feels to know you'd do anything to make her happy."

"I don't need to get my memory back to understand that. I haven't stopped loving Josie just because my brain is scrambled."

"You're not mad at her anymore, then?"

"Yeah, I'm mad at her. But that doesn't mean I don't still love her."

"And me?" he says, looking a little wary.

"What about you?"

"Are you still mad at me?"

"Yes. But it seems we're family, so I'll get over it."

He smiles. "When you walked away earlier, I was wondering if you'd ever speak to me again."

I shake my head. "I just needed some time to myself, like I said."

He lets out a slow sigh. "I'm so relieved."

"Because you thought I'd never forgive you?"

"Partly. But mostly because of Josie."

"Why Josie?"

"Because I knew how in deeply in love you were with the woman I knew as Lexi's sister. I could see you falling for Josie and I was powerless to stop it, even though it felt like your present was ruining your past. I was dreading your memory coming back, and you recalling the love you'd had for Lexi's sister, and what it might mean for you and Josie. Except I had nothing to worry about, did I? Because Lexi's sister and Josie are one the same person… thank God."

I smile at him, shaking my head. "That sounds a lot more complicated than it is, when in reality, the simple truth is, there's only one woman for me."

"It looks that way." He sits back a little. "Try not to be mad at Josie. None of this was her fault. She was told not to tell you about yourself. I was there when the doctor spoke to her. He was adamant it was in your best interests to be kept in the dark."

"I get that, even if I don't agree with it. But what I don't fully understand is why she didn't tell you who she was."

"She gave us a reason for that. It made sense to me."

"Did it?"

"Yeah. She wanted to be with you. I doubt her boss would have let her look after you if he'd known the truth, and that meant she could hardly tell me, could she? Besides, she probably thought I'd refuse to let her come here if I'd known about the connection between you."

"Would you?"

"No, of course not. But Josie didn't know that, did she?"

"No, I guess not."

He reaches out, putting his hand on my arm. "You need to tell her how you feel, Drew."

"I know."

I stand, and he looks up at me before slowly getting to his feet. "About Maisie…" he says, letting his voice fade.

I push my fingers back through my hair. "Yes… yes. I need to work something out, don't I? I need to… um… to…" I stop talking and look up into his dark brown eyes. "Would you think really badly of me if I told you I'm nervous?"

"What about?"

"Maisie. I'm responsible for her, but I don't even know her. It seems so strange that I wanted to have children with Josie, but now I've discovered I'm a father, just the word itself terrifies me."

"You were good at it, Drew. Really good."

"I'll have to take your word for that. The thing is, I don't feel like I can take her back to the cottage with me just now. There are things I need to discuss with Josie, and…"

He smiles. "I wasn't expecting you to take her with you right this minute. You've got an enormous amount of information to process, and you're right, you need some time with Josie... just the two of you. I was going to suggest that you come over later, or maybe tomorrow, and spend some time with Maisie. She can stay here with us until you're ready to care for her, and if it's easier for you, you can build up to having her come live with you, maybe just taking her for a few hours at a time. You don't have to do it all at once."

"Y—You're sure about that?"

"Of course. Although, to be honest, I'm also pretty damn sure that once you set eyes on her, you're not gonna want to let her go again. But we can take it in stages, if that's what works for you."

"Thank you."

He shakes his head. "You've got nothing to thank me for."

Somehow I doubt that, but that's a conversation for another day. "I'm gonna go talk to Josie."

"Okay. Be kind to her."

"I will."

He pats me on the shoulder and I step away, feeling better than I have in a while. Okay, so I'm still confused, and my brain still feels like cotton candy, but there seem to be a lot fewer holes in my story now.

He's right. I have got a lot to process, but there's no rush... not as far as I'm concerned. I know what I'm aiming for now, and even if there are still a few hurdles to face with Josie, I know we'll get there. As long as we're together, we can't fail.

I keep my head down as I'm walking, only looking up when I get to the cottage, letting out a surprised gasp when I notice the front door is open.

"Josie?" I rush inside, glancing around.

Everything looks as it did earlier, except for the addition of an envelope set prominently on the shelf above the fireplace. I stride over, seeing my name on the outside and I grab it, ripping it open, tearing the page from inside and reading…

'Drew,

I'm sorry. It wasn't supposed to end like this. It wasn't supposed to end at all. But I know you won't be able to forgive me for what I've done. I know I've lost you. I just wish I could turn back time and do things differently. Except I can't. Too much has happened and no matter how much I love you, it's too late for us now.

Josie x'

'Too late'? She can't be serious.

I re-read the note, then shove it into my pocket, running up the stairs.

My dressing room is a mess. She packed in a hurry, taking her things and leaving the drawers and closet doors open.

"For fuck's sake, Josie," I yell, slamming one shut.

I let my head fall, holding it in my hands. Why didn't I see this coming?

Probably because she told me she wouldn't run again… and I was dumb enough to believe her.

I thought we'd agreed, if she ever felt like this, she wouldn't run, she'd stay and talk. And yet, here I am, staring at an empty closet again. If I'd known there was any danger of her doing this, I'd never have left her by herself. I'd have followed her straight back here, and made sure she understood how much I love her, even if I am still mad at her.

"Oh, Christ…"

I rush out of the room, running down the stairs and straight out the door, closing it behind me. My sprint back to the main house takes no time at all, and I go around the back, finding Hunter sitting by the pool still. He looks up, frowning as I approach.

"What's wrong?" he asks.

"It's Josie. She's gone."

I pull out the note, handing it to him and he reads it, standing up as he does. He looks at me, handing it back, and shakes his head.

"I'll tell Livia what's going on, and I'll drive you into the city."

I nod my thanks, unable to speak, and sit down, waiting for him. It's a struggle, but I try to stay calm. Getting mad with Josie won't help. That's what drove her away in the first place. I need to tread carefully if I'm gonna bring her home again… and that's what I want, more than anything.

"You ready?" Hunter's voice makes me jump and I look up. He's standing beside me, a set of keys in his hand, and I get to my feet.

"Yeah. I'm sorry about this."

He shakes his head. "It's okay," he says, leading me around the far side of the house, where there's a double garage, with two cars parked in front of it… my Range Rover and his red Ferrari. We both head for the Range Rover, and he gets in behind the wheel. I'm not about to argue. If I thought I was fit enough to drive, I would.

"I take it we're heading for her apartment?" I look over at him as he starts off down the driveway.

"We don't have anywhere else to look."

I twist in my seat to face him. "What if she's not there?"

"We'll worry about that if it happens."

That doesn't feel very reassuring. "Why does she keep doing this?"

"Maybe she doesn't understand that arguments happen in relationships, and that you get over them."

"But why wouldn't she realize that? I told her she's my family."

He flips his head around, glancing at me as we get to the gate and it opens, letting us pass through onto the main road.

"You did?"

"Yeah. The last time she ran out, when we were at her apartment, I told her then she's my family. I…" I stop talking, remembering what we both said back then. "Oh…"

"Oh, what?"

"I just remembered something."

"Something from the past?"

"No. Something Josie said… or rather something she neglected to say. Again."

"What are you talking about?"

"Another lie. When she ran out on me last time, and we caught up with her at her apartment, she told us about how she couldn't have kids."

"I remember. I was there. That wasn't a lie."

"I know. But do you recall I said there was no guarantee I could have kids… that we couldn't be sure about it?"

He blushes. "Oh… yeah."

"I noticed her looking at you when I said that."

"Well, she would, wouldn't she? We both knew you already had a child. We just weren't allowed to tell you."

"Yeah… and look where that got us."

"I know. It hasn't worked out as well as any of us would have wanted."

"No shit." I suck in a breath, letting it out slowly and shaking my head. "Hiding things and keeping secrets, it's caused nothing but trouble. You know… after you'd gone to sit in the car, I asked her why she hadn't told me about her illness before and she said she couldn't, even though it wasn't about me. I thought that was odd, but I didn't question it too much. I was just so relieved to have her back. Now, I'm wondering if she chose not to tell me until she was cornered into doing so, in case she accidentally revealed something from our shared past."

"I guess that's possible."

"I think it's more than possible. It's highly probable."

"And? What's your point?"

"That it's another lie to add to the list."

"You've gotta stop thinking like that. They're not lies."

"What the fuck are they, then?"

He purses his lips. "I don't know. But it sounds like you're suggesting Josie was keeping things from you for her own benefit, which she wasn't. She was doing it because she believed it was in your best interests."

"Then she was wrong," I yell, and he takes his foot off of the gas, applying it to the brake and pulling up at the side of the road.

"Are you gonna talk to her like this when we catch up with her?" he says, slamming the car into 'park' and turning to face me. "Because if you are, I'm gonna turn around and take you straight back to the house." He stares at me. "She didn't lie to you." I raise my eyebrows. "Not intentionally."

"Maybe not, but look at where we've ended up."

"And this is all her fault, is it?"

"Why? Are you saying it's mine? I'm not the one who keeps running away."

He takes a deep breath. "No, but I heard her story earlier. Her childhood sounds kinda fractured."

"And ours wasn't?"

"It was. Entirely. But we always had each other. You, me and Ella. We had Pat and Mick, too, and I can honestly say we've never been alone, despite everything our parents did. You think Josie can say that? It sounded to me like she'd lived a solitary life, even when her mom was alive, but then her mom died when she was seventeen. Seventeen, Drew. When you were that age, you wouldn't have known where to start, and neither would I, but it seems like Josie fended for herself from then on. She didn't have anyone. She was used to being alone... even to cutting herself off when she had to. Think about it... she hadn't seen Lexi since Maisie's birth. That was a choice she made to protect herself from her feelings for you."

"But I don't understand it. She's not alone now. She's got me."

"Has she?"

"What does that mean?"

"What do you think?" he says. "She asked if you still loved her, and what did you say?"

"Nothing. But I was hurt. Surely, she understood that."

"She asked you the question, Drew. You had the chance to prove yourself to her."

And I didn't. I failed her. I close my eyes, opening them again after just a couple of seconds. "Shit... I fucked up, didn't I?"

"Yes."

"Take me to her... please."

He sits still, glaring at me. "Are you gonna yell at her?"

"No. I just wanna talk."

He doesn't say a word, but puts the car in 'drive' and checks the mirrors before pulling out onto the highway again.

What have I done?

I'll never forgive myself if I've lost her now, after everything we've been through...

Chapter Thirteen

Josie

Orla is standing at the nurse's station in the ER, staring at the computer screen, her brow furrowed, and I wonder if I can sneak past her. It seems mean when we've always been friends, but I'm not in the mood for conversation. Not today.

Unfortunately, she looks up at just the wrong moment, her face lighting up into a smile.

"Hello, stranger," she says. "We were wondering if we were ever gonna see you again." I smile, but don't answer. I'm not sure I know how. She clicks on the mouse a couple of times and then leans over the desk. "So, is this a flying visit, or are you back for good?"

"It's a flying visit." I'm definitely not staying. "I just need to see Doctor Sweeney."

"Ahh… and how is the patient?"

"He's okay."

That's a lie, but lying seems to be my forte… at least according to Drew.

"So, I guess you'll be coming back soon, will you?"

"I—I don't know."

I do. I know exactly what I'm doing, and it doesn't involve coming back here.

"It might be worth discussing your return with Doctor Sweeney, even if it isn't imminent."

"Why?" I'm intrigued. Her suggestion may be irrelevant, but I'd like to know what it means.

"Because they took on a temporary replacement to cover for you. Agatha Meadows insisted, evidently. She said it wasn't fair to expect everyone else to work extra hours to cover for you, and in the end, Doctor Sweeney agreed."

In a way, that makes things a little easier for me, and I nod my head. "Well… we'll see what happens." I make a show of checking my watch, even though I don't need to. It's not like I have an appointment or anything. "I'd better get upstairs."

She leans back, standing up straight. "I'd better check on the guy with chest pains in curtain four."

She comes around the desk. "Is it serious?" I ask.

"No. His ECG is fine, but we're monitoring him, anyway. I'd stake my life it's indigestion."

I smile and she smiles back, and I head for the elevators, pressing the 'up' button. The doors open immediately and I step inside, where I'm joined by a white-coated doctor, who's studying a file and absentmindedly presses the button for the third floor.

"What did you need?" he asks.

"I'm going to the third, too."

He nods, his eyes wandering downward slightly, appraising me for a moment or two before they return to the file he's still holding. I'm dismissed, but I don't mind in the slightest. It suits my mood.

When the doors open again, he moves aside, letting me step out ahead of him, and as I turn to the left, he goes to the right, and I make my way down the hall, grateful that Doctor Sweeney's office is outside of the main Neurotrauma unit. I can avoid meeting any of my colleagues and hopefully get this over with as quickly as possible.

The doctor's name is printed on a small sign stuck to the outside of the pale blue door, and I knock once, waiting until I hear him call out, "Enter."

I push the door open and step inside, closing it behind me. I can't fail to be reminded of the last time I was in here, when Doctor Sweeney told me of his and Hunter's plans, that Drew should return home to Newport to complete his therapy, and that I should join him. Of course, the doctor's intention was that I should remain Drew's nurse, and manage his recovery… not that I should become his lover, and make a mess of everything, including both of our lives.

He's sitting behind his desk, just like he did on that fateful day. Only now, he's studying a file and looks up as I approach him.

"Nurse Emerson?" He frowns at me, putting down the pen he's holding as he sits back in his chair. He's not wearing his white coat today, but is just in dark gray pants and a button-down shirt, undone at the neck. "What are you doing here?"

"I—I need to see you."

"Oh?" He waves his hand at the seat in front of his desk and I perch on the edge, feeling uncomfortable… and nervous. "Can I assume your presence here means there's been a change in Mr. Bennett's condition, and that for some reason, known only to yourself, you came all this way to tell me about it, rather than calling?"

He shakes his head, his frown deepening. "That's not why I'm here," I say. "But since you asked, there has been a development with Drew… with Mr. Bennett, I mean."

"In what way?"

"He worked out that Maisie is his."

"Maisie?" He looks perplexed.

"His daughter… the baby." How can he have forgotten?

"Oh, yes." His face clears. "He remembered her, did he?"

"No. He just worked out that she's his. He still has no memory of her, or of her mother."

"The woman who died?"

"Yes."

He sits forward again, resting his elbows on the table. "This is unfortunate. We're going to have to handle the next stage carefully."

"I'm afraid it's a little late for that."

"What do you mean?"

"Unfortunately, things came to a head, and Mr. Bennett's brother and I were forced to tell him everything."

"Everything?"

"Yes. It wasn't optional. If there had been any other alternative, I'd have taken it, trust me."

He stares at me for a long moment, then takes a breath, shaking his head. "Has Mr. Bennett had any memories of his own yet?"

"No, nothing of any significance."

"I see." He thinks for a moment. "This changes everything. Having his past revealed to him like that could bring about a rapid return of his memories. It… it could prove very traumatic for him." I feel even worse now, given my real reason for being here. "Do you think he'd consider coming back into the hospital?"

"No. But…"

"In that case, we'll have to reassess the situation."

"Please, Doctor… I didn't come here to tell you about Mr. Bennett's condition, or to discuss how his treatment might change."

"You didn't?"

"No. I came to tell you I can't stay there anymore."

He frowns, blinking a couple of times, and then gets up, coming around his desk and leaning against it, right in front of me. "Why on earth not?"

"My reasons are personal."

"So you want to come back here? You expect me to just…"

"I don't expect you to do anything. I'm leaving the hospital."

He stands up again, staring down at me, his mouth slightly open. "Y—You're what?"

"I'm leaving. I've got some vacation time owing, and I'd like to take it now, rather than giving notice."

"You mean, you're resigning?"

"Yes." How many ways does he need me to say it?

"This is all very irregular, Nurse."

"I know, but I've been told you've hired a replacement for me, so I'm hardly causing you a problem, am I?"

"And what about Mr. Bennett?" he says. "What about your duty to him?"

I feel the prickling of tears behind my eyes and blink them away, swallowing down the lump in my throat. "I—I guess Hunter Bennett will be in touch with you. Or maybe he'll hire a private nurse from somewhere else. I don't know."

"Hmm… and you obviously don't think it's your problem." He shakes his head, disapproval pouring off of him. "I have to say, I'm disappointed in you, Nurse Emerson." He walks back around his desk, sitting down and facing me again. "I've always thought you were one of our more caring and professional nurses. I'd expected better from you. But if this is your attitude to your patients, I think both we and they will be better off without you."

That stings, more than he'll ever know, but I just nod my head and get to my feet. "Can I take it I'm free to go?"

"You can. I'll contact Hunter Bennett myself and suggest a couple of private nursing agencies he could get in touch with. At least that way, one of us will be looking after the patient's interests."

I suppose I ought to thank him, but I can't speak, and instead I just leave his office, closing the door softly behind me. I'm so ashamed, so overwhelmed with crippling guilt, it's hard to put one foot in front of the other, but I have things to do… and I need to get on.

I wander down the hall, barely aware of my surroundings, knowing only that I need to clear my locker before I can go home. I called in at my apartment before coming here, just to drop off my bag and check my mail… and to cry for a little while, by myself, but I couldn't afford to delay, any more than I can now.

I've already decided I'm leaving town… and I'm going to do it today. Selling my apartment can wait a while. At least until I've settled somewhere new. I don't know where I'm going yet, but I've got some savings, so I can afford to rent a small apartment, and nursing jobs are fairly easy to come by, so I have no doubt I'll find something… somewhere.

My sight is blurred, but I know my way to the nurse's lounge and let myself in, grateful that I haven't met anyone I know, and that there's no-one in here, either. The gray walls match my mood, but I don't have time to dwell. I brought a couple of bags with me from my apartment and I pull them from my purse, going over to my locker and opening it as I let out a sigh. I'm starting to wish I hadn't stored quite so many things here now, but there's no point in wishing, is there? Let's face it, if there was any point in wishing, Drew would still love me, and I wouldn't be here at all.

No. Wishing doesn't get you anywhere. It just makes life hurt more.

I square my shoulders, trying to pretend the pain in my chest isn't threatening to bring me to my knees, and I stare at the contents of my locker.

I occasionally take a shower here, so the top shelf is loaded with shampoo, a couple of deodorants, and body wash. There's a tub of hand cream at the back, and a toothbrush and tube of toothpaste. I dump them all into one of the bags, along with the hairbrush and pack of spare hair ties. My hand is shaking, partly because I'm rushing, but mostly because Doctor Sweeney's words are ringing around my head, torturing me. Everything he said was completely deserved, but that didn't make it any easier to hear… or to keep hearing, on repeat, over and over… and over.

The door opens, slamming against the wall behind it, making me jump and I turn, letting out a yelp of surprise when Drew strides into the room, a little out of breath, followed closely by Hunter.

"There you are. Thank God…" Drew comes closer, shaking his head, his eyes locked on mine. "We tried your apartment, and you weren't there, but other than here, we couldn't think where else to go."

"Wh—What are you doing here?"

"Looking for you, of course," he says, staring down at the bag in my hand. He frowns, his eyes darting up to mine again. "What's going on?"

"I'm packing my things."

"Why?"

"Because I've quit my job, and I'm leaving town." I turn around, grabbing my small notebook from the top shelf of my locker. "If I hurry, I can leave tonight."

"And go where?"

I turn around again to find that, although Hunter is still standing just inside the door, Drew has moved much closer, his body just a few inches from mine, the heat and confusion pouring off of him.

"A—Anywhere."

"You're so desperate to get away from me, you'll go anywhere?" he says and I look up into his eyes, struggling to breathe as he reaches out and takes the notebook from my left hand and the bag from my right, and drops them to the floor. Then he steps even closer, so we're almost touching, and I gaze up at his troubled face. "I've never been to anywhere, Josie. The way my brain is right now, I wouldn't remember, even if I had. But if you go there – wherever it is – I'll follow you. I'll find you, and I'll bring you home."

My mouth drops open, a slight choke escaping my lips. "Y—You… you…"

He raises his right hand, cupping my cheek and closing the final gap between us, so his body is pressed against mine. "I'm sorry."

"What for?"

"I'm sorry I didn't tell you how much I love you when you asked. I should've done. That was a mistake."

"You mean you still love me?"

"I never stopped. Not even for a second." I find that hard to believe. I saw the look in his eyes earlier. There wasn't much love there. I open my mouth to say so, but he moves his thumb, clamping it across my lips. "That wasn't the only thing I wanted to say 'sorry' for."

I open my mouth and he moves his thumb, letting me speak. "Why? What else do you think you need to apologize for?"

"It's not an apology, as such, but I wanted to say sorry about Lexi."

Now I'm really confused, partly about what he's saying, but also because he's brushing his thumb back and forth across my lower lip, and it's very distracting. "I—In what way?"

"In the normal way that people say 'sorry' when someone dies. I know you keep saying you weren't close, but I think you wanted to be. Maybe I'm reading too much into things, I don't know… but when all's said and done, you and she were family. She died in that car accident, and I can't imagine what you went through when you found that out. You learned that your sister was dead, that Maisie had lost her mom, and that I was unconscious… all in the blink of an eye. It must have been horrendous."

"Yes. It was."

"And yet you put your own feelings to one side so you could look after my daughter… and me. I know you think you were being selfish, but I think the opposite is much closer to the truth. You couldn't mourn. You couldn't even mention your own grief. It was all about me and Maisie. I haven't acknowledged that yet, and I should have done. I'm sorry, Josie, for what happened to your sister… that you won't get to find out if you could've been friends."

Tears well in my eyes, blinding me for a moment. "Thank you." I suck in a breath, waiting for my blurred vision to clear, for his perfect face to come back into focus. "I don't understand, Drew."

"What don't you understand?"

"Why you're here? You're supposed to be angry with me, and you have every right to be."

"I know. And I am angry with you, but that doesn't mean you have to run away from me. You said you wouldn't do it again, after the last time. You agreed you'd stay and talk."

"I didn't think you wanted to talk."

"I said I needed some time alone. I know I didn't handle things very well, but the last thing I needed was for you to run out on me again. We're in a relationship, Josie… or I thought we were, and while I may not be very familiar with relationships, or how they work, my understanding is that you're not supposed to run every time the going gets tough… unless, of course, you don't love me."

"You know I love you. I—I just didn't think you loved me anymore."

"That's my fault. I should have made that clearer… but don't you get it?"

"Get what?"

He brings up his other hand, so he's cupping my face. "I don't remember my past. To me, it feels like I've had two lives; one before the accident and one after… and I've loved you in both of them. You, and no-one else. You're it, Josie. No matter who I am, or what life I live, you're mine, and I'm yours." He rests his forehead against mine. "Please, baby… if you're scared, or worried, or unsure, I'm the one you should turn to, not run from."

"But you were so mad at me."

"I know. The thing is, we can't keep doing this every time something happens." He's right. It hurts too much. He tilts his head back, looking into my eyes, narrowing his own. "There's more to this, isn't there? There's a reason you're so quick to fly… to say it's too late, even when it isn't." He must've read my note, then. I regret writing it now. I regret all of it, but most of all, I regret leaving him. "There's something I'm not seeing… something that's not necessarily to do with us." He sighs, frowning. "Is this something to do with your past?" he asks, his hands moving down to the sides of my neck, his thumbs caressing my jawline. "Was it your mom? No… your stepfather. Did he used to get mad at you?"

"Not me, no. But he used to get mad with Mom."

"And did she run?"

"No. Not until he cheated, and even then, she didn't really run. She just gave in, admitted defeat."

"So, what did she do when your stepfather got mad?"

"She stayed and let him yell at her... let him bully her, hurl abuse, and put her down."

"And you heard his?"

"Heard it and saw it. Regularly. It always made me run... so I could find somewhere to hide. I grew to hate the conflict, the shouting, the tension. I wanted to pretend I wasn't there."

He nods his head and closes his eyes, opening them again after just a few seconds to reveal the torture behind them. "I'm sorry, Josie. I shouldn't have raised my voice to you when we were back at the house. No matter how angry I was, I shouldn't have done that, and I promise I won't yell at you anymore. Okay?" I nod again, unable to speak. "Have I... Have I ever put you down?" he says.

I bring my hands up, resting them on his chest. "No, Drew."

"Do you think I ever would?"

"No. I didn't mean to imply you were like that. I just..."

He moves his thumb again, brushing it over my lips, cutting me off. "I may not remember it yet, but I walked into a party and fell in love with you, and from what I can gather, I've been in love with you ever since. I'll always love you, Josie, even when I'm mad at you." He puts his feet either side of mine, molding our bodies, his lips hovering over mine. "Except I don't think I can stay mad at you for very long... because I need you too damn much."

He touches his lips to mine, just as the door opens again, and we step apart, turning to see another nurse come in. She's wearing pink scrubs and I don't recognize her... not that I know everyone on this floor.

She looks from Drew to Hunter and then at me. "I didn't think men were allowed in here," she says, frowning.

"They're not." I bite on my bottom lip and Drew gazes down at me, shaking his head, and struggling not to smile. I'm not sure what's wrong with him, until he glances at my mouth, and I recall what he said about my bottom lip. It brings back memories of our first time together, and suddenly, out of nowhere, a raging inferno builds between us.

"I'm sorry," Hunter says, addressing the other nurse before he looks back at Drew and me. "Shall we go?"

"Where to?" I ask, feeling uncertain again, those flames not entirely extinguished, but dying down to a slight spark.

"What about Drew's apartment?" Hunter says, like he's sensed I'm not ready to be taken back to the cottage yet. "It's not that far away, and it's neutral territory for both of you. You can talk… say whatever needs to be said."

"Neutral?" I can't see how he can say that. "It's Drew's apartment."

"I know," Drew replies, stepping in front of me again. "But I don't remember it, and unless you're keeping something else from me, you've never been there, so…"

He has a point, I guess, and it's got to be better than standing here. "Okay. Your apartment it is." He smiles and the other nurse clears her throat, making her presence felt. "I just need to finish packing up my locker."

Drew looks inside. "Is there anything in there you can't live without, bearing in mind I'm evidently a multi-millionaire?"

He's wearing a mischievous grin and I can't help smiling just slightly as I glance inside the locker myself. "I guess not."

"In that case, let's get the hell out of here."

Drew

Josie's gone tense on me again.

We've been in the car for less than five minutes, the two of us sitting in the back, while Hunter drives, and I can feel the anxiety pouring off of her.

I'd thought she was reasonably relaxed by the time we left the nurse's lounge. She held my hand when I dragged her out into the hall, barely giving her time to grab her purse. She even giggled when I pulled her along to the elevators, and she stared up into my eyes all the while we rode down, even though Hunter was standing right in there with us. But when we got to the car, she came over all nervous, and now she won't even look at me. She's staring out the window, her hands in her lap, like I don't exist.

Is she having second thoughts?

God… I hope not.

I hope I haven't ruined everything.

I get that I just came on a little strong. It wasn't my intention to make her leave her things behind, or to use my wealth as a bargaining chip, but I wasn't thinking straight. I wanted out of there. My sole purpose was to get her somewhere private where we can talk, not to flaunt my millions. I hope I haven't offended her…

"Are you okay?" I ask.

She turns, startled by the sound of my voice, and nods her head, although I'm not entirely convinced. I give her a smile, which she struggles to return, and I move my hand along the seat, hoping she'll take it. She doesn't. She doesn't even seem to notice, and goes back to staring out the window.

"How much further?" I say to Hunter, and he glances in his rear-view mirror.

He said my apartment wasn't far, but now I just want to get there. I want to find out what's wrong, to make sure Josie's still mine, and she's not going to leave again.

"Less than five minutes."

I nod my head, wondering about the place I live and what it will be like, when a thought occurs... "How are we gonna get inside?"

"I've got your keys," Hunter says. "I've had them since the accident."

"Oh. I see."

It appears he's taken care of everything, which doesn't surprise me, and I sit back, looking over at Josie and wishing she'd turn my way.

She doesn't, but within just a few minutes, Hunter pulls into an underground parking garage. It's fairly well lit, and he drives around, parking in a bay on the far side before getting out. I join him and run around to Josie's side to help her. She accepts my hand and, once she's out of the car, I keep a hold of her. I'm not letting her go again... not now... not ever.

"This way," Hunter says, locking the car, and he leads us over to the elevators in the corner. There are two, but the one on the right opens first and we all climb in, Hunter pushing the button for the fifth floor.

"You mean I don't live in the penthouse?" I say, looking at him with a smile.

Hunter laughs. "No. That's more my style."

"So, you live in this building, too?"

He shakes his head. "No. I live in a different part of town. You bought this place before we inherited from Dad, and you chose it because it's close to your studio, which is why you haven't moved. You could've done, if you'd wanted, but you don't spend that much time here… or you didn't."

"I see."

The elevator doors open and Hunter steps out first. It makes sense, as he's the only one who knows the way. Josie and I follow, letting him lead us to the right, along a hall to the third door, which is numbered 512.

Pulling a key from his pocket, Hunter lets us inside. It feels warm, the air a little stifling and stale.

I stand, taking in my surroundings, trying to remember… but nothing's coming to me.

The space is quite impersonal. It's just a small lobby, with a dark wood floor and a couple of landscape photographs hanging on the white walls. I'm guessing I took them, although I have no recollection of the subject matter. The door to the left appears to lead to a bathroom, and there's a bedroom to our right. I glance inside, noting the vast bed, dressed with white bedding, the pale wood nightstands and closet, and the black and white photographs. Mine again, I guess.

"Is this my bedroom?" I ask, and Hunter turns.

"No. That's here." He nods to a door beyond the bathroom, and I step forward, still keeping hold of Josie, and look inside.

This room is quite similar to the other one, except there are signs of someone actually living here… a book beside the bed, a pair of shoes next to the dresser.

Hunter leads the way further into the apartment, to an open-plan living area.

"I thought you said this place was small," Josie says, looking around.

"He did?"

"Yes." She looks up at me.

"I don't remember…"

"It wasn't today," Hunter says. "It was when you were still in the hospital. We were trying to decide where it would be best for you to go while you recuperated, and I said that coming here would be impractical because it's not very big."

I glance around at the high ceilings, the enormous windows, the expansive living area, with dark blue furnishings, and I turn and frown at him.

"It's not?"

He smiles. "Okay, it's not that small, but there's only one bathroom here, and I knew that if you were both staying here, it could be inconvenient."

"Oh, I don't know." I glance at Josie. She blushes, and I wish I'd kept quiet now.

"Well… I wasn't to know how things were gonna develop between you," Hunter says. "Or that there was any history. But in the past, whenever Ella's stayed here, you used to make a point of staying away as much as you could."

"I don't remember Ella yet, but I imagine there's an enormous difference between sharing this place with my sister and being here with Josie." I look down at her again and, although she's still holding my hand, I can sense her discomfort.

"I'm more than familiar with Ella," Hunter says, "and you're dead right." We both laugh, although I'm aware of Josie's uneasiness. I think Hunter is too. He gives me an odd look, his eyes dropping to her. "Shall I fix us some coffee?"

"Sure."

He wanders to the other end of the room, into the kitchen area, which has white cabinets and granite countertops, and I turn toward Josie, knowing I need to say something, but scared I'll say the wrong thing and make it all worse… if that were possible.

"Is this bringing back any memories?" she asks, saving me the trouble of starting the conversation.

"No."

Hunter's phone rings, but we both ignore him as he pulls it from his pocket, speaking in muffled tones.

"Does it feel like your kind of place?"

"I don't know. I'm not sure what that is. The color scheme feels similar, but it's not very personal. Still, I guess if I didn't spend much time here…" I step in front of her, cupping her face in my hands and she gasps, looking up into my eyes. "What's wrong?"

"Nothing's wrong."

"Don't bullshit me. You're nervous. I can feel it. I just don't know why. Surely you know you're safe with me."

"Of course I do."

"Then why…?"

"I feel like you've brought me here to talk."

"I have."

"But I don't know what to say."

I smile, resting my forehead against hers. "You don't have to say anything."

"Then what are we doing here?"

"We had to go somewhere, Josie. We couldn't stay at the hospital…"

"Asshole." We both turn at the sound of Hunter's raised voice, and he glances over, shaking his head and stepping toward us. "Sorry," he says, looking at Josie, but she shakes her head.

"Are you okay?" I ask.

"Yeah, I'm fine." He holds up his phone, like it's an exhibit. "That was Doctor Sweeney."

I feel Josie tense beside me. She even takes a half step back and I look down. Her eyes have widened, her skin paling as she looks at my brother. He seems to have noticed her reaction, too, and moves a little closer.

"What did he want?" I ask and Hunter looks back at me again.

"He called to apologize."

"What the hell for?"

"To use his words, for Josie's lack of professionalism." He looks pained, but that doesn't stop Josie from flinching and I let go of her hand, putting my arm around her. She's so stiff, I can't mold my body to hers, but I'm not giving up. I keep a firm grip on her, regardless.

"Are you serious?"

"Completely. He was angry because Josie had walked out on you."

I turn to Josie. "You told him?"

She looks up at me, her eyes clouded with confusion. "Told him what?"

"About us."

"No," she says. "I just explained that I couldn't keep working with you. I didn't give him a reason… and then I told him I wanted to leave the hospital. He said how disappointed he was, and that he thought the staff and patients would be better off without me."

"That was a shitty thing to say."

She blinks a couple of times, like she's trying hard not to cry. "Was it?"

"Yes. It also isn't true. You did everything he asked of you, even when you weren't sure it was right, and you only left because it became personally difficult for you to stay. That wasn't your fault."

She shrugs her shoulders, like she's not convinced, and I wonder if her nerves are entirely due to our situation, or whether his words have hit home… if they're one of those conflicts she'd rather run and hide from.

I turn back to Hunter. "Why was he calling you?" I ask.

"To offer a few suggestions for private nursing agencies, where he said I'd be able to find someone to look after you."

"He said he was gonna do that," Josie says and I look back at her, knowing now that I'm right. I can see it in her eyes. She was expecting this call, although I imagine she hoped it would come later, when we weren't all together.

"To humiliate you?"

"No. He said he was putting the patient first, even if I wasn't."

"Except I wasn't your patient, was I?"

"Yes, you were."

"No. First and foremost, I was your lover." I hope to God I still am, but I don't think now is the time to say that. "It was more complicated than he realized, Josie. You can't take his criticisms to heart."

"Can't I?"

"No." Hunter and I both speak at the same time and she looks over at him, and then back at me.

"I let you down."

"No, you didn't. And before you argue with me, it's for me to judge how you made me feel, and no-one else."

"And how did I make you feel?" she asks, nibbling on the corner of her lip.

I pull it free with my thumb, because it's too distracting, and look into her eyes. "Scared."

"Scared?"

"Yes. When we couldn't find you, I was terrified. I thought I'd lost you." I lean in and kiss her forehead, then turn back to Hunter. "What did you tell Sweeney?"

He stares at me for a second, then shakes his head, like he's coming out of a dream. "I told him thanks, but you didn't need a nurse anymore." He glances down at Josie and then back at me, with a slight smile on his lips.

"No, I don't."

"Sweeney disagreed," Hunter says, tipping his head one way and then the other. "He said the next part of your recovery could be traumatic, but I told him we'll cope." He lets his eyes drift down to Josie again and leaves them there this time. "Did I do the right thing?"

She nods her head, and Hunter smiles, returning to the kitchen.

I can't help feeling a little relieved. We've got a lot to talk about, but that felt like Josie was saying – albeit silently – that she's willing to come home with me. That's a start. It's a step in the right direction.

"We don't have to talk, if you don't want to," I say and she looks up at me, frowning.

"We don't?"

I suck in a breath, deciding to take a chance. "If you're coming home with me, we've got time. We can talk later, or tomorrow… or whenever you're ready. There are things that need saying…"

"Yes, there are."

"But they don't have to be said all at once… and not right now."

She almost sags with relief, and while I don't know whether to be pleased or disappointed by that, I console myself that at least she's coming home.

For now.

She glances around, like she's looking for a change of subject, and I can't say I blame her. There's too much tension. It needs breaking, and her eyes settle on the enormous wall-mounted television, which seems to have some kind of sound system beneath it.

"It seems you like your home entertainment," she says, looking up at me.

"Yeah. I wonder what kind of music I listen to?"

"I don't know. We never played any at the cottage."

"No." I wander over, feeling intrigued by my tastes, and flick on the sound system. There's something already set up, and within a second, the room is filled with the sound of a piano playing… and then what seems to be a harp. At that precise moment, Josie bursts into loud tears behind me and I spin around, going straight to her, just as a man starts singing about the love of his life.

"What's wrong, baby?"

I take her in my arms, and she sobs against me. "It doesn't matter. You won't remember it."

"Remember what?"

She looks up at me, tears streaming down her cheeks. "This."

"What? The music?"

"Yes."

It obviously means a great deal to her, and I close my eyes, holding her close to me. "Who's singing?" I ask, wondering if it will help.

"It's Freddie Mercury."

That means nothing, but as other voices join in, harmonizing with his, I get a shiver down my spine, and the briefest of images flashes through my head.

"A red dress," I murmur, opening my eyes. Josie's staring up at me, smiling through her tears.

"Yes. I was wearing a red dress."

I clasp her cheeks in my hands, pushing my fingers back through her hair. "Was your hair shorter?"

"No. I was wearing it up."

"That's right." I nod my head. "There's nothing else. My mind's a blank apart from that. I'm sorry."

"Don't be sorry. I'm just glad you've remembered that much."

"Was it our first meeting? Is that why the song matters?"

"Yes. It was playing at that party… the one I told you about."

"I can't remember anything except your red dress and your hair."

"It's enough."

"Is it?"

"For now, yes." The music stops and then immediately starts again, and she sighs. "You've got it on repeat."

"Evidently. It must have been important." She smiles and leans in to me, her arms coming around my waist, a very different person to the one who looked so doubtful and anxious, just a few minutes ago. "Are you okay?" I ask.

She nods, looking up again. "I didn't mean to make you scared."

"It's okay. I told you, we don't have to talk now."

"I understand that, but I just wanna say… I—I never wanted to hurt you, or make you scared, Drew."

"I know. I said some things earlier which I shouldn't have done. Blaming you for what happened was childish. It wasn't your fault."

"You were so angry." Her eyes darken, like she's re-living those awful moments outside the house in Newport.

"I was."

"Even at the hospital, you said you were still angry."

"I know. But I'm not angry anymore. Like I said, I need you too much to stay mad at you for very long."

"You need me?" She gazes into my eyes, like she can't quite believe me.

"Yes. I think this piece of music proves that."

"It does?"

"Of course it does. I might not remember it now, but I clearly played it non-stop when I was here, presumably because it reminded me of you," I say, moving closer, and this time her body molds to mine. "I've needed you all my life, Josie."

"Which one? The one before the accident, or the one after?"

"Both."

I crush my lips to hers and as she sighs in to me, I know I'm as close to finding myself as I ever need to be.

Chapter Fourteen

Josie

"This won't take a minute. I didn't unpack my bag, so I just need to run in and get it."

I unfasten my seat belt and reach around to open the car door, but Drew grabs me, pulling me back and across the rear seat, into his arms.

"We're coming inside with you," he says.

"Why? I just said, there's no need." To be honest, now I know we're going back to Newport – or going 'home' as Drew insists on calling it – I just want to get there… to lie in his arms and feel safe again. The fact that we've had to call in at my apartment is an inconvenience, but a necessary one, as all my things are here.

"Yes, there is." He's adamant, his jaw firm, his eyes fixed on mine.

"I can carry a bag all by myself, you know?"

"I know… but there'll be more than one."

"No, there won't."

"Yes, there will." He twists in his seat, pulling me up onto his lap. "You're not coming to stay this time, Josie."

"I'm not? But I thought…"

"You're moving in." I open my mouth, but he shakes his head and I close it again. "Don't bother arguing. You know this is what you want, just as much as I do. We belong together. I think that much is obvious."

"But I can't pack everything… not now."

"I know, and you don't have to. We can come back another day and take care of most of it. I just want you to bring enough with you to convince me you're gonna stay."

I rest my head on his shoulder. "I'm gonna stay, Drew. If it makes you feel better, I'll even sell my apartment."

He leans back into the seat and places his finger beneath my chin, making me look up into his beautiful face. "You will?"

"Yeah. I was gonna sell it anyway, after I left town, so…"

He bends his head, touching his lips to mine, and then deepens the kiss, our tongues meeting in a heartfelt dance, until the sound of Hunter's deliberate cough breaks us apart.

"Did someone mention packing?"

Hunter and Drew took my bags upstairs the moment we got back, and left them in Drew's dressing room. I'll unpack them later… or maybe tomorrow, or the next day. It doesn't feel like there's any rush now, and that's just as well, because I'm exhausted, emotionally, as well as physically.

Hunter waved away my thanks before he left, and then put his arm around Drew's shoulders, walking him out through the front door. I can hear them talking in whispers, although I can't make out what they're saying and I stand still, waiting, wishing Drew would come back in.

I know it sounds pathetic, but even though he's held me all the way back here, I feel lost without him. I need the reassurance of his arms and his kisses and his words. More than anything, I need him to tell me his memories are real, to give me hope that it's all coming back to him… that our past and our future can merge, rather than colliding.

I jump at the sound of the door closing and turn to see Drew standing there, the two of us alone at last.

"What was that about?" I ask.

"Hunter was just reminding me to be kind to you." He walks over, taking my hand and leading me to the couch, where he sits, pulling me down beside him. "Not that I needed reminding."

I'm relieved to hear that. I'm feeling a little bruised after today, and I think I'd like to be bathed in kindness for a while.

He pulls me into his arms and I rest against him, although he quickly lets out a sigh.

"What's wrong?" I ask.

"You're not close enough."

He shifts down the couch, turning onto his back, and lifts me up on top of him. I lie out and he brings his arms around me, letting one hand rest on my ass.

"Is that better?"

"Much," he says. "I need you close. All the time." I nestle against him and he holds on just a little tighter. "Do you need anything?" he asks, in a drunken-sounding whisper.

"Just you."

He kisses the top of my head. "That's good to know… but I meant food, or drink. Are you hungry?"

"I probably should be, but I'm too tired to care."

"Hmm… I know the feeling. I was just saying to Hunter, I'm gonna leave meeting Maisie until tomorrow now."

I lean up, looking down at him. "You are? I—I assumed you'd have met her earlier."

"No. I went for a walk… like I said I would. Then I went back to Hunter, loaded with questions, which he answered, and then we talked about Maisie. I told him how nervous I am about being a father, and…"

"You're nervous?" I can't believe I'm hearing this.

"Yes," he says. "Suddenly discovering you have a child is a strange sensation."

I lower my head. "Hmm... one you wouldn't have to be experiencing if I hadn't kept her from you."

He clasps my chin, raising my face to his. "We're not going through all that again, Josie... especially not now. We're both too tired."

I nod my head, knowing he's right. "So, what are you gonna do about Maisie?" I ask.

"I've just told Hunter, we'll go over there sometime tomorrow. He's said we can take it in stages, if we need to... spend some time with her at the main house before bringing her back here."

"I think that's sensible in terms of your recovery. You've got a lot to process."

"Stop talking like my nurse," he says with a smile, but I can't return it, and his own fades. "What's wrong, Josie?"

"It's nothing."

"It's not nothing. Tell me what's wrong."

"It was something you said earlier, when we were all outside the main house. But you don't wanna talk about that now, and I think you're right. We should wait."

He shakes his head, just slightly. "What did I say?"

"It can wait, Drew."

"No, it can't," he says. "Tell me."

"Okay. It was about me being your nurse. You asked if that was all I was."

"I did?"

"Yeah. You'd just worked out that we knew each other before the accident, and you said, 'So, you're not just my nurse?'. It made me wonder if that was all I meant to you."

"Of course it wasn't." He closes his eyes for a second, opening them again, and planting a soft kiss on my lips. "A lot of what I said earlier came out wrong. That's why I don't want to talk now, in case I make the same mistakes again. But I have to tell you… you were never just my nurse. Not even when I was in the hospital and you were wearing scrubs and taking my blood pressure… and checking out my ass. You were always more than that."

I smile, resting my head against his chest, feeling the rise and fall. "Thank you for saying that."

"You don't have to thank me. It's the truth. I just wish I could remember more. No matter how hard I try, I'm still only getting a red dress and your hair."

"Stop trying so hard." I reach up, stroking his cheek with my fingertips. "It'll come back to you."

"I know. It's just that now I'm getting these tiny chinks of memory, I want it all back."

"Don't rush it. Doctor Sweeney was right about that. Some of what you're going to remember will be traumatic."

"You mean things like the accident?"

"Yeah, although there's a chance you might not remember very much about that, even when you get everything else back."

"I can't say I'll be sorry about that."

"No, but there are other things for you to consider… other memories. Like your childhood."

He frowns, confused. "You know about that?"

"I know a little."

His frown clears in an instant. "Oh… of course. You met my mom."

"How did you know that?"

"Hunter told me. I asked him to fill in some gaps… one of which was how we came to have so much money. He told me about our parents."

"I see. Well, I know your mom left when you were very small, but I don't know much about your father."

He looks into my face for a few seconds and then nods his head. "I'm not gonna tell you about it all now. I think it might be better to work it through with you when the memories come back."

"If that's what you want."

"It is. If I told you now, I'd be giving you Hunter's version, and while I don't doubt a word of what he's said, I'd rather tell you what happened from my own perspective."

"I think that's wise."

"You do?"

"Yes. Just don't force the memories and remember to talk to me."

He smiles. "I don't think I'm gonna forget that, baby."

I lay my head down again, and he strokes my back, his other hand still resting on my ass. It's comforting here. Lying on Drew is the best place to be, and even if the past is still another country to him, he's taken the first steps toward discovering it.

He shifts slightly beneath me. "I'm sorry," he says.

"What for?"

"I know we said we'd wait to talk some more, but…" I look up at him. He seems troubled.

"What's wrong, Drew?"

"Are you sure you're okay with this?"

"With what?"

He pauses for a moment, taking a deep breath and letting it out slowly. "With the situation. With me having slept with your sister. I mean, there's nothing I can do about it now, but…"

I wriggle up his body, so we're face-to-face. "Drew… I'm the one who went into this with my eyes open. I knew what I was letting myself in for. You're the one who had no idea about Lexi and the past you'd shared with her. But what your brother and I told you earlier was the truth. What you had with her was very transient, and neither of you took it seriously. Besides, she wasn't my sister... not really. We weren't related by blood." I stop talking, aware that I'm rambling. "Why do you ask?"

"Because I want to take you to bed, and I need to be sure you're completely happy with how things are."

"I am, Drew. Honestly. I've known all along about you and Lexi... and Maisie, and it hasn't made the slightest difference to how I feel about you."

He nods his head. "Put your legs either side of mine."

I do as he says, straddling him, and as he sits up, I go with him, squealing slightly as he twists around and stands, his hands coming beneath me as he lifts me into his arms.

"Why don't you let me walk? You're tired."

"I'm not that tired."

He carries me up the stairs and straight into his bedroom, kicking the door closed, before he walks over to the bed, lowering me down his body.

"It feels like a lifetime since we were last here," he whispers, pulling my t-shirt over my head. I recall our playful conversation this morning.

"It's a whole other world ago."

He nods. "But we can make this a better world, Josie. I promise."

He undoes my bra, releasing my breasts and leans down, kissing first one nipple and then the other, before he unfastens my jeans, pushing them down over my hips. His hands roam around behind me, and he squeezes my bare flesh.

"I'd forgotten you weren't wearing any panties." He pulls me closer, his arousal pressing into me, and I look up into his eyes.

"I hadn't." I undo his jeans, pushing them down, and let my hand slip around his erection. He gasps, his head rocking back as I slide my grip up and down his length, over and over, building up a steady pace.

"I'm sorry," he murmurs. "I can't wait." He kicks off his jeans, yanking his t-shirt over his head at the same time, and then he lifts me onto the bed, pulling off my jeans before he crawls up over my body. "I need to be inside you, baby. I need to feel you come."

I part my legs wide, pulling them up toward my chest and he pushes inside me. I let out a gasp as he joins us, relaxing into the stretch, until I'm so full of him I can't take any more. He rests his body against mine, completely still.

"We're home," I whisper.

"Where we belong."

I nod and he pulls out, plunging slowly back in again. He keeps it gentle, resting his hands behind my knees, holding me down, but loving me so tenderly, like he's worshipping me. I rest my hands on his biceps, his muscles flexing with every move, and I match his pace, pulse for pulse, breath for aching breath.

"D—Don't ever run from me again, Josie." His eyes bore into mine, his words uttered in a hoarse, stuttered breath.

"I won't."

"My heart is more fragile than you'll ever know. I couldn't take it if you left again."

"I'm not going to."

He releases my legs, moving his hands up so they're on either side of my head, and then leans in, kissing me… hard. His tongue finds mine and as he thrusts inside me, deeper and deeper, I feel that familiar quiver at my core. He must feel it too, because he breaks the kiss, gazing down at me.

"Please, Josie…"

His words are enough to push me over the edge, my body succumbing to pleasure, a myriad of starbursts tumbling through me in wave after wave of ecstasy.

I feel Drew plunge into me once, twice more and on the third time, he lets go inside me, my name a repeated howl that's almost anguished in its intensity.

My body is still recovering, still twitching against his as he turns us over onto our sides, holding me in his arms.

"Sleep, baby," he murmurs, his eyes already closing, exhaustion claiming him, and I drift into peaceful oblivion, knowing I'm safe at last.

"Brake! Hit the fucking brakes!"

I'm woken by Drew's shouts and flip over in bed. He's sweating, his body rigid, although his head is rolling from side to side.

"Drew?"

"It's okay. I love you. I won't let anything hurt you."

What? "Drew? Wake up." I raise my voice and he opens his eyes, sitting up, his breathing labored as he rubs his hands down his face. "Are you okay?" I ask.

He turns, looking at me, and then lies back, taking me in his arms. "I'm fine. It was just a nightmare."

"Tell me about it."

"No." I pull away from him, releasing myself from his grasp, and although he tries to pull me back, I hold up my hand, stopping him. "What's wrong?" he says.

"You said you'd talk to me, Drew, so don't shut me out."

"I'm not. It was just a nightmare, Josie."

"Yeah, a nightmare in which you just said 'I love you' to someone. I need to know who and why."

He lets out a long sigh. "Okay, I'll tell you." I can sense his reluctance and shift away slightly. He watches and shakes his head. "Don't do that, baby. You said you wouldn't run."

"I'm not running, but I need to know who you were talking to."

"It was Maisie. My dream, or nightmare… or memory – if that was what it was – it was about the accident." I move back beside him again and he puts his arms around me. "I can't remember very much of it, other than a feeling of powerlessness… of being out of control and wanting to save Maisie, but not being able to get to her. She was too far away."

He turns onto his side and I see the pain in his eyes, the reality of what he dreamed, or remembered, and I hug him. "It's okay, Drew."

He shakes his head, clinging to me. "No, it's not. If that was what it was really like, I don't want to remember anymore, Josie. I don't want it to come back."

There's no point in me repeating that it'll be okay, when I think we both know it probably won't, so I just hold him, and he holds me, until eventually, we drift off to sleep again.

I pop the last piece of pancake into my mouth and put down my fork, taking a sip of coffee, all the while, my eyes never leaving Drew's. He's sitting opposite me, holding my left hand, even while he eats, and doesn't show any signs of letting it go… not that I'm complaining.

We woke about an hour ago, and although we both agreed we were hungry and in need of breakfast, we needed each other more. Drew got up and pulled me into the shower, lifting me into his arms and taking me. It was very different to last night, which was tender and gentle, like a re-discovery. Our shower this morning was heated and frenzied. His lips were all over me, his hands and fingers everywhere. There was an urgency to our love-making that took my breath away, and I shudder now, just thinking about it.

"Are you okay?" Drew asks, finishing his pancakes and pushing his plate aside.

"Hmm… I was just thinking about this morning."

He smiles. "It was pretty memorable."

I can feel myself blush. "I wish you could remember more."

"What about? This morning? Trust me, I remember every second of what we did."

I shake my head. "That's not what I mean. I—I wish you could remember what you did before… with other women."

"Why would I want to?"

"Because it would be nice to think that at least some of what we do is different."

"Everything we do is different… because it's with you." I smile, and he clasps my hand a little tighter. "Are you thinking about what I think you're thinking about?" he says, narrowing his eyes.

"That depends on what you think I'm thinking about."

"Me, fingering your ass." My body convulses in a sudden shock of pleasure, and Drew smiles. "Guess I was right." He raises my hand, kissing my fingers. "You asked me before if I'd done anything like that, with anyone else."

"Yes."

"I think we both know now that you meant Lexi, didn't you?"

I nod my head. "I know I said I'm not worried about you and her, and I'm not, but…"

"Hey… it's okay. If the roles were reversed, I'd feel the same. I wish I could tell you with any certainty what went on between us, but I can't. Not yet. Hopefully I will, one day, but until then the only thing I can say is, I can't believe I would have done that with anyone else… including Lexi."

"Why not?" I ask.

"Because it feels like there's too much trust involved. There's something about the way you give yourself to me. I can't picture myself being in that situation with anyone other than you. Obviously, I could be wrong… but I hope I'm not."

"I guess we'll find out when your memory comes back."

"Hopefully. Do you want me to tell you, either way?"

"Yes. I need to know… and I don't want there to be any secrets between us."

"No. No more secrets."

He gazes across the table at me. "I hated keeping things…" I say, and he reaches out, touching his forefinger against my lips.

"That's enough, Josie. We're not going to talk about it. I know you were only doing what the doctor told you, and even if it backfired, it wasn't your fault. Regardless of all the things I said yesterday, I don't blame you."

I pull his hand away, keeping hold of it and lower it to the table, so all four of our hands are clasped together.

"There are still things we need to talk through, though."

"Yes, we do. About the future. We don't need to keep raking over the past. For one thing, I still don't really have one." He tilts his head to one side. "But I have a future, don't I? With you?"

"Yes, of course you do. If that's what you want."

"More than anything. Let's just leave the past and my memories to take care of themselves, shall we?"

I nod my head. "But only if you agree to talk things through with me, when you need to."

He pulls his hands from mine and gets to his feet, coming around the table and standing beside me. I look up and he offers me his hand again, this time pulling me to my feet and into his arms. "I'll tell you everything." He kisses the tip of my nose. "No secrets, remember?"

I smile, nodding my head, and he places his hands on my denim-clad ass, pulling me close to him, so I can feel his arousal.

"Wearing clothes is very over-rated, you know?"

"Hmm… but what if someone comes over?"

He bends, brushing his lips against mine. "There's no rule that says we have to answer the door."

He has a point, and I tilt my head back as he deepens the kiss. I'm not wearing any underwear and he squeezes me, groaning into my mouth, just as someone knocks on the door.

I pull back, smiling. "You see? This is why we wear clothes."

"Maybe. But you'll need to see who it is."

"I will?"

"Yeah. I've got a raging hard-on, so I think I'd better sit down and do my best to disguise it, don't you?"

I giggle, unable to help myself, and we leave the dishes on the table, wandering into the living room. Drew sits on one of the blue chairs, pulling down his t-shirt to hide the bulge in the front of his jeans, and I wander to the front door, opening it to find Hunter and Livia standing there, his arm around her shoulders.

"Sorry. Did we disturb something?" Hunter says.

"No." I smile.

"Yes." Drew's reply comes out at the same time as mine and I turn, narrowing my eyes at him.

Hunter laughs and I look back at him, noticing the slight blush on Livia's cheeks. It's the first time I've seen her since we met at the hospital, and she smiles at me, rolling her eyes.

"Don't worry. They're always like this."

I can't help smiling myself because at least Drew is doing something in character… something recognizable. And that's got to be good.

I step back, letting them into the cottage, and I close the door, offering them a seat on the couch. They accept, sitting side-by-side, and I move past Drew, heading for the other chair. He grabs my hand, though, pulling me down onto his lap and holding me tight against him. I can feel his arousal pressing in to me, and a blush creeps up my cheeks, although he stares across at his brother, unfazed.

Hunter is grinning broadly, his arm around Livia. "This feels odd, but I guess I should introduce you." He smiles at Livia and then turns back to Drew. "This is my wife, Livia."

"It's nice to meet you," Drew says. "Although I guess this isn't the first time."

"No, it's not," Livia says, smiling.

"We didn't come over just to make introductions," Hunter says. "And I'm sorry for disturbing your morning, but we wanted to tell you our news…" He glances at me, just for a second, something like sympathy in his eyes, and I know what he's going to say, even before he announces, "Livia's pregnant."

I feel the tug of anguish deep inside me, and while I should be getting used to it by now, I'm not sure I ever will. Drew holds me tighter, maybe sensing my distress, although he doesn't say a word. He doesn't need to.

Livia looks directly at me. "I'm sorry," she says. "This must be the last thing you wanted to hear."

"No. Not at all. I'm pleased for you. Truly, I am." I just wish it didn't have to hurt so much.

"We only found out this morning," Hunter says. "And I know it might seem that we're telling you really early, but…"

"You've wanted this for a long time," Drew says, finishing his brother's sentence and we all look at him, even though I have to twist on his lap to do so.

"Yes," Hunter replies. "How did you know?"

"You mentioned to Drew that you and Livia had talked about having children," I say. "He's probably thinking of that."

"No, I'm not." Drew sits forward slightly, bringing me with him. "As far as I was aware, Maisie was theirs, not mine, so I didn't question what they were doing about having kids. I assumed they'd already done it, if you see what I mean." He shakes his head slowly. "No… there's something else in the back of my mind about the two of you, although I don't know whether it's this, or if it's to do with something else."

Livia blushes and murmurs, "Oh, God," under her breath, and Hunter laughs, looking down at his wife.

"I don't know why you're embarrassed, babe. Drew might not remember everything yet, but he will one day."

"What is it I'm supposed to remember?" Drew asks.

"Just that, when Livia and I first got together, you nearly caught us in the act."

Drew chuckles, his body shaking beneath mine. "Perhaps that's one thing I'll pretend I forgot permanently... for your wife's sake."

"Man, you really have changed." Hunter tilts his head, staring at his brother. "The old Drew never passed up the chance to score points over me."

"I've changed in all kinds of ways," Drew says, hugging me tighter.

"So it seems." Hunter glances at me, smiling. "But I still can't work out how you knew Livia and I were trying for a baby."

"I don't know." Drew sounds thoughtful. "Is it something to do with a telephone call?" He looks at me, but I shrug my shoulders.

"It would have been before the accident, Drew. I wouldn't know."

He turns his attention to Hunter. "There was sunlight and I'm getting an image of domed rooftops. Does that make sense?"

Hunter smiles. "Yeah, it does. You were in Rome on that assignment, and you called me a couple of days before you came home. We talked about it then."

"That's when you told me?"

"No, you already knew."

"I did? How?"

"I told you just after Maisie was born. Livia was finding it kinda hard, what with Ella being pregnant as well, and you noticed she wasn't being her usual self, so I told you what was going on."

"Please tell me I didn't try to score points."

Hunter shakes his head. "No. I don't think you could've been more supportive. I couldn't always share my feelings with Livia, so it helped, knowing you were there."

"But surely you had Ella, too."

"We didn't tell her."

"Why not?"

"Trying for a baby is really personal… especially when it's not working out. Somehow, having you in my corner made it a little easier. It was like you said in that phone call, when you were in Rome, I had to be strong for Livia, but sometimes I needed someone to be strong for me… and that was where you came in. That's why I wanted to tell you our news. Because even though you don't remember, you've been there for me, and I appreciate it."

"Are you keeping it to yourselves, then?"

"Just for now. We won't be able to for long. Pat will almost certainly work it out if Ella doesn't get there first."

Drew takes a deep breath and I look into his eyes, seeing how happy and proud he is that his brother trusted him with this. It's important, I can tell, and I nestle in to him. He looks down, tilting his head to one side.

"Are you okay?" he asks. I nod my head, just once, and he tucks my hair behind my ear, his thumb caressing my cheek. "It's all gonna work out just fine, Josie. I promise."

I close my eyes, his lips dusting mine, and I let myself believe him… because when I'm in Drew's arms, anything feels possible.

Drew

I break the kiss, gazing into Josie's eyes.

As much as I liked hearing my brother's good news, and knowing I was there for him when he needed me, it had to be hard for Josie, and I'm aware of that… aware that their joy is something she can never share… never feel.

Our happiness feels tempered, moderated by this one sadness. Except it doesn't have to be like that. It's within my power to make it better, to take away at least some of the ache Josie feels for the one thing she can never have… never be. At least, in her eyes.

I kiss her again, just briefly, and turn to Hunter.

"I know we planned to do this later today, but I had a dream last night, which was a kind of memory, too. It was to do with the accident, and it's left me with this… this need to protect my daughter. So, do you think it would be possible for me to meet her now?"

Livia sits forward on the couch. "Of course," she says, answering for Hunter. "I left her with Pat while we came over here, but she's yours, Drew. She always was."

I smile over at her. "I'm grateful to you for looking after her for as long as you have."

"You don't have to be grateful."

"Oh, I think I do." Livia smiles at me, lowering her eyes, and I look down at Josie. "Are you ready for this?"

She doesn't know what I've got in mind, but she nods her head. "If you are."

"I am. That dream left me kinda rattled, and I guess hearing Hunter and Livia's news has made me wanna try being a father again."

She sucks in a breath, letting me know this won't be easy for her, although I'm hopeful I can make it better than she thinks, and then she gets to her feet. I copy her, waiting while Hunter helps Livia to stand, and we all make our way to the front door.

Outside, it's a warm sunny day, and I put my arm around Josie as we walk down the path to the rear of the main house. It's been a good day so far, starting off with that spectacular shower… and while I didn't think anything could be better than that, I'm not so sure now. If I get this right, it could make everything perfect.

Hunter opens the glass doors at the back of the house, letting us all into the kitchen. There's no-one here, but I can hear voices and Livia leads the way to a living room, with brown leather couches surrounding an enormous fireplace. It's very formal, but we pass on through and into the lobby before she guides us to a door, which opens into a much more informal living room. In here, there are four fabric covered couches, two in a dark blue, and two in a paler tone. There's a television mounted above the fireplace, and on the floor, lying on a cushioned, fleecy play mat, is the most beautiful baby girl I've ever seen. She's wearing a pink dress, with a white collar and a pink hairband with a bow on the side. Her tiny feet are kicking out as she waves her hands at the toy penguin and whale dangling from the wooden arch above her head. I'm mesmerized for a moment, just staring, but let my eyes wander to the two women sitting on either side of her. One is older, maybe in her early sixties, and is wearing a thin summer skirt and a white blouse. I realize this must be Pat and she looks up, her green eyes clouding with tears as she shakes her auburn head in disbelief. The other woman notices her reaction and turns toward me. I can see her face now, and the family likeness is unmistakable. This is my sister, Ella. I don't recognize her as such, but she's got the same dark hair as Hunter and me, cut in a short, pixie-like style, and her eyes are a similar shade of brown to mine…

"Oh, my God… Drew." She leaps to her feet, her hand over her mouth as tears well in her eyes.

"We haven't been introduced yet, but I believe I'm your brother."

She bursts into tears and I let go of Josie's hand and step forward, pulling Ella into my arms.

"I was so scared," she whispers into my chest.

"What of?"

She looks up, her cheeks stained with tears. "That we'd lost you forever."

I shake my head. "No such luck."

She slaps her hand against my chest, just as a man comes through the door. I remember him as the man who helped carry me up the stairs. He's tall, with dark hair and is really muscular, making the baby he's cradling in his arm seem even smaller.

"One son… suitably changed and refreshed," he says with an English accent, before he looks up and stops dead, staring at Ella and then at me. She steps away and I release her as the man comes over, holding out his free arm to put around her. She nestles against him, her head on his chest, and he smiles. "We haven't been formally introduced," he says to me. "I'm Mac… Ella's fiancé."

"I remember you."

"Really?" His eyes widen and he tilts his head slightly.

"Yes. You helped carry me up the stairs."

"Oh. I see. I thought you meant you remembered me from before."

"No. Sorry." I turn back to Ella. "I hate to disappoint you, but I don't remember you, either. The only reason I know you're my sister is because Hunter told me."

She looks really upset, and blinks back her tears, although it's Mac who speaks, shaking his head slightly. "Hey… don't let it worry you. You'll work it out when you're ready."

I glance down at the baby he's carrying... a little boy dressed in blue dungarees and a white t-shirt. He's gazing up at his father with total adoration.

"This must be Henry?"

Ella reaches out, cradling his head with her hand. "He's nearly a month old, and you've never met him."

"Until now... and I'm sure we'll make up for lost time."

There's a slight whimpering behind us and we all turn to see Pat has stood up and is holding my daughter in her arms. She looks up at me and I step closer.

"I'm sorry. I know you're Pat because Hunter explained about you and who you are, but all I'm getting is ice cream cake. Does that mean anything?"

She smiles, the tears in her eyes threatening to fall as she nods her head. "It was your favorite when you were little. I can make some for tonight, if you like... if you all wanna stay and have dinner together?"

I turn to Josie, who smiles. "I think we'd like that. Thank you."

I look down at my daughter as she turns her head to face me, her blue eyes fixed on mine, and I take a deep breath as Pat holds her out and I lift her into my arms. Maisie gazes up at me, and I feel the connection, like an unbreakable bond between us, as I pull her close to my chest. She snuggles and sighs, like she knows who I am, and I breathe her in. There's something familiar about the smell of her, although I can't remember what it is, and as I stare down into her face, she blurs before my sight, my cheeks wetting with tears.

Josie's standing beside me, her hand on my shoulder. "I've been here before," I whisper, and she nods her head.

"On the day she was born. You cried then, too."

I raise my head, looking at her. "Did I?"

"Yes. It hurt so much to see you like that."

"And does this hurt, too?"

She glances down at Maisie and then at me. "No." I'm not sure she's telling the truth, but before I can say anything, Hunter comes and joins us.

"Remember what I said before? You don't have to feel pressured to do anything too quickly. If you need Maisie to stay here for a while longer, until you're ready, that won't be a problem." He gives me a long look, like he's telling me that Livia's pregnancy makes no difference, which I'm sure it doesn't. What makes the difference is how I feel… not just about Maisie, but about Josie, and I shake my head at him.

"After the dream I had last night, I don't wanna let her go ever again. She's mine, Hunter. She belongs with me."

He smiles. "Then maybe you should spend some time together, so she can get to know her daddy."

"I couldn't agree more," I say and I take Josie's hand with my free one and turn to her, looking down into her eyes. "I think she should get to know her new mommy, too."

Josie blinks once, then twice, and then bursts into tears.

"We'll be in the kitchen," Hunter says in my ear and I'm vaguely aware of him shooing everyone from the room as I put my arm around Josie and pull her in to my chest, hugging her close, while being careful not to crush Maisie.

"Is this okay?" I ask. She nods her head, sniffling through her tears. "We won't let Maisie forget who Lexi was, but I want us to be a family."

She looks up. "So do I, Drew… so much."

I smile down at her. "I can't claim to remember very much yet, but one thing I recall very clearly is what it felt like to fall for you."

She wipes away her tears with the back of her hand. "Really?"

"Yeah. It's exactly how I feel now… like I'm falling for you, and I'm never gonna stop."

Epilogue

Josie

The last few months have been crazy.

I suppose it didn't help that neither Drew nor I realized that Ella and Mac were getting married at the beginning of December, so on top of everything else, there was a wedding to plan.

We all had fun, though, helping with the preparations, and the day was a tremendous success. We got to meet baby Henry's namesake… an old friend of Mac's who flew over from London and acted as his best man. He was lovely, and it was easy to see why Mac is so attached to him.

That was two weeks ago now, and they've just returned from their honeymoon in the Turks and Caicos, in time for the celebration dinner Hunter has organized for this evening. Pat and Mick are both going to be there, and Pat's preparing a feast for all of us in honor of the publication of Ella's cookery book and Mac's second novel, both of which are coming out next week. At least, that's the reason he's given everyone else for gathering us all together. I know differently. He spoke to me last week and gave me the real reason. He needed my advice, and I gave it, hoping I was doing the right thing. After that, he set the wheels in motion, making sure everyone could attend, including Livia's mom and dad.

We met Julianne and Connor a couple of days after Drew was re-introduced to his daughter. It was clear to me from my nursing background, that Connor's struggles are a lot worse than Drew's, so we didn't stay for long, and on the way back to the cottage, Hunter explained that Julianne and Pat have become good friends, the two of them often sharing a coffee together in the mornings while Connor's resting.

We're all really close, and I have to admit, I've missed Ella while she's been away. Livia and Hunter split their time between here and the city, and although I've shared in a couple of Julianne and Pat's coffee mornings, I've discovered that I enjoy having female company of my own age. I'm learning what it's like to have sisters at last, and to be part of a family... and I'm enjoying every moment.

As for myself and Drew, we've never been closer, or happier.

Maisie is eight months old now. She's thinking about crawling, but hasn't quite got the hang of coordinating her arms and legs, so she usually just flops onto her tummy, which seems to make her giggle and has everyone laughing.

Moving Maisie's nursery furniture back into the cottage was slightly chaotic, but Drew was adamant he wanted her with us, so we managed it between us. Everyone helped, including Livia, although Hunter wouldn't let her lift anything heavy, and kept checking she was okay.

"Ella's gonna guess Livia's pregnant if you keep doing that," Drew whispered to him as they maneuvered Maisie's crib into place at the cottage.

"I know. But what's a guy to do?"

Later, we all sat in the kitchen at the main house and ate the fabulous meal Pat had prepared. She presented Drew with his ice cream cake, and he looked up at her, a smile forming on his lips.

"It's just how I remember."

Pat's eyes glistened with unshed tears, and she helped him dish it up and hand it around to everyone. When I tasted it, I could understand why it was such a prominent memory for him. It was the best ice cream cake I've ever eaten.

Later, when Drew and I were alone, and Maisie was sound asleep in her crib, we lay in bed and he held me in his arms.

"You're sure you're okay with this?" he asked, turning toward me.

"Positive."

"You don't mind becoming an instant family?"

"No. You have a beautiful daughter."

"We have a beautiful daughter. She's ours, Josie."

I struggled to speak for a moment, but when I knew I could trust my voice, I told him about my conversation with Hunter on the day of his mother's visit.

"So you knew they were trying for a baby?" he said, tilting his head.

"Yeah, but I couldn't tell you."

"I know. It's okay. Why did he tell you? Do you know?"

"Because he wanted me to give him an idea of how long it would take for you to get better. Livia was finding it hard looking after Maisie when she wanted a baby of her own."

He nodded. "Oh, I see." He leaned in, kissing me tenderly. "I can understand that."

The look in his eyes told me he wasn't talking about Livia, but about me, and I rested my head on his chest and whispered, "Thank you."

It felt inadequate. He'd given me my dream come true… the family I never thought I'd have. But it seemed that 'thank you' was more than enough.

Maisie adjusted really well to living with us, and that was a good thing, because it was only a few days later that Drew's long-term memory started to come back, including recollections of the accident. I'd hoped he might never recall it, but that wasn't to be, and it was just as traumatic as I'd feared. I had to be there for him, to help him through it, and as his memory slowly returned, it came with more questions, both for me and for Hunter, especially as he tried to piece together moments from his past. That was when I learned about his father, and the business he'd founded, the role of a man called Ken Bevan, and his connection to Livia and her parents. I found it very confusing, but fortunately, Drew's recollections and Hunter's explanations helped make sense of it all.

Drew slowly rebuilt his past, adding layer upon layer, from things like the foods he liked and didn't, to the password for his laptop… until the day he recalled a conversation he'd had with Lexi, in her car, just minutes before the accident. I think that was why he'd blocked it for so long, just out of fear of having to recall the moment of impact again. When he finally explained it to me, he revealed Lexi had admitted to him that she'd been seeing someone else, and that she wanted to move to Boston.

"It was just like you said."

I nodded my head, handing Maisie to him, so I could get on with making the lunch.

"How did it make you feel?" I asked him.

"I think I was a little mad at her to start with. I'd already told her about you…"

I almost dropped the carton of eggs I was holding. "Y—You had?"

"Yeah." He scratched his head. "I basically asked her permission to date you."

I put down the eggs and turned to him. "What did she say?"

"She laughed and told me she was fine with it. She said she thought I'd be good for you."

I looked up into his eyes. "She did?"

He moved closer, tilting his head. "Yeah. She told me a little about your background, and she said you'd been lonely. I remember, I didn't like the sound of that. I wanted to do something about it."

I smiled up at him. "And you did."

"Yeah... eventually."

I leaned up on my tip-toes, kissing him. "It was worth waiting for." He smiled, and I opened the carton of eggs. "You haven't explained why you were mad at her."

"That's simple. I'd asked her if she was okay about me seeing you, which she was, and then she promptly told me she was already living with someone. Manuel, wasn't it?"

I nodded my head. "Yeah... and I guess I can see why that got you riled."

"I thought she should have told me earlier."

"That's what I said to her, when she told me about him... that you had a right to know another man was living with your daughter."

"Precisely."

"You didn't fight, did you? That's not what caused the accident?"

"No. She accepted she should've told me sooner, and I explained that I'd need some time."

"To get used to the idea?"

He shook his head. "Funnily enough, that's what she said. But that had nothing to do with it. I needed time to find a house in Boston."

I frowned, surprised by his answer. "A house? What for?"

"For Maisie. I knew my apartment wasn't suitable for a baby, or a small child, so I wanted to buy a house instead. Somewhere other than here that I could call home. I offered to help her out financially, if she needed it, but she said 'no'. I guess because her boyfriend didn't want me interfering."

"Maybe." I moved a little closer to him. "Are you still thinking of buying a house there?"

"No. Why would I?"

"For when you need to go there… for work."

He shook his head. "Work doesn't seem so important right now. Watching Maisie grow up and being with you are my chief concerns. So, I was thinking I'll probably sell my apartment and my studio."

"You'll give up photography?"

He smiled. "I didn't say that. I enjoy taking photographs of you… and of Maisie, and I might build a small studio here, just for fun. The thing is, I'm not gonna do anything that takes me away from you."

And that's exactly what he's done. He's sold his apartment, and I've sold mine, too. When we went back there, we discovered Maisie's travel cot in the guest bedroom. To be honest, I'd forgotten I even had it, and it was a reminder of that last night with Lexi. She was snatched away the very next day, and that thought made me cry. I think that was the first time I realized what I'd lost, and Drew held me and let me weep.

We kept the cot… not because we needed it, but because it was a reminder not to take anything for granted.

He's rented out his city studio to another photographer, and the building work on the studio here will begin in the spring.

The other thing we'll be doing in the spring is visiting Lexi's grave for the first time. We decided to go on the weekend before Maisie's birthday, in April, and we've invited Manuel Ortega to join us. Drew said it felt wrong for him to be left out, and although Manuel was surprised to hear from us, I think he was pleased to be invited.

Whether we'll make it a regular thing, I don't know yet... but time will tell.

Either way, we owe it to Lexi to raise her daughter in the best way we can, and knowing she gave Drew her approval feels like the cherry on the icing on the cake of our happiness... sealing our love.

Hearing him tell me about Lexi was a special moment. It was almost as special as the moment, a few nights later, when we were lying in bed together, relieved to have settled Maisie in the nursery, and he turned to me, pulling me into his arms.

"I—I wanted to talk to you," he said, sounding nervous, which surprised me. It wasn't normal for Drew to be unsure of himself.

"Oh?"

"Yes." He studied my face for a second or two, then swallowed hard. "It's about my past."

"You've remembered something else?" I wasn't sure what more he had to recall. It felt like we'd touched upon every aspect of his life over the previous weeks. But the look on his face told me there was more, and it wouldn't be easy... for either of us.

"Yes."

"Is it to do with the accident?" I couldn't think what else would make him look so despondent.

"No. It's to do with my relationships... or rather, the lack of them."

"Oh."

He held me tighter. "Hunter was right about that. I didn't have relationships to speak of. I've been patching it all together over the last few days, and I don't think I was a very nice guy."

I smiled at him, raising my hand and cupping his face. "I didn't hear Lexi complaining."

He smiled back, although it was a half-hearted effort. "Maybe because she wasn't looking for anything more out of it than I was.

But there were others... women I wasn't so kind to. Hunter had already told me about one, but I've remembered others."

"What do you mean when you say you weren't kind?"

"I wasn't cruel," he said, frowning. "Not deliberately. Most of the time, things ended naturally, like they did with Lexi. It was just that, with some of them, they were looking for something more serious than I was, and when that became obvious, I left."

"Every time?"

He nodded his head. "Until I met you, the thought of settling down, and of only ever being with one woman, was... frankly, terrifying."

I smiled. "And now?"

"I never wanna be with anyone else again."

I leaned in, kissing his lips, just briefly. "Stop beating yourself up. You can't change what happened."

"I know. I just wish I'd been more considerate."

"Well... look at this as a chance to be better."

He nodded his head and kissed me, taking a little longer over it, his hands settling on my ass and pulling me on to his ever-present erection. I let out a sigh, and he pulled back.

"There's something else."

"Oh?"

"I've remembered quite a lot of detail about my sex life... and you said you wanted to know."

I couldn't deny I'd said that... but when faced with the reality, I wasn't so sure. He rolled onto his back, bringing me with him, so I was straddling him, and I stared down at him, waiting until he smiled, and I felt my body relax. He must have felt it too, because he raised me up, lowering me over his arousal, penetrating me deeply, our bodies joined. Then he pulled me down, my breasts hard against his chest, and moved one hand behind me, finding my tightest hole and brushing over it, making me squirm against him.

"This is mine," he said.

I leaned up, resting my hands on his chest, and looked down at him.

"I'm all yours. Remember? I was a virgin before we…"

"I know. My first."

"Really?" I couldn't help smiling. "You'd never slept with a virgin before?"

"No."

"Are there any other firsts?" I asked, feeling nervous again and dreading that he'd say 'no', and burst my bubble.

"Yes." I almost giggled with relief. "Most important, I guess… I've never made love with anyone I've actually loved before."

"That's good to know."

He smiled. "Hmm… I thought so."

"Anything else?"

"Yeah. I've never brought anyone else here before… not that I really brought you here, but you know what I mean."

"I do," I whispered, smiling.

"Also, I've never had sex standing up…"

"Seriously?"

He shook his head. "You didn't let me finish. What I was gonna say was I've never had sex standing up in the way we do. In the past, with other women, it's always just been a matter of convenience, or something to do for a change of scenery, but with you, it's so much more. It's the way you cling to me when I hold you in my arms, the look in your eyes when you give yourself to me." He let out a sigh. "I've never done that with anyone else."

I shuddered, recalling how good that felt. We didn't save it for the shower, either. Not any more. Drew had taken me that way in the kitchen, the living room and the bedroom… oh, and the dressing room. I'd almost forgotten that…

"Why not?" I asked.

"I don't know. I guess it's about trust again. It's about you trusting me not to hurt you... like this." He circled his finger over my anus.

"You mean...?"

He nodded his head. "It was just like I thought... I've never touched anyone there before." He gazed into my eyes, and I stuttered out a breath as he flexed his hips upward, going deeper inside me.

"Do you want to do more than touch?" I asked.

He paused, gazing into my eyes, and then closed his for a second before he breathed out, "Oh, fuck... yeah."

He pulled me closer, kissing me hard, and then rolled us over so I was on my back. I stared up at him, biting on my bottom lip. "Y—You will go easy, won't you?"

He bent his head, nibbling at my lip to free it, and then rested his forehead against mine. "You know I will... at least until you're begging me for more."

I giggled, and then he kissed me again, and spent the next two hours showing me what it's like to have everything.

And oh, so much more.

"I'd know that smell anywhere," Drew says as we enter the main house through the kitchen doors. I'm holding Maisie and he closes the door behind us, keeping out the December chill. "It's Pat's beef chili."

She smiles over at him, her eyes misting slightly. Drew and I might be used to the fact that his memory has completely returned, but the rest of the family are still getting used to it.

"It's still got an hour or so to go," she says, putting the lid back on the pan and resting the spoon beside it. "Everyone's in the den. I'll join you in a minute."

He nods his head, smiling at her, and we wander through the house, into the lobby, and through to the 'den' as Pat calls it. To me, it's too tidy to be a 'den', but when you have two living rooms, you need to differentiate, I guess.

Everyone is already here, including Mick, who I've only met briefly before. For such a large man, he's very unobtrusive, with gray hair and a friendly face, and I like him. Livia's mom and dad are sitting together on one of the many couches. Julianne is just as pretty as her daughter, with blonde hair, which she's wearing loose around her shoulders today, while Connor's coloring is darker… but that's not surprising. He's not related to Livia, even if he is her dad.

In the corner, there's an enormous Christmas tree, decorated with white lights and wooden toys. I know there's another such tree in the library at the back of the house, but the one in here gives off a lovely, festive glow.

"When are we actually gonna get to see this famous cookery book?" Drew asks Ella and she turns, narrowing her eyes at him.

"Monday," she says.

"Are you gonna write another one?" I ask her, sitting on the couch opposite Julianne and Connor, while Drew perches on the arm beside me.

"No. The publisher offered, and Mac's agent was really keen for me to take the deal, but I'd rather be a full-time mom."

"Never thought I'd hear you say that," Hunter says, and Ella shoots him a glance, just as the buzzer sounds, letting everyone know there's someone at the front gate. He gets up, leaving Livia behind in her seat. "I'll go get that."

"It's okay. Pat's in the kitchen. I'm sure she'll answer it." Drew looks up at him, but Hunter shakes his head.

"She's busy."

He leaves the room and I glance down at Maisie, who's struggling to stay awake. "Do you want me to take her upstairs?" Drew says, leaning over me, but I shake my head.

"She's no trouble."

"You just like holding her, don't you?"

"Yes."

He smiles and kisses my forehead before turning to Mac. "Is your new book out yet?"

He shakes his head. "That's launching on Tuesday, but I guess Hunter wanted us to get together and celebrate while everyone's here."

That's not strictly true, but I'm not about to say that.

"Are you writing anything new?" Julianne asks and Mac turns to her.

"Oh, yes. I've already finished the third book. That's with the editors, and I'm about half-way through the fourth one. I've got at least three, or maybe four more in the pipeline in this series, and then I might move on to something different."

"Goodness. That must keep you busy."

"It does. But I really love it, and there aren't very many people who can say that about their work."

"That's t—true," Connor says, stammering over his words, which he tends to do.

"It's a detective you write about, isn't it?" Julianne asks.

"Yes. A female one, who also happens to be a doctor. That was Ella's idea, so if anyone should take the credit for my success, it's my beautiful wife, not me."

"Hardly," Ella says. "You still have to write them."

"I know. But they wouldn't even be published if it wasn't for you."

He leans over and kisses her, just as Hunter comes back into the room, followed by the woman I know to be his mother. I'd expected this, but what I hadn't anticipated was that she'd be with a man. He's in his early-fifties, with salt and pepper hair and steel-rimmed glasses. Both of them look nervous as they glance around the room, and the man puts his arm through Lindsay's as Hunter coughs, getting everyone's attention. A silence falls, just as Pat comes in behind the small group, dodging past them, a blush on her cheeks, as she walks over and sits beside Mick. I'm not sure if she knew Lindsay was coming tonight, but I think she might have done.

Hunter steps a little further into the room, ushering Lindsay and the man to follow, and then looks at Drew, and at Ella, who are both staring at him, equally confused.

"Drew… Ella… I want you to meet our mother."

Drew sucks in an audible gasp, but it's Ella who reacts. Without a second's hesitation, she pulls away from Mac and jumps to her feet, taking a step forward.

"How could you do this, Hunter? You told me she'd been to see you after Drew's accident, and I explained I wanted nothing to do with her."

"I know, and I heard you. That's why I told Mom she couldn't come to your wedding, even though she wanted to."

Ella narrows her eyes. "Don't make it sound like you've done me a favor, when you've so obviously invited her here tonight. This is a family celebration. She doesn't belong here."

I can see the hurt on Lindsay's face, and the surprise on Hunter's. He's clearly taken aback by his sister's outburst.

"Is that true?" Drew says from beside me. "Did you invite her?"

"Not exactly. After I'd told Ella about Mom's visit, Mom and I had a long conversation. She was upset about Ella not wanting her to come to the wedding, and she asked if she could visit afterwards. I couldn't say yes or no straight away. We had to wait for you to be well enough, but once you were, I spoke to Josie and she…"

Drew leans forward, looking down at me. "You knew about this?"

I nod my head. "Don't get mad. Hunter asked if I thought you were ready and I said 'yes'." I glance at Ella, just briefly, and then look back at Drew. "I appreciate it's not just about you, but there are things your mom needs to tell you, and putting it off isn't gonna help anyone."

"You think?" Ella says, glaring at me.

I suck in a breath, but before I can reply, Hunter gets there first. "Don't blame Josie. It was my decision. I told Mom she could come tonight, providing she accepted the outcome." He moves a little closer to Ella, looking down into her upturned face. "If you decide you never want to see her again, that's fine. She'll respect that. But at least hear her out before you jump to any conclusions."

Ella glances over his shoulder at her mother, just as Mac gets to his feet, coming to stand beside her. "It can't hurt to listen, can it?" he whispers.

She shrugs, but doesn't answer, and I look up at Drew. "Are you mad at me?"

"No. I wish you'd told me, but I guess you were worried I wouldn't show."

Hunter turns, smiling at him. "I was more worried you'd tell Ella and she wouldn't show."

"No shit," she mutters, folding her arms across her chest. "But having ambushed me, I guess it would be interesting to know why our mom abandoned us."

She tilts her head, looking directly at Lindsay, the older woman blushing as she sucks in a breath, her eyes wandering over the assembled faces.

"I—I hadn't expected there to be so many people here." She turns to Hunter. "I thought it would just be the three of you."

Hunter shakes his head. "We're the family you left behind." He holds out his arms to Livia and Mac and myself. "These are the people we love. This is what we made of ourselves without you." Lindsay looks over toward Julianne and Connor. "They're my in-laws," Hunter says. "They're part of the family, too." Lindsay opens her mouth, but then snaps it shut, hesitating for a moment before she nods her head and glances at Pat and Mick, who are sitting side-by-side. She frowns and turns to Hunter, raising an eyebrow. "Our father hired Pat and Mick to care for us and look after the property when you left. Pat raised us. She did your job when you weren't here to do it anymore. She has more right to be here than you do, so you either talk in front of her, or you can leave."

Pat stares at Hunter, blinking hard, fighting back tears, while Lindsay flounders, unsure of herself until the man beside her steps a little closer.

"I'm here, Lin. I'll help you. But you need to tell them. It's what you came here for."

She takes a deep breath and looks back at Hunter again. "Would you mind if I sat down?"

He nods, stepping aside so she can sit in the corner of one of the couches, the man perching on the arm beside her. Hunter returns to his seat as do Ella and Mac, and we all stare at their mom, waiting.

She's twists her fingers in her lap, biting on her bottom lip and then she looks up, making direct eye contact with Hunter.

"You want to know why I left, but to tell you that, I'll have to explain how I came to be here in the first place."

"Okay."

She sighs, and glances up at the man beside her, who nods his head, and rather than looking at any one of her children, Lindsay gazes at the low table in front of her.

"When I first met Theodore Bennett, he was just making a name for himself in the advertising world. It was at a party, and I was there with my parents…"

"Your parents?" Hunter says, surprise evident on his face. "How old were you?"

She turns her head, looking at him. "I was a couple of months shy of my sixteenth birthday. My father knew Theodore, and they talked about work for most of the evening, although he spent a lot of time staring at me. I was flattered, in the way that teenage girls can be when an older, attractive man pays attention to them. So, I didn't think too much of it when I came out of the ladies' room later in the evening and found him waiting for me. When he pushed me up against the wall and kissed me, I enjoyed it. When he told me he'd fallen for me, I believed him. I let myself be swept away, and I agreed to meet him the following evening." She stops talking and looks up at the man beside her again. He smiles and gives her another encouraging nod of his head. "He waited for me in his car, on the corner of the street where I lived with my mom and dad, and then he drove me to his place." I feel Drew tense beside me, although I daren't look up at him. I daren't move for fear of breaking the moment. "He didn't bother with the niceties of food or drink. He said he couldn't wait, and he held my hand as he took me upstairs," she says, with a slight crack in her voice. "He was very reassuring… and then afterwards, he took me home. I didn't see anything wrong in what we'd done. We were in love… or so I thought. I certainly believed myself to be in love with him, and when he asked if he could see me again, I couldn't believe my luck."

Hunter sits forward, his hands clasped tightly together, his knuckles white. "Didn't it occur to you that what he was doing was statutory rape?"

"No. I didn't even think it was odd when he held my hand in the car and told me I couldn't tell anyone about us. I liked the fact that there was an 'us', and that he said it would spoil what we had if other people knew about it. He was very… plausible. Either that, or I was very gullible. One way or the other, though, I believed every word he said."

"So you kept seeing him?" Hunter asks.

"Yes, three or four times a week. Sometimes even more than that... until I realized my period was late."

"You were pregnant?" Drew says and his mom nods, just once.

"With me?" Hunter tilts his head.

"Yes."

"How old were you then?"

"Sixteen. Just. I'd had my birthday five days before I found out I was pregnant." There's a collective gasp and Lindsay looks down at the floor, her cheeks flushing.

"What did you do?" Livia asks, resting her hand on her slightly swollen belly.

"I told Theodore." Lindsay looks up again, taking another deep breath. "I'd waited until we got to his house, thinking we could sit and talk, but all he did pace the floor. After about half an hour, he drove me home again, making me promise not to tell a soul. I didn't see him for a few days, but when I did, he proposed. He'd bought a ring, and everything... which I stupidly thought must have meant he really loved me."

"So, you accepted?" Hunter says.

"Yes. And we were married within weeks. Not long afterwards, my mom died. She'd been sick for some time and, while my parents had been surprised – even shocked – by my decision to marry Theodore when I was so young, I think they thought we were rushing our wedding plans so she could see me walk down the aisle. My father was devastated by her loss, and believing me to be happy and safe with Theodore, he went to stay with his family in North Carolina, and eventually he moved back there, which suited Theodore perfectly, because it meant he was no longer under any kind of scrutiny. He persuaded me it was in my best interests to drop out of school, making sure I lost contact with all my friends, and because there was no-one to contradict him, he could say anything he liked about me to anyone who asked. So, he told his friends and colleagues I was twenty, not sixteen, and that we'd known each other for years before marrying. I didn't know he was doing any of that at the time. As far as I was concerned, we were perfectly happy together. His hours were long, but that was to be expected when he was building his business. He was doing very well for himself, too. He bought us this house," she says, looking around and sighing. "I loved living here, even if it meant we only saw each other at weekends. He stayed in the city during the week, but I didn't mind. I had so much fun decorating all the rooms and getting ready for our new baby." She glances at Hunter with a loving smile and, although he's clearly struggling, he smiles back. "Everything was going so well, or at least, I thought it was… until I was about seven months pregnant."

"What happened?" Hunter asks.

She bites on her bottom lip again and sighs. "Your father used to come home on Friday evenings, and I'd always go to the grocery store in the afternoon to get in some supplies. I got held up for some reason. I think there was an accident, or something… anyway, by the time I came back, he was already here. His car was parked out front, and I let myself in, calling out that I was home. He didn't reply, so I went through to the kitchen, and dropped all the groceries on the floor when I saw him having sex with another woman up against the wall."

"Asshole." Drew's whisper is so quiet, I'm fairly sure I'm the only one who heard him, and I lean in to him as he hugs me closer.

"He brought a woman here?" Ella says, speaking for the first time since Lindsay started her story.

"Yes. It was a deliberate act on his part. He wanted me to find them like that… to know what he was doing. She was tall, slim, probably in her early twenties. Her underwear was… quite sophisticated. He kept his arm around her while he told me he didn't want to sleep with me anymore. I was too fat, evidently, and he'd brought Bridget with him to keep him amused over the weekend."

"Are you kidding me?" Drew sits forward, looking over at his mom. "He brought his lover into your home and expected you to accept it?"

"Yes." She looks up at him. "He gave her directions to one of the guest rooms and told her he'd join her in a minute, and then she left, picking up her clothes from the floor. Once we were alone, he told me he'd been seeing her for a couple of months." Her voice falters. "He told me she understood his needs, like I never could… because she was a real woman, not a little girl. I reminded him I wasn't a little girl, I was his wife… and I was expecting his child, and he hit me with the back of his hand, right across my cheek."

She touches her fingers to the side of her face just as Hunter shoots to his feet and Drew follows, the two of them staring down at their mom. I raise my hand, putting it into Drew's, and he gives me a gentle squeeze.

"I know you're gonna ask why I didn't leave?" she says, looking up at them.

"No, I wasn't gonna say that at all," Hunter replies, glancing at Drew.

"Neither was I."

Lindsay seems to deflate with relief. "I thought about it," she says, defensively. "But I had nowhere to go, and no money of my own. Theodore had seen to that. My father was still recovering from Mom's death, and I didn't feel I could burden him with my problems. So, I buried my head in the sand and pretended it wasn't happening." She focuses on Hunter. "I went into labor three weeks early, which I guess wasn't surprising under the circumstances. It was a Wednesday, so Theodore was in the city, and when someone at the hospital called to tell him what was happening, he said he couldn't get away."

"So you gave birth alone?" Ella asks, the experience of labor still fresh in her mind, I guess.

"Yes. Theodore arrived at the weekend, as usual."

"Did he come alone?" Drew asks through gritted teeth and their mom shakes her head. "You're kidding, right?"

"No. He brought Bridget with him. She'd been a regular visitor ever since that first time, but after Hunter was born, I told him I'd had enough. We had a baby, and I wasn't willing to tolerate having his lover in the house any longer."

"What did he do?" Ella asks, her voice little more than a whisper, her face as white as snow.

"He stopped coming here altogether, although he made it clear he wouldn't be faithful. He'd gotten a taste for other women, he said, and Bridget had introduced him to a friend of hers. It seemed she liked to share…" Her voice fades and her cheeks flush slightly. "He liked that too, evidently, and told me I could never hope to satisfy him again… so there wasn't much point in trying. He slammed out after that and we barely saw each other. To be honest, I didn't mind in the slightest. I had you…" She turns to Hunter. "And I didn't need anything else."

"You were sixteen," he says, frowning and shaking his head.

"I know. I grew up quickly."

A momentary silence descends while we all take in Lindsay's story, and I tug on Drew's hand, getting him to sit back down again. Hunter follows suit, putting his arm around Livia and kissing her forehead. I think he's more shocked than the rest of us, although Ella's leaning on Mac, too.

"If it's not a stupid and insensitive question," Drew says, leaning forward to look at his mom, "how was I conceived?"

Ella glances at him, and then looks at her mom. "Me too."

I notice a frown crossing Hunter's face, and he turns to Ella, his eyes filled with concern. I'm not sure what that means, and no-one else seems to have noticed his discomfort. They're all looking at Lindsay.

She turns, focusing on Drew. "As Hunter got older, your father spent a little more time here. He'd maybe come back once every six weeks or so, I guess... something like that."

"What about birthdays and Christmas... and Thanksgiving?" Ella asks.

"He missed a lot of birthdays," Hunter says, answering for his mom. "Even I remember that."

Lindsay smiles. "I still tried to make them special," she says, and Hunter nods in acknowledgement. "As for Thanksgiving and Christmas, he'd often work right through them. At least, that was what he told me he was doing, and I didn't care enough to question him. That was why I was so surprised when he came home the week before Christmas... completely out of the blue. He arrived late in the afternoon, in a foul mood. I'm not sure why, but everything I did was wrong. He hated the Christmas tree, and criticized everything I'd done around the house, the way I'd wrapped the presents, and every meal I cooked. He clearly didn't want to be here, and after a couple of days, I'd had enough and I answered back." She stops talking and takes a breath. "A—Afterwards, when I was lying on the kitchen floor, crying in pain and shock, I asked him why he'd r—raped me, and he laughed and told me it wasn't rape. It couldn't be rape, he said, because we were married. But I knew that was wrong. I'd been pushing him away, screaming at him to stop, and he hadn't. He'd forced... he'd..." A slight sob leaves her lips and the man beside her puts his arm around her shoulders.

"Do you want to take a break, Lin?"

"No," she says through her tears. "I want to get this over with."

"You mean there's more?" Drew's voice is a shocked whisper and his mom nods her head, looking over at Ella.

"Was it the same with me?" she says, staring at her mother. "Because if it was, I don't want to put you through having to tell it."

Lindsay shakes her head. "It wasn't the same... not exactly." She leans forward, resting her elbows on her knees. "Your father was seeing Doreen by then."

"Doreen?" Ella says, sounding surprised.

"Yes. I'd known about their affair since the moment it started."

"How?" Hunter asks.

"He fell in love with her," she says simply.

"Um... who's Doreen?" I ask, and Drew turns to face me.

"She was our father's secretary while he was alive, and for a while, she was Hunter's too... until she left, and he hired Livia."

I nod my head, and he smiles, returning his gaze to his mom. "Your father and Doreen might have worked together for years, but after her husband's death, everything changed between them, and finding love changed him. It was too noticeable to miss. He still hardly ever came home, but when he did, he was calmer, easier to deal with."

"So you got along better?" Drew asks.

"I wouldn't go that far, but we tolerated each other more easily... at least until that night..."

"What night?" Ella sits forward, as though she knows the next part of the story is going to be about her.

"The night you were conceived, Theodore came back from a function he'd attended with Doreen. She never used to let him stay the night because she had a young child, and although I know it used to make him angry, it never used to bother me, because he stayed in the city. On that night, though, he brought his resentment back here. It was late by the time the taxi dropped him off, and I was asleep in bed, although he still came barging into my room, cradling a bottle of whiskey. He sat at the end of my bed, swaying and drinking, still wearing his tux, as he bemoaned his lot." She pauses for a second. "H—He wasn't violent that time… just drunk and fumbling. To be honest, I think he thought I was Doreen, and while it was unpleasant, it was nowhere near as frightening as the previous time. The next morning, when he woke up and found me beside him, he was horrified by what he'd done."

"More so than when he'd raped you?" Hunter says.

She looks over at him. "Of course. In his eyes, there was nothing wrong with what he'd done before. This time, he'd betrayed Doreen, and he jumped out of bed, staring at me and saying, 'What have I done?'. He was terrified she'd find out, which of course she did, when I discovered I was pregnant… again. Theodore had no choice other than to tell her, although I know he was scared she'd leave him. She did, I think… or maybe she just threatened to. I can't remember now…" Her voice fades and she sits back slightly, looking up at Drew, then at Ella, and finally at Hunter.

"If what she told me is true, she left him," he says. "She resigned from the company and told him she wanted nothing more to do with him."

The room falls silent, and everyone slowly turns and looks at Hunter. It's Ella who speaks first.

"Y—You mean you knew about this?"

"Yes," he says. "Doreen told me."

Ella sits right forward. "But you didn't tell me?"

"How was I supposed to tell you something like that?" She stares at him for a long moment and then lowers her head, sinking back into Mac's arms. "I couldn't, could I?" Hunter says. "Not only would it have been difficult for you to hear, but when Doreen revealed her side of the story, I didn't know whether what Dad had told her was the truth. I couldn't see any reason he'd have lied about something like that, but what benefit would there have been in me telling you something I couldn't verify? I couldn't see how it would have served any purpose. If I got that wrong, then I'm sorry." Ella nods her head in silent acknowledgement and Hunter turns to his mom. "Doreen told me she left him and was getting ready to leave town and take her daughter with her, when Dad arrived at her apartment and begged her to forgive him."

"I can't imagine your father begging for anything," Lindsay says, shaking her head.

Hunter shrugs his shoulders. "Those were Doreen's words."

"And did she? Forgive him, I mean?" I ask.

He nods his head. "Yes. She wasn't sure it was the wisest thing she'd ever done, but she loved him." He frowns, turning to his mother. "Sorry if that isn't what you want to hear."

"I don't care, Hunter," his mother says. "I barely cared then, and I certainly don't now."

Drew sucks in a sharp breath. "So…" he says, shaking his head slowly from side to side. "None of us were born out of love."

Lindsay gets to her feet, pulling away from the man beside her and walks straight to Drew, standing in front of him. "Please don't think that. I loved you all."

"Then why did you leave us?" he says.

It's a simple enough question, and Lindsay's shoulders drop as she says, "Because of Ken Bevan, I suppose."

I notice Livia tense, and something about my expression obviously catches Lindsay's attention. She follows my line of sight, turning to look at Hunter and Livia.

"What's wrong?" she says.

Hunter keeps a firm hold on Livia, looking up at his mom. "I've got something to tell you."

"Oh?"

"Livia is Ken Bevan's daughter."

Lindsay darts across the room, her movements as fast as they are unexpected, although Hunter leaps to his feet, putting himself between Livia and his mother.

"How could you?" she screams.

"It was real easy, Mom. I fell in love."

"With Ken Bevan's daughter?"

"Yes. But you need to calm down. I didn't know who she was when we met. Even Livia didn't realize the connection until it was explained to her. She's not responsible for what he did, any more than I can be blamed for what my father did."

Julianne gets up and steps into the fray. "I was Ken's wife," she says.

Lindsay turns toward her. "You're Julianne?"

"Yes. And I'm sorry for what he did. But as Hunter said, Livia isn't responsible. Neither am I. My first marriage was hell. Nothing like as bad as yours, but still hell. Regardless of that, though, I never wanted to make my child suffer for the actions of my husband." Julianne tilts her head. "Do you?"

Lindsay stares at her for a moment and I think everyone in the room sees the moment she backs down, her body deflating in the wake of Julianne's wise words.

"You're right," she says, turning to Hunter. "I'm sorry. It's just that everything changed after Ken Bevan stole the money from your father. I'd tolerated his women… even his love for Doreen. He'd abused me. He'd raped me…" She stops talking and swallows down a sob, and the man who came in with her gets up, going to her, and putting his arm around her shoulders. "I'd taken so much from him, and then it just got worse. I didn't think that was possible, but he was so angry and bitter about the money... and that's when the violence started."

"Violence?" Hunter looks down at her, frowning. "You mean, other than when he slapped you around the face?"

"Oh, that was nothing."

I doesn't sound like 'nothing' to me, and judging by the look on Hunter's face, I think he agrees.

"But I don't remember any violence," he says, sounding confused. "I've spoken to Doreen about what happened back then, and she didn't mention our father being violent, either."

"He probably wasn't violent to her. He loved her. And besides, she didn't know everything."

"But surely, I'd have noticed?" he says.

Lindsay shakes her head. "I hid it from you for as long as I could."

"What does that mean?"

She leans in to the man beside her, like this part of her story is going to be hard to tell... although how it can be harder than what's gone before, I don't know.

"It means that one evening, he beat me so badly, he broke four of my ribs. Ella was asleep in bed, and the two of you were playing in different parts of the house. None of you saw or even heard what he'd done, but I knew I had to get out. So, I waited for him to leave, then I called a cab, took the three of you, and went to the hospital."

"You mean it was real?" Hunter says, his voice barely audible.

Lindsay looks confused. "What was real?"

"The reason you went to the hospital."

"Of course it was real."

"I—I remember being at the hospital, but I thought you'd faked an accident, so you could get away," Hunter says, shaking his head.

Lindsay lets out a sigh. "I'd never have done something like that. And it wasn't an accident, believe me. When he arrived late that afternoon, I stupidly thought he'd come home to spend Thanksgiving with us. In fact, it transpired he needed some documents to do with the money Ken had taken. I think his intention was to go straight back to the city, once he'd found them. The problem was, he'd misplaced them, and he blamed me. There was nothing accidental about what he did next." Lindsay pauses, taking a breath. "I remember, I was lying on the kitchen floor, and he was standing over me. I honestly thought he was gonna kill me, but he didn't. He left. That was when I took my chance."

"You mean, that was when you called the cab?" Hunter asks, his face pale.

"Yes. I don't know how I made it to the phone, but I did, and when we got to the ER, they took the three of you to a room and called the police. Unfortunately, your father arrived first. No-one ever explained how he knew where we were. I've always assumed he came back here for some reason, found we'd gone and put two and two together. I guess I'll never know the truth of that, and it doesn't matter. The fact is, once he arrived, he took over. He persuaded the hospital staff I had mental health problems. He told them I was having a breakdown, that I was so sick, I didn't even know how old I was. I didn't realize, but he'd taken away my driver's license. I don't know when he did that. It could have been that day, at the hospital, or some time before. All I know is, when they queried my date of birth for the third time, and I told them to check on my driver's license, it wasn't there. I had no other identification on me, and somehow he convinced them this was part of my 'illness'. He claimed I was taking medication for my supposed mental health issues and that the drugs affected my memory, which was why I'd given them the wrong date of birth. According to him, I was really four years older than I was claiming to be. He was friends with the mayor and a few prominent businessmen, and he wasn't averse to dropping their names into the conversation, while he lied and said he'd seen it all before. He said I was delusional, that I'd inflicted the injuries on myself by throwing myself down the stairs, and that he was scared for my safety, because things seemed to have escalated more quickly than usual. The police arrived, and he repeated the story to them, adding that he was concerned for the welfare of his children… that he was worried I'd hurt the three of you next. I denied it all, but he had an answer for everything, and somehow whatever he said sounded more plausible. Before I knew it, someone came and strapped me to the bed. They were talking about sedatives and hospitalizing me, even while I was screaming at them to let me see my children. It all happened so fast after that, I can't remember the chain of events very clearly. I just remember crying, begging them to let me see you all, and being given an injection, which made everything go hazy."

"Jesus Christ," Drew says. "Hunter was right… at least in part."

I look up. "What do you mean?"

He glances over at his brother, who's standing, his head bowed, clearly in shock. "Hunter has always maintained that Mom didn't want to leave… that Dad drove her away."

"N—Not like this," Hunter says, his voice cracking. "I thought it was his behavior that made Mom leave… of her own free will."

"I know," Drew says. "And all my life, I wanted to believe you. You're the only one who remembers any of it, and I so wanted it to be true. I thought it was wishful thinking on your part. I thought you weren't willing to face up to what had happened…

to the memories of Mom walking out on us." He shakes his head, averting his gaze to his mother. "Now, I wish you had," he says. "I wish you'd just left us."

"Why?" She's horrified by his suggestion.

"Because he'd tortured you enough already. He'd abused you in so many ways. But to do that to you… to take your children by force…" He lets his voice fade and turns, stroking Maisie's head, the concept more real to him than any of us.

"I would never have left you, if he hadn't made me," Lindsay says with more strength in her voice than I've heard all evening, and I look up at Drew.

"Are you okay?" I whisper. He nods, although he doesn't answer, and just stares deep into my eyes. "I love you."

"Even after hearing that? Even after knowing where I come from?"

"Yes. You're not your father, Drew. And I love you more than ever for being you."

Drew

I smile down at Josie, grateful she's here to support me. I need her tonight, more than I think I ever have… because the last twenty minutes have been the most shocking of my life.

I thought regaining my memory was the worst thing that could happen to me. Having to re-live the accident and knowing there was nothing I could do to prevent it, or to save my baby girl… that was horrendous. But this…?

To know what my father did to my mother…

To know how I came to be born…

Mom coughs and we all look at her. She's turned and is staring at Hunter.

"I wrote to you," she says. "When I was lucid, they let me write."

"I never received any letters. None of us did."

The man beside Mom lets out a long sigh, shaking his head and she looks up at him. "Theodore must have intercepted them," she says, turning her gaze back on Hunter. "I wrote to you, though. I promise."

Ella sits up. "How long were you in the hospital?"

"Nearly three years." Ella's eyes widen, her mouth dropping open. I can't help gasping. *Three years?* "I'd probably still be there now if it wasn't for Braydon." She looks up at the man who's still holding her, gratitude and love filling her eyes.

"Why? What did Braydon do?" Hunter asks.

"He saved me," she says, quite simply.

Braydon smiles. "I don't know about that, but I moved here from Chicago, and I went to work at the hospital as a resident psychologist. After just a few one-to-one sessions with your mom, I realized there was nothing wrong with her… other than the damage your father had done. She certainly wasn't psychotic, or a danger to anyone… not even herself."

"Braydon arranged for my discharge," Mom says. "And although I wanted to contact you, he reminded me I'd have to go through Theodore. We both knew I wasn't strong enough for that."

"So you just left us?" Ella says, shaking her head.

"Don't make it sound easy," Mom replies. "It wasn't. But I'd written and heard nothing back. I assumed Theodore had told you stories about me… made you fearful of me."

"He never said a word about you," I say, recalling his silences, his rebuttals whenever one of us raised the subject. "He refused to talk about you at all."

"Th—That's not strictly true." I turn at the sound of Hunter's voice.

"What are you saying? I'm pretty sure I don't have any holes in my memory now. As far as I'm aware, you've always told me…"

"I know what I've always told you," he says. "And it's not your memory playing tricks. I lied to you, Drew… to you and Ella. Dad told me once, why Mom left."

Before I can say anything, Mom steps forward, releasing herself from Braydon's arms. "What did he tell you? Did he say I was crazy?"

"No. He told me you didn't love us enough to take us with you."

"Oh, my God." She raises her hand to her mouth, but then pushes it back through her hair. "Was he implying I'd just walked out, abandoning you? Or did he mean I'd left with another man?"

"I always assumed the latter," Hunter says, shrugging his shoulders before he turns to me and then looks down at Ella. "I promised myself I wouldn't tell you what Dad had said because I wanted to protect you from his cruelty. If I was wrong, then once again, I'm sorry."

Sometimes he can take the big brother thing too far, but in this instance, I'm grateful. I wouldn't have wanted to hear that, when there was no hope of having it contradicted. "You weren't wrong." I smile at him while Ella just nods and leans back in Mac's embrace.

"I loved you," Mom says, looking first at Ella, then at me, and finally at Hunter. "I loved all of you, and I still do, but I couldn't be sure your father would let me have any kind of relationship with you, and rightly or wrongly, I assumed it would be too difficult for you to hear from me after such a long time. Ella would have only been six years old when I was released, and Drew just nine. I didn't know how they'd handle me coming back out of the blue, especially if their father had fed them stories about me being insane. The last thing I wanted was to scare them…" She pauses, stepping a little closer to Hunter. "And I knew you'd look after them. You were good at that. You'd looked after me for long enough."

"I'd tried," he whispers.

"Even though it wasn't your job." She smiles up at him and he shakes his head, but doesn't speak. I'm not sure he can. "When I didn't get any reply to my letters, I figured you didn't want to know me anymore, so we moved away." Mom turns, going back to Braydon. "To England."

"That's a long way to go," Mac says, tilting his head to one side.

Mom looks over at him. "You're British?"

"Yes. I know what it means to cross the Atlantic and start again. It's an enormous commitment… and I didn't have any family to leave behind."

"It wasn't a decision I took lightly," Mom says, gazing up at Braydon. "I missed my children every minute of every day. Maybe I was weak. Maybe I should have tried harder, but Theodore had stolen all the fight from me. I had nothing left."

"What did you do when you got to England?" Mac asks.

"We settled in a tiny village in Cornwall. Braydon opened a private practice in the nearest town, and we did our best to be happy… which was hard for me, without the three of you."

"Did you have any more children? The two of you… together?" Ella asks, blinking hard against her tears.

"No." Mom's answer is blank, her voice monotone, and Braydon steps a little closer to her.

"I said earlier that there was nothing wrong with your mother, other than the harm your father had done… but you need to remember he'd done some considerable damage. Physically, there was no reason your mother couldn't have had more children, which was a miracle in itself, considering what your father had done to her. But I think to have had another child, while the three of you were absent from her life, would have destroyed her."

"Did our father divorce you?" Ella asks, still looking at Mom and still clearly desperate for information. She reminds me of myself, wanting all the blanks filled at once.

"No," Braydon says, answering for our mother, who looks exhausted now and seems to need a little time to recover. "I believe he'd have divorced her, if he could. I think it's one of the reasons he treated her so badly… because he wanted his freedom and couldn't have it. She knew what he'd done, you see? She knew he was a rapist, that she'd been underage when they'd first had sex together. I imagine he either knew, or found out, that there's no statute of limitations on statutory rape, and if your mom had her freedom, she'd be able to tell anyone and everyone what kind of man he really was. Maybe he was also worried about what might come out during the divorce proceedings. Either way, he needed to feel he could exert control over Lindsay and everything she said. Staying married to her, but preventing her from having any contact with the three of you, was the best way of doing that, even if it meant he wasn't free to do what he wanted with his life."

"I remember now…" Hunter says, shaking his head. "Doreen told me our father had always maintained he couldn't leave you," Hunter says, turning to Mom. "It made little sense at the time, but it does now. His behavior bound him to you."

Mom nods her head. "And me to him, unfortunately. He still held that fear over me, even if I hadn't heard from him or spoken to him for over twenty years. I didn't even realize he was dead until I got back here."

"Seriously?" Hunter's surprise is obvious. "He died nearly three years ago."

"I know, but he's not a household name in Cornwall, and I wasn't a beneficiary in his will, so there was no reason for anyone to contact me." She stops talking and looks around at us. "To be honest, I wasn't completely sure he'd have left the three of you anything in his will, either. Part of me fully expected him to leave it all to Doreen."

"He left her a very specific eight figure sum," Hunter says. "But most of it came to us."

"At least he got that right," she whispers.

"Don't give him too much credit," Hunter says, letting out a sigh. "I've often wondered why he left us so much."

"So have I," I say and he turns to me, nodding his head.

"I know, and in talking to my lawyer about something else last week, I've realized one important factor that none of us had ever taken into consideration before."

"Oh?" Ella and I both turn to look at him, although it's me that speaks.

"Yeah. The date of his will. It was before he got sick… before he took the company public. When he wrote and signed that will, his cash value was significantly less than it was when he died. He left us the house, and whatever remained of his estate, after Doreen had been paid her legacy. That was how it was worded, and if things had stayed how they were, we'd have had to sell the house, and probably our shares in TBA to pay her."

"You're kidding," Ella says.

"No." He shakes his head. "When you come to think about it, it makes more sense than him suddenly developing a conscience."

It does. But there's one thing I still don't understand. "You've always maintained he knew he was dying, so why didn't he change his will?"

"I'm guessing he ran out of time. His cancer developed more quickly than anyone thought it would. Who knows? Either way, I don't think he intended to make us millionaires."

"It sounds more like he intended to bankrupt you," Mom says and we all let out a collective sigh.

"He probably did," Hunter says. "But changing the subject slightly, if you weren't aware of Dad's death, then you won't have heard than Ken Bevan died in a car accident."

Mom shakes her head. "No, I hadn't," she says, glancing over at Julianne. "When did that happen?"

"Just after Christmas," Julianne says. "I can't say it was a great loss to humanity."

Mom smiles. "No. Probably not." She shakes her head. "I only came back because I read about Drew's accident… which was a complete fluke." She turns, looking at me. "It was on the Internet. Someone had posted something about the young lady who was driving the car. She was a model, I believe?"

"Yes." I nod my head, although now doesn't feel like the time to go into details about Lexi and everything that happened between us.

"I can't remember most of the article I read, but your name popped out at me, and I saw you'd been injured. I—I had to come back. Braydon couldn't come with me then, because he had work commitments at his practice." She turns back, facing Hunter again. "When I came to see you, I wanted to tell you everything, but I couldn't… not by myself. I should have realized that would be a problem."

Braydon kisses her cheek, and she stops talking. "Your mom still struggles with what your father did to her. She was nervous about coming back, even though she had to, to make sure Drew was okay. When she discovered your father was dead, she called me and we agreed, there and then, over the phone, to move back here. She wanted to be close to you all, to see if she could rebuild her relationship with you. I stayed behind in England for a while, to sell the house and wind up my practice, and we've bought a house in Providence. I'm going to start another practice there, if I can… and…" He looks around at Ella, me, and Hunter. "And if you're all in agreement, we'd like to get married."

Mom glances up at him and then turns to us. "I—I need you all to forgive me… if you think you can."

There's a prolonged and awkward silence, during which you could hear a pin drop. None of us seems to know what to say until Pat coughs and we all look over at her. She's sitting still, holding Mick's hand in hers, and she glances around the room. "What's wrong with you all?" she says, shaking her head. "Do you honestly think your mom needs your forgiveness? Because if you do, I got something very wrong when I raised you. She's a victim of your father, just like the rest of you… only worse. And I didn't raise you to be victims. I taught you to rise above what's been done to you… to do better. To be better." She stares at Hunter, as the eldest. "So… be better."

Hunter nods his head, stepping aside and pulling Livia to her feet before he moves closer to our mom.

"This is my wife, Livia," he says, placing his hand over her tiny bump. "And our daughter, who you'll get to meet in a few months' time. Her name will be either Talia, Poppy, or Skye."

"Not Talia," Livia says, looking up at him. "I've changed my mind about that."

"Again?" he says, smiling. "We've only known the sex for five days, and I think we've gone through about eight names already."

"I know."

"Are Poppy and Skye still in the running?" he asks.

She nods her head and turns to our mom, offering a tentative hand. I guess she's nervous about her father's involvement in Lindsay's story, but Lindsay reaches out and pulls Livia into a hug, kissing her on the cheek.

"I'm sorry about earlier," she says. "I overreacted."

"Don't worry. It's nothing compared to what Hunter did when he first found out."

I chuckle and Ella laughs out loud before she stands, dragging Mac out of his seat.

"This is my husband, Mac," she says, going over to Mom. "I'm sorry I didn't invite you to our wedding."

"That's okay," Mom says. "I think it was probably for the best. I wouldn't have wanted my dramas to spoil your day."

Ella blushes. "Our son, Henry, is asleep upstairs, but I have no doubt he'll put in an appearance very soon. He should wake up at any moment."

They both step aside and I stand, offering my hand to Josie. She takes it and I pull her up, along with Maisie, who she's still cradling. I don't let go, but lead her over to Mom and she smiles at Josie… a friendly face, I guess.

"You've met Josie," I say. "But you met her as my nurse, not my fiancée."

Everyone gasps, but no-one louder than Josie and she turns to me, looking up into my eyes, as I grin down into her bemused but beautiful face.

"Fiancée? Since when?"

"Since now. Everyone else is either married, or getting married." I nod toward Mom and Braydon. "I figured we should join them."

She shakes her head, which doesn't feel very promising. "Is this your idea of a proposal?"

"No." But this is very spur of the moment, so the thought that I've had any ideas about this is almost comical. I reach out, taking

Maisie from her arms and turn, handing my daughter to Hunter, who grabs her with a smile on his lips. Then I turn back and drop to one knee, taking Josie's hands in mine. "Okay... there's nothing like doing this in front of an audience." I've only got myself to blame for that, and I take a deep breath, looking up into Josie's eyes, the words coming naturally, now I'm here. "Even when I didn't know anything else, I knew I loved you. When everything was dark, you were my beacon of light, guiding me back to where I belong. You're my ray of hope, Josie... my everything... my dream come true. All you have to do is say yes, and make the dream a reality."

She smiles and I smile back as she nods her head and whispers, "Yes."

I leap to my feet, pulling her into my arms, and I kiss her as everyone gathers around, congratulating us. There are kisses, pats on the back and hugs, and then Hunter hands Maisie back to me, and I turn back to Mom again.

"Who's this?" she asks.

"This is Maisie. She's your granddaughter."

I hand Maisie over to Mom and she lets her tears fall as she gazes down into Maisie's beautiful face. Josie looks up at me and I know this is right. We've completed the circle.

I lean over and kiss Josie, just as Hunter coughs and we turn to face him.

"If we're in the mood for making announcements, then I've got one, too."

I groan, unable to help myself. "You're not thinking about buying back the rest of the shares in TBA, are you? Because if you are..."

Hunter shakes his head. "Hell, no. In fact, I'm thinking of doing the exact opposite. That's why I went to see my lawyer. I'm giving up my position as CEO."

Livia smiles and I get the feeling she knew this was coming, even if it's a surprise to the rest of us.

"What are you going to do, then?" Ella asks.

"I'm going to be a father." He rests his hand on Livia's bump and she places hers over the top. "I'm going to get right all the things our father got wrong... like being there when our daughter takes her first steps, and when she says 'Daddy' for the first time." He smiles at me and Ella. "Neither of you have gone back to work since the accident, and Henry's birth."

"No," I say, grinning. "I'm enjoying being a father myself."

"I noticed." Hunter chuckles. "And I was thinking, maybe the three of us could do something together for once."

"I hope you're not suggesting we start a new business, because I really don't have the time... and besides, I can't think of a single thing that involves an advertising man, a photographer and a chef."

"Neither can I," Hunter says. "But that's not what I had in mind. We all have our shares in TBA still, and I'm okay with leaving them where they are for now. That's more that enough involvement in business for me."

"Me, too." Ella nods her head.

"Good... so I was thinking we could do something completely different."

"Like what?"

"Like being better." Hunter glances at Pat with a smile. "I was thinking we could take some of our money and do some good... give something back."

"Is this you railing against Dad again?" I ask and he nods his head.

"Absolutely. I think we've established he never meant for us to have his millions, so let's do something he'd have hated." I have to laugh and Ella soon joins in. "I haven't worked out what yet," Hunter says. "But I'm sure if we put our heads together, we can come up with a few ideas."

"I like the sound of that," I say, holding Josie a little closer as Ella goes over and gives Mom a hug, taking care not to crush Maisie, and the two of them rest their heads together, while Mac moves in and shakes Braydon's hand.

"Shall we all go eat?" Pat says, raising her voice above the hum of conversation.

"Oh… um…" Mom seems embarrassed.

"We'd like you to stay," Hunter says, looking at me and then Ella. I nod my head and she does, too. "We can talk about wedding plans."

"Whose?" Ella asks. "Mom's, or Drew's?"

"Both," Hunter says with a laugh and I shake my head at him, although I don't mind in the slightest.

I bend and kiss Josie as everyone files out of the room, Mom still holding Maisie in her arms.

"Thank you," I whisper, and she looks up at me.

"What for?"

"For giving me back my family."

"I didn't."

"Yes, you did. Without you, I'd still be floundering around, trying to remember who the hell I am. And now I know…"

"Oh? And who are you?"

I smile, kissing her again. "I'm the luckiest man in the world."

The End

Thank you for reading *Mistaken Intention*. I hope you enjoyed it, and if you did, I hope you'll take the time to leave a short review.

Printed in Great Britain
by Amazon